Saints and Vagabonds

Saints and Vagabonds

A novel

Nancy Veldman

ISBN-13: 9781530301522
ISBN-10: 1530301521

'Tis grace has brought me safe
thus far...
and grace shall lead me home.

Prologue

I was told once
that I had the brains of Einstein
and the hands of
a great surgeon.

But now I had no home.

A bottle of Smirnoff
was lying at my feet
empty as my pockets,
and I had nowhere to go.

I had just decided that morning,
sitting on my bench,
when I heard the foggy sound
of a boat at sea,
that I was going to change.

But my heart had other plans.

CHAPTER 1

❦

My heartbeat was the only thing I was aware of as I awakened in bed on the fourth floor of the Cardiac Center of Fort Walton Beach. It took me a few moments to put things together, and then I remembered I'd had a heart attack on the beach on my way into town. I barely remembered the trip in the ambulance, but one thing stuck out in my mind. That was the first time I had to tell someone I had no address. No place I called home. Somewhere out there was a bench that had my name on it. And that's about all I had to call my own, except the clothes I wore into the hospital. The shame of not having a place to live outweighed the fear I had about what was going on with my heart. But I hadn't seen the doctor yet. So everything could change in a second. I found that out the hard way.

My past was a blur of drinking, sleeping and hanging out with other drunks. Work barely existed; just enough to get the money I needed to buy more liquor. That was what I called my life. But it was gone now. I could no longer continue on that road or I'd be dead. And the future I faced depended greatly upon what the doc would tell me about my heart.

I had plenty of time lying still in the quiet of my hospital room to think about things. I got sick of looking at the green lunchroom- colored walls, so my gaze drifted to the window, which was my only contact with the world outside. I had asked the nurse to raise the blinds so I had full view of what little I could see. At the moment the view was mostly sky and little edges of the tops of buildings near the hospital. My eyes focused on a flock of birds flying north. Their brains were the size of a tiny pea and yet they seemed to have it all together. I, on the other hand, couldn't stay sober and focused for ten minutes. I had just begun to realize how pathetic I was when the doctor strolled in with a nurse behind him.

"How's it going, my friend?"

I hadn't remembered us becoming friends, but I nodded and forced a smile. Granted it was weak, but I'd just had a major heart attack. So smiling wasn't on my "to do" list. "Hello, Doc. Dying to hear what's going on in my chest."

Dr. Franklin Harrison nodded and pulled out my chart. He was tall, blond, and handsome. You could tell he worked out but there were dark circles under his eyes. "Well, buddy, you've had a major heart attack and after running a few tests, we see that you have three major blockages. Two large arteries connected to your heart and one smaller artery behind the heart. We're probably looking at a triple bypass pretty quick here."

He was a man of few words. "A triple bypass? How soon are you talking about, Doc? I got things I need to do."

Harrison laughed and closed my file. "If you want to be around to do those things, to do anything, you better plan for this surgery pretty quickly."

I rolled my eyes and frowned. "You serious? Is there no other way to fix this?"

"Well, that's exactly what we're trying to prevent! I'm not promising, but there is a slight possibility that we could do stents in two of those arteries. The surgery is to prevent your death. Not cause it. I will look at your tests and make that decision before the day is out."

The information hit me like a ton of bricks. After all I'd been through, it felt like the world had collapsed around me. Life to me had become like a wrecking ball, swaying back and forth, bringing so much demolition. The love of my life was gone, my career as a doctor was on hold for an indeterminate amount of time, and then this massive heart attack. What little self respect I had was somewhere in the rubble, along with my ability to look people in the eyes. Love was an ideal of the past. Compassion and concern for others was covered over by the raw instinct of survival, which was now being called into question. I strained to digest the information Dr. Harrison had just imparted to me, and the best way I knew to do that was by walking. I had learned that tidbit of information on the streets when I had nowhere to go—just get up and walk in a straight line. I glanced up at the life-giving fluids that were dripping into my arm, and decided that I could tackle the challenge of dragging it with me up and down the hospital halls.

The nurses nervously allowed me a fifteen minute window to walk the halls. My head was light and swimming as I eased out of bed, making sure the wheels of my IV machine would survive the trek. *Open heart surgery.* The words echoed through my chemically fogged brain as I headed for the hallway in a knock-kneed fashion, taking small deliberate steps. *A private room,* I thought to myself, smirking. *I bet that costs a pretty penny. More than the seven dollars and sixteen cents I had in my pocket when the ground came up to meet me on the back beach road.*

The thoughts soon drifted as other rooms came into view on my way down the dimly lit hallway. My peripheral vision picked up the concerned looks on the faces of the family members of my new neighbors. As I walked past a closet marked "Supplies," I was struck momentarily by the thought that the two men leaving the room and locking the door more resembled doctors instead of the orderlies or janitors one would expect to see. When I finally passed the now locked closet door, another thought crossed my mind. *Ether. Why would the odor of surgical supplies be seeping out of a janitorial closet?*

My medicated brain tried to juggle the pieces of a new puzzle, but my musing was interrupted by the insistent voice of a nurse. She gently gripped my elbow, telling me that the duration of my journey had reached its limit. Time to abandon my walk and return to the crisp white sheets that were my only refuge from the world.

The stale-smelling pillow, soiled by my own unwashed hair, cradled my head all too quickly. The pain of the IV being wiggled in the back of my hand and the sounds of people fussing around me momentarily crowded out the thoughts of ether, bypasses, survival and doctors. Sleep settled on me like a thin warm blanket and my mind emptied as the silence drew closer to me. Never before had sleep come so easy in the middle of the day. I drifted to sleep like a small child, unaware of anything going on around me. As I moved in and out of sleep, it almost felt like I had been drugged with ether. *Ether.* There that word was again! My eyes popped open as if I was startled. *Ether.* The word flashed in my mind like a red neon Budweiser sign. Dr. Harrison smelled of ether when he was standing near my bed talking to me. That wouldn't be all that strange accept ether wasn't used in surgery anymore. A long fitful period was followed by my constantly being awakened, no longer able to discern real visitors from dreams. Bizarre images came and went and a vague discussion about stents with Dr. Harrison. Looking up, I thought my IV had been moved over my right shoulder and I suddenly felt a pinch in my thigh. I felt myself drool, and it ran down my cheek to my shoulder. Whatever they gave me to relax was working.

CHAPTER 2

THE SUN POURED into my room as I tried to focus on my size twelve feet at the foot of the bed. Above them was the vaguely familiar face of Dr. Harrison looking at my chart. "Are you with us, Matt?"

My reply was nearly inaudible. "Yeah, maybe."

Dr. Harrison continued to speak in a commanding tone. "We've put stents in two of your arteries that will keep them open for now; with proper care and medication we may have prevented surgery. But—" He paused and raised his eyebrow, which suddenly reminded me of my father. "You are going to have to do your part in this recovery. I'm not kidding here. Be sure you're taking the meds prescribed; if you fail to take them, you will be back in here and you may not make it out again. Have I made that clear to you, Matt?"

I swallowed. My throat was incredibly dry. "Crystal. Do you have to sound so glum?"

"The good news is that we're going to have you out of here in days, not weeks. How does that sound to you?"

I shook my head to clear my thoughts. *Exactly where was I going when I got out? Back to the park bench?* "Oh yeah, Doc. That's great news. Thanks so much for everything you've done for me. I guess this was pretty serious, huh?"

Harrison took his glasses off and looked at Matt squarely. "You almost didn't make it. That's how serious it was. Had no pulse when you came in here. I'd say that was a pretty close call."

With that, he turned and walked out of my room. For the next few days I walked up and down the halls, feeling stronger and stronger. I noticed that the activity around the closet continued and became more and more aware of the characters that seemed to make frequent stops there. Unseemly characters that were out of place in such a sterile environment. Yet, two doctors would often appear and enter the closet and leave with a briefcase in their hands. I watched from a hidden vantage point of the south stairwell. On day two of my surveillance, I noticed two well-dressed gentlemen approach the closet, and a Hispanic man entered the closet about three minutes behind them. He was carrying a satchel and I silently made a bet that he would come out empty-handed. I was correct in my assumption.

I returned to my room with thoughts racing in my head. Surprisingly, I found my personal belongings in a plastic bag on my bed. Wendy, one of the nurses on my floor, was waiting for me by the bed. "You've been voted off the floor by all of us on the night shift!" There was a twinkle in her eye.

"I don't blame you guys one bit. I'm sure I haven't been the best patient on this floor. Not by a long shot."

She laughed and left the room and I dressed, smelling the stale cigarette odor and beer on my worn out clothing. The odor clung to my clothes like a bad dream. I was ready to leave but the paper work seemed to take hours to complete. They had to fill out forms for my aftercare plans and prepare my prescriptions.

I began my customary pacing, which increased as I continually looked at my watch. I felt like a lion pacing in a cage. I looked towards the closet as I paced up and down the hallway, and suddenly Dr. Harrison and another doctor came out of the closet. Their eyes met mine briefly, and both men hurried to the awaiting elevator. I smiled with relief, noting that not only did they fail to lock the closet door, but Dr. Harrison had not recognized me in my street clothes.

I waited until I saw the elevator closed and I headed quickly to the closet to see if I could find out what was going on. Something didn't "smell" right and I was just crazy enough to want to find out what that was. I reached for the door, looked both ways, and ducked into the closet.

Fumbling around for the light, I cut it on quickly and scanned the small room. It was dusty and crowded with boxes and cleaning supplies but I could smell the coke. I had used it for years so I knew what it smelled like. As I was just about to kneel down to dig underneath a pile of boxes, I heard someone turning the doorknob. I jumped up, opened a small broom closet, and pulled the door shut. I could hear someone enter and then leave. I was holding my breath and feeling a little weak, but as soon as they left, I poked my head out the door and hurried to the nurse's station, where I picked up my discharge papers and my prescriptions. Dr. Harrison had given me my orders, to fill the prescriptions he prescribed and take care of myself, or I'd have another big one and probably die. Walking out of the hospital, I felt elated that I was alive, but depressed that I had nowhere to go and no one who cared whether I lived or died. I had pretty much run off all of my good friends on my way down. I faced the harsh fact that I really didn't know how to find my way back up.

CHAPTER 3

ON ANY GIVEN night, when the city had settled in for the night, and there was hardly any traffic on the roads, a single lone figure could be seen walking in dark areas of town down by the harbor under the Destin bridge, or on the hills along the harbor between buildings. He had a heavy coat on, a hat with a brim, and he was carrying heavy blankets in his arms. It was cold and his breath was floating up into the air as he passed many sleeping men hidden from sight. Forgotten men. They walked the streets by day and hid in secret places by night, hoping not to be seen by policemen doing their rounds, shining their lights into the cracks and crevices along the harbor.

Joseph Mason had taken on a task that would never end. No one wanted this job. But he loved it. He actually was smiling as he walked from sleeping body to sleeping body, covering these men with warm blankets and leaving them some food. They never woke up when he touched them, but in the early morning when the sun was beginning to peep through the cold winter clouds, these men raised their heads and discovered they'd made it through another night without shivering to death.

It was an unspoken gift of grace that Joe laid down. He really felt compassion for these sleeping giants of the street. They lay in places most of mankind wouldn't walk through in broad daylight. But on the street, after years of nights spent alone, these men understood what would hurt them and what wouldn't. They also knew who they could trust. And Joseph became a man who was trusted on the street. When it was cold, their body temperature dropped and there was a high risk of death among the street people. Joe was determined to lower those numbers by keeping them covered with blankets and coats.

He had certain favorite areas to walk and one of them was on the harbor near RT's. One particular night he'd been through most of the town area and decided to go to a hidden place on the harbor where he'd seen a park bench stretched between two buildings. As he headed towards the bench area he saw a man sleeping on the bench with one arm hanging off. He was out of blankets and extra coats, so he took off his leather jacket and laid it over the man.

He was about to walk away, but something about this man was pulling him in. He stood there watching the man sleep, shivering because he'd given up his jacket, and then he heard the man whimper in his sleep. He walked over to him, bending down to see if he was okay, and he saw a tear rolling down his cheek. The light from a distant street lamp was shining through the tree limbs and reflected on the tear. He reached his huge hand over the man's face and wiped the tear away. Then he turned and walked back to his car, which was parked down the street in a well-lit parking lot next to a pharmacy.

All the way home he couldn't get this man out of his mind. *What was that tear from? What made this guy take a bench on the street?* He knew better than to go too far in that direction of getting attached to these men. But for some reason, even when he lay down that night to sleep, this one man was on his mind. He said a silent prayer for the men he'd touched during his walk, and especially for the one man he'd shared his leather jacket with. He shivered as he lay underneath several blankets in a warm bed. It haunted him to think about how his father had lived on the street. Anyone could end up there. Anyone.

"But for the grace of God go I," he whispered into the darkness of his room. And someone heard. Someone.

For a few hours I sat in the park on my bench, which felt warmly familiar to me, and thought about my life. It was a sunny day, and the beginning of fall was scattered in the trees and the air. It smelled different in the fall and it brought back memories of when I was a young boy going fishing with my father. I'd been abnormally emotional since the heart attack and my eyes filled with tears when I pictured him in my mind. Philadelphia was colorful in the fall and I missed the massive trees that lined the streets. My parents had no idea what I'd just been through; I didn't have the heart or stomach to tell them. There was nothing they could do, anyway. Luckily I did have a cell phone, but I needed to pick up some money pretty quick to renew my contract. My last phone call to them was before the heart attack and the stents put into my arteries to avoid the knife. I decided to not let them in on the heart issues. I was pretty private about my own life, which had ruined several relationships along the way. I'd been told many times that I had a lot of words but none of them showed what was inside of me. That's the way I liked it, but it was tough on relationships. Intimacy was elusive to me and I didn't see a change coming any time soon.

It was getting dark and my stomach was growling, so I headed over to the Coffee House to eat a cheap meal. All I had was the seven dollars I had entered the hospital with. When I walked through the door I spotted a seat next to the window at the back of the restaurant, so I quickly headed to it and sank into the faux red leather seat. The tall lanky waitress yelled a greeting and I nodded, noticing I had a headache coming on. I put my head in my hands and closed my eyes for a moment and jerked back to reality when the waitress came up and asked what I wanted to eat.

"What can I get ya, buddy?"

"I'll take a number four with coffee. And make that with sausage instead of bacon."

"Sure. You okay? You look a little pale." She studied me closely, running her tongue across her stained teeth.

"I'm fine. Just a little hungry is all." I sat up straighter and forced a smile. She didn't buy it, but I acted like I didn't notice it. I stretched and yawned and decided to head to the bathroom to wash up a little. I wasn't that dirty after being in the hospital, but I would've killed for a hot shower. I checked my beard and my teeth, ran my fingers through my wiry brown hair and went back to my seat. Dinner was already waiting for me.

I got lost in eating my food, relishing every bite, and was unaware that someone had come in the door. As I was taking an oversized bite of egg and toast, I saw a man walk up and stand by my table. I raised my eyes slowly, with my mouth full of food, and gazed into the face of a handsome older man who looked like a preacher. I nearly choked on my food, but managed to chew it up fast and swallow it down with water.

"Sorry, man. I was wondering if I could share this booth with you. I couldn't help but notice you were alone, and I hate to see a man eat alone."

I didn't feel like company but I nodded and took another bite. He shook my hand and introduced himself. "Brother Joe here. What's your name?"

I wiped my hand off and shook his huge paw of a hand. "Name's Matt. Matt Collins."

"Nice to meet you, Matt Collins. So you live here in Destin?"

"Sure do. Been here a little while. How about you? How long you been here?"

"Well, it's a long story. But I've been here since I was four years old. That's a long time. And I've seen things change around here in the last twenty years. Believe me."

The waitress came up and took his order and he picked up the conversation where he left off. "So what do you do, Matt? You live around here?"

My stomach knotted up. I was trying to think of a way to answer his question without cluing him in on the fact that I was homeless. "Right now I'm kind of between jobs. And I live in town here. How about you?"

He looked right through me with his dark brown eyes. His face was full of deep wrinkles and his big hands were worn and weathered. But he had a warmth about him that I was drawn to, and that was a big surprise because I hadn't been drawn to anyone for years. I had deliberately closed myself off from most people because I didn't like where I was in life.

"I live in the parsonage near St. Luke's Presbyterian Church on Main Street. You should come hear me on Sunday. You might enjoy it, Matt. And I'd love to have you."

I nodded again and forced a smile. He didn't know I had no clothes to wear to church. All I had was the clothes on my back. I didn't even have a pillow to rest my head on. But he was kind and I didn't want to ruin his meal by complaining about my situation. Besides, I had caused all of this myself. So I had no one to blame but me.

Brother Joe ate his meal in silence, noticing everything and saying nothing. I felt transparent as I sat there dabbing at the last bit of egg on my plate. I was afraid to look up but he didn't wait for that. He snatched that window of opportunity and drove a truck through it.

"Matt, you got a place to stay? Are you living on the street these days?"

I was disappointed that he read through my words. I didn't lie too well and maybe that was a good thing since I was sitting across from a preacher. I paused and allowed myself to look him in the eye. There was a peace about him that suddenly found its way across the stack of plates and half eaten slices of toast to me.

"Yeah, Brother Joe. I got that park bench across the street there. I'm pretty much homeless right now. But I'm making it okay."

Dead silence. Then he spoke to me in that deep bass voice with a rasp that seemed to me to suggest years of talking.

"I've got a nice apartment next to the parsonage, right above a garage, that is empty tonight. Why don't you come home with me and stay there tonight? There's no need for you to be out in the park as long as I have this room empty. You okay with that?"

I didn't want to give in, but I was still a little weak from the surgery. A bed sounded pretty good to me after feeling the boards of that bench digging into my back. I hadn't had a full night's sleep in a long time and even though I loved seeing the open skies at night, I would give all that up for a room with a window and a good mattress. So even though my response was slow, he got the message loud and clear.

"I would appreciate that so much. You have no idea. I have some health issues, but if I can help you in any way, please let me know. I'm not much for taking help from strangers, but right now that bed sounds awfully good." I nodded and Brother Joe grinned and shook his head.

"I'll take you there after I finish eating. It's been a long day and I'm ready to turn in. But I think you'll be pleasantly surprised when you see where you're staying."

CHAPTER 4

Joseph Mason was a giant of a man who had wanted to be a preacher since he was seven years old. It came on him early in life and never left. Like a brand in his side, the call of God guided him through his life and affected every decision he made in life. He loved football when he was younger and could have made pro. But other plans were in the making, and he followed a different path that didn't get dirt under his fingernails, but instead gave hope to those with no hope.

He spent his early years feeding the hungry and talking on the street to the homeless. He had a real heart for those men out there who were broken. The garage apartment had been used for years as a safe place for a man to stay, and then Brother Joe would begin working his magic on the broken soul until finally a whole man emerged from the garage.

His own father had died on the street so the street became his walking ground, his patrol several times a week, to check on the men who were lying on the ground. The longer a man stayed on the street, the less likely he'd ever go back into mainstream society. So Joe tried to get them fresh off the merry-go-round. When their feet hit the ground and they headed underneath the bridge, he'd spot that new face and grab him. Matt was getting close to being unreachable, but Joe was going to try hard to save him.

As he pulled up in the driveway, he pointed to the garage and Matt swallowed hard. "Here's your new place to live for a while, Matt. I hope you are comfortable. If you need anything at all, just holler. I'm right next door." With that he handed Matt the keys to the apartment.

"I don't know quite what to say, Brother Joe. I'm—" Matt looked at the ground and sighed. It was just too overwhelming for him to verbalize.

Joe interrupted quickly. "Man, don't thank me. Just go in there and enjoy the sanctuary that little apartment offers and don't forget breakfast with me at 7:00. I love punctuality." With a wink he turned his large frame around and walked into the house.

Matt stood there for a while staring at the door and then headed to the garage apartment, anxious to get inside and see what his new digs would look like. When he unlocked the door and cracked it open, he was shocked to see a fully furnished apartment with a tan sofa, rich leather chair and ottoman, photos on the wall, full kitchen, and a fireplace. He walked through the rooms smiling, waiting to see the bed. When he entered the small bedroom it was filled up with a king size bed with down covers and huge pillows.

He dove into it head first and burst out laughing. He laughed long and hard and suddenly his laughter turned to tears while he let out the loneliness and pain of the time spent on the bench. At the moment it felt far away. But later in the night, when he fell fast asleep, he dreamed of the park bench and the coldness of the night. When he woke up, he was shivering underneath the down covers. He pulled them up over his head and snuggled down into the bed, thankful for this one night safe inside a small apartment on Main Street. Off and on memories came running through his mind, but all he had to do was open his eyes and he knew his life had changed. Taken a turn. He had a chance, a small window of opportunity, to make right choices and turn his world upside down. The wrecking ball that had destroyed everything he owned was now a dim memory being replaced by the kindness of one single man he barely knew. The jacket that lay on the chair had been given to him by someone, one night when he was sleeping. He had a feeling there was a story behind it.

Across town in his rundown apartment near the brickyard of houses that were hidden by a broken down fence and live oak trees, a man poured white snowy powder out on his coffee table. His body was shaking and he felt so tired. Sick. He didn't know the way out. He knew he was in trouble big time. But tonight all he wanted to do was pull the powder into his body and sit back and let himself float away. He had a gig tomorrow night. He needed to be busy. But tonight he had nothing. He was nothing. And the powder was his only friend. Odd that something so snowy white would cause such darkness.

CHAPTER 5

———— ⚜ ————

I woke up with the sun cutting across the comforter, warming the room and rousing a thirst in me for some strong coffee. The remnants of last night's headache were hanging in the back of my eyes and I stretched and climbed reluctantly out of bed. I checked my watch and realized I was expected to breakfast at 7:00 and the hands of my watch were fast approaching that time. Racing around to find my dirty wrinkled clothes, I dashed to the sink, splashed water on my face, and threw my shoes on.

When I knocked on his door I heard a faint "Come on in!" I opened the door and walked into the living room.

In his booming voice Brother Joe greeted me. "Morning, Matt! How'd you sleep?"

"Man, I slept better than I have in years."

"You hungry?"

"Yeah I could eat something." I was actually starving but would die before I said it.

"Well, pull up a chair and dig in. I've got a hungry man's breakfast ready for you. But let's say a quick prayer before you swallow it whole."

I bowed my head and closed my eyes. His raspy voice rumbled like thunder in the small house. But somehow it felt good to hear his prayer.

"Okay, let's talk about you, Matt. Tell me your story."

I didn't talk to anyone about my life, but he was pretty insistent and I owed him for allowing me to stay in that apartment. "It's a long story, Brother Joe. Too long for this meal. But I have made my share of mistakes, drank too much liquor, and lived a life that was full of partying with the wrong people. A heart attack later, I finally decided to face the changes that needed to take place in my life. Only I don't have the means to do it. I'm homeless and jobless. It's hard to go up when you have nothing."

Joe smiled. "Tell me about it. My father was homeless and died on the street. But he was a good man. Just couldn't see his way out. I don't want you to make that mistake, Matt. Don't look down. Give every opportunity you come across great scrutiny lest you miss that one chance to dig your way out."

"I plan to do just that. I was going this morning to see my friend Paul. He's in a band and plays at RT's. You familiar with that place?" I felt stupid asking a preacher about a bar.

"As a matter of fact, I am. A good friend of mine hangs out there and I've sat many a night with him, talking him out of a dark hole."

I was surprised but glad he could relate to the place. "Paul has been a good friend for years and I know him well. He'll help me find something to do, some sort of job that will help me get on my feet."

"Well, I'll be checking in on you every day about this time. If that's good for you, I'd like to eat breakfast with you while you're around."

"It's an honor, Brother Joe. I appreciate what you've done. You won't have to ask me twice. Food is something I didn't see much of on the street."

After a long nap that I badly needed, I left the apartment and started my long trek into town. It was a cloudy day and I acutally enjoyed the pace. When I walked into RT's, I scanned the room for Paul. I saw him on the stage doing a sound check and waved at him. He spotted me out of the corner of his eye and nodded in cheerful recognition. Same Paul I knew before. Hadn't changed a bit. I quickly ordered a Coke from the waitress and took a seat. Paul completed his sound check and stepped off the stage, and headed in my direction.

"You got a smoke?" His usual greeting to me.

"Sure. You need one?" I laughed. Always hitting me up for a cigarette. Did he really smoke or was he just trying to rag me?

He lit up and grinned. "What's shaking, man?" He was the only fifty-year-old I knew who was stuck in the '50s. His long brown hair bounced when he talked. He was tall and lanky and his jeans had about twenty holes in them. Pretty drafty. He wore no socks and loafers that had holes in the soles were on his feet.

Our conversation was interrupted every time a female patron walked by. "Nothing much. But I'm off the street as of yesterday, man. Got an apartment to stay in that's fully furnished. Bouncing back pretty good from a heart attack. Pretty cool, huh?"

"Man, I had no idea you were in that kind of trouble. Got you a girlfriend now?"

"Nope. Just a friend who wanted to help me out. But I need some work. That's why I came by. I figured you'd help me out in that department."

Paul eyed the crowd as they walked in like he was taking inventory. He seemed unusually relaxed before the show, quiet and confident, unlike the extrovert lead singer, Derek. Paul referred to the lead singer's showiness as "LSD." Lead singer disorder. Without Paul, Derek would still be flipping burgers at the Pancake Hut. He eyed my glass with the stir stick in it. I could see he was puzzled so I cleared the air.

"Just Coke, man. Just a Coke. Relax."

He laughed and relit the cigarette. The lighter glowed in his fingers, calloused from years of practicing in his double-wide.

I knew Paul's story pretty well. He was a quiet man with little education. He had run away from his simple surroundings in Defuniak Springs to the streets of Pensacola and later Mobile, where he learned to care for himself, taking jobs that required little or no I.D. He supplemented his meager income by selling pot until he earned a position of "muler." Then he could deliver speed for a local biker gang. The money was good but the risk of prison was high.

When his dad fell ill with a stroke he returned to a life in Defuniak. He'd saved enough money to buy a two acre lot with a trailer on it. Along the way, he'd picked up a Les Paul guitar from a doper who couldn't pay for his tab. Taking care of his father gave him time to learn the guitar and after he'd put some time in, he really made the guitar sing. He formed a band called "Underdogs" and spent a lot of time at the basketball courts persuading kids to stay off drugs. Oddly, he delivered them, knowing kids might end up using. "A sort of irony that I have to live with every time I look in the mirror," he once commented to me, shaking his head in disbelief.

Paul sipped his drink and studied me. He knew I loved privacy, especially lately, and attempting to respect that, he stepped out on a ledge by asking some questions. "Did the doc tell you when you could go back to work?"

I squirmed in my chair, feeling pathetic in my filthy clothes. I glanced at my nails, which were still a little dirty and ragged. I had an old school way of looking at things; I hated not working more than I hated having no money. "He said I could do what I felt like doing. But not to lift anything heavy. I suppose I should apply at one of the hotels around here for a front desk position. That would be an easy job for me to start off with."

Paul spit out some of the Coke he had in his mouth, and he looked like he was trying hard not to react to the comment. "You'd die in that job, man. There's no way you would last as a front desk clerk in a hotel. With a brain like yours, you'd be bored in five seconds."

I couldn't help but let the laughter out that was rising up in my throat. It felt good to laugh about such an uncomfortable subject. I looked at Paul and raised an eyebrow, waiting on the rest of his response.

"There's no doubt you could do the job, but come on, Matt. Reach higher than that. You're too smart for that. I'd rather you sit in the band for a while than lower yourself to that kind of work." He reached for a rectangular box he had laid on the seat beside him. He slid it onto the table and pushed it in front of Matt.

"Ever see this thing before?"

"What? The box?"

"No! What's *in* the box. Raise the lid and see."

I looked inside and saw a Lee Oscar twelve key harmonica. I raised my eyes to see my friend grinning from ear to ear.

"So you ever played one of these bad boys before?"

"Maybe in school, a long time ago. This one's a nice one. I didn't have anything like this when I was a kid."

"Well, pick it up. I was thinking about adding it to the instruments we're using and wondered if you'd like to sit in on a session to see what you could do!"

I paused, taking it all in. "You joking, Paul? 'Cause I been in too raw a place to have you joking with me about that. I know you take your music seriously and I wouldn't want to mess anything up with you and the guys in the band. I'm not that good."

"Look, you need something to do, and I want this sound in our music. They charge twenty dollars for a stand for one of these harps. I'd rather give the twenty to you and see what you can do."

We parted with the traditional tap of our fists together. I felt like I'd had been corralled into doing a gig with Paul, but deep down I was pleased. It kept me off the streets and that was always a good thing. I headed back to the garage and listened to my stomach growl. I'd become accustomed to going to bed hungry and this night was no different. It was early for me to be going to bed and just as I was about to doze off, lying on the bed with my clothes on, I heard a quiet knock on the door. I cracked open the door and stared right into the face of Brother Joe, who was grinning.

"Hey, Son. Brought you dinner. And don't tell me you aren't hungry. I saw the way you shoveled your food in at breakfast. Enjoy this and see you at seven."

I laughed and locked the door. This guy was beginning to grow on me. It was hard not to like him. But I also knew Brother Joe had an agenda. I wolfed down the beef stew and cornbread, savoring the last few bites. I lifted the napkin and found two brownies underneath that were still quite warm. I picked up one of them and smelled it. The aroma brought back memories of my mother who had loved to cook. Warm brownies and cold milk. A tough combination to beat unless you had vodka.

I saved one brownie for tomorrow and swallowed the last bit of milk and set the tray aside on the bedside table. I got up, brushed my teeth with a toothbrush that Brother Joe had left for me, and looked at my image in the mirror. I could have used a haircut and my gums were bleeding a little from the lack of brushing. Looking around for something to cut my nails, I found a nail cutter in one of the drawers in the cabinet so I clipped them and cleaned them out. I also found some mouthwash and swished it around and spit in the sink. Clicking the light out, I dove into the bed and was asleep in seconds. My dirty clothes lay in a pile on the floor and my shoes were beside the rug near the door.

Later that night, Brother Joe quietly opened the door and took Matt's clothes and washed them so that when he woke up, he'd find them folded at the foot of his bed. He would only do this once for Matt, but there was a reason. A man on the street was hard to reach. He kept to himself and was very private. Joe knew Matt would never let on that he had no money. He would never talk about his needs. So if he wanted this homeless man to make it off the street, he would have to keep a close eye on him, because a homeless man who used to be married to the bottle could be slippery.

CHAPTER 6

THE SMELLS OF scrambled eggs, bacon, fresh strawberries, and home-made biscuits hit me as I walked into Brother Joe's house. My stomach was growling but I acted like I was barely hungry. The plate went from full to empty in about three minutes, which gave me away.

"Guess you don't care for my cooking, buddy."

I smiled sheepishly. He had a way of getting to the point. "Yeah, well. It's tolerable."

He laughed a big booming laugh. "So how's it going so far? You found a job yet?"

"You might call it that. My friend at RT's is pushing me to sit in on the next gig there. Not sure if I will, but it's a way to pick up some change while I recoup from that last heart attack. The stents seem to be working."

"Sounds like fun. You play an instrument?"

I laughed lightly. "Not much. But he handed me a harmonica yesterday that was ripe. I loved it. I'm gonna try to make some noise with it today. I'll let ya know."

"Keep your eyes open for all opportunities that come along. And by the way, I sure like that jacket you have there."

I touched the leather jacket that was on the back of my chair, grinning. I still didn't know where it came from. "Thanks. It gets the job done. Kind of chilly out there these days. Sure appreciate having a room to sleep in. It gets pretty raw out on the street in the winter."

Brother Joe looked down and shook his head. "Watch yourself today, Matt. None of my business, but now that you're on your way up, there will be things coming your way that will try to bring you back down. I'm just saying."

I laughed at his quip and gave him a high five. "I hear you, brother. I appreciate the hand up more than you know. That bed feels like heaven to me. And this breakfast. You didn't have to do that, ya know."

"I'm not sending you out there each day hungry. That would be stupid of me. Just watch yourself. I don't want you back on the street. Not now. Not ever."

I grabbed my coat and headed out the door. I felt a little overwhelmed with his kindness as I pulled the jacket close to me and buried my hands into my pockets. Down in the corner of my right pocket I felt something metal and pulled it out to see what it was. I was shocked to see it was a cross. *How did that get in my pocket? Whose jacket was this, anyway?* I put the cross back in my pocket and hurried back to my apartment to catch another nap. My body was still weak from the heart attack and the hundreds of nights without sleep on the bench. Paul would be waiting for me at RT's later and I was anxious to see how that harp would sound with the band.

Even though RT's had been open for a few hours, it still had a smell of yesterday's beer and smokes. I headed towards Paul and the band, noting that they all looked sleepy from a late night. They were busy setting up as I stepped up on the stage, and I noticed that the harmonica was sitting on a stool near the back. Paul grabbed my arm and the others slapped me on the back. A nice welcome for my first time in a gig.

"Hey, dude. How's it going?" Paul yawned and pointed at my stool.

"I'm good. Nervous about playing with you guys. Not sure yet what I'm gonna do."

"You'll figure it out once we start. Just try to hear the key and play a little in the background. You'll know when you're ready to come out front more. Okay?"

"Got it. But I'm going be quiet for a while and just listen to the sounds you guys make. You'll hear me working it in here and there."

I sat on my stool and looked at Tommy, the drummer. He was the oldest of the group, and even though his arms were built, he had the face of an old man. He'd lived hard, apparently, and he could chew gum and chain smoke simultaneously. He had upper body strength and could last for hours, carrying the beat into the night. He credited his energy to the little trips he made to the men's room before the show and sometimes in between songs. He was never that quiet about his use of the white powder. He seemed to get shaky if he waited too long for his next drag.

Mac Perkins was the bass player and he was phenomenal as a musician. He looked cool in his John Lennon glasses and his raspy voice just screamed "rock star." Five minutes of listening to him play convinced the toughest audience that he knew what he was doing.

Ginger Smythe was the keyboard player and she was a tough cookie for a woman. Being a single mom and a musician had caused her to be savvy about working and saving enough time for her twin boys. She could belt out the songs, but sometimes it was nice to have her sing a solo on a quiet tune that caught the ear of the audience. She had a Southerner's voice and it blended famously with Mac's when they sang together. The keyboard did very little to hide the hot little figure that begged to be center stage, topped off with the brown eyes that sucked you in with her sad story.

Derek Woods was lead singer and a wolf in disguise. All the ladies liked him and he knew it. I enjoyed watching him work the crowd but he could slack it down a little when it came to women. His voice was good enough that it would have attracted most of the ladies, but he couldn't leave it at that. He smoked heavily and drank while singing. I didn't care for that, but who was I to criticize a drinker? I had lived on a bench and had nearly killed myself with booze and snow. I just hated to see someone else crash their life.

Paul spoke hurriedly as they were setting up the gig. "You guys know Matt. Well he's gonna sit in on the gig tonight and see how it goes. Just give him some slack and we may hit on something with this harp. I've wanted to add another instrument to the sound so it'll be fun to see how it turns out. He's a friend of mine. 'Nough said."

I shook my head and smiled weakly. I felt like a fifth wheel but knew it would pass. "Thanks, guys. I'll try not to mess you up too bad."

"Matt, we got you here by Tommy so that you can just sit back and listen to the sounds. Once we get comfortable with you we'll give you a mic and put you out there for the crowd to hear. I have a feeling you're really gonna dig this."

Paul pulled me aside and whispered low in my ear. "We'll pay you sixty dollars a show and ten percent of the tips; are you in?"

It was way over the top and I slapped his hand. "Heck, yeah, I'm in. Are you nuts? This beats sitting on that bench any day of the week."

The music started and it took me a bit to find the chords. I embellished a little and Tommy rolled his eyes. "We've created a Bob Dylan here, guys." Everyone laughed.

In between sets Tommy stopped by my stool and talked low into my ear. "I know you're off the sauce but you still do some blow now and then, don't ya?"

I winced at the mention of snow and shrugged him off. His breath was bad enough to turn a grizzly around. "No way, man. I'm clean. I gotta stay clean this time."

"If you change your mind, I got a visit from the Snowman and was going to toss you a line, but hey. It's just more for me if you turn it down."

The set started and the music kicked in and the crowd went wild. I sat on my stool enjoying the connection with the audience and got lost in the sounds my new buddies made on stage. It was nice for a time to be a part of such talented people. They looked rough, except for Paul. But man, they were good. The harmonica got heavy as we settled into a third set of songs and I was beginning to really loosen up a bit. It was like everything I had learned as a kid was coming back to me, and with prompting from Paul and Tommy, I let it all go. By the fourth set, the mic had been placed in front of me and I was having a ball.

It didn't slip my attention that Tommy was heading to the men's room way too often. I mentioned it to Paul. "Man, how many times does he go in there a night? It's dangerous. He's gonna get busted, Paul. And you guys might be dragged into it. I can't let that happen to me right now. I'm on my way up."

"I've tried to hold him back but he won't listen. He's crazed by the stuff. You can try to talk to him but I'm afraid he's headed down a one-way street."

Suddenly some people in the crowd came up to us and asked who was playing the harp. I blushed and ducked out to take a smoke outside. When I came back in, Paul was waiting to start the last set. I was tired and decided to sit one out. I pulled a chair up at a table and kicked back to listen to the band I was fast becoming a part of. My hand dropped into my pocket and felt the cross down in the corner. I thought of Brother Joe and what he had said to me before I left his house. My eyes were distracted, watching Ginger swaying to the beat of the music. Her voice could take me places in my mind. But I strained to stay focused on what my plan was. I didn't need a female in my life just yet. Especially one with twins.

When the night was over I thanked the members of the band and walked with Paul to his car. "Man, you have no idea how much I enjoyed tonight. Thanks for letting me sit in with your band. It felt better than I thought it would. Hope I didn't mess things up for you guys."

Paul looked me straight in the eye. "Seriously? You sounded great. I was glad you were in there and the crowd seemed to like what you did. How 'bout joining us tomorrow night for another set? It won't be as long a gig, but you will get some needed practice."

"Sure. I'll do it. About the same time?"

"Yep. We play at 8:30. Don't be late. And stay clean. You're looking so much better."

"Got it, buddy. Thanks again."

I put the money he had handed me in my wallet. It felt weird to have cash in my pocket. But it felt good. I made a decision right then and there to not look backwards and regret anything.

CHAPTER 7

———— ⚜ ————

NEW JERSEY WAS having a heck of a winter. The snow on the size twelve Herman Survivor hiking boots was slowly forming a puddle of water that was growing by the minute as it melted and trickled down the laces to the floor. Hunter Pierce had just discarded them in his dorm room in Seton Hall and had taken his post near a window, which was the only light left in the room. The moonlight came alive in a white haze that illuminated the courtyard of the school.

His mom, Irene, had been so proud to hear he'd been accepted to Seton. That seemed a lifetime ago as Hunter stared outside the window at the snow clinging to a willow tree, causing it to resemble a dandelion in full bloom. Tiny drifts quickly formed through the wrought iron fence bars that gated the dorm area creating a blanket of silence over this playground of academia. The frost that crystallized on the window served as a movie screen to one of winter's darkest ballets. The silence he felt was punctuated by huge gusts of wind, and the sidewalks were slowly getting lost in the white fluffy snow. His eyes found the park tables that looked like Styrofoam statues of old men playing cards, sculpted by old man winter.

The microwave beeped on the counter and disrupted his thoughts as he grabbed his hot chocolate that had been purchased at the local convenience store. He peeled the lid from the squeaky cup and put his nose down close to smell the aroma and let the steam warm his face. His mother's voice kept returning to his mind because lately he'd been thinking about trying to locate his father. Especially since her death. He stared out the window with her words running through his mind.

"When your dad was young his head was full of lofty ideas, like you, Hunter. The Ivy League schools eluded him so he worked hard to put together a list of schools that would accept him so he could pursue a career in the medical field. Your father was a blue collar doctor that outworked every starched shirt he competed with. He would be so proud of you if he knew you'd been accepted to Seton Hall. He would raise his glass in a toast to you, Hunter. If he only knew."

"Mom, you talk about him like he was a saint. Yet you never told him about me."

"He could have been a saint, Hunter, with his intelligence and great stature. But his love for booze was frightening to me as I watched him destroy everything and everyone around him, including his own mind. The liquor quieted the violence but it also dimmed what made him special to me. It was unbearable to see; my own father was a drunk. I couldn't live through it again with your dad. When you were born I wouldn't take his calls. Your smile has haunted me and I have watched as you acquired his persistent drive as you grew up."

*She never told him I was alive. . . .*His thoughts drifted away as his roommate came stomping into the room.

"Man, it's frigging cold out there!" Lonnie exploded, as he shook off the snow from his surplus jacket. "You trying to save energy or something?" He flipped on all the lights and frowned at Hunter.

"Sure am. Doing my part, if you don't mind." But Hunter's words fell like bricks to the floor. He wasn't really paying attention to his loud friend.

"I can't wait to get back to South Carolina. Sure hope it's warmer. Warm enough to bring out the bikinis on Myrtle Beach!" He grinned and winked in Hunter's direction, oblivious to the faraway look in his eyes.

Hunter responded weakly with a nod.

"You headed back to Philly for the holidays?" Lonnie reinserted, trying to get his friend to talk.

Hunter stared out the window, getting lost in the sea of white. "Yes, well, old Hunter is gonna do some hunting this year."

Lonnie stopped pacing and sat on the edge of his bed. "Chasing skirts?"

"No way. Bigger prize than that." Hunter avoided any further questions by heading into the kitchen to get a Coke. He had been fatherless for twenty-one years and it was time he tried to get some answers to questions that had haunted him all his life. He went into the bedroom and squatted down, pulling open the bottom drawer of his nightstand. He lifted out an old hardback copy of *Jane Eyre* and slipped the out the laminated bookmark. It was his mother's obituary and his eyes welled up with tears as he scanned the words. He was in awe of how lovely she looked, even in a faded black and white photo. He whispered to her in a low voice, "He may have scared you, Mom, but he doesn't scare me. I'm gonna find this guy no matter what."

Hunter plodded through calf-deep snow on his way down West Orange Boulevard. Four more blocks, he thought, then left into the area locals called "the Badlands," and then three more lights to the Greyhound station. Hunter was delighted at the way his hiking boots crushed the drifts under his feet. He smiled as he rehearsed the details of his plan in his mind. He would take the forty-five minute bus ride to Aunt Jenny's in Mt. Laurel. After a nice meal and visit with his aunt he would get a good night's sleep and go through his mother's things. Once he had a good place to start he would take his mom's Chevy into Philly. Between his cell phone, laptop, and what clues he could dig up, he was willing to use his whole break if needed. *How difficult could this all be, anyway? Three days tops*, he mused.

As he made the turn towards the bus depot the snow got grayer and slushier. An old Ford Escort sped past him, sending a wave in its wake. He weaved over to the far side of the sidewalk to evade the wall of water and soft ice that pelted him as he ducked out of reach. But not fast enough. "Damn!" He let a curse slip as he shook off the cold wet snow and proceeded down the road. Shaking off the snow, he didn't notice the approach of the sixty-something Italian guy wearing a denim vest over what looked like three flannel shirts.

"Hey, buddy, can ya spare a buck or two so I can get down to Philly and scare up some work?"

"Can't, man. Don't have any." Hunter stepped around the man, moving a little faster down the sidewalk to avoid further contact with the bum.

"How 'bout some loose change you can spare?"

Hunter shook his head. He set his sights on the gray, white, and blue sign on the Greyhound Bus Station, and silently quickened his pace. Wasting no time, he wondered where people like that came from. *Can't they just keep a job? Do they think we're gonna just hand 'em money? Do I look like Mother Teresa or something?* He yanked on the double doors, entered the depot, and took his place in line with the holiday travelers. Husbands were hugging their wives goodbye and people were laughing and talking together. He stood in line feeling as if everyone had a companion except him. The line was dragging and he allowed himself to wish that his mother was meeting him instead of his aunt. Then the thought occurred to him. *I wonder if this Matt guy would really hit it off with me, or would he rather not know I'm alive? We could go to a Sixers' game. He probably has season tickets.*

Hunter paid his money, got his ticket, and sauntered over to one of the six lines forming near the back of the room. There were more people getting off the bus, being greeted by noisy cheers. Again he felt the loneliness creeping in as he walked to the big blue bus with the sleek happy looking dog on the side. Busy workers tossed luggage under the passenger compartment. He felt like he was almost being herded like cattle as he found his cadence of step and wait. Step and wait. He slowly ascended the stairs, trying to stay ahead of the loud lady behind him. The high school student ahead of him kept holding him back to an arduous pace.

Once on the bus he spotted two empty seats. Half falling, he stooped and climbed into one of the seats. He settled down and spied two attractive coeds, perhaps from Seton Hall. The thought buoyed his sagging spirits that maybe they might join him at some point so they could swap cell numbers on his way to Mt. Laurel. He daydreamed that perhaps they even lived near his aunt and they could go out and check out some bands in the area.

He was snapped back into reality when a vaguely familiar voice entered his head. It was that rude panhandler cramming his backpack into the overhead compartment right above his head. *No way! God, don't let this be true.* The vagabond plunged into the vacant seat next to him, stirring an invisible cloud of liquor and unwashed human flesh into the air.

"Paco's the name," the guy blurted out as he plopped down in the seat next to him.

Hunter saw the two coeds passing by and knew his dream was never going to be a reality. As luck would have it, he was going to sit next to this guy the whole trip.

"My name's Hunter," he said, not hiding the disdain. Paco's breath did little to hide the fact that the money he'd begged on the street was now in the cash drawer of the liquor store across the street. This was going to be a long ride. Hunter stared out the window, watching buildings go by, dreading the conversation he was fated to have with this wrinkled, smelly man next to him. He really wanted to sit and think about the man he called his father. But there was no way Paco was going to sit there quiet on the long bus ride. Leaning his head back against the seat, he closed his eyes and thought about his mother and all the things she'd said about his father. He was dying to know what he looked like. What he sounded like. His thoughts were interrupted by a rough voice and he didn't have to open his eyes to know whose it was.

"Where ya headed?" Paco coughed and spit travelled a foot in front of him.

"Mt. Laurel." Hunter was blunt.

"I'm headed to Philly to scare up some work."

"So you said." Hunter looked out the window as cars whizzed by. Shadows seemed long, and street lights were just coming on as the two men made their way to their respective destinations. Paco seemed to really want to talk so Hunter struggled to pull his mind into the moment. He had nothing to lose and there was no one else to talk to.

"I'm gonna be in Mt. Laurel for the next couple days." He could tell Paco was listening.

Paco unscrewed the stop of a pint of O'Shaunessy's Private Stock. A bright orange sticker on the cap read $3.99. It smelled acrid and cheap. The smell of bourbon was repulsive to Hunter, who had never been a drinker. He avoided even being around it if he could.

"Take a sip, man. It's good stuff."

Hunter shook his head. "Nope. No thanks. I don't drink."

"'Sup, man? I didn't get any backwash in it yet."

Hunter winced. "Never cared for the stuff."

Paco shrugged. "All the more for me."

Hunter watched as Paco, who was weirdly becoming his confidante, gulped the foul-smelling liquor down like it was water. "Some gulp," he said as he watched Paco take a pull on his bottle. "We still got forty five minutes 'til we hit Mt. Laurel, and Philly is another hour down the road."

Paco grinned and whipped open his denim vest revealing another bottle. "I brought reinforcements," Paco said, settling even deeper into the soiled gray cloth seats. "So why you off the sauce, you sick or something?"

"Not hardly," said Hunter, remembering a promise he'd made to his mom years ago. *Before she got so sick.* Hunter's mind trailed off. *Before she got so sick. Before she died.* His eyes began to tear in the darkening bus.

"You meeting your folks for the holiday?" Paco's question jolted Hunter back to the present.

"No, man. No folks here. Not yet, anyway." The vague answer piqued Paco's curiosity and his eyes bore down on his young companion with a quizzical stare.

"Mom and Dad split up before I was born and my mom passed away six months ago, after a two year illness." Hunter got quiet and turned his face towards the window.

Paco's voice trailed off. "Ouch, kid! All alone just like that, eh? Damn, I guess you just never know."

Paco's style allowed his human side to appear from underneath the baggy, torn clothing. "Dude, I'm sorry to hear that. Damn sorry. Well she suffered for two years; I guess her suffering is over now. Where is your dad?" Paco persisted in questioning him.

Hunter found himself letting out more information than he'd planned to say to this stranger. "Mom never told my dad he had a son. She said she didn't want to be involved with his demise. When she was sick I begged her to contact him for help with bills and stuff. But she suffered in silence. He has no idea I'm alive. And no idea she is dead."

Hunter changed the subject. "Where you from, Paco?"

Paco's face lit up. *I bet it's rare to have anyone take an interest in his story without soliciting a few sips of his whiskey*, Hunter thought.

"Well, I wasn't always the guy you see today. I grew up in a hard working family in New Rochelle. I made varsity in both football and track. I was fast. I could run, man, really run. Got a full ride to Purdue and was looking at a degree in nuclear engineering. I was gonna get my degree in June but I was drafted and it wasn't the NFL. I was running with a hippie chick in those days. After burning my draft card I showed everyone just how fast I could run; we went clear to Ottawa, where I rode out the war. In '79 we crossed the border back into New York where I lived in a commune near White Plains. Man, we smoked a lot of dope in those days. After I got amnesty I finally got set up with a job at Three Mile Island."

"So how did you end up on the street?"

"It's a long story, Son. And I bet we don't have that kind of time."

"Aw, come on, Paco. Don't leave me like that. You've obviously been on the street a long time. Give it up."

Paco swallowed and looked out the window. "I was a draft dodger. I was under the radar and flirted with disaster. The engineer job held me up for a while but when disaster hit, I had no foundation to stand on. When the plant closed I had no job and began to drink. The rest is history. I fell back on my survivor skills I'd learned long ago. The street became my friend. I had nowhere to turn and I was tired, Son. Tired of dodging life."

Hunter sat there quietly, thinking about what he'd just heard. If a man as intelligent as Paco could end up on the street, that said a lot about the uncertainty of life. How far a man can go in society and be as brilliant as Einstein, and still end up living on the streets. What was this guy's real name? And how far down did he go before he let go of his name?

Paco got sleepy from the liquor he'd swallowed and leaned his head back against the seat. His eyes closed and he was asleep before Hunter could finish their conversation. It was more than obvious that the life he'd chosen to live had taken its toll on him. He looked old and beaten down. Odd that Hunter had been so against talking to him, but somehow had gotten Paco to open up and tell him his life story in five minutes. He wondered how people survived outside the world of jobs, home and family. *There it was again, that word "family."* In the ride that transpired he and Paco had swapped dreams and plans. Hunter mused at how the older bum had so quickly earned his confidence.

As miles sped by, they were nearing Mt. Laurel, and Hunter began to get anxious about getting off the bus. As Paco's snoring became less and less tolerable, the lights inside the bus turned on. They'd reached Mt. Laurel and Hunter slid past his sleeping friend and prepared to exit. As he stepped off the bus he felt his spirits rise. Soon he would embark on his brief adventure and the waiting arms of Aunt Jenny. As he walked away from the bus towards the depot he turned and saw Paco sound asleep, leaning against the window. He wondered if he'd ever see the old man again. The thought occurred to him that maybe he should have left an address or phone number with the guy. But it was too late now. He could see Aunt Jenny waving to him in the crowd.

CHAPTER 8

———— ⚜ ————

THE ROOM WAS dark and humid when I walked into RT's. Someone was sitting on a bar stool smoking, even though the bar was supposed to be smoke free. I could see a curl of gray find its way up to the ceiling, disappearing in a cloud of smoke that moved along the edge of the room. I was sweating from the walk to the bar along the beach road and it felt good to sit quietly before the chaos began. I picked up my harmonica and began a slow mournful tune, just loosening up to get ready for the faster pace of the band. *Moon River* floated out of the harp and I lost myself in feelings that had been hidden, coming out in the notes that lifted up in the air. My eyes were closed and when I opened them I was looking at Paul, who was standing motionless right in front of me. His eyebrow were raised up, which usually meant he was annoyed.

"Dude. Where did that come from?"

"What? You don't like it?" I grinned, thinking he was annoyed at me for playing such an old tune in "his" bar.

"Are you serious? It was awesome. It was frigging amazing. Where did that come from?"

"I was just killing time before you guys came out. It was nothing. Really."

"Well, don't stop. What else you got hidden in there? Dang. It sounded really sick. I'm ready to hear more."

I laughed and slid off the stool shaking my head. "I never know what angle you're coming from, Paul. Totally blew me that you liked that. I was just clowning around."

"Well, do it more often. That's what we want, even when we're doing a rock tune. Just jazz it up a bit and you got it, dude."

He called the rest of the guys up on stage and they all got tuned up and were ready to play in five minutes. It was second nature to them.

Ginger winked at me and began a strong chording on the keyboard, and Tommy kicked in on the drums. He looked rough but what else was new? I didn't know how he'd lasted this long with all the snow he was taking in. His lips were white. No telling what his teeth looked like by now. Paul, Derek, and Mac picked up the beat and the song took off. I was struggling with finding the key but finally picked it up and let my mind go, just listening to the melody line and letting the harp slide. The place began to fill up, and when I opened my eyes people were filling up the front tables and ordering drinks. The night had started and we were into our first set. I was already picking up the lingo and this was only my second night with the band.

I had a perfect seat on the stage near Tommy, so I could watch the whole band and the audience, too. Paul had worn some ripped jeans that I'd considered throwaways when I was on the street. But he looked cool in them, along with a black t-shirt with the name of the band on the front. His thick brown hair was slicked back and his white teeth showed up in the heavy lights that were almost blinding at the front of the stage. Ginger was wearing boots, jeans and a red shirt tied in a knot at her waist. Her hair was long and a little ragged looking, but she was beautiful in her own way. Nothing to me. But a good friend to Paul and the gang. I was learning about her and all her issues. She was a strong woman and was good for the band. And I could use a friend.

Derek was the showman of the group. He loved the limelight and fought for it with Paul. His voice was stronger but Paul could rip out your heart on the high notes. So they made a good pair at the mic. The girls loved them and that just egged them on. I loved being in the background and kept it that way through the whole night. Even though Paul wanted me to move up to the front of the stage at the end, I ignored his leading and remained on my stool near Tommy. But I got stronger on the harp and blew some heavy notes and drug them out. It was good and I knew it. But I was still learning.

There were some tough looking guys in the back of the bar that I'd seen earlier talking to Tommy on the side of the building when I walked up. Sitting near them was a man that looked vaguely familiar. I strained to get a better look at him but the lights were in my eyes and everything past the first couple tables was pretty dark. Near the end of the night, the man in the back got up and walked to the door, looking back one more time before he left. The light hit just right as he turned and I noticed that it was my heart doctor, who I hadn't seen since my stents were put in place. He was dressed in jeans and a black pullover so it was tough to recognize him, but as soon as I knew it was him, memories flooded back of the hospital and the smell of ether.

The night was going smoothly and we switched to some Eagles songs, and the crowd started dancing. This was my favorite time in the bar, because the focus was off of us. They were just having fun now. We were in a groove and nothing was stopping us.

"Matt! Did you catch that?" Paul's voice snapped me back to reality.

"Uh, no. What's up?"

"We're doing another song. The crowd doesn't want to go home."

I looked at Paul and grinned. He was loving this. "Okay, dude. What're we doing?"

"The last tune over again. They loved it. Only this time, move your stool up front. The girls are screaming for that harp sound. You're getting good, man. I think that juice you lived on for so long has given you some soul."

I laughed, but on the inside I winced. That juice had nearly taken me down. It didn't give me soul, it nearly took my soul out. I moved my stool to the center front next to Paul and Derek and gave it all I had. I didn't even look at the crowd this time, but kept my eyes shut and felt the movement of the song. Everything that I'd ever been through was coming out on this song. And the crowd went frigging crazy.

We ended on a powerful note and Tommy slammed the drums down all at once. I looked out of the corner of my eye and noticed he didn't look too good, but it was too late. He leaned over and fell off the stool he was barely sitting on. Hit the floor like a ton of bricks. No one noticed because the crowd was so noisy, but I grabbed Paul and Mac and we pulled him off the stage. He was sweating profusely and red faced. Mac opened the door of his Honda and we shoved Tommy in the front seat. We headed to the ER at Mercy Central, and we all knew this was serious. Tommy may have overdone it this time on the snow.

We were sitting in the waiting room anxious to see how Tommy was doing, worried that he'd done himself in. Paul tried to head back to the room where they were working on him. The nurse stopped him at the door.

"Sorry, we don't want anyone back here right now. We're doing all we can to save your friend. As soon as I know anything, I'll come and tell you."

"With all due respect Miss, he's our drummer. Our best friend here. He'd want us to be back there with him, ya know?"

She stood her ground and the look in her eyes told Paul more than he wanted to know. "Sorry. But not this time. It's pretty serious. You better wait here in the lounge. I'll be back shortly."

She disappeared and Paul came and sat down with me and Ginger and Mac. Derek came in shortly after he'd parked the car and had a smoke. He was shaking his head.

"He didn't look good, dude. He didn't look good at all.

Paul put his head in his hands. "No he didn't. He may have gone too far with that white powder. Stubborn. Just plain damn stubborn."

"Aren't we all?" I decided to add my two cents into the pot.

"Yeah, we are. But he was playing with fire. White fire. You know that as well as I do."

"Where was he getting his stuff? You guys have any idea?" I asked quietly.

They all shook their heads. Mac answered in a low voice. "Dude, it's easy to find. He had his own source, I'm sure. But we didn't ask questions. He wouldn't listen so we dropped it. He was one of the best drummers around so we put up with it, knowing he'd probably overdose at some point. But what do ya do?"

I shook my head. It was too much for me for one night. "I'm headed home. Let me know how he's doing. I know you guys will want to hang out here until you know something. I'll be at my apartment, so ring me no matter what time it is. You got my number, Paul."

It was cold as heck outside and I had a long walk ahead of me. Paul wasn't thinking when he let me leave. But I pulled my coat up around me and started out towards the apartment. I listened to the traffic racing by and the pounding of the waves coming in to shore. Suddenly my heart raced as I felt all the emotions rushing back in. It wasn't that long ago that I'd been homeless. I stood up and stretched and headed back towards the apartment. I owed Brother Joe my life because in reality I deserved the bench. But what I got was hope.

It took me about forty-five minutes before I saw Main Street looking back at me. I turned down the road and the wind picked up, making it hard for me to breathe. I tucked my head into my coat and trotted a little, trying not to think about Tommy up there struggling for his life. But in the back of my mind was the face of my doctor and those goons in the back of the bar. And because I had used drugs not so terribly long ago, it was easy to smell drugs on others. The signs would be there plain as day. And it didn't hurt that I had discovered the janitorial closet with snow in it about four feet high.

As I got closer to the parsonage, I spotted Brother Joe standing in the kitchen window. It was late and I was surprised to see him still up. *Does the guy ever sleep?* I fought the urge to knock on his door and walked directly to my apartment and unlocked the door. I was freezing and my feet were getting cold. I hurried to the bedroom and yanked off my coat, took my clothes off and jumped into a hot shower. It felt good to just stand there and feel the hot water running over my head and back. I was tired but the hot water felt so soothing that I leaned against the wall and enjoyed the warmth for about ten minutes, and then shut it off, dried myself off, and headed to the kitchen.

My eye caught something odd sitting on my table, and I finished heating up some hot water for a late night cup of coffee and walked over to the table. My eyes were hurting from the cold but not so bad that I couldn't recognize a new computer sitting on my table. A new computer. *What in the world is Brother Joe doing?*

I sat down and opened a fully loaded laptop. Ready to use. I jumped up and opened my front door to see if his lights were still on, but they had been turned off. He was no dummy. He knew I'd want to thank him, and that wasn't what he was about. What a guy! There was a note on the table that had been shoved under the computer. I lifted the flap and pulled out the folded piece of paper, looking at the scratchy note written to me.

"Thought you'd like to have a computer to talk to the world. You've been shut off for a long time and I think it's time you reached out. You never know what you'll find. Have fun, Matt! Bro. Joe."

I sat back in shock at this man who'd found his way into my life. Who was this guy? And what made him sit down with me at the Coffee House? He seemed so comfortable with me. Like he already knew me. It was crazy. But he'd been nothing but nice to me since then; he'd offered me a place to live so I could get off the street. *I don't think he knows what he did for me. Or maybe he does.*

I was so tired from the long night and worrying about Tommy and the rest of the band. The bed was calling me so I closed the computer and headed back to the bedroom. When I lay my head down on the pillow I was out in five seconds. Comatose.

CHAPTER 9

⚜

THE OLD BUS engine fired up again, roaring in low gear through the side streets of Mt. Laurel, gently sloping up the wet on ramp to the highway. The headlights illuminated the snowflakes until they resembled a shower of falling stars as the bus sped toward Philadelphia. Paco snored in his warm retreat from the elements outside. His eyes darted open from time to time but then he settled back down as the warm air in the bus offered him a long awaited respite from winter's harsh treatment. Before he knew it he was being bumped and brushed by passersby unloading at the Philadelphia station. The inside of the station glowed with the reflection of yellow lights on a dull gray wall. It was time to get off the bus.

"Wake up! We're in Philadelphia!" A voice invaded Paco's sleep. "End of the line, buddy. You got to get off the bus."

Paco quickly staggered to his feet. Nothing seemed to go smoothly enough, as the backpack jammed behind the safety cables in the overhead compartment. After tugging it back and forth a few times, he felt it finally spring free, and he headed for the door of the bus. Pushing his way through the crowd like a linebacker for the Eagles, he stepped into the cold, feeling the bitter December air, but it did little to sober him up—it just made him shiver as he pressed his way into the station.

He instinctively checked his stash to make sure he had a couple belts to fortify him for the night ahead. He was happy to be back in Philly and was looking forward to seeing a few of his pals when he suddenly remembered his conversation with the young boy. *What was his name?* Paco strained to retrieve memories from the blurry bus ride from South Orange. *Fisher . . . uh, Fisher. No, Hunter. That was it! Hunter, the med student from Seton Hall. Nice kid.*

As he rested in an unlit outside corner of the parking lot, he secretively retrieved the bottle from his breast pocket and took a healthy sip. He rehearsed the memory of the recently orphaned boy on his quest for his long lost dad and smirked at the boy's idealism. Paco had heard all the warning signs; his dad was a drinker, and his mom probably knew more than she ever told the boy. *Hell, I would have a better chance of finding that guy than Hunter would. He's an Ivy League kid and his mom might have had some will money or a nice insurance settlement. I bet that kid would pay a nice finder's fee in exchange for the whereabouts of his dad. If his dad is still alive.*

The wheels spun in Paco's dimming brain. The whiskey was working to settle his nerves and help him concoct great schemes. He laughed at himself and then he shook off the thoughts and hurried to the men's room. After relieving himself he bent over the sink to splash water on his face to help chase away the whiskey induced slumber. He cupped his hand and brought the pool of water to his face, trying to rehydrate himself as he washed. His head hummed in unison with the buzzing of the bluish fluorescent lights. He tried to gather his thoughts long enough to come up with a plan for the night. It was about 9:00 and he had a few hours to kill before he camped out for the night. The cold weather is gonna make tonight a real challenge, he thought, as he reached into his pocket and felt the twenty dollars and grinned. Just enough to get him through the night. Grabbing his gear he braced himself for the trek to a bar called Nicky's. It had been years since the neon N had burned out but everybody in town knew the name.

Pushing open the bus station door, he trudged through the snow and ice, weaving his way through the back alleys and side streets. The Budweiser sign glowed in the distance, urging him to quicken his pace. As he walked he reflected on his visit with Hunter. Something inside him really hoped the kid would soon be reunited with his dad. Yet, if this guy Matt followed a path like his own he would be a little tougher to find than the kid expected. Paco soon dismissed the thought of helping Hunter as he opened the door to Nicky's. The smell of stale beer and the sound of Patsy Cline made Paco feel right at home. He set his back pack in a conspicuous location near the coat rack, so he could keep an eye on it from his seat. The dimly lit bar provided shelter from the cold for as long as he could keep a beer in front of him. He bellied up and ordered a draft from an unsmiling bartender who only acknowledged him after Paco pulled the money from his pocket. He surveyed the rough-looking crowd and hoped he might talk his way into a pool game for the night's entertainment that might also net him a few more dollars.

The stools were vinyl and the legs wobbled as Paco settled in at his table. He kept a close eye on his backpack because that was all he had in the world. Other patrons were scattered all around the bar, including two boys about twenty years old. They were overdressed but were enjoying the abundance of cheap beer. It was obvious that the older lady next to them had played the Patsy Cline tune on the juke box, because she looked so annoyed at the noise they were making. Beside her there was an older guy fighting sleep, and the bartender had his eye on him to make sure he stayed awake. Someone else at the other end of the bar, wearing a wool coat, was also watching the old timer, hoping he would fall asleep. Paco knew this crowd well and he knew his first game would be with the younger boys but he was really looking for a game against the guy in the wool coat. He walked over to the boys, keeping his head low.

"You guys up for a game of cutthroat?"

Both kids shrugged and nodded, much to the relief of the Patsy Cline fan. Paco handed the lanky kid his dollar and said, "Money breaks, right?"

They grinned and nodded. Oddly quiet. The lanky one racked the balls while his buddy and Paco picked up their sticks. As Paco rubbed his stick he glanced at the guy in the wool coat and was not surprised to see he was watching. He broke the rack with a lame break. As the colorful balls scattered across the green felt, he sipped his beer and noticed happily that none of the balls dropped. The two boys dropped two balls each. Paco quickly saw his one ball resting near the corner pocket. He hit it dead on and it gently fell in the hole, but the cue ball followed it in. The lanky guy got lucky and sunk three more but got over zealous with his final ball. The pudgy guy was about to take his shot when the man with the coat put his dollar on the table and announced he would take on the winner. The kid only scattered the balls more. Paco cheerfully sunk his remaining five balls and acted surprised as each one fell. He downed his beer with a single gulp and walked to the bar for a refill. The two boys walked up and bought him a beer and the bartender tossed a chip beside Paco's glass insuring he would get two beers for the price of a pool game. Before he could get the glass to his lips, the man in the coat walked up.

"Name is Burt."

Paco nodded and drank some of his beer. Burt picked out his stick and strutted to the table. It was obvious he had no intention of losing. He bounced each stick until he found the heaviest. After Paco took another sip, he racked the balls for his new best friend and Burt slammed the cue into the awaiting balls. One spun into the side as the cue came to rest with a good line on the four and six.

"Damn!" Paco blurted out. "Good thing we're only in for a beer."

"We could make it interesting." Burt stared at Paco. He pulled a single from his pocket and laid it on the edge of the table. Predictably, Burt won the next game in two rounds and Paco started chalking for game two. Burt racked and went to refill his beer. Paco tossed him a chip.

"Glad you're giving me a chance to get my beer back." Paco kept a stolid expression as he lined up his break. "I thought we were gonna make this game interesting. You thinking five? Ten would make it a short night for me."

"Let's make it a short night then," Burt replied with a smirk.

Paco broke and hit solids and ran seven more, and missed on the eight. Burt only got five but buried the cue ball so deep in the corner that it was going to take two banks to even tap the eight ball. Paco bent to line up the shot and remarked in a low voice, "Glad it wasn't twenty."

"Got you scared now, man." Burt lifted his glass confidently.

Paco mumbled under his breath. "Oh, hell, no guts no glory." He popped the shot like he had twelve times last month and as the eight ball dropped into the pocket he retrieved his pint and sipped it as the bartender tried to wake up the old man. Burt tossed the twenty on the felt and retreated to his chair. He got his coat and headed for the door before Paco had even put his stick back in the rack. As Burt opened the door quickly, the cold air blasted in so hard all the patrons could feel it, and then just as suddenly Burt slammed it shut.

Paco sauntered to the bar, a blast of cold air returned, and he saw Burt coming back through the door. Before Paco could turn around, Burt had grabbed his backpack and run out of the bar. Instinctively Paco bolted after him because everything he owned was in that backpack. He snatched the door open and saw Burt climbing into an old Ford truck. Paco grabbed Burt's torso and hurled him into a snow bank. The backpack tumbled to the sidewalk beyond Burt's head. Paco yelled at Burt.

"Don't get up, man. I got my pack and this is finished."

Before the words were out of his mouth, Burt was back on his feet speeding toward Paco. The two men collided and Burt pulled a knife. Paco caught a glimpse of the shiny blade as it ripped across his arm and the two men hit the snow. A crowd gathered at the doorway, shouting. Paco stood up, startled by the attack and grabbed his pack and ran through the snow. The bartender was calling the police, but Paco would be long gone, his footprints covered by the snow that was now coming down in sheets.

CHAPTER 10

⚜

OUT OF BREATH and tired, Paco knew he better find a place to camp out for the night. *Man, the South Side can get ugly this time of year.* He zigzagged through the side streets of south Philadelphia, moving like an alley cat. He knew where he was headed. The old ramp garage near the ancient federal building would be a good place to camp tonight. He was making tracks for it as the wind gusted between the ramshackle houses that stood as his momentary wind breaks, and he moved along towards his destination.

Paco eased up the side of the ramp garage, surveying it carefully to see if there were any unexpected changes since he camped there two months ago. Many a time a good plan like this would get messed up by some construction. *Nothing like a construction company to drive you out of a safe haven*, he chuckled to himself. Good spots were hard to come by in the winter. Soon he was over the wall and entering a stairwell, and he could smell the urine of fellow campers as he climbed the concrete step, feeling his way to find his bunk for the night. His backpack clamored on the concrete as he pulled out his blanket and the old pair of jeans that would serve as his pillow. He remembered the flashlight he had stuffed in his pocket and pulled it out, noticing that the battery was weak. He shined it across the floor to check for rodents and bugs, and the word "Kenmore" jumped out at him as he stumbled upon an abandoned cardboard box large enough for a man to camp out in. His bad knee was aching as he bent down to get into the box, pulling his backpack in with him.

The night was bitter cold but the wind was unable to get its fingers around him, so he felt safe enough to sleep. His shoes had holes in them, and the pants he wore were baggy. His hair was thinning and gray and his eyesight was poor by regular standards, but not in comparison with the eyesight of those men who had lived on the street for many years. He had put the box against a wall to keep somebody from walking up on him from behind. That gave him a tenuous sense of security. He wrestled around to find some position where the more padded parts of his body were hitting the ground. This was getting more difficult as he aged because his muscles were atrophying a little. He pulled his bottle of whiskey out and took the last swig, feeling the warm liquid hitting bottom. His eyes were heavy and as the thoughts of the young man he met on the bus slipped from his mind, he let the elusive blanket of sleep overtake him. He was hoping as he dozed off that the whiskey would keep him out for the rest of the night.

As he slept, some stray feral cats scurried across the floor, hunting for any sign of unforgotten food or scraps that someone else had left. In middle of the night, the temperature dropped to a deadly level and Paco stirred in his box, shivering. A veteran of the street, he knew it was time to build a fire or find a place where a fire was burning.

He climbed out of his box, discouraged. He'd just found that box and now he had to leave it. The forgotten task of checking the weather reports now interrupted his sleep. A little foggy and huddled up, he stood up and got his wits about him and made a decision to head back to the bus station. It was a long walk, but at least there would be heat and if he was lucky, he still had several quarters to keep the television on. That way, they couldn't kick him out. He grimaced, remembering one time when he had spent a full night sitting up in a stall in the men's room. Odd as it might seem, the little pride he had left he wanted to hang on to. As he forged ahead to reach the station, he deliberately moved his arms to create as much heat in his body as he could. When he arrived, he found dozens of people milling around, late night travelers who were bleary-eyed and eager to get to their destination. He fit right in except for his tattered clothing.

⚜

Hours passed and Paco dozed off, leaning his head against the wall. He was not the only person using the bus station for a shelter from the bitter cold. Exhaustion took over and he fell asleep as the passengers walked by him without notice. Paco's head drooped to his chest amid the late night confusion and chatter of the Philadelphia Bus Terminal. Schedule announcements and luggage castors blended to a dream-like drone.

The faint hum of florescent lights that made sleep increasingly uncomfortable also disguised the footsteps of the African American security guard who landed right in front of him. He cleared his throat and spoke in a deep voice. "Where ya headed for, buddy?"

Paco snapped to a groggy state of attention, instinctively misleading the security guard, hoping to buy time.

"Hey, I'm catching the 8:15 into Mt. Laurel, man."

"There is no 8:15 into Mt. Laurel."

Paco's face fell and he could already feel the temperature dropping around his body, knowing he was going to have to go outside or face loitering charges. He saw the guard make a quick decision to ignore the obvious as he looked down at him. "Okay, buddy. I need my seat back by 8:00 in the morning. No excuses. You still here by 8:00, I'm calling the man."

He turned and walked away, and Paco silently thanked a God he hardly ever spoke to for a merciful guard and for a warm place to be. Thoughts of Hunter and the conversation he'd recently had seemed to haunt him. An unfamiliar ring of responsibility was chiming inside his heart, even though he was homeless and starving. He acknowledged that the kid had cast his spell on him and now he was about to be drawn into the drama of finding the errant Dr. Collins. His mind was racing, trying to recall the days when he was an engineer and frequented the bars in the hospital district where doctors often imbibed. An emerging sense of purpose began to surge in his veins but the exhaustion was beginning to take its toll. He leaned his head against the wall and this time he gave in to the weighted feeling of delayed sleep. And night gave way to early dawn.

CHAPTER 11

⚜

AUNT JENNY'S HOUSE was just like he remembered it. It was a bit cluttered but there was some sense to the clutter. A purposeful arrangement of what meant something to her. The paintings over the sofa looked outdated and the leather couch was worn looking. There were plants in the window sills and music was playing softly from an old receiver on a bookshelf.

Aunt Jenny was definitely someone who lived in the past. Hunter found himself sitting at an old familiar table, eating one of her famous bowls of chili. Sweat was forming on his brow, but he loved every spicy bite. He asked for seconds on chili and watched a smile turn up the corners of her mouth as he put warm buttered Italian bread into his mouth. She didn't seem to mind the mess he was making and the crumbs that had found their way to the floor underneath his chair. He carefully studied his beloved aunt, hoping to see the opportunity to enlighten her about his real plan for the winter break.

Breaking the silence, he blurted out his thoughts. "Did you and Mom talk much about Matt Collins?"

Aunt Jenny kept her facial expressions unreadable. "I see you love my chili like you always did. You're asking me a question like that and I haven't seen you in months. You could ask how I was doing."

Hunter swallowed and grinned. "You know I'm crazy about your chili. There's never been any question about that, right? I've just been doing a lot of thinking and I want to find this guy Matt. So I was wondering what Mom ever told you about him."

Jenny stood up and walked over to the sink, rubbing her chin. The wind was howling outside and there was a chill in the house. She'd known this subject was going to come up at some point and resented for a moment that Irene died before the boy got so curious. "Honey, I know you're getting older and I figured this would be on your mind. I will say that your mom and I did talk about Matt a time or two. I've got some things downstairs of your mother's. After you get a good night's sleep, you can shuffle through it all and see what you can find. Might be some old photos and letters in that pile. I knew you wanted some of your mother's things so I didn't throw anything away."

Hunter felt nervous inside. "Do you know where he worked? Can you remember who he hung out with?"

"Honey, you need to see what you can find when you look in your mother's things. That will jog my memory about our conversations. It's been a while, you know. Let's get a good night's sleep. I want to hear all about your college life and how you're doing in school."

Hunter was disappointed because all he'd thought about the entire bus trip was finding Matt. But he knew his aunt was right; he knew he needed a good night's sleep. He gave her a hug and found his way back to his bedroom and turned the radio on by his bed. He kept the sound down low and sat on the edge of his bed and looked around the room. It was like time had stood still. The pictures on the wall were the same as when he was a young boy. His bedspread was the same patchwork quilt, with just a single pillow at the head of the bed. She had a blanket draped over the foot of the bed that he'd used to use to make a fort. There were airplanes he'd made as a young boy. Model planes. He laughed and got up to brush his teeth. He reached for his toothbrush and thought about Paco. *How does he ever get to brush his teeth? Does he even have teeth anymore? And why do I even care about that old drunk?*

He laughed at himself and changed quickly into his pajamas. The room was chilly and he dove into bed, pulling up the covers and yanking the blanket off the footboard. The sheets were cold so he shivered for a few minutes until his body heat warmed the covers. Paco would be shivering about now if he was sleeping outside. *How does he take the cold?* He was getting up there in age and it would be tough to sit outside all night trying to keep the wind off his body. Hunter burrowed into the covers further, pulling the blanket over his head. Paco kept creeping into his thoughts as he drifted off to sleep. Paco and an elusive man named Matt.

Morning came and the sun was beaming through the thin curtains at the window near his bed. He stretched and yawned, listening to his stomach rumble. Hunger was the first thing he felt when he woke up every day. But this morning he was excited about the possibilities that might open up when he went downstairs to the basement to see what his mother had left behind. It was a shot in the dark, but he really wanted some information that would help him trace down his father. *His father.* That had a weird ring to it. He sat up on the edge of the bed and stepped into his jeans. It was cold in the bedroom, almost like a window was cracked. He swore he could see his breath as he headed to the bathroom to brush his teeth. A whiff of bacon came wandering through his doorway; Aunt Jenny's way of getting him out of bed. He smiled and the hunger pangs he'd ignored came back with a roar.

"Hunter! You better get in here. Your breakfast is getting cold!"

Hunter grinned. She was trying to sound tough. "Okay, Aunt Jenny. Coming right down."

He flew down the steps three at a time, only to see her frowning when he walked into the kitchen.

"You're gonna kill yourself at some point on those darn stairs. Now you ready to do some investigating today?"

"It's all I been thinking about! Are you kidding?"

"I know you've got some mighty big expectations, Hunter. You need to settle down and realize your father may not even be alive. We have no idea where he is, Son. No idea what he's doing. He was a pretty rough character at times. I want you to have your eyes wide open about this."

Hunter tucked his head down and ate quietly. He didn't want to hear that he wouldn't have a chance in hell of finding his dad. He was determined to find something out about him one way or the other. Alive or dead, he was gonna track him down. He swallowed his eggs whole and started down the basement stairs, passing his aunt on the way down. "Don't worry. This won't be the first time I've been disappointed."

The stairs were old and creaky and several boards were loose. He tripped on the last step and stumbled into some cobwebs hanging down from the top of the stairwell. Swiping his hand across his face, he tucked his hands into his pockets to keep warm and looked around. It was dimly lit and he had to squint to see what was piled around the edges of the room. It looked like yard sale trash that needed to be thrown out. He shook his head and walked over to the lone window that was full of dust and cobwebs. He grabbed an old rag lying on a stack of papers and wiped the window out, allowing more light into the room. He saw filing cabinets and suitcases, books, and old blankets. Finally his eyes spotted his mother's trunk with a red ribbon tied on the handle. His stomach was full of butterflies when he walked up to it. He was ready to know the truth about his father, but now that it was time to see what his mother had left him, he hesitated and sat down on two suitcases stacked on top of each other near the trunk. His heart was racing and he felt the presence of his mother in the room. He almost was afraid to look.

He put his hand on the trunk and lifted it up, leaning the back of the trunk against an old broken chair. Inside were piles of letters, a few pieces of clothing, books, a couple of hats, and a metal box that had a clasp on it. He fingered the clothing and picked up a blouse and brought it up to his nose, breathing in any remaining smell from his mother. He flipped through some of the books and laid them back into the trunk. Smiling, he lifted up one of the floppy brimmed hats and put it on his head, remembering how his mother looked in the hat.

He got lost in the piles of letters and papers she had left in a drawer in the house that were now neatly piled into one side of the trunk. For a few minutes he forgot the purpose of his search. But suddenly his mind cleared and he grabbed for the metal box and sat up straight. His whole life history might be in that one box and as bad as he wanted to find out who his father was, he was scared to see the truth. He'd lived so long on rumors and short statements about his father and now he had a chance to perhaps find out what really happened.

CHAPTER 12

THE BOX HUNTER had in his hand was about fifteen inches long and eight inches wide. It was wood and metal; he discovered this after he opened the lid. There was a musty smell but nothing was damaged. It was probably just like she'd left it the last time she'd looked inside the box. He hated to disturb anything. This was holy ground to him.

The first thing he found was a movie theater stub. Two of them. He found a stack of greeting cards bound by a rubber band. He tried to take the band off and it broke and snapped his finger. He shook his hand and opened the cards one by one. They all were signed "Love, Matt," or "I love you, Baby, Matt." He smiled. *So he did love her.* He placed the cards back in a stack and laid them in the box. Underneath the cards was a leather journal. He didn't know his mother had kept a journal. *Interesting.* He felt intrusive as he opened the journal, being careful not to bend any pages. This would be something he would cherish all his life. It wasn't just about finding Matt.

The basement was getting colder, or maybe he was just nervous. He shivered and zipped his hoodie up, trying to keep some body heat in. He opened the first pages, noticing her writing changed from day to day. Sometimes she printed, sometimes it was in cursive. And there were pages he could hardly read at all. He scanned the pages looking for comments about his father. His fingers ran down the sentences as his eyes hungrily looked for any small bit of information on Matt. He found notes written about the first few months of their relationship. He grinned, knowing he was close to something important. His mother had no money, so the affair was not about money. He must have been attracted to her and that made him feel some better. Then his eyes spotted some comments about Matt being a doctor. A neurosurgeon. That was impressive. *So he wasn't some fly-by-night that had no education. I wonder what happened to him. What made them break up?*

He kept on reading, hoping to find more information, but most of the writing was about her day, her job, and how much she loved Matt. *Apparently he was the love of her life and she never mentioned the importance of that relationship to me my whole life. How did she keep it such a secret? And why?*

He was deeply disappointed that he didn't find something more about his father in the journal. He put it back in the box and looked around for more papers, anything that would tell him about Matt. He lucked upon an article from a medical journal that had a front page article written by Matt. That was impressive, but it wouldn't help him locate the guy. He also found an old shirt that was definitely a man's shirt, and two photographs of them posed together at the beach. He stared at the man in the photo; it was difficult to see his face clearly because of the hat he had on his head, casting a shadow across the top part of his face. *Not bad looking, though.* He stood up and brought the photographs over to the light from the dirty window, tilting it to see if he could see Matt's face better. He frowned, wanting so much to know this man who was his blood. His history. His mother was smiling; her head was leaning back and she was laughing. She looked happy. *Why didn't it last?*

He pushed aside some of the papers and on the bottom of them was a sealed envelope with his name on it. His breath caught when he put his hand on the envelope. Why did his mom write him a letter?

He leaned back and took a deep breath. This was getting creepy. What did she have to tell him that she had to write in a letter? And when was she going to give it to him? Obviously she died before she could do it, but he still felt weird about it. They'd never really had secrets from each other, so this had to be pretty serious. He grabbed the envelope and ripped it open and unfolded the letter. His eyes watered just seeing his mother's handwriting. It was the neatest he'd ever seen her write. A tear ran down his face as he read the letter out loud.

Dear Hunter,

I know if you are reading this, I am gone. I had planned originally to give this to you when you went to college. But somehow I never got around to it. Please forgive me. You and I never had secrets, as that was a promise we made when you were younger. However, I had my reasons for withholding the information that is in this letter. I hope you will understand why someday.

Your father, the man you wish so much to meet, is named Matt Collins. He was a doctor. A neurosurgeon. A very brilliant man. I want you to know first of all, he is a good man and has a good heart. But he was an alcoholic when we were dating and also did cocaine. When I fell in love with him, I guess I thought things would get better. But they did just the opposite. They got worse. I lived my life for him, Hunter. But I had you and then I put my whole life into you. Matt couldn't take the responsibility of having children, so I left him when I got pregnant and raised you on my own. I never told him I was pregnant. He just thought I left because of the drinking and drugs. That was part of it. But the real reason was I knew he didn't want kids.

He was born in Philadelphia and practiced medicine at St. Francis Hospital. I met him at a party and we hit it off immediately. I want you to know we were happy. I did love him. But he had a temper, and he drank way too much. At times we were happier than we had a right to be. But towards the end, his drinking was his true love, and I was second. It was no life for a child, so I decided to leave Matt and raise you on my own.

I pray one day you find your father and get the answers to the questions that you've had since you were old enough to ask about him, if he's still alive. I know you always wanted a father in your life, and I hope that dream comes true before Matt dies. I love you and want you to know you've been a joy to me all my life. Through all the financial problems we had and all the lonely nights I cried, you were always there for me. I will miss seeing you grow into a man, but if you turn out half the man your father is, you will have achieved greatness. The only flaw is that I don't believe he realizes just how brilliant a man he is. I will go to my grave loving him, if that brings you any peace.

You were the light of my life.

Love, Mother

Hunter leaned back again on the seat and looked down. His hands were shaking and he could hardly fold the letter to put it back into the envelope. He felt his throat closing up and he tucked the letter in his pocket and closed the trunk up. He suddenly wanted to run. To get as far away from everything he knew as he could. His mother was gone, and he had no idea where to find his father, or even if he wanted to be found. He felt mixed up, alone. He ran up the basement stairs and into his room. He started packing, throwing all his stuff into his suitcase and slamming it shut. He was lost in his own world and didn't see his aunt standing in the doorway.

"What's the matter, Hunter? Did you find what you were looking for?"

His throat was so tight he could hardly speak. "Yeah, you might say that."

Seeing his hands shaking, she moved a little closer. "Come on, angel. I know this is tough on you. We can work through it. You don't have to leave."

He turned and looked her in the face, shaking. Tears streaming down his face. "Don't you see, Auntie? I feel like I have no one. My mom is gone. My father may not want to be found. I'm heading back to school where I belong. It's the only place I belong now. I'll keep in touch with you. And I appreciate the chili and the talks we had. But I gotta get outta here real quick or I'm gonna lose it."

"I understand, Hunter. But I wish you'd stick around long enough to work through this. I don't want you to leave upset."

He smiled. But he knew it wasn't a real smile. "I'll be fine. I'm just not over all the things I saw in that trunk. My life's about to take a different turn, Aunt Jenny. And I can't promise you how it'll turn out. But I can promise that I'll come back to you soon. Don't you worry."

As he walked out the door Jenny shook her head. The boy had been through too much. How much could a young man take without cracking? She hoped she never found out.

CHAPTER 13

⚜

I AWOKE TO the sound of my cell phone ringing. Through sleep-glazed eyes I saw Paul's name on the screen. It was 6:00 am. *After a long night what could he want?* I sat up, pushed the call button and heard Paul say, "Hey Matt, it's Paul. Tommy is dead." A long silence followed and my thoughts were spinning as to what to do next.

"Are you okay, Paul?" I asked, my throat as dry as I ever remembered it being.

"Yeah, I'm okay. Just wanted you to know."

"Man, I don't believe it! What the heck happened? Was it bad coke or just too much?"

"Damn it, man, we should've seen it coming. I just always figured he would straighten out in time."

"Who we got to sit in on drums tonight?"

"I haven't gotten that far, dude. I just called you first. Been at the hospital all night."

"You need me to come over there?" I asked.

"Thanks, but I'm okay. I'll give you a call after I get things figured out. Sorry to wake you up with this news, dude. But my head is kinda spinning. It barely seems real."

"Yeah, I hear ya!" I couldn't say any more.

Paul hung up. I swung my feet to the floor and just sat there. The scene whirled in my head. Tommy had taken way more than the usual bathroom breaks. *Damn it, why didn't I see it coming? Those thugs came in with. . . .*My thoughts were interrupted by Brother Joe knocking on my door.

"Sorry to bother you," Joe said, "but I couldn't help overhearing you talking and was wondering if you would help me eat some of these waffles? They're good when they're warm but once they get cold, well you may have to use a steak knife on 'em." As always, Joe's good-natured way got me out of my own head for a minute.

"Sure. Be right there." I threw on my jeans and headed for the bathroom. Waking up in this place was a pleasure compared to that bench. I could remember the last time I woke up to mosquitoes buzzing around my face. The water from the faucet felt good on my face. Couldn't wait to join Brother Joe in his now famous breakfast talks, wondering what silly joke he was going to make today. Sure beat waiting for the bag lunch they handed out at St. Ben's. Or having to wait in line with the grumpy homeless guys that were my only company for a while.

Joe greeted me in his customary fashion when I came in the kitchen. He took the frying pan lid off the plate that held my waffle, and a wisp of steam rose in the air.

"That looks good, Joe." I took my seat. Joe studied me as I applied liberal amounts of butter and syrup. When I took my first bite, he spoke quietly.

"While I was at the store I got that new spread that's better for you than butter. I can't have my star harmonica player adding more cholesterol to his diet just because I like having breakfast with him."

"Hmmm," I grunted. "I think I'm a former harmonica player, Joe."

"You quit the band already?"

"No man, I didn't quit but our drummer Tommy bought it last night.

"Bought it?" Joe asked quizzically.

"He died," I said out loud. "I think he got a hot shot or something."

"Hot shot?" asked Joe. His frequent need for clarification got the conversation off to a laborious start as we enjoyed our waffles and coffee.

"Well, we used to call it that when someone got either bad dope or took too much at a time."

Joe looked saddened by the news. "I hate hearing about victims of addiction." I could see he was sincere and I began to speak more slowly and deliberately. I wasn't used to having someone to share news with so I didn't want to be insensitive.

"Tommy had a coke habit. We all thought he would snap out of it. But lately Tommy had been keeping company with a couple of thugs. I saw those same thugs at the hospital while I was there recovering from a heart attack."

Joe looked surprised but interested. So I continued.

"I'm getting the feeling these guys are in cahoots with my heart doctor over in Ft. Walton. I was never gonna say anything but damn, Joe. Tommy's dead." Joe stopped eating and leaned forward to listen. His look was the one I'd grown to love. He showed genuine concern and he always had a grasp on the big picture.

"Are you telling me you think you're doctor had something to do with your drummer's death, Matt?"

My answer was as uncertain as I was at that moment. "I've been around bars and around dope for a big chunk of my life, and I've learned how to watch people. And I've got a strong feeling these dots all connect."

"It's a very strong accusation, Matt. A man's career is at stake if you're wrong."

A sound warning, I surmised. "Yeah, I know."

"Your follow-up care is with this same physician, is it not?" Joe questioned. I simply nodded in agreement.

"Son, I know this guy's death shook you up a bit, but you can't afford to tarnish a man's reputation just because he was at the bar that same night."

"So you think I ought to shut up about the whole thing?" The conversation now had a life of its own.

"No, that's not the answer, Matt," Joe stated flatly. "You got to have some kind of straight story before you alert authorities. If people went to the cops every time they had a suspicion the police would never have time to stop a real crime, don't you see, Matt?"

"I wasn't thinking cops," I shot back at Joe.

"Silence is a poor answer, as well. Then you inadvertently become part of the conspiracy of silence." I listened as he continued.

"If what you're saying is true you have to report it. If what you're saying is just your own grief, it's best not to hurt reputations and stir up trouble over nothing."

"Joe, when I was in the hospital I watched the same guys who were at RT's, and they appeared to be operating out of a closet at the hospital." Joe's eyebrows went up. I clearly had his full attention so I continued.

"These three guys were coming and going at the hospital and one of the thugs went into the men's room with Tommy at RT's. I know a guy when he's geeked up and Tommy was definitely geeked. No question in my mind! In fact, that night he took his life." Joe slid back in his chair a few inches from the table and gave me his undivided attention.

"Matt, you can't go to the cops half-cocked. You're going to see your doctor today. Why don't you ask him? I'm sure there's an explanation to all this and you can put your suspicions to rest." That sounded good because the thoughts were beginning to cycle around in my brain and I was feeling uneasy about the whole mess.

"I really want you to get over this drinking thing and the stress of suspicion can't be good for a man who just had a heart attack. If this doctor is lying you'll feel it in your gut when you talk to him. But Matt, if this doctor's up to no good, he's not gonna come out and tell you."

I sighed at Joe's assertion. I didn't want to believe there was a connection. I didn't want to be involved at all. But I had to see the doctor at 11:00 and I decided that I would simply ask him if he'd heard what happened. If he knew too much he would hang himself. Just as I was about to head out the door, Brother Joe put down the dish towel and cleared his throat.

"You want a ride to the doctor? No sense in you taking the bus, and my schedule is open today. What d'ya think?"

His kindness was killing me.

CHAPTER 14

DR. FRANKLIN HARRISON had arrived early at work and was going through his daily appointments when his eyes fell on Matt's file. He froze in his chair as he recalled seeing Matt at RT's. He was jolted out of his stare when there was a knock on his office door. When he opened it he was stunned to see Mickey and Louis still in the same clothes they had had on the night before.

"Hey, come on, guys," he moaned as they entered into his office. "Didn't I tell you no surprise visits where I work? It's a hospital, for heaven's sake!"

"Yeah, Frank, well it's our office, too," Mickey reminded the doctor as he and Louis took their seats in the leather chairs facing Harrison's desk. Louis casually put his feet on the desk as they sipped their convenience store coffee.

Frank despised the overly familiar use of his first name. These two goons had no respect for his education or his position. He listened to them, as they had enough on him to send him to prison, not to mention ruin his career. He rued the day that his addiction to the white stuff had depleted his finances and drove him to get in bed with this distribution ring. Mickey's voice grated on the doctor as he spoke.

"You ever find a way to get that stuff up to Atlanta? We got a lot of money riding on that gig. What have you got for us?"

"Come on, guys," Frank pleaded. "We just had this discussion last night. No courier is gonna risk that kind of weight for less than four grand. And you guys don't have that kind of margin on this load. You think I'm gonna put it in my golf bag and run it up there and pretend I'm on my way to Augusta? Hell, no! I do enough dirty work for you two and as soon as I pay you the twenty-five thousand I owe ya, we're through, right?"

"Are you through crying yet, Doc?" Louis asked as he sipped his coffee, looking unmoved by Frank's speech.

"Look, we move the first shipment in cheap, we undercut the other distributors, and we clean up on the future business. By this time next week we will be making regular runs there and someone is gonna be getting a cool five grand for sixteen hours' work. And you're telling us you ain't found no one in this flea bag town that wants to earn that kind of scratch? I mean, come on, Doc, it's a real no brainer. A payday like that don't come from the tooth fairy, right? Second, the old man is starting to wonder what team yer batting for here. We gonna move this load or what?"

At that point Harrison's eyes fell back on the file marked *Matt Collins*. And as the two goons began to get restless, a smirk cut across his lips.

"I got our guy. A while back I had a patient in here with a massive heart attack. His name is Matt Collins and he's coming in today to do a stress test and re-up on his meds. After we review his labs." Mickey and Louis just looked lost. No idea what the doc was babbling about.

Dr. Harrison continued. "This guy's so broke he can't pay attention. And I spotted him playing in that rock band last night when that drummer went belly up. He looks like he'll do anything for a buck and I'm gonna be talking to him at 11:00 today, if he didn't freak out over his buddy dying. This kid's in frail shape and he's our boy to make the move to Atlanta. I would bet anything."

Mickey laughed at the doctor's last statement. "Doc, if you're betting anything, you're betting your life."

As Matt walked into the doctor's office he braced for the worst. He knew in his heart that if the doc figured out he was onto him, things were gonna blow and it could get ugly. But he had to do it. He and Paul needed answers. Tommy's family deserved answers. Matt had seen it a hundred times in Philadelphia. Damn snow had no mercy. No mercy at all. Even before the lifestyle took him down he'd seen it in others. The parties, the girls, the morgaged futures. It was all part of the game and nobody won but the snow. He looked around the room quickly—nice office, pretty secretary, Berber carpet, mahogany desk and bookcases. But not the extravagance he'd expected. His gut told him that this guy had something to do with Tommy's death but he just had to hear the doctor connect the dots himself.

"How are you today, Matt?" Frank barely looked up from the computer screen.

"I'm great, Doc. At least I feel great. Anything in those labs make you think otherwise?"

"No, your labs are pretty good. I think the blood pressure should come down a few points. But otherwise you seem to be stable." Harrison paused, rechecking the computer screen.

"Any pain or discomfort?"

"A little bit," Matt admitted, standing with his hands shoved in his jacket pockets. He looked at Harrison and felt the lump in his throat subside enough to speak his mind.

"Here's the deal, man. When I first met you I smelled ether on you. The way you were sweating, I could tell you had a nose for the powder."

Harrison's face fell as he continued. "And I was poking around in that closet of yours and watched the action as people came in and out. I saw enough in my ten days there to figure out you had a little side business going on, or at least a bad habit. But I don't care. We all got our hobbies. But I saw you and your thugs at RT's last night and a friend of mine is now dead. That same friend would probably be alive today if you hadn't shown up at the club." The words flowed like a river.

Frank stood up and checked the door, and then turned to face me. "Who do you think you are, talking that crap to me? Do you have any idea what you just stirred up? I think sleeping in that park has skewed your logic a bit. That drummer had tombstones in his eyes for years. He couldn't get enough of that stuff. But I heard you've reformed or something. Yeah, that's right," Frank continued. "I spotted you with the drummer and did some asking around myself. You may have a few friends at that bar but you got nothing to save you from the wrath you just opened up with your mouth." He paused and brushed some lint off his pants with a sneer.

"So what did you see when you poked around in that closet?"

Matt could feel his blood pressure rising. "I saw your stash, Doc. Yeah, that's right. Either you or one of your stooges got sloppy and left the gate open. And one of your guys was in the men's room when Tommy took his last line of blow."

As Matt raised his voice Frank's face turned red with rage. He moved towards Matt and shoved him into a chair. A smile raced across Matt's face but he shut it down fast.

"You smug little punk. Let me tell you what you saw. You saw enough snow in one week to keep a pretty big crew afloat. We all get our beaks wet from time to time; you should know that better than anyone. Yeah, I did my homework on you." He poked his finger in Matt's chest as he spoke. "Guys like you die all the time and a coroner and colleague of mine doesn't like to waste taxpayer money to find out why. You already got two stents in your chest you're never gonna pay for, and you're on enough blood thinner that I could take you out with the back of my hand. But today is bonus day for you, kid."

Matt stood up and returned his icy stare. "Don't call me 'kid,' Harrison."

"That's 'Dr. Harrison' to you, punk, and don't you forget it! You're gonna get a call tonight and your gonna answer it. I got some guys that need you to take a drive. If you want to stay alive you will take some snow up to Atlanta for us. You open your mouth, you die. You open the package, you die. Am I making myself clear, Matt?"

Harrison was on a roll. "You opened a very dangerous door. But my friends are very forgiving. You play ball with us and you might get back on your feet. You mess with us or cause us the least bit of anxiety and you're a memory."

"Hold on a minute, buddy. You—" Matt tried to interject but was cut off.

"I'm giving you a real break here. Don't be stupid. The Gulf is full of people who have gotten stupid. Consider this an opportunity. Don't ask questions. You can make some real money. You do anything that even looks out of line, you'll wish we hadn't brought you back from that heart attack."

"Are we finished here, Doc ?" Matt asked, walking towards the door.

"Yeah, just be at RT's tonight at eight. I want to introduce you to your new best friends. If a cop should even stop in for a drink, you die by mistake. It's that serious, Matt. See you tonight."

When Matt hit the hallway Joe was already standing. He had so much adrenaline pumping he could hardly speak.

"Let's walk, man." Matt couldn't even smile. They were back at the car in a flash and Joe broke the silence.

"How were your labs?"

"Fine."

"You and the doctor talk about anything else?" Reaching in his pocket, Matt retrieved a mini-recorder and handed it to Joe.

"It's better if you don't know what's on the tape right now, but if anything happens to me you get that to the cops stat, okay?"

"What's going on, Matt?" Concern showed on Joe's face. "And where did you get a recorder?"

"Oddly enough, Joe, I got it from Tommy. He had given it to me to record the band and practice my harp parts between gigs. He said it helped him on drums. He had no clue it was gonna help us uncover the details around his death."

"We're gonna have to put this somewhere because if the cops find out about this, they'll come after you. I'll keep it in the parsonage. But you're taking a big risk here, Matt. Should you go to the cops now? It seems like the best move to make. These guys are not joking around. They'll kill you without hesitation."

"I have no choice now. I have to do this. We better get home. Those guys are gonna contact me fast. I wish I knew what to expect."

Joe shook his head. He wasn't happy with how this thing had turned out at all. He took the recorder and stuck it in his pocket. When they pulled up to the house, he got out and started up the walk to the house.

"Let me know as soon as you hear from them, Matt. They may have already put cameras up in your apartment. It depends on how much risk they think you are. Stay watchful, Matt. This is serious."

Matt nodded and walked up to his apartment. The door was unlocked. Joe was right. Someone had already been there. He walked in slowly and the door slammed behind him. He was staring into the eyes of two thugs who had guns aimed at his head.

CHAPTER 15

⚜

PACO'S HEAD SNAPPED back to an upright position. His nerves were on alert as he looked around the bus station. It was clear to him that the sun was coming up and he needed to make tracks. Grabbing his back pack, he headed for the door.

He hit the morning air and cleared his head as he walked down the sidewalk. His back was stiff from sleeping sitting up. The familiar hunger in his belly drove him forward. The snow sloshed around his ankles as he watched the City of Brotherly Love wake up. Soon cars began to move in the street as he made his way through the city. Paco reminisced, remembering he had been around this town before the Walmarts and the Office Depots made every town look the same. But his thoughts were soon interrupted by the throbbing pain in his arm and the queasy feeling that told him it was time for a beer. Then he smiled as he recalled his twenty dollar windfall that put a little over forty dollars between him and the inevitable withdrawal symptoms.

A corner gas station he spotted looked like it would provide him with an opportunity to ease a little of the suffering of his painful existence. He walked in and checked with the clerk to make sure they sold beer at this hour. The clerk did little to hide his disgust as he spoke in a broken Middle Eastern accent.

"You can buy beer but no drink in front of store."

Paco knew exactly what the guy meant as he surveyed the cooler in front of him. Full of choices, he settled on a forty-ounce bottle of Steel Reserve. It was cheap but had enough alcohol to chase the bees out of his head. He reached in and removed the bottle from the rack and quickly carried it to the counter as the owner turned to ring up the $1.67 for the beer. Paco quickly stuffed two cinnamon rolls in his bloody sleeve, watching the clerk closely to make sure he hadn't been observed. On his way out he stopped to look at the headlines in the morning paper, but the icy stare of the store owner made it clear that it wasn't a good time to catch up on his reading. He hit the frosty air again; this time he was watchful for a place to tend to his arm and enjoy his breakfast as best as he could.

The traffic continued to pick up and Paco soon found a vacant bench in a small city park. Bending down he cleared the snow from the bench with his good arm, then sat on his back pack as insulation from the cold metal bench. He surveyed the snow-covered park for footprints and saw none, and he looked forward to his privacy while he unscrewed the top of his beer. As he pulled the cinnamon rolls from his sleeve he was not happy to see how much of his own blood was on the cellophane. A sick feeling in his gut told him he should get some help with this, but he was going to have to see to it himself. He carefully rolled up his sleeve and made a makeshift bandage out of a clean t-shirt he had in his backpack. He wet the shirt with a little of the whiskey that he had saved from his bus trip and winced as the new bandage settled into place. He then took a sip of his "antiseptic," replaced the bottle in his pocket, and settled in for a leisurely breakfast, followed by some thoughtful planning. He used to enjoy the simple life the streets offered. Now it seemed a blur of pain and a constant pursuit of relief; he rarely found another fellow hobo that wasn't plagued by voices or bent on stealing his stuff. Paco took a bite of his cinnamon roll remembering the last friendly conversation he had. The pleasant company of Hunter was kind of a rest from the constant search for food and shelter. To live on the street required vigilance and a strong stomach.

"I bet Hunter's dad wouldn't last a day on the street. The spoiled life of a professional would hardly prepare a man for the demands of street life," he whispered into the air. *Although*, he thought for a minute, *hell, I feared that years ago, but I pulled it off.*

He returned to his thoughts of Hunter and wondered if a man with no future could be of any benefit to a boy trying to reconnect with his past. While he sat there, the chill became far more tolerable as he emptied the beer can. Paco continued to spin thoughts on how he could be of service to the lad. The more he pondered, the more Hunter's quest became his curiosity. Then the thought hit him like a clarion bell. *What have I got to do that is more important than a boy finding his dad? Who else is gonna take time out of his life to help him? Probably no one. After all, who helped me?* Paco shook his head in a moment of indulgent self pity.

He jumped to his feet with a sudden sense of purpose, leaving his beer three-quarters empty. He left the park in search of a library where he felt certain he would get the answers he needed to find Matt Collins. *Hunter and I are now comrades. We'll find this guy Matt. He may not want to be found but we'll do it.*

An old song rattled through his brain as he weaved his way through the well-known streets. He pictured himself as the boy's only hope. His arm still throbbed as he burst into the library and stood in line to use the computers. He was rudely aware of his appearance as he eyed the other people dressed nicely who were standing in line. Repeating Matt's name over and over in his mind, he wondered where in the world this guy could be. He paced, as it took about thirty minutes for a computer to become free.

Finally he was in front of a computer that was faster and smaller than the ones he'd used at the nuclear plant. Paco fumbled his way through Google and found the public records. He recalled how it felt to tap out the keys wearing a shirt and tie and heading home at night to his apartment near Three Mile Island. His mind reveled for a moment in the comfort of the sofa and a twenty-five-inch console TV. His mind cycled to the bills and the possessions that owned him and to the fights with his girlfriend, Summer.

Soon Paco's time was up and he'd had only a few hundred Google hits once he narrowed it to a search in the Philadelphia area. One name continued to surface all the way down in Alabama and a few more in Texas but he could eliminate them. Paco's allotted computer time was up until the next day.

Back out on the street, Paco set his sights on finding a place for the night. While on the computer he'd seen a warning that the temperature was going to hit the low twenties. He knew he'd better stay sober enough to get a bed or a cot at one of the city's homeless shelters. Might even get a square meal. Of course, he often had to sit through some preaching, but once inside he could collect his thoughts and maybe find a friendly game of cards.

Paco hoped the line wouldn't be too long at the River Road Rescue Mission. There he could get a pretty good breakfast as long as he was out by 6:30. The vagrants then had to start lining up at 1:00 the next day. Paco's walk to the mission was about ninety minutes. He would be way early but might be able to panhandle a bit on his way over. He found a busy spot near a bus stop; the crowd was tough but he managed to get about twelve dollars in folding money and six dollars and fifty cents in loose change. Paco continued his trek, shaking his head at the loss of dignity in such an endeavor.

The River Road Mission held about ninety men. On nights when the temperature got below thirty degrees the cots came out and the first hundred and fifty men were in great shape 'til breakfast. Then they had to split food for ninety men. But in those conditions, complainers were few and opening a man's mouth to complain was a good way to be shunned by the other refugees. Worst case scenario was that in numbers like that there were twice the thieves, twice the male prostitutes, and twice the crazies.

"Yeah," Paco said aloud. "It's gonna be a long damn night."

Paco's guess was right after the first twenty guys tried to bum cigarettes. He had already seen enough. He'd been number twenty-three in line and was assigned a bunk—a top bunk with an asbestos mat like the ones in the jails. In fact, he found a sticker confirming that the mattresses were, indeed, donated by a local penitentiary. It occurred to him that the mattresses were no longer good enough for convicts, but beggars couldn't be choosers.

His arm burned in agony as he dragged himself to the top bunk, plopping down on the hard mattress. He rolled to elevate his arm, peeking under the bandage. He tried in the dim light to assess the amount of infection in his arm. The dried blood obscured the layer of white infectious fluid that was beginning to form.

"Dammit!" He muttered under his breath. I got to find a clinic. *This thing is gonna get bad.* No telling where that knife had been. The puncture wound alone was gonna require a tetanus shot. Let alone staph or MRSA. This is gonna cost me time in helping Hunter. Oh well, a one-armed man is not any less help than a two-armed man. We just got to find this Matt guy.

As he lay there amid the snoring and the body odor of the forty homeless men that shared his dorm, a hand stretched out and gripped his shoulder. It was a kid who had to be sixteen at most. "Hey, man, I'm hurtin'. Have you got any pills? I mean, it's gonna go bad for me if I can't get some kind of dope to settle me down."

"Shut up, kid, yer gonna get us kicked out and I ain't sleepin' in the snow for no junkie."

Paco reached into his backpack and gave the kid his last corner of whiskey. "Here, kid, maybe you'll sleep better; drink this."

The kid disappeared in the dark. Paco noticed the yellow hoodie the kid had draped around his waist. Soon the kid was gone as well as his last swallow of whiskey. *I hate these places,* he thought to himself. wishing it was warm enough to camp out. Wishing he could find Matt. Wishing his arm was better, wishing he knew were Hunter was. There were too many blank spots in his world at the moment.

The next morning found the men packing up, getting ready to brave the cold. As Paco stepped into the hall he saw a gurney being wheeled down the hall. Hanging out from under the blanket that covered some unknown corpse was the yellow hoodie.

"Oh, my God!" Paco said. "The kid didn't make through the night." The transport guy just nodded.

Paco's head hung a little lower as he helplessly moved for the exit. Feeling like a zombie, he realized he didn't have the stomach to stand in line for the morning meal. He felt badly for the kid with no name, and now no life left.

As Paco headed down the sidewalk the ambulance passed him slowly. Paco stopped on the sidewalk for a silent goodbye to the noisy kid in the night.

CHAPTER 16

---✤---

I HAD NEVER been put in a position where I had to stare down the barrel of a gun. But I could tell by the looks on their faces these men meant business. I tried hard not to panic. My time on the street had hardened me to stone, but these guys were playing hardball. There was no room for error here. I shrugged and nodded, trying not to show any fear.

"Okay. I get it. I'm ready to hear where you want the delivery. So can you take the guns down and talk to me?"

The two thugs lowered their Beretta 45s and glared at him. "The one called Mickey said, "You seem to think you're running the show, dude. You got it all wrong. You live if you deliver the goods. Got it? Now shut up and listen up."

I swallowed a lump that had slid up into my throat and stared at both men. "You don't have to bombard me with your threats. I'm here to do the job. Where do I deliver? And what do I do with the vehicle after I'm done?"

Louis, a huge brute with one eye gone, slapped a key into Matt's hand. "You drive the van to Atlanta and don't stop on the way." He handed Matt a wrinkled scrap of paper. "These are the directions to the warehouse where you will deliver the van. You'll find your own way home. No mistakes. No cops. You get it?"

I nodded. My brain was thinking fast about a way of escape from the two men.

"Your van is wired so we will know where you are at all times. We can hear every word you speak inside that van. When you get home, be prepared to make another run shortly. We want all of this snow delivered before Friday."

"I never promised a second delivery."

75

"You don't get that choice. Dr. Harrison owns you now. You answer to him. You're lucky to be alive, punk. So don't push it." Mickey looked like he was about to explode.

I decided to be quiet as the two thugs were only following orders, or, at least, I guessed they were.

"When you arrive, one of our men will be there to collect the paper. Nothing can scare the delivery or fireworks will go off. Bodies will drop like flies. Do you get that? Don't act suspicious. Don't shift on your feet. Just stand there and stay calm. One single thing goes wrong—one little fly landing on the pudding, and this whole thing will go up in smoke."

"I'll deliver it like you want. When do I leave?"

"You leave at midnight tonight. We'll be watching every move you make. Don't try any funny stuff, dude. All eyes are on you."

I nodded and the men went out the back door and disappeared behind the parsonage. Joe knocked on the front door right after the two thugs left, and I broke out in a sweat. I had to answer the door because Joe knew I was home. But I knew I was being watched and the house was probably bugged.

"Hey, man! Come on in. You okay?"

Joe smiled but I could tell he knew something wasn't right. He'd seen a van parked in the driveway so he must have figured something was up. "Sure, sure, I'm fine. Just checking on you, Matt. You heard from anyone? That doctor call you yet?"

I froze but tried hard to act calm. "Nah. Haven't heard from anyone, Joe. Just relaxing in the house. Thinking of going out for a bit. Thanks for coming by."

I knew Joe could feel me pushing him out the door. I watched him slip over to the parsonage to get something and head out to his car. He jumped in and backed out of the driveway, moving down the street out of sight. I picked up something to drink from the refrigerator and grabbed my jacket and walked out to the van that was parked in my driveway. I looked around and didn't see Joe anywhere, so I pulled out and headed down the street to the interstate. I hit the pedal, noticing the drag on the engine. I smiled, thinking I'd hate to try to make a getaway in such a slow vehicle. Hopefully I could make the delivery and get the heck out of Dodge. I had no idea how this drop was going to go down, but I wanted it to go smoothly so I would get out alive.

It was pitch black and not much traffic on the road. The radio was broken and even though I had my cell in my pocket, I was afraid to use it. The van was bugged so anything I said would be heard. I tried hard to concentrate on the road and let my mind recover from the two thugs greeting me with guns aimed at my head. A few headlights came my way, blinding me for a few minutes. Otherwise, it was a black night with only my own thoughts to keep me company.

I spent hours trying to figure out all the scenarios of how this thing could play out. Worst case scenario I would get killed. I tried not to worry because I'd made that decision when I decided to confront Frank about what he knew. It was time now to suck it up and get the job done. I wanted to find out where the drop off was and who all the drug lords were. This was big and I would notify the cops as soon as I could get back home. I just tried to keep the speed steady and not break the law. I didn't want to draw attention to the van.

As I turned over every possibility both good and bad in my mind, I never saw the lone black car way back in the distance following me. The car had stayed just far enough back so as not to be seen easily. I drove all the way to Atlanta without ever noticing the car. A shadowy figure in the night with the eyes of a soldier. Or a guardian angel.

It was cold and dark. I pulled up slowly to the drop off point and turned off the van. I was tired and sleepy and had to drink black coffee to keep my focus.

Just as I was getting out of the van, the doors opened up on the warehouse and six men walked out with guns pointed at me. I froze in my tracks as a man dressed in black walked up beside the van. The others called the thug "Coon," and he apparently worked for Frank. He spoke out loud to the six armed men.

"I'm here to take the paper. We got the snow. Now let's get this thing done without a hitch."

"You bring any eyes with you?"

"None. We're alone. It's a clean ride here, man. Now let's let this thing go down and quit the words."

"Open the back doors of the van and step aside. My men will come up and check out the count. If anything looks crazy, bodies will drop. Is that clear?" A briefcase was sitting on the ground in front of the van, and a huge brute was standing beside it, his gun at his side.

"Crystal."

You could hear a pin drop. No one moved for a moment. Then suddenly, like a shooting star, electricity was in the air. The hair stood up on my arms. Coon saw the briefcase of money and reached for it, and bullets started to fly. Coon fell to the ground and the other men rushed toward the back of the van. I grabbed the briefcase and went around the other side of the building to find a side road. Another way out. I ran as fast as I could, holding the case close to my body. I'd worn black so it would be difficult to spot me, but my shoes had a light rim of silver on the sole. Just as I was turning a corner on the road a car pulled up slowly and a man rolled down the window.

"Get in, Matt. Get in the car."

My mouth shot open and I strained to see the face in the car. It sounded like Brother Joe. I got closer to the car and saw Brother Joe grinning at me, waving frantically. I jumped into the car and Joe took off like a bullet in the night. Smoke poured out of the back of the car as the tires screamed. I couldn't believe Brother Joe could drive like that. But the goons were not far behind.

What I didn't know was how far out of Atlanta the goons would chase us. I was hoping they wouldn't cross the state line. We heard shots being fired but Joe was flooring the car. If the cops stopped them, all the better. But Joe wasn't waiting to see who followed who. He was heading back to Florida as fast as his car would take him. He came to a split in the road and turned left. About five minutes later the goons were in his rearview mirror. He turned right down a side road and swerved back onto the on ramp of the interstate. The speedometer moved rapidly to one hundred miles per hour but it felt like we were crawling. He took an exit ramp off and went right back on, hoping to confuse the guys behind him. He changed lanes and got behind a semi that was traveling light, and then went off the next exit again. The chase was bringing them to the state line and I was holding my breath that the goons would give it up.

Fifteen minutes later there was no sign of them. I blew out a sigh of relief, but Joe was still worried.

"Do you realize what you nearly did? You could have gotten killed back there! Was this worth your life?"

I could see he was sweating and I became concerned about how this was affecting him.

"Are you okay? You shouldn't have come here, Joe. You risked your own life without even knowing the whole situation. I was willing to take a chance just to find out what this doctor was up to. After all, he was planning on doing surgery on me! Can you imagine the risk he is putting his patients under? As a doctor, I couldn't allow that to continue. Now I know what is really going on. I know my instincts were correct."

Brother Joe laughed loudly, leaning his head back. "Well, that makes me feel better! You kill me, Matt. You come from living on a bench to risking your life on a drug delivery just to check out your doctor. Man, what a day this has been! Let's get home."

I sat back in the seat smiling but still shaking. I knew it had been a close call. If Joe hadn't shown up I would've been shot down. Somehow death didn't scare me. Not after the bench. But the thought also crept into my mind that the good doctor wasn't about to let the money disappear. I knew I had to take it to Frank before they came after me. I couldn't waste any time doing that, or I'd be a dead man walking.

"I need to get to Dr. Harrison with this briefcase, Joe. I mean pronto. They're gonna come after me if I don't."

"Have you looked inside that thing? How do you know if it's full of money?"

"Why would they chase us if it was empty?"

"It's worth checking, buddy. You risked your life for it."

"You're right. Lemme check this out." I pulled the latches on the briefcase and peered inside. It was full of hundred dollar bills bound in rubber bands. I slammed it shut, my heart racing, and spoke with a voice that was shaky.

"It's full of paper, Joe. We got the money. I need to call Frank right now and tell him I got the money. He's heard by now that the deal went south. He's gonna be worried about this money."

"Good idea. You will save your life if you call him now."

CHAPTER 17

———— ⚜ ————

A FORMIDABLE SNOWSTORM was moving across New Jersey and Hunter was nearly blinded walking to class. He was dreading his advanced chem course but didn't want to miss a class. He was more determined than ever to get through the next few years and qualify for med school because he wanted to continue in his father's footsteps. That seemed odd since he'd never met his father. But the fact that he was a neurosurgeon made all the difference in the world to Hunter. He pulled his coat up around his neck and bent into the wind, but his ears were frozen.

Holly Carrington passed him and waved, smiling that killer smile as she walked into class. He really liked her but she was avoiding conversation like the plague. He was hoping she would warm up to him because there was a party Friday night at the frat house and he wanted to ask her to go with him. He was mesmerized by her face. It stopped traffic. The beauty of her whole spirit took his breath away. But he couldn't say that to her. She'd freak out. She'd think he was crazy.

He sat in class taking notes, trying to focus. Professor Jones was boring, as were all of the other professors. But his aim was to finish best, to win. So he tried hard to focus and retain as much as he could. Without even trying, his mind would wander to thoughts of Matt Collins. He was dying to see his face. To know what he was like. But it seemed a daunting task to dig up enough info to find the man. *Why does he have to be so invisible? Does he ever think about my mom?*

So many questions ran through his mind as he left class and headed to anatomy with Mrs. Elliott. She was beautiful but cold as ice. And as he trudged through the snow he entered the building and stomped the snow off his shoes. His toes were frozen. He had a bad habit of wearing his boots with no socks. They were lined with fur inside, so the socks seemed redundant. However, today it was cold enough to freeze an Eskimo and he realized the no sock thing was going to have to go.

He sat down at a desk in the back and stretched out his legs. He felt tired and discouraged until Holly Carrington walked into the class. Her arrival got his attention fast, and he sat up straight, running his fingers through his thick brown hair. He was tall, handsome, and strong. He ran five miles a day no matter what was coming down out of the sky. And this winter it had been snowing every single day. He hadn't seen the sidewalk or a blade of brown grass in months. He waited to see if Holly would notice that he was sitting in the back of the class, but she acted like she didn't see him.

After class, he walked to the front of the room, hoping to catch her when she was headed out the door. He couldn't find her, got discouraged, and decided to head over to a local coffee house to eat a bite before his next class. The street was busy in spite of the poor weather and a truck whizzed by, dumping wet icy snow all over Hunter's pants and jacket. He ducked but it was too late. He stood up and brushed himself off as best he could and pulled hard on the door to Bob's Coffee House.

The place was noisy and packed with students. He grabbed a stool at the counter and sat down, feeling the icy water drip down the back of his neck. Shivering, he ordered a latte and pulled out his cell to check for messages.

He didn't see Holly coming in the door. His head was down and he was erasing sent messages when she grabbed the seat next to him. When he looked up, he nearly fell off the stool. He was so stoked he was speechless. Finally he got his wits together and smiled a goofy smile. She turned her head for a second to look at him and grabbed her phone to answer a text. His latte arrived, steaming, and he put his hands around the cup to feel the heat. Life was good. *Coffee and a beautiful girl. How bad could life be?*

Holly ordered her drink and kept herself busy texting and sipping her coffee. He was invisible to her and he had to do something to break the spell. He finally got enough nerve to speak as she got off her stool to leave.

"Holly, how was anatomy today? You find that a tough course?"

She turned and gave him a look that made a bead of sweat appear on his brow. "You talking to me?"

"Yeah, I was. Do you mind?"

"I hate that class. Professor Elliot is retarded. Could it be any more boring?"

Hunter hopped off his stool and grabbed his coffee, nearly spilling it on the floor. He noticed a slight grin on her face. "She's a nerd," he commented. "But we have to make it through this course if we are gonna make it in pre-med. Where are you headed now?"

"Back to the dorm. I'm not feeling good and need a warm bed to take a quick nap."

"Sorry you feel bad. Maybe we can have pizza one night next week. When you feel better."

Holly grinned for a moment but it disappeared into the freckles on her face. Her eyes were brown but light showed through them. Almost translucent. Her hair had a little auburn tint to it, and it was so long you got lost in it. Hunter sat there looking at her, struck with how beautiful she was. He snapped himself back to reality and reached out his hand.

"Hunter Bentley! Nice to finally talk to you, Holly."

She barely touched his hand and put her solemn face back on. "Nice to meet you, Hunter. I've seen you in class. I'll be around. Catch ya later."

Hunter sat back down at the bar and watched her sashay out the door, never looking back to see if he was watching. But he was.

The rest of the day was a blur for Hunter. A mixture of professors moving their mouths and memories of the five seconds he'd had with Holly. He headed back to the dorm, dreading the mushy wet snow and the wind that had picked up since he started his day. Each footstep was a chore and he was getting sick of the cold. His mind wandered away from the pretty girl he'd developed a massive crush on to Paco and their last conversation. He suddenly wished he'd left his cell number with Paco. Some way to contact him. It was too late now, but he could've used some help in finding his father. As annoying as Paco was, he was a cocktail of the corporate world, street life, and humor. That was a combination Hunter would most likely never see again in his lifetime.

He hit he dorm room ready to crash on his unmade bed, when his roommate came bursting through the door. "Hey, dude. Wassup?"

"Nothing, man. Pure nothing."

"You sick or sumthin'?"

"Nah. Just tired. This cold is ridiculous. What you up to?"

"Just got back from chemistry. Professor Hoffman is such a jerk. Threw a test at us with no warning. You know how important that grade is to me? Damn. Can't get a break. Not one."

"I know, dude. This is tough, but we knew it would be. There's no room for the weak. You and I have to be tough to get through this because pre med is gonna be worse. I've heard some war stories that would make you change your career path!"

Lonnie shrugged and grinned. "Yeah, yeah. Hey! I almost forgot. This dude called you. Didn't recognize the voice. Was kind of rough."

"What'd he say?" Hunter perked up.

"He wanted me to tell you he called. Said his name was Paco. Who is this guy, Hunter?"

"Paco? Tell me what he said! I need to talk to this guy." Hunter's heart was racing.

"Take it easy, dude. He said he'd call you back tonight around eight. Said he had something to tell you."

Hunter sat down on his bed and put his face in his hands. He rubbed his face and pushed his bushy hair back out of his eyes. He was hoping for a miracle. But he'd take anything. Any clue about his dad. He checked his watch and grimaced—three more hours. He had some studying to do, so he pulled out his books and computer and typed some notes up.

Lonnie's face was a big question mark "So who is this dude 'Paco'? You gonna share that info with me?"

Hunter rolled his eyes towards his nosy roommate and frowned. "It's just an old guy I met on a bus. Nothing, really."

Lonnie wasn't buying it. "An old dude you met on the bus, huh? Well, what's he want with you? What does he have to tell you?"

"If I knew that, I'd be out eating the biggest hamburger I could find. But instead, I have to sit here and study so that I'll be around when he calls back. Now you gonna let me get this done or just sit there staring at me?"

Lonnie threw his head back and laughed a deep laugh. "You got your pants in a wad, dude. I was just asking is all. It seems weird for an old dude to be calling you. I'm hoping you haven't gotten yourself into some trouble or something. That could be bad right now, you know. We can't mess up. There's no room for error."

Hunter looked at Lonnie and shook his head. "You're letting your imagination go rampant, dude. Relax. Old Paco is a new friend of mine. I have no idea what he's gonna tell me but I'll let you in on it as soon as I know. Is that fair enough? Now can I study?"

"I'll leave you to your computer. That seems to be the only date you have lately. I'm meeting Candace at five near the Meat House on the corner. You decide you need to get out for some fresh air, head our way. She's bringing her girlfriend."

Hunter turned his head slightly, leaning his chair back on its legs. "Oh, really? Who's she bringing?"

"You don't know her, anyway. Quiet girl. Holly Carrington. I'm sure you don't know her."

The legs slipped on the hardwood floor and Hunter went crashing backwards into the bookshelf on the back wall. He rolled over and stood up, straightening his shirt. He was embarrassed but his mind was racing. "Oh, I know her all right. I just saw her today. What time did you say?"

"Five. That's less than an hour from now. So if you're coming, don't be late. You have to be back here by eight, remember?"

"I remember, dude. Just save me a seat. And don't tell her I'm coming. She just might leave."

Lonnie walked out, shutting the door behind him. Hunter clapped his hands over his head and shouted. There was no way he was going to miss this chance to see Holly again. But he would have to cut it short so he wouldn't miss Paco's call. He sat back down at the computer and finished his notes for anatomy, then ran through them quickly, his mind in and out of focus. *Paco. The dude is pretty clever to have tracked me down. Pretty smart in spite of those ragged clothes. Wonder what he has to say? What has he found out?*

A new feeling of hope was growing in Hunter's mind. But just for a second, a one chance in a lifetime moment, he was going to put the thoughts on hold about Paco, and enjoy staring at the most beautiful girl he'd ever seen in his life. And somehow he had to do that without letting her know her eyes were shooting arrows into his heart.

CHAPTER 18

⸎

THE PAIN IN his arm forced Paco to the waiting room of the Westbury Clinic. He'd found help there before. The doctors at Westbury provided flu shots every year for the homeless. Paco was sure he was going to need a tetanus shot. He gave his name at the window and took his seat amid the rows of chairs. He hated places like this; they were so clean and sterile they had a way of making him feel even more unkempt than he was. He scratched his thickening whiskers and looked at the sick people waiting to see the medical team. They were lined up like sick cattle waiting to be given a miracle to make them better.

Paco grew impatient quickly and he got up and walked over to the water fountain. As he bent down to take a drink, he wondered how many sick people had used that spigot ahead of him. He put his thumb on the lever and the arc-shaped stream of water began to flow. As he carefully took his drink he could see his own reflection in the shiny stainless steel bowl that served as a shallow sink. An unflattering reflection was looking back at him. Because he rarely ever saw a mirror, he winced at the sight of his hair and beard.

Before he could sit back down, the nurse called his name and took him to a room in the back. As they entered the tiny examination room she sat on a stool and pointed to a table with white paper on it. "Please remove your jacket, shirt, and undershirt."

He did as he was asked but was uncomfortably aware of his dirty body. She held out a bin for him to put his discarded clothing in and he felt the chill in the room. His body was gaunt and scarred from years of living on the road and he could feel her looking at him. The nurse let out an involuntary gasp when she saw the homemade bandage. Paco felt embarrassed but peeled the now filthy bandage off his arm. He looked at her with a frail smile.

"Where do I put this?" She silently pointed to a stainless steel wastebasket. He tossed the rag in and the lid snapped shut. His wound glistened in the fluorescent light.

The doctor came in and Paco tried to stand to be polite. "Please remain seated," Dr. Fleming directed him. He turned to the nurse. "Please disinfect the wound."

The nurse squeezed the liquid surgical soap out of a green bottle. It reminded Paco of some stuff his mom had kept in her medicine cabinet. His trip down memory lane was cut short by a stinging pain from the soap.

"Ouch!" Paco said as he squirmed on the examination table. The wound appeared under the wave of painful liquid. "Man, that hurts worse than when I cut it."

"How did you do this?" She had her left eyebrow raised in question.

"Well, I was helping a guy change out a window and cut my arm on the broken glass."

She shook her head and threw a quick look at the doctor to see how he was going to respond. Dr. Fleming tuned Paco out as he reached for the sutures. As if she'd been silently coached, she eased up to Paco's left arm and injected him with a tetanus shot as the doctor stitched away. Paco wiggled at first but then relaxed and let the man do his job.

"You've had stitches before," Dr. Fleming said flatly. Paco just grunted in agreement as the doctor removed his gloves and washed his hands. He sat down and scribbled out what looked like a couple of scripts and handed them to Paco. Before he could ask, the doctor spoke in a cold tone.

"Take the antibiotic three times a day. It'll clear up the infection in that wound. The other med will help with the pain which will pass in a week. You should come back in and let me take those stitches out by the time the pain meds are gone." He paused and made some notes without looking up.

"Can you afford the pills, buddy?"

"Well, that depends on how much they cost."

"No more than two to three hundred dollars." Paco nearly fell off his chair. Noticing his reaction, Dr. Fleming added a solution to the problem he knew Paco was facing. "Okay, the reason I ask is this clinic has its own pharmacy if you're indigent." The doctor studied Paco's eyes to see if they registered. "That means—"

Paco interrupted with a vengeance. "Pretty astute observation by you, Doc."

Unmoved by Paco's sarcasm, Dr. Fleming stood up and pointed to the right. "Follow the yellow line on the floor and you'll see a window. Hand these to the clerk and she'll have you fill out an application. As best as you can keep that arm elevated when you sleep. Have a good day, Mr. Sansone."

Paco stood up and made his way to the pharmacy. When he got there he found yet another waiting room. He slid the prescriptions under the glass at the window, and a form was passed back to him. He filled out his name and used his sister's address as he'd done a hundred times. He found a chair and grabbed it, looking at the yellow, red, and blue tape lines on the floor that were used for directions around the clinic. He noticed the pale yellow walls, smudged and covered with fingerprints. The venetian blinds hung down, covering the wintery Philadelphia horizon. A certificate of appreciation hung on the wall across from his chair. Paco looked close so he could see who was presented on behalf of the people of the Commonwealth of Pennsylvania. Next to a series of photos there were groups of physicians who donated their time to the Westbury Clinic.

As Paco looked closer, he chuckled at the hairstyles that had changed as the decades had passed. He saw funny names on the groups of doctors; one name was *Dr. Zoran Barbaric*. "Glad he didn't put my stitches in," he whispered under his breath. His eyes then landed on a group of physicians posing by the clinic's entrance. He saw a man who looked like an older version of Hunter, his bus companion. The caption read: "Row two: Dr. James Reed, Dr. Matthew Collins."

Paco nearly fainted. *What are the odds?* He was astonished.

"Raffaele Sansone?" The clerk yelled across the room. In his shock he barely recognized his given name."Mr. Sansone, your prescriptions are ready."

Paco rushed back to the window and tapped on it. "Hey, lady! Uh . . . ah, ma'am, I'm Raffaele. Please can you tell me about a guy in this picture?"

The clerk looked disinterested and insisted he sign for his scripts.

"Please, ma'am, it's important that you tell me about this doctor!"

"The personnel office is down the hall. Follow the blue line till you see the exit, then turn left, and you will find the personnel office."

Paco grabbed the white bag containing his medicine and followed the blue line. He found the personnel office locked and he rang the buzzer. The door buzzed and he entered and was greeted by a slender brunette wearing a white blouse under a forest green suit with a skirt that was cut narrow but came nearly to mid calf. Her head tilted back so she could view Paco through heavy brown glasses that had slid down her nose. Paco was so excited he trembled when he opened his mouth.

"Hey, I need the contact information for Dr. Matthew Collins."

"I don't believe we have a Doctor Collins on staff, sir."

"That would be correct," Paco said, using his best diction. "He would have been here in 1993."

"Are you one of his patients?" she asked. Paco could see if she was moving to look at a file or anything, so he hedged a little.

"Yeah, he, ah . . . he took out my appendix."

"Sir, we have many surgeons on staff that can help you. We don't release personal information on any of our physicians."

"Well, it's very important, ma'am. I have to see him. You see, it's about his son." Paco, now desperate, resorted to the truth.

The unnamed lady in the green suit excused herself and disappeared behind a cloth covered partition. Paco was beaming with anticipation as he pictured the look on young Hunter's face when old Paco came to the rescue with the lowdown on Matt Collins. He pictured the scene in his mind of Hunter being united with his father and it made him smile. The lady returned with a calling card from the American Board of Medical Associates, commonly called the AMA.

"You may contact this agency to get professional information." Her expression was blank as she handed the card to a perplexed Paco.

"I understand that you have rules, but the man has a son who is searching for him. The boy's mom just passed away. I'm appealing to your sense of pity. I'm sure his address is on some form back there or the next place he went to work. Please. You got to give me something."

Her expression was unmoved by Paco's plea. "Sir, we have our rules. Have a nice day." Her attitude had slipped from unhelpful to indifferent as she dismissed Paco a final time. "Good luck, sir."

Paco was discouraged at her lack of interest. As he turned to the door he could feel the heat of disappointment combined with embarrassment burning his ears as he walked to the exit. The winter air did little to cool his head as he returned to the sidewalk. After walking a few blocks he saw a clock on the wall of a bank. It was 2:30 and he realized that he had to head back to the mission or face being outside in the cold all night.

He found a bench at a bus stop and he stopped to rest. His backpack thudded into a snowdrift as he sat down. His arm still hurt a bit so he swallowed a pain pill. The *mattress at the mission'll be a little more tolerable while I'm on the pills.* He liked the way they made him sleepy, insuring that the snoring and the constant noise in the mission would be tuned out. It was a sure thing that the pain in his arm also would be less likely to keep him awake.

As the bus pulled up, Paco stood, grabbed his pack, and climbed aboard. He remembered the bus he had boarded a few days ago when he was sitting next to young Hunter. He remembered the boy's pain as he described his mom's passing. *I wish that uppity chick at the clinic could have met Hunter. She would've produced an address on Matt in a snap. Instead she turned a deaf ear to me.*

As the city bus pulled to the curb Paco recognized the surroundings. He was going to wind up about two blocks from the mission, which saved him a lot of walking. Paco jumped from the final step of the bus and as his feet hit the icy sidewalk, he momentarily lost his footing. His feet skidded out from under him and he reached out and grabbed the bus stop sign, preventing himself from hitting the ground.

He walked gingerly across the snow and ice after the close call. The lower temperature made walking a little more laborious. The soft crunch of snow had been replaced by the harsh crackle of ice and frozen snow. The wind was bitter and cold, making Paco crave the warmth of the shelter that night. He carefully made his way back and arrived there a few hours before check-in time. The staff had decided to open the day room of the mission, allowing all of the patrons to get warm. Before the evening meal he found a few guys that were playing hearts and joined them. And the next couple of hours passed pleasantly for Paco.

The food was warm and tonight there was plenty. Paco was happy to have gotten seconds of some kind of hamburger Stroganoff. The noodles were a bit over cooked and mushy. But the gravy was warm and not as greasy as Paco remembered it. The guys that played cards with him accompanied him to dinner and they continued their sporadic laughter throughout the meal. The three snuck around by the dumpster to share one more cutting drink that would burn all the way to their stomachs before bedding down for the night.

"Man, it's cold out here, dude." Rufus shoved his hands in his pockets and blew out a mouthful of smoke.

"Least we had a good meal. I been on the street so long my feet are black. Got no shoes half the time," Murphy remarked, looking down at his brown work shoes. His soles were half gone.

Paco shrugged and took a swig. "Lucky to have a meal and bed tonight. Wouldn't last out in the cold on a night like tonight."

The men shook their heads in agreement and headed back inside. It was time for lights out.

After checking in, Paco went to the bunk and slipped out of his shirt. He was happy to have gotten his wound tended to and was glad to have his pill for sleeping. He crawled up to the top bunk and flopped to his back. He used his shirt to prop up his arm as he was instructed. As the lights dimmed, darkness and disappointment settled on him heavier than his wool blanket. He breathed out a deep sigh and was asleep before anyone else in the room began to snore.

CHAPTER 19

———— ✦ ————

Joe silently started the long drive back to Destin. There was no need to stop for coffee when we were on pins and needles. He looked in his rear view mirror where I was beginning to stir after a long nap.

"Welcome back," Joe said, as I shook my head, hoping the events of the night were a bad dream. The suitcase was proof that it wasn't a dream at all.

"Hey, man, you need me to drive a while?"

"How was your nap?" Joe was deliberately ignoring my offer to drive at least 'til I was more awake. I couldn't believe my eyes as I opened the suitcase again. As if to reassure myself it was all still there.

"We got a boatload of money here, Joe. You know, partner, we could make for the coast," I prodded just to see his reaction. There was none.

"Hey come on, Joe, what would you do with your half?" I asked him in a jovial tone.

"Matt, I don't even like to tease myself with such notions. That kind of money sure won't buy happiness."

"No, it won't buy happiness, but we could sure rent some for a while." I laughed. Joe smiled. He knew I wasn't serious.

"Let's take the Defuniak Springs exit and we'll stop at Paul's," I strongly suggested.

Joe glanced back in the rearview mirror. "Are you sure you want to involve anyone else in this mess?"

"Well, you know your place is hot as a pistol. At least at Paul's we can stretch our legs, get coffee, and clear our heads. We got a long day ahead of us when we hit town."

"I think you're right, Matt. If what I saw at that drop scene was any indication, we're in harm's way 'til we get that money back to its rightful owners, or to the authorities."

"Authorities?" My eyebrows must have disappeared into my hat. "What do I tell the cops? 'Hey, I ran into a little trouble while delivering cocaine'? No, man, I got to figure a way out of this mess. I'll go to the cops when the coast is clear."

"We will." Joe corrected me.

"Joe, you've helped me so much already, and you really stuck your neck out for me over and over. I really don't want to see you get caught up in all this."

"Hey, I'm already in it. But the goal is to get out of it as peaceably as we can."

I was agitated. "No, Joe, the point is to take out the damn doctor that tried to kill me tonight and was successful at taking Tommy down. Who knows how many others? We got to bring this guy down now. It's a matter of survival."

"Matt, you've just seen firsthand what can happen to you if you persist."

I just looked out the window as the Florida sun was peeking over the horizon. The light streaming onto the highway felt more like the searchlights after a jail break. This morning, like never before, I wanted to be invisible again. Like so many mornings that began on the bench, light brought with it only the fear of being seen. I remembered what I liked to call "bright light fright." Every car that would pass the park carried a fresh set of eyes to behold all of my mistakes. Being seen in public felt like I was being exposed for the failure that I had become. This morning took exposure to a whole new level. Exposed to the cops. Exposed to the fact I didn't know how many bodies went down in Atlanta. Exposed to the creeps whose money Joe and I were lugging around.

There was some relief when we pulled off the highway. Fueling up at the local Stop 'n' Go was tense but it provided Joe and I with a big cup of coffee and a tank of gas. When I went in to get the coffee, I asked the clerk if she knew where Paul Becker lived. She gave me some vague directions and I paid for the coffee and gas with the money from the drop. Then I slid the receipts in the rubber bands that held the money together. I was going to account for every cent, whether they paid me or not. The country roads looked like a peaceful oasis from the drama we'd encountered the previous night. It felt so good to see palm trees again. I felt for a moment like we were players in some kind of gangster movie. We had seen firsthand these guys were playing for keeps. I was afraid to call Paul in case the phone was bugged, so we had to hunt for his house in the dark using the clerk's weak directions.

I looked at Joe as he drove. He had such a quiet confidence about him. If I had taken his picture no one would have guessed he'd just bailed me out of a Wild West show. He was tapping the steering wheel to the beat of a song on the radio, which seemed totally out of character for a man of the cloth. But so was getting involved in a drug drop.

"My stomach is in knots over what our next move is. You seem happy to be on the ride." I studied him as I gave him the directions to Paul's house. "Turn left at the next street on your right. It's up that hill in the woods a little. He lives in a trailer. Double-wide."

"Got it, man." He showed only understanding. But I could tell he had one eye on every car we passed. He made a great wheel man. But I had to figure a way to keep him out of it; it was me the crooks wanted. Joe just steered the car as if he had done it every night of his life. I sipped my coffee as we got closer and closer to Paul's house. As we pulled in the driveway it looked like no one was awake yet.

"I'm walking out front to keep an eye on the road, Matt. You go check to see if Paul's home."

I walked up to the back door and knocked. I glanced at Joe as I tapped on the window. "You look like you're loving this way too much," I whispered, attempting a joke. There was no response to my first few taps so I knocked a little louder.

"I'm cool on the outside. But this probably isn't the best idea you've had, coming here to Paul's. Get it done, Matt. We can't be out here all day."

Paul finally came to answer the door. His hair was a mess, and he was in his jeans with his belt unbuckled. And he looked confused.

"Hey! What's up?" He eased out of his storm door to join me on the back steps.

"Got something to talk to you about."

"Who's the dude?" He asked pointing to Brother Joe.

"He's my new guardian angel. I'll fill you in, Paul. Can we walk in the woods? I've got to bring you up to speed on a few things, and I'm in a real spot. I am too wound up to be inside right now, but man, we got to talk."

"Sure, you settle down a sec and let me throw on some shoes. We can walk in the woods; I got a deer stand I want to check out, anyway. And it will give us a chance to chill and talk a while."

"Cool." Paul disappeared to retrieve his shoes. I walked over to Joe and talked in a low voice.

"Hey, man, we're gonna talk. I trust Paul. If anything looks suspicious, you yell. Okay?"

"I'm cool with it, Matt. Walk around to the back of my car. Got something for you."

He pulled out an old Colt .45 and a snub nose .38. I took the .38 and he grinned.

"I was glad we didn't have to use them last night."

"You mean you were packing the whole time and didn't tell me?" I rubbed my chin and frowned.

"It never came up in conversation! But I would hate to get separated without you having some company."

"Damn, Joe, you just got this thing covered, don't you? I can smell the oil on the .38. You've taken care of this thing, haven't you?" Just the feel of the handle in my hand dropped my blood pressure by twenty points.

"We're gonna get this money back to the doctor and soon you'll be able to get back to what you do best." I looked up to see if he was going to smile.

"May I ask what that is, Matt?" Joe asked. I chuckled.

"Looking out for the likes of me."

As Paul re-emerged from his doublewide, Joe's eyes met mine. I felt a little choked up and spoke under my breath.

"Joe, you've become such a good friend so fast I hardly know how to—"

"We'll talk later." Joe cut me off before I could finish.

I turned and was surprised to see Paul sporting a twelve gauge. "What's up with the cannon?" I asked with a big grin on my face.

"Well, we might spot Bambi while we're looking at the tree stand. Hate to miss an opportunity." Paul had stuffed an old hunting cap over his long brown locks. He was quite a sight.

"Hey, Joe!" I laughed, pointing with my head toward the back seat where the money was. "Don't make me chase you out to California or anything." Joe laughed, letting me know he knew what I meant. As if we were in a scene from a movie, Paul and I headed into the woods. I glanced back at old Brother Joe at the corner of the double wide watching the road. *What a trooper.* I had a gut feeling nagging at me that I ignored as I walked with Paul to the woods, but I felt covered with Joe on watch.

Paul surveyed the scene as thoroughly as I did and he spoke right up. "Man, you two are up to something, Matt. What in the world are you doing?"

"Paul, remember the thugs in the bar the night Tommy died?"

"Yeah, they're around once in a while. But I try to ignore dudes like that. Especially since I got in a mess down in Mobile. I hate that life and the crap that goes with it. Tommy never knew how to say no. Why you remembering that?"

"You're not gonna believe this but those dudes worked for my heart doctor."

"Get out!" Paul said, disbelief dripping from his words.

"When I could have confronted him, these goons roped me into making a delivery for them."

"Oh, crap!" Paul said, as if my words resonated with some memories from his not so distant past.

Paul listened intently as we walked the thickly grown path to the deer stand. As we talked, I gave him every detail of the adventure. The forest was heavily vegetated and had a rich green smell to it. Soon the gun play and the drama of the previous night slipped away in the lush green woods.

Paul paid attention as I relayed the details of the ill-fated drop. As we got to the deer stand he looked intent, like he was straining to get his mind around the adventure. His eyes stared into the distance as he processed the gravity of my words.

We looked around the deer stand. Paul glanced at me and said, "You been through a lot, Matt. How is your chest?"

"No problem so far." I shivered, remembering what we'd come through.

At the foot of the tree stand Paul looked off in the distance as if straining to take it all in. As he gazed at me, he asked, "When did all this go down?"

"Last night. I stopped here because it's bound to be too hot at Joe's place and we got to get the—"

Paul's eyes nearly burst from their sockets. "Last night? Where is this money?" He sounded afraid of the answer. "Are you on crack? You're on the run from some half-baked kingpin with his money, and you decided I needed some heat in my life!"

"Paul, I didn't know what to do." I could see he was trying to restrain his tongue. But it wasn't working for him.

"Dude! Guys get killed every day for that kind of bread! Important people, connected people die for that kind of loot. Guys like you and me don't even make the morning news, we just fall off the map. I can't believe you did this, Matt. This is not like you. This is not the behavior of a man trying to fix his life. You're gonna get us killed!" I raised my hands and motioned for him to settle down.

"Paul, I know this is heavy but I didn't have a choice." Paul punched the door of the deer stand.

"There's always a choice, Matt, always a choice." He calmed himself by reaching into the deer stand and retrieving a five gallon bucket of corn and then he came back down the three step ladder. His gun was resting against a tree. He lugged the bucket out to a clearing some fifty feet away and scattered the corn on the ground.

I walked up behind him and the silence grew uncomfortable. "Is that legal?" I asked him, never having seen anyone bait a hunting ground before. Paul's back was to me and I couldn't see his face but his body was heaving with a strange rhythm. In a moment I recognized it as laughter. His cheeks were wadded up in a nervous laughter as the irony of the question overwhelmed him.

"Legal?" he asked. "You been running cocaine all around the country, stealing money from bad guys, and you're asking me if it's legal to put some venison on my table before spring. Man, you're hysterical."

I got his point and couldn't help but laugh. He made a funny speech as he held his hands up in surrender.

"I seen it all now; this gun totin', drug runnin', cash stealin' gansta is gonna bust me for jackin' deer."

I was embarrassed that I'd even asked the question. I picked up his hat that had fallen to the ground and handed it to him, still chuckling. He hugged me and spoke quietly.

"C'mon, man, let's get you off the hook with these guys so you can turn me in to the nearest game warden."

CHAPTER 20

FRANKLIN HARRISON WAS pacing feverishly back and forth in his office. His desk was covered by a white powdery film.

He'd been hitting the stuff hard since he got a call from Atlanta. The kingpin had sworn threats into the phone about how the deal had been handled. The money now unaccounted for was nowhere to be found. Matt must've really screwed the deal up and now Coon was dead.

Frank's mind was a whirl as he used a card to scrape out one more line from his desk drawer, sniffing hard as the powder took its affect. The snow did nothing to soothe his wired up nerves. He had to find Matt. *Please, God. Somebody please tell me I didn't send that loser on his first mission. If that guy got his hands on the money he'll be in Mexico by now. I'm sure of it.* Frank's brain was racing. A knock tapped on his door and he hurried nervously snatching the door open.

"Thanks for getting over here so quick," Frank remarked, while Mickey and Louis filed into his office.

"Don't tell me there's a problem, Doc," Mickey said as he headed for his chair.

Louis yawned. "Yeah, the last thing we need is a surprise. Come on, Doc. Let's split up the dough so we can get the boss off our backs." Harrison put his elbows on his desk, gripping his own short brown hair. He was looking paler by the minute.

"I just got off the horn with the kingpin. All hell broke loose at the drop last night." His fingers were sweaty as he shoved his hair off his face.

The two goons hit their feet in unison. "Don't joke around Frank, it's not funny," Louis blurted out.

"Man, I wish it was all some kind of joke," was Frank's lame response. Mickey leaned across the desk. "Talk to us, Frank. What happened?"

Frank was struggling to clear his mind. He began pounding the top of his desk with his fist. "That idiot I sent to do the drop ran with the money after things went haywire. Where did he go? I bet he got the money. He was a mess, no ties to keep him here. He could be anywhere."

"He was your boy, Frank. If the money is missing, it's your neck. You know that." Louis chimed in, adding to Frank's anguish. "What do we know about this kid? His hospital records say 'homeless'. Some next of kin somewhere in Philadelphia or something. I bet he got the money, got spooked, and headed north."

Frank chuckled."With his heart condition he couldn't have gotten far on his own. They found the van near Coon's body. That means he was probably on foot. We gotta find him. You two got any bright ideas?"

"Well, I thought we saw him that night when their drummer bought the farm. He was playing harmonica next to him that night at RT's," Mickey remarked, raising a bushy eyebrow.

"Go back to town. Find out what you can on that band. We got to get some leverage on Matt or he's gonna be trouble." Frank wanted to put some distance between himself and the two thugs.

Mickey fired back at Harrison. "Hey, lemme check something out." He grabbed his cell phone and fished around his contact list and highlighted the name *Eddy*. In seconds he was calling. The phone rang and went right to voice mail.

Mickey yelled into his cell phone. "Eddy, this is Mickey. Gimme a call as soon as you get this. You got to help me out." Then he hung up and looked at the doctor.

"I got nowhere with that play but who else do we know that knows about that band? Who hangs out at RT's that can give us the 411 on this kid? I'm thinking he'll come back here."

Harrison had heard enough of Mickey's input and was growing impatient with the talk. "No way! You guys are barking up the wrong tree. That man's gonna run off with that money and I'm gonna be screwed."

Louis spoke. "Yeah, Frank's right, Mick. That kid's gonna hotfoot it with our bread. It's a big country. Where we gonna find him?"

"There has to be someone in this town who knows how to find this guy. He ain't no kid; he's fifty-somethin', ain't he, Frank?" Mickey growled.

"Yeah, something near that. He has to have an ex or a girlfriend or somebody we can sit on 'til he shows up with the money. Now help me think."

Louis and Mickey raised eyebrows at each other as Frank jumped up from his desk. "We got another problem."

"What's that?" demanded Mickey.

"We lost the van, too. We gotta get another one ready by next week or we're gonna be dead meat. That's no problem since that old chop shop near I-10 can alter another ride for us by the time we piece together a new shipment. But we gotta get that bread or there won't even be another shipment."

Frank was shaking when he looked at the two men. "That guy is stepping on the hose of our whole operation. We got to keep him on our side; if he goes to the cops with the money, we're in up to our neck. You are right; we need someone close to this Matt character to sit on 'til the guy plays ball with us. But who?" He sat back down behind his desk and tapped a pencil against the computer. He was firing up. "You two better get over to RT's and start asking questions about Matt Collins. We need someone close to him or the rabbit will run."

Mickey jerked as his cell phone sprang to life in his pocket. "Cool, it's Eddy. Hey man, I'm glad you called me. Yeah, okay, look, Eddy. Here's the deal."

Frank spoke over Mickey and said, "Don't you dare tell him anything!"

Mickey hit mute and stared at Frank. "Hey, I wasn't born yesterday. You got us in this mess so let me and Louis get us out! Now shut up and lemme work." He hit un-mute and began speaking again.

"Hey, um, Ed, sorry 'bout that. It was my girlfriend givin' me some grief. Ya know how they do, right? But hey, you know that band that plays at the bar you work at? The one with the drummer who went deep six the other night? Yeah, right, okay. Well my father-in-law wanted them for his birthday party. How do I find these guys? What do ya know about 'em? Are they always at the bar when you're workin'? Uh, huh, yes."

Frank felt like the conversation would never end. Mickey continued. "Yeah, there's a girl who plays keyboard, right? Is she with any of the members?"

The repetition was driving the doc crazy, and from the impatient look on Louis's face he could tell Louis was ready to explode. "Who was the dude playin' harmonica? Who does all the booking ? Oh he does, eh? Yeah dats da guy my father-in- law will need to speak with, right? I'm gonna slide you a few extra grams to pretend we didn't have this talk, okay? Yeah, it's a surprise party we don't want nobody hearin' about ahead of time." Louis rolled his one good eye at Frank as Mickey concluded his call.

"That was a ringer—"Mickey began.

Louis interrupted him. "Yeah, we heard, now Mickey, shut up and talk."

"Well, make up your mind already," Mickey stated with a glare at Louis. "Look, here is the 411 on this Matt guy. We put the squeeze on him over at this church he's been stayin' at. I guess this guy was quite the boozer and has been on the streets a while."

"Cut to the chase," Frank demanded.

"The guy's not close to anybody, see. The band leader Paul lives near the chop shop, and he took pity on the guy and let him jam with the band. None of 'em got any money. The only guy Eddy thinks is close to Matt is some preacher who took him in a week or so ago. Me and Louis are gonna stop at this preacher's house and find out if Matt made it home."

"Frank, you do know we're talkin' kidnappin' here?" Mickey added, wiping sweat from his brow.

"Listen, you two," Frank said in a low voice. This Matt guy can connect the dots from us to a body in Atlanta. I don't have to tell you what that means. I don't care if we start taking scalps from here to Atlanta and back, I want this guy. With or without the money. Get me?"

"Yeah, we hear ya, Frank."

"This run is getting messy. If we're not quick we're gonna be three of the bodies. Right now let's get this resolved," Frank said as the two goons left his office.

Frank propped his elbows on his desk and laid his head in his hands. *What in the world am I doing? This has gotten way out of hand. And now I've dragged a patient into the mix. All I need is a murder on my hands and I'll spend the rest of my life behind bars or dead.* It was too late to pull back. All he could do was walk through the hole he'd just created in his life.

Louis and Mickey jumped into the white Dodge Charger. It shone like a race car as they sped back to Destin. "Let's get back to that place by the church first. No one is gonna be around RT's 'til afternoon. Shoot, we could be in front of the grand jury by that time," Mickey blurted out in frustration.

Louis tried to correct him. "No, man, it takes a while for the grand jury."

"Shut up and drive; it was a figure of speech." They both laughed. They knew if the heat was on they could blow town in any direction and start all over in some new city. But they both had a stake in the recovered money. Within fifteen minutes the charger rolled up in front of Brother Joe's and they eased up to the door. The place looked pretty much as it did when they got the drop on Matt. They went to the back door and knocked. When no one answered Louis made a suggestion.

"Shoot the lock off the door, Mick."

Mickey just shook his head. "Yeah, why not get all the neighbors involved?" As he reached for his wallet, he took out a roughed up credit card and inserted it in the door. After a little fumbling he flattened the latch and they were in. The two split up as they searched each room, staying in contact with each other as they moved around. They ran up on a roll top desk with some papers on it and a mini-recorder. Mickey picked it up and looked at it for a moment.

"Look at this! The old man probably used this to record his lectures or whatever you call it. You know, where the guy gets up and talks at those Jesus meetings." He threw it down and looked around for any other items that might have something to do with Matt. Suddenly his eyes focused on two photographs sitting on top of the desk. One was a photo of an older man who looked fragile. The other was a photo of a pastor in front of church.

"Hey, Louis. Look at this! I bet it's Brother Joe. Now we know what this guy looks like. We need to keep this in mind as we go lookin' for Matt. This guy might just be the ticket we need to get Matt to turn over the money!"

"You're right, dude. Glad you saw that 'cause we're gonna need all the help we can get. The boss isn't gonna take any excuses. The money has got to come home."

Finding the house empty of clues on Matt, Louis was the first to head across the lawn to Matt's apartment and when Mickey showed up, the two of them began tearing up the room. They were hoping to find an address book or wallet or a photo album but they found none.

"Damn it, man, this guy lived pretty close to the bone," Louis remarked. All they found were a few shirts and some jeans folded up in a backpack and a laptop computer under one of the pillows on a king-sized bed.

"You're right. Makes him a bad risk to skip with the cash."

"Yeah, sucks, don't? He could replace this stuff fast enough and be set up in Canada or anywhere with all that loot."

"Yeah! Wish the old preacher was here so we could track this guy down. If we don't grab someone he is gonna be slippery as an eel." They continued through the apartment, shuffling through drawers, but found nothing they could use.

The two hit the door and in minutes were heading down the road. "Let's head out to Defuniak, man, so we can stop and find this guy named Paul. Hope he's close enough for us to lure Matt back. If not, this is gonna get ugly," Louis said as he gripped the wheel. The ride took about fifty minutes and they stopped and gassed up at Gas 'n' Go. Mickey went in and got a pack of cigarettes and saw a cute young brunette working the cash register. Making no attempt to conceal his approval, his words drooled out of his mouth.

"Hey, uh, sweetie c'ere. I gotta ask ya something." The brunette approached Mickey giggling, as Louis gassed up the charger.

"What can I get for you, sir?" Her smile was like cotton candy to a child.

"Look, sugar, me and my buddy were looking for a friend of ours. You ever hear of Paul Becker, the lead singer at a bar called RT's?"

"Wow!" she giggled. "You're the second person to ask me that today. Like I told the other guy, he lives on Old Pine Road; third or maybe the second place on the left. His dogs are out front sometimes, so be careful."

"Oh, thanks," said Mickey. "Hey, maybe you and me should go listen to the band sometime, eh?"

"I don't go to hear too many bands play, you know, school and all."

"School?" This one might be jail bait, he realized.

"Yeah I go to—"

Before she could say another word Louis burst through the door. "Hey, Romeo! C'mon, we're burnin' daylight here." Mickey straightened up and threw a five dollar bill on the counter and removed two Cokes from the free standing cooler. The two were back in the car before the girl could make change. Mickey cursed at Louis for making a scene.

"I got Becker's location while I was in there. It's right around the corner."

The two sped off and approached Paul's house carefully. As they neared the location they slowed down and stopped near the opening of the driveway. Standing in the driveway was a man who looked just like Brother Joe.

"That's the guy in the photo! That's Brother Joe. What in the world is he doing here?" Mickey was shaking his head.

"Don't know, man. We need to figure out where Matt is. And Paul! I'm gettin' out to see what's going on here."

"Hold on, dude. Get your gun out. This guy may be packin' and we'd be walkin' into a trap."

"Got it. Let's go." Louis climbed out of the car and headed straight towards Joe.

The two men stepped away from their car and walked quickly towards the preacher. Brother Joe seemed to sense their tension and knew who they were in an instant. He held his gun by his side, as the two men aimed their guns at him.

"Drop your gun, preacher. Where are Paul and Matt?" Mickey sounded angry.

"I came here to talk to Paul, gentlemen. He's supposed to return any minute."

"Where's the money, preacher man?"

"What are you talking about? What money? What's going on?"

"Where's Matt?" Louis asked angrily.

"I have no idea where Matt is. That's why I'm here to see Paul."

"What's with the gun?" Mickey pointed to Joe's gun, which was still hanging at his side.

"Because I'm out here in the middle of nowhere, strange area, and I want to be able to protect myself. Obviously, it was a good idea. You two just showed up and have your guns aimed at me. Now you tell me what's going on."

"Get in the car. You're comin' with us." Louis grabbed Joe's gun and threw it in the front seat.

They grabbed Joe's arms and led him to the car and shoved him into the back seat. They hopped into the car and sped off, leaving nothing but a trail of dust behind them.

Matt and Paul walked the serene path back to the house and Paul assured him he'd been in worse scrapes.

"What these guys want is their money. They don't want to kill anyone; its messy business. You got to make it easy for them to get the money back so they don't get jumpy." He related some similar experiences he'd had while muling speed for the motorcycle gangs back in his youth.

"Man, the rules were different then," he continued. "Back then it was shoot now ask questions later.'"

As they got back behind the house they could hear the dogs inside going crazy. They stopped. Something had gone wrong. Matt walked to where Joe had been standing and his cell phone was lying on the ground. "He's gone," Matt said to Paul, frozen in his tracks. The car was untouched. Paul had run to the trailer to see if Joe had gone inside, and Matt spotted fresh tire tracks by the road. They walked to the road together and looked at each other in disbelief.

"Yep, he's gone." Paul was shaking his head in bewilderment.

Walking back to the car Matt looked at the suitcase in the backseat of the car. The money was still intact but Joe's life was at stake. He guessed both he and Joe knew they had only one move left to make. Matt had to return the money to Dr. Harrison and get Joe back before he got killed.

"Nothing ever turns out the way we plan it. I never wanted Joe to be involved in the first place. Then he had to show up at the drop point and now look what's happened. He's an older man. And he's a good man. He doesn't need to get hurt over some stupid drug deal. These people are ruthless. Life means nothing to them. I'm outta here with this money. You stay here. I thought it was a good idea for you to get involved, but now I see what I'm up against. These guys will kill at the drop of a hat. And I don't want you or Brother Joe to get hurt. We already lost Tommy, Paul. I sure don't want to lose my best friend."

Matt jumped into the car and pulled out, burning his tires as he left Paul standing in the driveway. His heart was racing, but the car wouldn't go fast enough. He slowed down as he entered Defuniak Springs, heading towards Destin. The last thing he needed was to draw attention to his car and have a cop stop him. No explanation in the world would clear up the question of why he had a suitcase full of money in the car.

CHAPTER 21

THE GAS STATION was dirty and there was rust on all the gas pumps outside. The name had long since fallen off the awning and the man working behind the counter was as old as the building. Paco felt right at home when he walked in and asked where the pay phone was. He sauntered around looking for something cheap to buy to eat. He was starving. He was always hungry. But today he was excited because he was finally going to talk with Hunter and share what he'd found. He kept checking the clock over the counter, anxious to hear Hunter's voice again. Odd how they struggled at first to even have a decent conversation. Now all he could think about was talking to the young man again.

There was a noise in the background that was coming from one of the refrigerators—a droning noise that drowned out any conversation inside the station. After eating a piece of chicken and coffee, Paco went to the bathroom and washed up. It felt good to splash the cool water on his face. He looked in the mirror, frowning at the gray hair sticking out in all directions. His teeth were falling out one at a time, yellow, gritty and cracking at the edges from opening cans. His eyes were a faded gray blue and his skin had weathered like a great oak tree. He shook his head, trying to keep his mind focused on what he wanted to say to Hunter. He was such a young man with high hopes about finding his father. Age had put a lot of wisdom under his belt, even out in the weather. It was a good place to come face to face with reality. What was really true. And he had an inkling, a whisper of the truth about Matt Collins. But he had decided not to speak it out loud to anyone, for in his weakened state of belief he feared it might make it come true.

At exactly 8:00, Paco put the money into the phone slot, listening to the coins clinking into the bottom of the phone. He waited for the ring. He was holding his breath that Hunter would answer. His money was running out and he would have to find odd jobs to pick up more. He wanted to continue his search for Matt, but he had to have enough money to live on.

After four rings a voice was on the other end of the line. Paco strained to recognize the voice but could not.

"Hello? Is this Hunter Bentley?"

"Hold on. I'll get him for you."

Paco waited, tapping the phone cord against the wall. His heart was racing and he was anticipating the conversation.

"Hello? This is Hunter."

"Hey man! It's Paco."

"Dude! What's up? You doing okay?" Hunter grinned.

"Sure. I'm fine, Hunter. How's school? You studying hard?"

"That's all I do. So where are you, Paco? What you been doing?"

"I've been moving 'round some. Ya know? Life on the street, Hunter. Never staying in the same place too long. The reason I called you was I've been trying to look for Matt Collins. And one day I was in a medical clinic for a cut I had on my arm, and I saw some photographs on the wall of some of the doctors who'd worked in the free clinic."

"Oh, hey. That's cool, man. So how's your arm?"

"That's not why I called, Hunter. I saw your father's photograph on the wall. Matt Collins was a doctor in that clinic and was one of the notable doctors recognized for his work."

Hunter stood in the hallway of his dorm with tears in his eyes. *So my father is a pretty good man after all. He has to be, to have worked in a free clinic.* He wiped his face quickly and cleared his throat.

"Wow! That's cool, man. So did you find out anything about him? Did the clinic have any information?"

"Nah. They wouldn't give me anything. 'Course I look pretty rough, ya know. But at least we did find out he used to work there. That shows what kinda man he is. We just don't know where he is now."

"I appreciate the call, Paco. You didn't have to do that. I know it's tough out there for you. Are you able to stay warm?"

"Don't worry 'bout me, kid. I'm fine. Been doing this for too long. But I want to tell ya something. I been thinking 'bout you since you got off that bus. I can't get ya outta my mind, man. This thing about your father has been haunting me. I'm gonna find this guy if it takes a year. I want you to know that. I'm not gonna stop looking 'til I find him."

Hunter was taken aback by the degree of intensity in Paco's voice. The caring. "You don't have to do this. You gotta be barely making it out there, Paco. It's freezing outside. Just take care of yourself, man. Don't worry about my father. I'll find him someday."

"It's too late now, Son. I've committed myself to this and I'm gonna stick with it. It kinda gives me a purpose. And I haven't had that in years."

"I wish they'd been able to give you more information about Matt. How are we ever gonna track this guy down, Paco?"

Paco could feel the hopelessness in Hunter's voice. "Son, I promise you one thing. I can't say how, or when. But we're gonna find him. It's just a matter of time. I'm out on the streets and one day I'm gonna run up on someone who has seen him or knows about him. The more people we come in contact with, the better our chances of finding him are. Do you see that?"

"Yeah. I sorta do. I really appreciate what you're doing Paco. It's hard for me to let you do this. Do you need anything? Where are you staying?"

"Don't worry 'bout me, Hunter. You forget how long I've been doing this gig. But I know all the ropes and I can handle it. It's cold outside and I do struggle when it gets this cold. But there are places to get outta the weather, and I seek them out. I'm gonna be fine."

"That's not a very convincing argument, but it'll have to do for now, Paco. I need to run back to the library." Hunter paused, wishing he had more time to talk. "Just keep in touch with me, will ya, man? I'll be doing my own research from here. But my hands are kinda tied up with school and all."

"You study hard and enjoy this time. It won't last long, Hunter. Trust me on that one. Just enjoy it. I'll be out here digging up answers for you. I'll call when I can. If I find anything, I'll call."

"Thanks, Paco. I hope I hear from you soon. Here is my cell phone number, in case you need to reach me. It will be easier this way."

"Cool. Thanks, Hunter. I got it written down on my arm. We should've thought of this sooner."

Paco hung up the phone and stood there rubbing his white bearded chin. He was hungry and tired. His knee was aching and he needed a shower. But what he wanted to do most was find Matt Collins for that young man. He looked around the gas station and spotted a cooler with beer. He walked over and got two cold beers and sat down at a table in the corner and drank them slowly. His stomach was growling again and he had just enough change to get a honey bun. It tasted good going down. But later that night he was going to need some protein. He decided to find some work and earn enough money to carry him through this dog hunt. He knew of a man he could count on for some light construction work. Grabbing his hat and coat he walked out the door waving at the old man behind the counter. His step was a little light because he had a new purpose and as the cold air hit his face, he pulled his coat up around his neck and walked into the wind. It was gonna be a long night and a cold one. He knew he'd better find another place to stow up for the night.

Hunter walked away from the phone with a tiny bit of hope. Paco had turned out to be quite a guy and he hoped that he would be able to dig up some information on Matt. As he walked back to this room he let his thoughts ramble through the notes he'd seen in Aunt Jenny's basement. *My father was a respectable man, highly esteemed by his peers. Would he be shocked to know he had a son? Was it stupid to think that he might want me in his life?* So many unknowns he had to face before he got some answers. He wondered how he'd feel when he found Matt. What he would say to him. His emotions were moving from zero to ten when he walked through the doorway of his room. Lonnie slapped him on the back as he passed by the television on his way to the kitchen.

"What's up, dude?" He was stuffing a sandwich into his mouth.

"Oh nothing, man. Just a phone call is all."

"That old man again? What's he want?"

"He's looking for my father. Get off my back about it, okay?"

"Hey, lighten up, dude. I was joking."

"Not funny tonight. Not funny. I'm heading to the library to study. You staying in?"

"Yeah. You seemed to really like seeing Holly tonight. Didn't think you'd show up."

"She's a nice girl. I was lucky to have a chance to talk to her. She wouldn't hardly speak to me 'til now."

"She's speaking now, dude. No way you could miss that." Lonnie shoved Hunter and laughed.

"I like her. But let me do it my way, man. I'll make my move when I'm ready."

"Yeah, I know how you are, it'll be freakin' Friday before you get enough nerve to ask for her cell number. I'll be out of medical school before you take her out!"

Hunter laughed and grabbed a Sprite and then walked back through the living room to get his notebook. "See ya later, man. It wouldn't hurt ya to crack a book now and then. Ya know?"

Hunter walked out and shut the door, shaking his head. Holly was beautiful. He had loved sitting next to her and listening to her talk about her family. But they were both covered up in papers, tests, and studying. There was no time for romance for the next two years. Still, somehow he'd have to find a way to take her out so they could get to know each other. As long as Lonnie was around, no one got a word in edgewise. He smiled, remembering her hair. The fragrance of freshly washed hair had drifted up to his nose.

As he approached the library, he pushed on the huge walnut doors and walked in. Far in the corner of the room, near a window, was a lone figure of a girl with her head bent over a stack of books. He squinted to see who it was, and shrugged. A chance in a million he'd know her. Pretty, though. He carried his books to a table halfway back and sat down facing her. When she looked up, she smiled. And his stomach left his body as he recognized the face. Holly! And he had a mother ship of an exam tomorrow that he had to ace.

She nodded as she went back to her studying, as if to tell him she shared in his dilemma. He felt a warm feeling come over him as he tackled the notes in front of him. He concentrated with all he had on the words he was reading, but his eyes kept wandering to the pretty girl his young heart was falling for.

Twelve hundred miles away, Matt Collins was fighting for his life. And for his best friend's life. He had no one in the world to care if he came home at night except Brother Joe. So it was his main goal in life to protect Joe from any decisions he made in his own life that were risky. He had to find it within himself to seek out the right path for his life. To change the dark patterns that had made up the web he'd gotten tangled up in that brought his life down to a park bench. The smell of that bench and the shame he felt sleeping there, wounded, would remain in his brain for a long time. He could close his eyes even now and see the ocean with its huge waves coming into shore. The roar he fell asleep to, night after night. The salt air. The seagull's call. The hunger that nearly ate the inside of his stomach. And the sleeping giants who remained out there in the night, who he once thought of as his brothers. Joe had pulled him off that bench and given him a roof over his head. But he knew it wouldn't take much to bring that bench back into his life along with the emptiness and the hollow feelings.

He snatched himself back from falling into that black hole. And he knew he had to save himself and Joe from Dr. Harrison. But he wanted to avenge Tommy's death. And he wanted to keep someone else from having to call that damn bench near the water, home.

CHAPTER 22

———— ⚜ ————

CRUSTY FROST HAD formed on his eyelids and his feet were numb. Paco had stumbled upon a lean-to shack near the edge of a small grouping of trees and grabbed it before some random hobo moved in for the night. It was on the edge of winter and the cold was bitter. He woke up stiff and starving. His first thought was water. But it had been that way for many years and he was accustomed to it. He knew most of the small towns around Philadelphia like the back of his hand, which helped him find water and food when things were hard. He was out of money and needed a job fast. He stood up and rolled up his tattered sleeping bag, tied it to his backpack, and walked outside. The sun was peeking through the gray clouds of another winter day and few cars were on the road in front of the stand of trees. He started walking towards town and tried to remember Chuck's phone number. He'd worked for Chuck for many years, off and on, and could always count on a small job to give him some cash. Chuck was used to his moving around and allowed him that freedom in their friendship.

The soles on his boots were thin and full of small holes. His socks were getting soggy, and that led to the risk of frost bite. His jeans were torn and the hem on his pants was ragged. He had the same gray brimmed hat on his head that he'd worn for the last ten years. It was weathered but he still loved it. Because he was so mobile, he didn't allow himself the luxury of collecting a lot of extra clothing, so he just put up with the holes and worn pants and hat because it was easier. He had gotten used to the looks from other people when he was walking on the highway or in town. It wasn't their fault. They were just curious. At first he had hated it, but now he hardly noticed.

He knew it would be tough to find another pay phone, so he went inside Frank's Cash 'n' Go and asked to use the phone. Mabel, the elderly lady behind the counter, winked at him.

"You back again, travelin' man?"

"Yeah, back again. You care if I make a local call, Mabel?"

"Nah. Help yourself. Doesn't cost nothing."

"I'll only be a minute. Thanks, sweetie."

She smiled and turned to check out a customer. Chuck answered on the fifth ring. Paco was just about to hang it up.

"Paco, is that you? You dirty scoundrel! Where in the hell 've ya been? I been thinking I'd hear from you pretty soon now."

Paco laughed and coughed up some spittle. He looked around for someplace to spit but ended up swallowing. He made a face and answered his friend.

"Hey, man. How are you? I been walking all over the place, catching odd jobs when I can."

"I know how you do, man. We been friends for years, ya know. So what's up? You need some cash?"

"Yeah. I've got me a project I'm working on. Something good for a change. And I am gonna need some money to keep on moving around. I got a ways to go and I'm broke. You got any work for me?"

Chuck's laugh was raspy. Paco recognized the sound of lungs going bad. He coughed and coughed and finally cleared his throat. "Yeah, I always got something for you to do. Meet me at the old Miller's house on Martin Avenue. We got some repairs to do. That'll keep you and me busy for a week. It pays good and it's not hard on the body. Ya know?"

"Sounds like a plan, man. Thanks a lot. I knew I could count on you."

"I'll be there today at 10:00. See ya then, Paco."

Paco hung up the phone and smiled at Mabel. Her teeth were nearly gone but she always had a smile.

"Thanks, Mabel. Take care of yourself, old gal. I'll be seeing you before too long."

She handed Paco a hot cup of coffee and a sugary honey bun. "You old gnarly coot, you. You been out on the street too long, buddy. Your body's wearing out like mine. Stay warm, is all I kin' say."

Paco headed out the door whistling a tune he'd forgotten the name of. He had a plan and was glad he was going to be working for a week. It gave him something to do and he could earn good pay.

Paco was determined and when he made up his mind, nothing and no one could change it. He sat in the sun and drank his hot coffee and pastry. He desperately needed a hot meal with plenty of protein. The work would require some strength and lately his diet had been filled with junk food. Unfortunately, that was the diet of a homeless man, as he knew too well.

I-95 unfolded before Paco as he looked out the side window. He had finally gotten a ride from the truck stop to Wilmington. Paco had befriended a black truck driver by the name of Roy. Roy was a short fellow with a medium sized Afro and smooth ebony skin that belied his fifty-five years. He also had a full set of teeth that seemed to be permanently on display through his easy smile. The truck driving comic loved to tell jokes as he and Paco passed the sixty miles to Martin Road and the promise of short term employment.

"How long you gonna be in Wilmington?" Roy asked.

"I got a quick job to do. Then I'll head back to Philly after I get some green paper in my pocket."

Roy laughed a deep laugh and pulled out of the truck stop, shifting gears like a pro. Paco knew he could tell his passenger had been on the road a long time, yet he had a nonjudgmental way of talking to him. Paco loved Roy's laugh, which he knew was his way of coping with the harsher realities life had sent his way. He drove a gasoline tanker and had driven one for thirty years. He loved grabbing gears and pushing that sixty-thousand-pound truck down the road. To Paco he looked like a king in the seat of that Peterbilt rig, passing judgment on drivers who didn't follow the rules of the road. He also always served as judge of a highway "beauty contest," remarking on the appearance of every female that passed him on the road. Between jokes he sang harmony with the Motown sounds rolling out of his radio. Paco and Roy had a common love for the road. They quickly agreed that nothing helped put troubles behind you like a long stretch of highway. Somewhere in the midst of the stories and the jokes and the pretty girls who drove by them, they sang together in harmony.

The levity and the warmth inside the truck made Paco feel drowsy. As they got close to Wilmington Roy spoke up, smiling. "What you gonna do with your thirty percent of our first million dollar album?"

"Thirty percent? Why, it's old Paco they'd be lining up to see at those concerts. In fact, I was gonna offer you forty percent if you drove the tour bus, too." The daydreaming song stylist laughed.

"Seriously, Paco, what would you do if ya had a million?"

"Well I got a project in mind that is close to my heart, Roy, my man. A while back, on my way from New Jersey to Philly, I met a cool kid. He's searching for his dad. His mom just died and his dad don't even know he's alive. And he's a good kid, too."

Roy shook his head. "My old man was MIA for a while. Mom raised us by herself out in Waco, Texas. Dad left right after my little sister was born. But we would see him now and then. How did you get mixed up with that?"

"I just rode with the boy on a bus. Since then I been trying to help. So many kids go bad these days. I mean what else do I have to do with my time? The president hasn't been inviting me for dinner."

"I'm gonna stop to make a call. According to my GPS, where you're heading ain't that far from the station I have in mind."

"Cool! As long as it ain't a police station."

The two broke into another chorus of laughter. A few minutes later Roy pulled his rig to a stop.

"Paco, my man, this is the end of the line. You keep your eyes open for my rig and we can do it again sometime."

Roy reached out his hand and Paco gripped it. Paco could feel something in Roy's hand. Looking down he could see it was a fifty dollar bill.

"Hey, dude, you don't have to do that."

Roy smiled one last time. "You just use that to help find that boy's daddy. I'll see you on the flip side, Paco."

Paco's location was a twenty-minute walk from Old Martin Road. As the big rig pulled back out onto the road Roy let out a blast with the air horn and Paco waved gratefully. He saw a Roast Beef Shack and got himself a sandwich, then made the walk to Chuck's jobsite. The house was about three-fourths of a mile up Old Martin Road and was easily recognizable because there was a pickup with Chuck's name on the side of it. Paco walked up the sidewalk and went to the door and tapped on it. Chuck yelled out quickly.

"Come on in!" He met Paco in the hall way.

"Hey, old timer!" Paco yelled. "You ain't aged a bit since we worked together last."

"Yeah, I see ya still haven't learned how to lie."

The two of them shook hands chuckling. It was easy to see they were happy to see each other.

"So, boss man, what are we working on here?"

"Uh, we gotta patch and paint the whole place and I got to put wainscot in the kitchen. I'm really gonna need a pair of hands moving the appliances." Chuck playfully jabbed Paco in the gut and laughed.

"And, of course, I got to dock ya for taking so long to git here!"

Paco was unfazed. "That's cool, 'cause I hurt myself shaking hands with you and have to hit you up for an extra day's pay." The old friends agreed it was a tie and went right to work.

The days flew by and Chuck let Paco stay on his sofa while they worked. Chuck was a big man and a youthful sixty-five year old. He was balding but handsome with some long arms. He had a tough exterior and never could keep a steady helper, largely because he was a perfectionist. He was a little short on his people skills. Paco knew he fit right in because his time on the streets had taught him not to take Chuck seriously, and Chuck's ranting and raving rolled off his back with relative ease. The fact that Paco had plenty to eat and a roof overhead made the work almost pleasurable.

Friday came quick and the two men finished ahead of schedule. Paco was on his way back to Philly with a little bankroll in his pocket. In his usual fashion, Paco stopped at a saloon. The Bandstand was an old joint down by the river and Paco couldn't wait to see if any of the old crew was around. His life had just bumped up a notch after working a week with Chuck. He had money and a purpose. That alone was an improvement to his normally nonexistent life. He was old but he wasn't dead.

CHAPTER 23

As I SPED down the highway toward Destin, I reached over and turned on the radio. Joe had set the channel for easy listening, but I switched over to classic rock and started listening to a tune I remembered from the '70s. As I put my foot in the throttle and rolled down the highway, my mind was punishing me for what had happened to Brother Joe. *If those idiots hurt him I would never forgive myself.* The knot in my stomach was bigger than ever. I watched my rearview mirror closely. The last thing in the world I needed was a speeding ticket. I noticed that my driving had grown more daring since I had quit drinking. All those nights of driving with one eye closed—how stupid can you get? Now I was racing against the clock. Every minute that passed was another minute of peril for Joe.

I fought back a smile as I recalled Joe pulling up at the drop point. The old man didn't know he was my only friend and now it was time to get him out of a jam no matter what the cost. The road was feeling solid under my wheels and I was making great time. As I weaved between lanes, I couldn't help but remember my speedy ambulance ride. Every moment had counted, just like it counted now. I remembered that the craziness was supposed to stop when I quit drinking. How did I get so deep into this mess with Frank Harrison? Paul had tried to help by letting me sit in with the band. Then Tommy had died. Now Brother Joe was in over his head. I needed to make some changes.

My self assessment was cut short when I saw lights flashing behind me. *Of all the doggone luck. Where in the world did that county sheriff come from?* Before pulling over I slid the gun under the seat and made sure the case full of money in the back seat was covered up. I could hear the gravel on the side of the road as I pulled over and stopped. I turned the radio down as I rolled down the window, and watched in the rearview mirror as the cop jumped out of his car and slowly eased up to my car. I was nervous as a cat but I tried to act calm.

"'Morning, officer." I tried to smile through my racing thoughts. All I could think of was the gun and the money, as the events of the last forty-eight hours raced through my head. *A simple speeding ticket, that's all he wants to give me. Play it cool, Matt.* I popped open the glove box and retrieved Joe's registration and insurance card. Reaching into my pocket, I pulled out my wallet. It felt like I was moving in slow motion as I tried to pull myself together. Finally I could hear the sheriff talking over the pounding in my ears.

"I clocked you at seventy-five miles per hour. The speed limit is 55. That's a lot of points on your insurance. Can I ask why you were going so fast?"

"Well, I was running a little late and was hoping to make up a little time." He shook his head as he returned to his vehicle. I looked at the thick brush along the highway, now brown and stripped of life. The cop returned to my window.

"Mr. Collins, I just ran your license and it came back clear. The laptop in my cruiser has been acting up and I was on my way in to get it serviced when I pulled you over. I've decided not to issue you a citation today, but I'm gonna give you a warning. This could have cost you over two hundred dollars in fines. Please be more cautious when obeying our traffic laws, especially speed limits." He paused.

"I see you are driving someone else's car. Is there a reason for that, Mr. Collins?"

I swallowed slowly, dry as a cork. "Joe Mason is a good friend of mine. He gave me permission to drive his car."

The officer nodded. "You have a good day, Mr. Collins."

As he was handing the paperwork and my license to me through the window, I could've shouted. I was so relieved. Yet I was afraid to even show that emotion for fear of stirring greater suspicion.

"Thank you, Officer, thank you very much. You have a good day now." He turned and headed back to his cop car. I leaned forward and rested my head on the wheel. My knees were shaking. *Thank goodness.* Man, this could have ended badly. The money, the gun, and the high speed all pointed to trouble. But I was free to spring Brother Joe and that's all that mattered right now. I eased out on the highway and went the distance into Destin at exactly fifty-five miles per hour.

Walton County came into view as I turned onto Highway 98. I supposedly lived in paradise, but at this moment it almost felt like hell. Joe was in danger and could be hurt if I didn't get a grip on things. I knew I had to handle this doctor with kid gloves. Any wrong moves and Joe would pay the ultimate price for caring about me. I just couldn't let that happen.

I crawled through the back streets of town and watched the stores open for business. As I headed for Fort Walton my mind began to focus on the situation at hand; all I had to do was get Joe out, return the money, and get out in one piece. If this situation taught me anything it was the fact that the primary benefit of being on the wagon was staying out of sticky situations. Too bad the good doctor hadn't figured that out yet.

That thought was a profound turning point in my thinking. I had been so eaten up with Tommy dying that I had yet to think clearly on this whole mess. If Doctor Harrison had intended to get wrapped up in the drug trade, he never would have gone to school all those years. *Somewhere in that guy is a heart to help people.* How did he get so mixed up in a racket that only brought grief and anguish to families like our drummer? Shoot, that guy didn't set out to be a drug dealer any more than I wanted to be a harmonica player. I chuckled. That doctor doesn't realize we got way more things in common than our profession.

The sand on the side of the road reflected the sunshine. As I rolled down the highway, the few red lights I had to stop at took forever. I rolled into the bus station and quickly locked the satchel in a locker and stuffed the key in my leather coat. Then I walked into the restroom and rinsed off my face. I looked up in the mirror and studied my reflection. I smirked. It'd been a long time since a young idealistic doctor looked back at me in one of these. I studied the toll that age, hard living, and weather had taken. I suddenly found it difficult, if not impossible, to hate Frank Harrison.

I realized that he would be having a lot of trouble in his future. I didn't want to add to it. As I walked back to the car, I wondered how deep Frank was in. I wondered if I'd had my heart attack sooner and shared my destructive path honestly with the doctor, perhaps none of this would've gone down. At that point I stopped my crusade to hurt the doctor. I began wishing we both could be part of the solution and no longer part of the problem. Looking around for paper towels, I found only a hand blower. I hit the switch and rubbed my hands under the air stream. Then I twisted the stainless steel jet upward and dried my face and hair. The stream of air was so hot I flinched.

I jumped back into the car and headed for Frank Harrison's office. Once there I couldn't help but look at the staff that had once saved my life.

Dr. Harrison's receptionist stood as I entered her zone. "Do you have an appointment? There are already people in his office."

"I think he will see me." I smiled at her and told her my name was Matt Collins.

As soon as the receptionist said my name into the phone the door flew open and I was motioned in by Dr. Harrison. As I walked in I could see how nervous he was and I could relate to the way the lid was boiling off the top of his secret life. As I looked around at the room I saw Mickey and Louis and Brother Joe. I looked at Joe and asked him if he was all right. Before Joe could answer, Louis shoved me against the wall and patted me down.

"He's clean."

"Is that fun for you?" I winked playfully. Then we just glared at each other for a few moments.

Frank spoke up sternly. "Okay, okay guys, knock it off. We're all on the on the same side here. Matt, were the heck is our money?"

"No worries, dude. The money is safe. And let's get Brother Joe outta here. This is between you and me, Doc. We don't need an audience, do we?"

Frank was looking at me eye to eye and I could see he understood. Then he looked at Brother Joe and spoke quietly. "Thanks for cooperating, man. I'm sorry it came to this. But there's one stipulation here, buddy. What happened here can't go any further than this room, Padre."

"As long as Matt remains safe there's no reason for anything that happened today come to the attention of anyone outside of this room."

"Thank you, Joe. Hey, here's a little something for your collection plate."

He held out a few one hundred dollar bills. Joe looked back at him and assured him that he didn't want to take any money to remain quiet. And he walked out with dignity.

"Joe, your car is out in the parking lot, I'll be out in a few minutes." I paused and looked at Frank.

"Okay, the money is in a safe place. Can we talk in private?"

The doctor knew I was referring to Mickey and Louis. "Guys, I'll call you this afternoon. If I have any issues, I'll pull you in."

Mickey was reluctant to leave. He started to speak up but the doc pointed to the door. "It's under control."

CHAPTER 24

— ⚜ —

I FELT LIKE it took way longer than it should have to get Mickey and Louis out of the office. As we sat down, I waved the key at the doctor. I could see the relief in his eyes.

"Gets pretty tense in your line of work, Doc."

He sighed, and for the first time in days he let a smile come to his face. I leaned across the desk and tried to copy one of Brother Joe's deep soulful looks.

"Dr. Harrison, the last time I was in this office we were talking about how I was going to stay alive. Now men have died and God knows how many lives will be ruined by one single shipment. How did this get so out of control? You can level with me. I'm really not trying to cause you trouble."

The doc's eyes looked like those of a deer in the headlights. For a moment I thought he was going to tear up on me.

"I got to tell you, Doc. I was once in the medical profession and I understand that we're all human. Lord knows I fell hard. For me it was coke and booze. Now you're going to get your money and all is well except for Coon. Look, I locked the money in a special locker." I paused and looked straight into his eyes. "Here is the key. When I get Joe home safe, I'll tell you where the locker is. But listen to me, Frank. I worked hard for you last night. Without me, you would've lost both the product and the money. I got a feeling that would've left you in a bind. Come on, man, can't you satisfy my curiosity a little?"

The doctor looked at me and his shoulders slumped as if a weight had been removed from his body and mind. "I used to love doing my job. You know how there's a special feel when people around you are depending on you to get them well. My first year in Tallahassee, I was as full of ideas as any twenty-seven-year-old med student. I loved going to work as much as I loved going home. My wife was great; we had twins, and life was so full of smiles. Then she miscarried and I wasn't there to help. Then we had our youngest, Stevie, who had Down's syndrome. Man, my wife had her hands full. Things got worse as the bills piled up. I was working harder and harder but there was never enough of anything. Not enough time, not enough money, and not enough desire to correct the issues I was facing at home and at work.

"Stevie lived three years and then died in his sleep. It was like he just forgot to breathe. Every time I looked at my once beautiful wife, I saw the pain I had brought her. And I began to feel useless as a husband. It was easier to stay at work than to come home. One night at an office party someone gave me a line of snow. Gave me a metal tube and showed me how to snort it. It was like discovering life all over again. I had energy, I could talk, and I could work 'til all hours and never tire. Matt, that dope is sneaky—you know it is. I began to use more and more to get the same euphoria. At home things were a mess and we were losing the house. My wife seemed to hate me. And I was using more than six hundred dollars a day just to function. Well, at that rate it doesn't take long to get in a hole. These guys you met were quick to offer credit and the bottom opened up.

"As my life sped out of control this guy stepped up. Let's just call him 'the kingpin.' He made me a loan. Got my house out of default. Everything I thought I wanted seemed to be right in front of me. For a week or so there was light at the end of the tunnel. The kingpin offered to square my debt if I helped him 'move some weight', as he called it. I got into it just to get him off my back. Then I gave in to temptation and helped myself to the stash. Before long I was deeper in debt than when I started.

"The kingpin put me in charge of distribution. When you came along, I thought I could get out by using the mule fees for my spiraling debt. I thought we were home free. I never wanted Tommy to die. The boys handled all retail sales. I got a cut. But I had no control over who sold what to whom."

"Frank, I've heard enough. I admire your honesty about it. You're in deep, man, and I wish I could help. But I got my own set of problems. All I need from you is your word that you won't hurt Joe. I'm not going to cause you any trouble. After all, Doc, who is gonna fix my ticker when I need it?"

The statement drew a funny look from Harrison, as if he was reflexively flashing back to being my doctor. I had seen that look before in a mirror in Philadelphia. Before he could say anything I opened up again.

"I guess we are finished here." I started to stand.

"Matt, it would really help me a lot if you'd help with another run. It's a pickup this time. It'll be clean, professional. No nervous Nellies like last night. I think after this we can both walk away."

"You're asking a lot, Doc. I been clean since that last heart attack. I don't need heat from the law or any other baggage. This drama is part of a past I regret deeply. I've paid my dues, man. I hate the whole scene."

"Matt, the job pays five grand for a night's work."

"It's not about the money, Doc, it's really not. I almost got a friend of mine killed. I can't go down that road."

"I respect that, but you have to see the spot I'm in. I've leveled with you. I need to get out and you could use the money. We can do this."

I sat there stunned. My head was whirling and yesterday all I wanted to do was get these guys busted, and busted hard. Now I just wanted out and I wanted this doctor out. I really needed to get some fresh air. But I also wanted to put that kingpin down. He was the real villain in this whole deal. I had to put my fears aside and do this thing right.

"Doc, I hate this, but I'm gonna do it. Just remember if things don't go just like you think, I'm still in your corner. And Joe is out of this, right?"

"He's out. I can promise you that he will not be harmed. And I personally will have your back. But you have to do everything I say, Matt, or you're on your own. Understood?"

"I hear ya, buddy. Get in touch with me when you are ready to relay the details. I'm outta here."

Frank agreed and I was on my feet. As I reached the door I looked back at the doc.

"When this is all over we're just gonna have to get a cup of coffee together." I reached in my coat pocket and retrieved the keys. "Look, man, the loot is at the Greyhound station locker number 13. I got to get Joe back to the house before he has my head on a platter."

We looked at each other and for the first time it seemed to me we saw each other as equals. We both had crashed over our addictions. And we'd both lost everything for snow. I had some decisions to make and every single step now was critical. There was only one person in the world that I could trust to help me think clearly and he was waiting for me outside.

I stepped out of Frank's office searching for Brother Joe, knowing he would be close to the car. I walked out into the afternoon sun and felt its warm embrace. There was a park across the street and after taking a few laps I found Joe relaxing on a bench. He looked so peaceful and I was glad he was out of harm's way. From about twenty feet I yelled at him.

"Hey buddy, you in the mood for a sandwich?"

"On one condition," Joe remarked with a raised eyebrow. His cheerful smile belied the nightmare we had just shared. I looked at him curiously.

"If I drive and I pick the radio station."

We both burst into mild laughter. "Hey, man, that's two conditions!"

"Exactly, Matt! I've seen you eat and it's not a sight for the timid." Our laughter continued until we got to the sub shop.

"I can't wait to bite into one of the five dollar foot longs."

After we got our food and sat down I noticed Joe silently blessing his food, and I couldn't help notice how I admired this guy more and more as each day passed. I broke the silence after he said grace.

"Joe, you should have made me drive straight to Frank and give him the money."

Joe just looked up from his sandwich quietly. "It was your choice what to do with the money, Matt."

"But Joe, you could have been killed."

"That's not the point."

"What is the point then?"

"The point is, I wasn't killed and you made the choice to give back the money. Matt, not everyone would've done that."

"I had to, man."

"No Matt, you chose to. You're beginning to show some character."

"You're my best friend. In many ways my only friend. No amount of money was worth letting you get hurt."

Soon we were on our way home and I brought the conversation back to life.

"I had quite a chat with that doctor." Joe glanced at me silently from behind the wheel. His look allowed me to continue.

"Yeah, he's not a bad dude; in fact he's been through a lot. I don't hate him like I did."

"Is that bad?"

"No I guess not. But I just don't have the drive to get him busted like I wanted to yesterday."

"So justice is only for the guys you don't like?"

"Well, no, I guess not. You always give me these puzzles to work on. You might want to boss me around a little more. Then I would know where you're coming from."

"You're a smart man. I can't tell you what to do; I'm not here to judge you. Think before you act. And the less words said the better. One more thing. Just because a person is nice doesn't mean he can't make a bad mistake. Your doctor friend made a bad mistake. And you jumped in with him, granted for other reasons. I hope this thing can be salvaged without any other deaths. Especially yours."

CHAPTER 25

As we turned back on the highway we both noticed a guy known locally as Jimmy Nubs. Jimmy usually flew a sign by the side of the road begging for donations. He was well known around the shelters and food pantries. I watched as Joe studied him when we passed by.

"You know Nubs, Joe?"

"Yes, I've met Jimmy. He's a hard case." Joe seemed to sigh as he spoke. "Jimmy lost all his fingers after turning states' evidence on a drug dealer in Atlanta."

"He told me it was a punch press in Pittsburg that got him. I guess the story changes to suit the company." I laughed. "It depends on if he's thirsty for beer or whiskey, which story you get. He loves to panhandle that one."

"Everyone has a story. Even you."

"Speaking of stories, Joe, I need to go to the cops. But I really want to help the doctor get back on his feet. A felony like that will ruin his career even if he flips on the rest of the organization. I really want to bust up this ring without hurting the doctor's reputation."

"You still intend to talk to the cops?"

"I got to do it, man. People are dying here. I can't just ignore that."

"Well how you gonna to play this one out?"

"Well, I promised the doc I would participate in a pickup."

"Didn't we just go through this?"

"Yeah, except this time I'm gonna involve the cops. I'm taking no more chances with my life and I'm sure not gonna put you in a bind again. All I have is my story and that tape. I'm gonna get Frank to get me more details about the drop and give the information to the cops. I just wish I could get them to go easy on Frank. They want that kingpin dude; he's the troublemaker here. Frank was just caught in the mix. Not much different from me, Joe."

"Or me," Joe said. "Last night I transported you and a bunch of money across a state line."

"Yeah, if you hadn't been there I might've been in the same shape as Coon. Dead."

Joe interrupted. "Yep, I did what I had to, to save you."

"I appreciate that, Joe, but Frank only got involved to help his wife and kids. We take this kingpin out of the picture and fewer innocent people get caught up in his web." I paused, rubbing my eyes. "I want you to stop up here; I feel a need for a walk. I'll catch up with you at home. I got to walk this off. Are you okay with that?"

"Sure, man. Go for it. I'll talk to you when you get in. Thanks for the conversation. I understand where you're coming from."

I jumped out of the car and headed for the beach, pulling my shoes off and wandering up to the water's edge. The air still had a January feel to it as put my footprints in the snowy white sand. The sun was sinking low as I walked. I loved the sea, always had. As a kid I would walk with my uncle to a cool fishing spot he always seemed to find. He and my aunt would take me camping on the Jersey shore and we would fish out in the Atlantic surf. The fish we would haul in were always great. My uncle made sure we only kept what we would eat after the pictures were taken. When we would fish the inland rivers and creeks, I loved catching carp. They seemed big when I was a little boy but they tasted awful. Yet I would endure a poor meal of boney carp again to feel the thrill of the next catch.

I had moved to Destin nearly ten years ago, I realized, as I made my way on the long stretch of beach. The big sign at the entrance to Destin read "Worlds Luckiest Fishing Village' and always reminded me of the days of my youth when thoughts of fishing consumed my whole summer vacation. I thought of my mom and dad and how out of touch we'd become. I wondered how they were and made a mental note to call them.

Dr. Harrison's life and mine were so similar. He, too, had a brilliant streak. And a once happy family. I thought of all of the unhappy moments that had brought me to this point. Then I said aloud, "Man, if I don't help him out, he's gonna wind up just like me." I didn't wish that on him. I normally avoided the police like the plague. If they were tipped off about this fiasco, the police would just arrest everyone and let the courts sort it out. And that would spell trouble for Frank as much as it did for me. I couldn't blow the whistle and ruin yet another career.

I stood up and began my walk home. I was sure going to enjoy that bed tonight. But I knew that when I woke up tomorrow I'd better spring into action on behalf of Tommy, Coon, and Frank. This destructive machinery had to be stopped. The kingpin and his cronies were peddling nothing but heartache and the cops had to be made aware so appropriate action could be taken. We lived in paradise but another force was riding underneath all the magic. The dragon needed to be slain.

I reached my apartment and plopped down in my leather chair and clicked on the television. Nothing was on except the news so I turned the sound down and laid my head back against the chair. I was playing with the big boys now and I wasn't that experienced. I had used cocaine but I never sold it. Frank wasn't that schooled in the snow, either. I just couldn't see turning him in if there was a chance for redemption.

I thought about walking over to talk to Joe and jumped out of my chair and opened the front door. Just at that moment I saw his car pulling out. *Where in the world was Joe going at this time of night, after the kind of day we had?* I decided to follow him, even though I had a headache the size of Texas. I ran out the door and stayed to the sidewalk so that he wouldn't see me following him. I had a feeling he was headed down to the water.

I was right in my assumption. As I ran along the highway I saw him turn up ahead of me down a side road that led to the harbor. I was out of breath and slowed down as I approached a row of benches. I sat there, watching him move around like he was invisible. I noticed he had on a gray coat and hat and was carrying blankets with him and a brown sack that looked heavy. I stayed in the shadows and kept near a wall so he couldn't see me. Joe had told me earlier how he moved among the sleepers at night, covering them. But now I was seeing firsthand how he did it. How much he cared for these men who lived outside in the cold.

Slowly Joe moved down a hill that was covered in small, leggy live oaks. There was some underbrush which hid the boxes that some men had dragged down there to sleep on to keep them dry for the night. Even the few who were awake didn't seem to mind his presence among them. And that was rare. For I had learned quickly not to talk to anyone. I wanted no contact with the world that I'd stepped off of. The pain was too great and it would've all come flooding back had I struck up a conversation with anyone who was in the real world.

Joe didn't seem to want to talk to them. He only brought them food, water, and a blanket or coat. A coat. I kept repeating that last thought over and over in my head. *Is that where I got my leather jacket? Did Joe give me his own jacket?* My eyes burned with tears as I ran back to the bench I used to sleep on. It was right near the barrier that held back the water during hurricanes. Because I was up a little higher I could see the water very clearly.

My bench was hidden from Joe's view and he wasn't looking for me outside. But every once in a while I caught a glimpse of him moving around. My body was shaking as I faced the realization that Joe had given me the coat. And when he saw me eating at the Coffee House he had come over and asked to sit by me. He had known me all along.

It was hard to fathom that a man could be so giving, so caring, to men whom the world turned away from. The homeless were embarrassing to most people; they made society feel uncomfortable. They were an undeserving lot of bums who needed to get a grip and earn their own way. But Joe somehow felt differently about us. He saw through the dirt and ragged clothing to the man underneath it all. He reached out in such a quiet, nonthreatening way that one couldn't help but respond. But he had really caught me off guard. He had sneaked into my life and given me hope again before I could resist. And what did I do? I dragged him into a shooting match with some goons and nearly got us both killed. I couldn't help but laugh, but inside I knew how crazy it was.

I had gotten lost in my thoughts when Joe walked up on me. My breath nearly stopped when I saw his face.

"Son, what are you doing out here in the cold night? I thought you'd be fast asleep by now."

"Nah, just thought I'd see what you were up to. I saw your car pull out, Joe. I was worried after such a long day."

"I do this all the time, Matt. You know that. I'm fine out here and I have no doubt that any of these men would defend me should someone try to attack me."

"I bet they would, Joe. But I have a question for you. And I want the truth. No more hiding."

"Sure, Son. You can ask me anything."

I stood up and looked him straight in the eyes. "Joe, did you give me your coat one night out here in the cold? Did you find me lying here and cover me with your own leather jacket?"

Joe turned his head towards the ocean and took a long deep breath. When he turned back to me he had tears running down his cheeks. "Yeah, I did find you sleeping here one night when I was walking around. I've been around here for years and seen men come and go. There was something different about you, Matt. I could feel it when I was standing over you. I knew you had to be cold and I was out of blankets. So I took off my coat and laid it across your upper body. You stayed on my mind for days. When I saw you at the Coffee House I grabbed that opportunity to see you again and talk to you. I was hoping I could talk you into staying in the apartment. And you did. I was never happier than when you said yes."

I was shaken by his response. The pure honesty of it. "How can I ever repay you, Joe? You saved my life by pulling me inside. I owe you for that." I tried to take off my jacket but he put his big hand up.

"Don't do that, Matt. That jacket is yours now. You earned it. Man, you went through hell out there and I don't think you've worked through everything yet. I hope it means more to you now because you know I cared."

I was speechless. Joe was going beyond anything I knew another human being would do, to help me find my way back to a life. "I resented it at first, I have to admit. I mean, hell, I was a doctor, for heaven's sake. I'm not an ignorant man. But something larger than me took me down. And most of those guys out there are in the same boat; drinking to kill the pain. You know that as much as I do. I know now that killing the pain with liquor isn't the answer. But back then it sounded pretty good."

"It's the addiction, Son. And the inability to process stress. We all have to learn to cope somehow. I see a different look in your eyes now than I did the day I saw you in that Coffee House. You look stronger and you look me in the eye."

"You have a way of creeping in. I wasn't gonna let you in. I wasn't gonna let anyone in. You learn that on the street, ya know? But how could I resist those breakfasts with you? They were "killer." There is no way to repay you for what you've done. And to think you found me on the bench asleep is insane. Some of those men out there will never be seen. They are masters at becoming invisible. I stayed in the shadows all the time because of my height, and because I avoided conversation like the plague. But those men you don't see are the ones who need help the most, Joe. Find them, will you? I'll even show you where some of them are."

Joe grimaced and nodded. "I'll take you out one night with me and we can find them together. It might do you good to place a blanket on a man. One broken man covering another. We're all broken Matt, one way or another."

I stood up and dusted the sand off my jeans. I shook Joe's hand and started walking towards the road. I turned back to say goodbye to Joe, but the preacher was already gone. He'd left his hat on the bench and I started to grab it. But I changed my mind and decided to leave it for the next guy who might find his way to the bench.

CHAPTER 26

———— ⚜ ————

THE BANDSTAND WAS an old bar down by the river and an old favorite of Paco's. As he walked into the sparse parking lot he could easily see that the place hadn't changed much. Actually, it hadn't improved at all, and neither had the other rundown joints along the strip that added to the downtrodden appearance of the whole area. The black and white tiled floors and stainless steel trim made it look a lot like an old burger drive-in. Pictures of Ricky Nelson, Buddy Holly, and Dick Clark lined the walls. The restrooms had life-size posters of Elvis on the men's room and Marilyn on the ladies' room. Each booth had 'fifties style mini juke boxes. The bar was stainless steel trimmed with pink neon that had faded to something akin to orange from years of cigarette smoke. There was a dance floor that hadn't been used much since the '80s, but had tables strewn around it now to accommodate small parties or folks that wanted to talk away from the bar. Pinball tables were abundant for people who wanted to kill time while they drank.

The music was lively and the afternoon crowd was stirring. The place did the bulk of its business at lunch because it served burgers as well as beer. In Paco's circles this was upscale. And Paco was feeling rather good; the work and rest had brought his color back a bit, though he had a sick feeling that was going to change after a night of entertainment. While Paco ordered his first draft, he began to size up the clientele. He searched each face, hoping to see a familiar one, other than the one staring back at him from the mirror behind the liquor bottles. There were none. He kept his pack near his feet and ordered a bag of chips with his second beer, studying the condensation gathering around his glass. The door opened and four guys entered noisily. Paco recognized them well enough to remember three of their names—Woody, Randy, and Joey. Randy saw Paco first and approached him slowly. Paco stood and the greetings were warm and cordial.

"Hey, dude! How's it going?" Randy's voice was as rough as it had always been.

"Good, man. Just sitting here relaxing for a minute."

Randy sat down quickly and ordered up a beer. Paco was happy to have company if only briefly. There was always a chance that a party could break out and he would again have a couch to crash on. The revelers decided to grab a table and a fresh round of drinks. Paco moved to their table and got the lowdown on the locals, the usual conversation of who had died, who was in jail, and who seemed to have disappeared into thin air. Paco was just happy his name wasn't on the obit list. After two more rounds the conversation lagged.

"Hey, dudes, enjoyed listening to the latest news, but I'm gonna head out." He suddenly was eager to head back to Philly. If he walked all night he wouldn't get to sleep until he got back. The burst of energy provided by his nerves abated, and his thoughts turned to a favorite spot he had slept in before, not far from the bandstand.

"What's your hurry to get back to Philly?"

"I been doing some private eye work," Paco said as the beer inspired his grandiosity. A surprised look sprang from Randy's face.

"Private eye work?" Randy's laugh echoed in the bar. "What are ya talking about?"

"Just kidding around," Paco said. "I been looking for a local guy down there named Matt Collins. Got some info for him but I got to track him down first."

"You wouldn't be talking about Matt Collins from the north side, would you?" Randy asked, seeming to strain his memory.

Paco's eyes lit up. His experience at the clinic a while back had taught him to expect the unexpected when it came to tracking down a total stranger.

"North side?"

"Yeah, I knew a quiet guy named Collins back a couple years ago. Haven't seen him in quite a while.

"Tell me more," Paco pressed.

Randy shrugged. "Not much to tell. I would see him 'round the old haunts on the north side but he kept to himself all the time. I saw him at Ruby's grill. He was talkative one night. We tipped a few."

"No!" Paco interrupted. "The Matt Collins I'm talking 'bout was a surgeon. Ruby's is a dive, man. You sure it was Ruby's you saw this guy at?"

"Yeah, I had a day labor gig over that way and popped in. There were only a few of us around so he stood out because he was quiet. I think he was watching the financial channel while we were all throwing darts. Maybe the World Series was on. But Matt had just had a bad run in with the law. In a real fix, as I recall. Man, it's been quite a while."

"Hard to believe we're talking about the same guy. Matt Collins was a surgeon over on the West End." Paco told himself it was impossible they were talking about the same guy, but there was a catch in Paco's gut that made him think a trail may have opened up. Hunter had said Matt was a hard drinking man. Drinks were pouring like Niagara Falls in the Bandstand and Paco tried hard to stash the information in the back of his brain. The last thing he remembered was Randy passing out on the floor.

Paco woke up the next morning in the back of a van that must have belonged to Randy. It was chilly so he retrieved his pack and started moving quickly. To walk off the cold he headed up the road and got as far as the on-ramp to I-95. He stuck his thumb out and began hitchhiking to back to Philly. Paco studied the people driving by him, and as usual on Saturday morning; the cars seemed full of moms headed out for their weekly shopping. Didn't look like a good morning for hitching a ride, but an old rusted pickup stopped and a gnarly old farmer told him to get in. His cold feet overrode his gut telling him not to get in, but his gut feeling was wrong this time. The old man was friendly but quiet. So the ride was a reprieve from the last blast of winter chill. Paco leaned his head back against the seat and dozed off, the remnant of too many drinks and not enough food floating through his mind. When he finally opened his groggy eyes, he asked to be dropped near Ruby's Grill. The old man grumbled something and stopped two blocks away, which made Paco walk farther than he wanted to, but he was grateful for the ride so he kept his mouth shut for a change.

Ruby's grill was a crazy little bar on Philly's north side. Total capacity was about three hundred but about two hundred regulars kept the place in business between weekends. The crowd was really quiet even for a Monday when Paco eased in through the door. Feeling pretty grungy, Paco took a seat on the short end of the L-shaped mahogany bar and asked for a beer. He was more aware of his dirty clothing than usual as he looked around the bar. The place was a study in brown; wood bar, wood booths, and wood paneling. The walls were lined with black and white photos with yellow edges, framed when the bar was in its heyday. Back in the '40s and '50s, when the shipyards had millions of workers, Ruby's had featured a full menu. Now it was beer and liquor, as the place only appealed to a handful of regulars, none of whom could remember when those days were.

Paco struck up a conversation with Chic, the day bartender, who was a fixture to all the regulars who frequented the bar. His slender face and dark-rimmed glasses were offset by his crisp white shirt and bow tie. Chic was an old school bartender and he had a quiet, almost bashful manner. He was extremely polite and always set a napkin to the left of the beer. After discussing the weather and the Phillys and the Sixers, Chic grinned as he wiped off the bar.

"Where ya' been, old man? Haven't seen ya' in a while."

Paco laughed and raised his bushy eyebrow. "Nothing wrong with me, buddy, that a drink won't fix. Say, do you remember a doctor by the name of Matt Collins?"

Chic stared off into space as if trying to recall. He excused himself and walked back to the old fashioned, two-feet high, wood-toned cash register. He grabbed a small notebook and after flipping through it, he came back to Paco with a refreshed memory.

"Matt Collins. Yes, I remember him now. Gosh, I been here six years and so many guys have come and gone. But for some reason I remember him pretty well, as a matter of fact."

Paco couldn't conceal his delight and since he still had a bit of a bankroll left over from the Willmington job, he tipped Chic upon ordering another beer. The bartender's face lit up as Paco handed him the gratuity.

"You know, I wasn't sure who you were talking about 'til I checked the book. But this guy used to come in quite a bit. Everyone called him some other nickname that I can't recall. You looking for him?"

"Yeah, kinda. I just got some news for him. You know where he lives?"

"Man, ya know I did see an address somewhere. I'll be right back. Ya need another YuengLing?"

"Yeah, man, worked up a real thirst last week."

Chic smiled when he returned. He'd taken the time to put Matt's address on a Post-it note. And he placed it next to Paco's third napkin. Paco held it as if it were a winning lotto ticket.

"This guy, what was he like? Was he a brawler or quiet? I just want to know everything you remember about him." Paco felt for a moment as if he were researching his own father.

"I recall that he was a really great conversationalist. Always pleasant, very polite. Had a tab here but he ran into a real tailspin. He might be hard for you to find. I recall some legal trouble he'd gotten into. No small affair. His personal life disintegrated in front of him so we eventually had to shut him off."

Chic paused, rubbing his face. "Geez, Paco, I'm kinda remembering as we talk. Matt used to come in with his colleagues from work. I can't recall what hospital he was working for. He'd gotten a huge grant for some kind of research. Drank the finest Scotch and he always entertained well. There was some commotion about how the grant money was being dispersed. Started coming in early in the morning after staying too late at night. Man, the bottom came up to meet him. It was a sad thing to watch."

Paco couldn't believe his ears. He felt like he was in a bit of a daze, as if he were hearing bits of his own life. "Yeah, I can feel ya'," he commented, realizing he was setting up his own sad story one glass at a time. He shook off his daze. "Can I have another draft, man?"

Chic nodded. "Sure, buddy. This one's on me. You've put a lot away for one night. This needs to be your last one, ya think?"

"Dude, that's my favorite kind," Paco laughed as he took the YuengLing.

"As I recall, he lived in Franklin Square. Could be wrong, buddy. But his tab says '165 Franklin Square.'"

"So Franklin Square is where he lived, eh? Isn't that off Liberty Street in the old section?"

"Yeah, that's been really upscale since the late '80s. He must've had a fortune in that house. Hey, if you're gonna go there, I can drop you on my way home. I get off in a bit."

Paco was enthused. "Can I get a cup of coffee before I get so drunk I'm no good to anyone?" He didn't want to be juiced if he happened to run into Matt. Of course, that was dreaming. The guy seemed to be as slippery as an eel.

Chic pulled up to the corner where the gate was at Franklin Square. Paco could feel his luck was holding when he noticed the guard shack was empty. He swiftly headed up the sidewalk undetected. *165 Franklin Square*, he repeated to himself like a mantra. The chill hung in the air as the sun streamed through the brownstone houses. Even in the eerie light of sunset the turn of the century elegance was unmistakable. Paco felt slightly out of place the more he surveyed the homes. Some had lights on and he could see inside. Children played quietly behind wrought iron fences. They seemed less noisy than the kids playing in the streets of center city or riverside. The sidewalk was in pristine condition and the cars in the garages were worth more the he could make in his lifetime.

Paco rang the bell at 165 and waited; his heart raced with anticipation as he saw shadows moving inside, proving someone was home. After what seemed an eternity, a very attractive black haired lady in a gray jogging suit answered the door. She peered over the top of her rectangular reading glasses. Paco was stunned at how lovely she looked. She smiled politely.

"Can I help you?"

Paco nearly burst. "I'm lookin' for Matt Collins."

The lovely lady smiled. "I'm sorry. There's no Matt Collins here."

"Well, ma'am, it's very important that I find him. You see, his son's very sick and it's very important that he find out."

"Hold on one moment." She answered, shaking her head. Paco hated bending the truth but he was too close to be stonewalled again. The lady excused herself. She yelled behind her to her husband.

"Charles, there's a man out here that's looking for Matt Collins. Wasn't that the previous owner's name?"

A handsome young man also appeared in the doorway. "Hi ! I'm Charles. Matt Collins hasn't lived here for some time now. We purchased this home years ago; I think it's been eight years already. I'm very sorry." At that moment the dark-haired lady appeared with a stack of mail and slid the stack into Paco's arms.

"Would you please give these to him when you find him? We keep getting them and the post office has no forwarding address for him. He seems to have vanished."

Paco's heart fell. His buzz was ruined. He tried not to allow his face to show disappointment but it wasn't working and he felt it. "Well, thanks. Hey, you got a bag for this?"

"Sure. Be right back!" She returned with a shopping bag from Saks Fifth Avenue.

Paco bent bent down as he poured the stack of junk mail and surgical equipment catalogues into the bag. He took the handles between his fingers and excused himself.

"Thank you for your time. I'll be sure to give the mail to Matt if I ever track him down." At the moment, though, the thought occurred to him that there that there might never be any such meeting.

CHAPTER 27

—— ⚜ ——

PACO'S FEET FELT like they weighed a hundred pounds as he walked back toward the street. The tall young man eyed him warily as he left, apparently waiting to make sure Paco was a safe distance away before he reentered his home. Paco couldn't erase the look that he imagined would be on Hunter's face as he heard the utterly disappointing news that Matt Collins had again eluded being found. Paco cursed as he walked and felt almost a tinge of hatred well up for the man who seemed as invisible as he often tried to be himself.

He opened the bag and looked at the mail that belonged to Dr. Matthew Collins, a proven surgeon, a generous man donating his time to the poor and forgotten. A man who commanded a high dollar research grant but who had lost his prestigious name and job by what appeared to be the pursuit of one more drink. Paco wondered about Matt; how much pain could drive a man to trade it all for one more drink? Or one more little party? How did he deal with the fact that he'd allowed so much to slip through his fingers? He realized as he was wondering about Matt, that he was looking into a mirror. It was sobering, to say the least. But somehow it always seemed worse when someone else fell. Paco sullenly stared at the trade journals, the medical junk mail, and the advertising, all of it addressed to a man who had turned his back on his own life.

He reached down and put the magazines and paper and all of the correspondence into a heap inside a rusty trash barrel. As he reached into the bag, his eye fell on one single letter that was handwritten to Dr. Matthew Collins. The postmark read July of the previous year. The discouraged private eye folded the letter into a plastic bag that had held some of the junk mail, put it in the bag, and and zipped the seal shut.

The letter felt thick; perhaps it was a long love letter from some gal who wanted to marry a doctor. Paco arranged a few pine branches over the pile of debris that filled the bottom of a trash drum. He took a deep swig of a new pint of whiskey he had picked up at a nearby Circle K and dribbled the whiskey over the abandoned junk mail. Then he set the flame and as the fire grew, the flames gave Paco's discouraged face an eerie glow. Thinking of the waste in Matt's life made his whiskey taste sour in his empty stomach.

He'd strangely grown to love young Hunter. The boy had so much promise, so much potential. Paco's investigations so far had allowed him to accumulate a story he didn't have the spine to tell the kid. It would've been so much easier if Matt had met his fate in front of a bus. People didn't make it out there for long. Especially someone soft and cultured like the famous neurosurgeon Matt Collins. No, the odds of Matt being alive at this point were slim. He dreaded any further investigation because every fact only would produce more misery for Hunter.

As the fire warmed Paco's face, the cold moisture seeped into the holes of his shoes like an infection of frost. The cold moved up his leg and he could feel the coldness meeting up with the warmth and comfort generated by the fire. His feeling of physical comfort did little to assuage his sense of disappointment in his discoveries about Hunter's dad.

Paco thought of all of the similar stories he'd heard over the years. How few of them, if any, truly ended happy? His thoughts drifted toward himself and the hopeless pursuit of comfort through one more drink. All of the traveling, all of the odd jobs—they were all part of the main-tenance of an irresponsible lifestyle. His meeting with Hunter somehow no longer seemed coincidental. The quest for Matt Collins had caused him to examine himself. And like an eerie reflection in a mirror, the image that was coming into view of Matt was a way of confronting him-self. And he wasn't liking what he saw. Paco tried to focus on the task at hand.

He shook off the feelings that were sweeping over him and took another sip of his poison. His attention became focused on the leak in his boot and how frozen his foot felt. He shoved both hands in his pockets and his knuckles skated across the sandwich bag. Sitting on an upturned crate he unlaced his boot, pulling it off his foot. He then removed the cardboard form inside the boot, pushed the letter encased in plastic underneath the cardboard to plug the leaks in the bottom of his boot, and then he carefully replaced the cardboard form. The warmth began radiating immediately and the problem was solved. Paco then stretched out in front of his artificial campfire and drifted off to sleep.

Somewhere in the early hours of the morning, Paco woke up coughing. He was freezing. His fire had gone out and the world around him was quite dark. He felt around for his pack and stuffed his blanket into it and stumbled to his feet. Embers still glowed among the ashes, but a few handfuls of snow quickly extinguished it. Paco knew he was closer to the road because he could see light piercing the thick brush he had called home for a few hours. As the light became more abundant he could see clouds of frost in his breath and noted that the temperature had really dropped in the night. Because the whiskey had dulled his senses, the cold had escaped his notice until he was moving about. After what seemed like an eternity he found a twenty-four-hour fast food joint. He needed a shower in the worst way. He went in, cleaned up in the restroom as best he could, and got himself a cup of hot coffee. He knew it was time to call Hunter, so he collected his thoughts and looked up the nearest pay phone. Then he had to solicit change for a five from the cashier.

Hunter's sleep was disturbed by an early morning call. He looked at his phone and didn't recognize the number. Just as he was about to dismiss the call, a smile broke on his sleepy face. He hit the call button.

"I bet this is my old pal Paco."

"The sound of your voice cheers me up, man. Hey! How's it going, Hunter? Been a while. Just wanted to touch base."

Hunter was warmed by the old man's voice. "The question is; how are you doing, man?"

"Making it fine, Son. Got more important things to talk to ya 'bout today. Dude, I got some news about your dad."

"Really? You're devoting more time to this than I've been able to. Whatcha got?"

"Well, kid, it's like this. Your mom said Matt was a drinking man, right?"

Hunter sat up as if bracing himself for the worst. "Yes, yes, she did." Hunter was listening intently.

"Well, kid, your dad did some really cool things. He was like a genius or something. But my trail went cold. Seems like he had a little bad luck. Hunter, it's my experience that guys like this, well they don't get back up after a fall like that. And well, like I said, my trail went cold. My thinking is that Matt Collins don't want to be found, even if he could be found. Look, kid, I'm trying to tell you the best way I can. I want you to be happy, Hunter. And my friend, the best way for you to stay happy is to stop looking for this guy. I know he's your dad and all. But I always say, don't ask questions 'til you are truly prepared for the answer."

Hunter sat on the bed. *Before I've even had coffee, Paco is persuading me to give up a search for the one man I want to meet more than anything else in the world.*

"Paco, you put a lot of time and effort into this search. I'm so grateful. Look, where ya staying? You keeping warm?"

"Yeah, I been working and stuff."

Hunter realized Paco was trying to sidestep his concern. "So when you coming back to the Garden State?" Hunter tried to keep the subject light.

"I'll look you up when I get back to West Orange. You been getting good grades, kid?"

"Yeah," Hunter replied. "Nose to the grindstone and all. Paco, you need some money or something? I mean I don't have much but—" Hunters voice trailed off as Paco jumped in.

"No, dude. I told ya, I been working. Don't worry 'bout old Paco." He sneezed then sniffled.

You didn't need to be a pre-med student to know the weather is taking its toll on the old guy, Hunter admitted. He reached out with his words. "Hey, Paco, man, why don't we—"

Again, the question was interrupted. "Of course we'll get together soon, kid. I miss ya. Look, kid, I got to get going now. I'll call you soon, okay?"

"Sure, Paco. I'll look forward to it."

The call went dead as abruptly as it began. Hunter's bare feet were on the floor as he sat up in bed. He wondered how he could help this guy who had taken such an interest in his quest. He also wondered how the old bum had gotten under his skin so thoroughly. The very roughness that had turned him off was now drawing him in like the pull of a magnet. He hoped more than anything that they weren't looking down a hole that had no end. An empty rabbit hole. But no matter how much Paco insinuated that it was a dead end trip, there was no way he was going to stop looking.

Paco hung up the phone and headed back to the burger joint to get another cup of coffee and let the sun warm things up again. His heart was less heavy having talked to Hunter. Paco felt as if he'd done all he could do for the moment. If Matt Collins was down, he sure wouldn't want his son to see him in that shape. *Well, it's a load off my shoulders, anyway.*

Yet, as the load slipped from his shoulders, so did the sense of purpose that he felt yesterday. He turned to walk up to the fast food place when he heard a horn and turned to avoid the little red Jetta that almost ran into him. With a closer look Paco recognized it was Chic waving him down. The Jetta pulled into a slot and Chic jumped out and greeted Paco with a handshake.

Chic was obviously on his way to work by the way he was dressed. He wore pressed jeans with a tuxedo shirt and little black bow tie. Only a bartender from Ruby's would dress like that. The outfit was topped off with a brown pair of penny loafers and brown argyle socks. His hair was slicked straight back and water still glistened on his black hair. He looked fresh and sharp and seemed more lively than usual to Paco, maybe because he hadn't gotten to work yet.

"I was driving around before work hoping to find you," Chic began. "After we talked I couldn't get that Matt character out of my head, and began to puzzle about him. I called a buddy of mine who drank with him a couple of times. And I remembered this guy had borrowed money from Matt or vice versa. So, anyway, I called him out of curiosity and he not only remembered Matt but kept up with him for a while." Chic handed Paco a business card with a man's name and number on it. The card read *Blake Connelly*, and the phone number was local. Paco gripped it, trying to grasp what his eyes and ears were telling him.

"I thought this guy fell off the radar for good. I'm surprised you found this."

"Thanks, but I'm not so surprised." Paco was cut off by Chic's insistence. "I think you'll find out this guy has some interesting news for you. Call him. It can't hurt. I told him you'd be in touch."

Paco finally got a word in. "Hey, man, I'll buy you a cup of coffee. Come on in."

Chic relented and joined Paco. Once inside the two men sat down and Chic took his time stirring in cream and sugar. While Paco eagerly sipped the hot black liquid, his head was spinning. He felt the pull of the mystery stirring inside him again as he quietly listened to Chic.

"Yeah, Blake seems to think that this guy Matt is down south. Seems to remember him talking about the time share business. He said something about some emails he'd gotten from Matt as recently as last summer. I think he said Biloxi or someplace like that."

Paco sipped his coffee. "I just told his son that he didn't want to be found. After you told me what you did, I figured Matt was down for the count."

"Don't be so sure, Paco. I watched him closely and knew he'd been through his share of rodeos. He seemed to have a quiet strength. I figure he licked his wounds for a while but he may have bounced back."

"Nah," said Paco. "For guys like that, the street is usually their last stop on the way out."

Chic looked at Paco and studied him for a moment. "How'd you make it out there so long, Paco? You been doing this for so long you probably don't remember your other life. I mean, it's tough out there. And you're not in the greatest of health. How you making it, man?"

Paco stared into space and his eyes glistened. Chic was right. He'd been outside so long he barely remembered what life was like on the inside. But part of what he'd learned to survive was to never show his weak side. And that included Chic. "Man, it's a breeze out here when you get used to it. Oh, yeah, I have my bad days and all. But you'd be surprised how innovative you become after you've had to scrounge for food for about five years or so. I'm living proof it can be done. Don't worry about old Paco."

Chic laughed, but inside he didn't believe a word the old guy said. He saw a weakening in the old man since the last time he'd seen him. His chest sounded worse. "Oh, I know you're okay, Paco. But you were talking about Matt not being able to make it long outside. Is it because he was so high up in the food chain? That kind of person can't suffer as long as you?"

"I don't know if that's it, Chic. But a guy like Matt wouldn't be on the street unless he was at rock bottom. He had to have given up completely and lost all that he had. I'm guessing he was ready to die when he came face to face with a park bench. It would be tougher for him to get along with street people. The language is different; there are rules out here. Corporate world isn't liked very well on the street. I ran between being a hippie and a scientist. So it wasn't so far for me to fall."

"A whole new world, I can imagine. Well, I'm glad you're doing well, old man. Kind of like having you come 'round now and then." Chic smiled at Paco and stood up, ready to head out the door. "You take care, Paco. Keep in touch any way you can. And good luck with finding anything more about Matt. You just might be surprised at what you find."

Paco watched his friend walk out and suddenly he was washed with loneliness. He never thought too much about himself and how he'd survived for twenty years outside of mainstream society. It had become so much a part of him that he didn't think about it. But Chic had unknowingly placed a mirror in front of his face and he was shocked at what he saw. It was overwhelming to see that broken man face to face. He was an educated man. He had had a great career. What in the world caused him to slip off the edge of society and fade into the background?

No one had reached out to him. No one had whispered hope in his ear. He was lost forever in the world of sleeping giants. He got up and walked out of the coffee shop and found the nearest bench to sit on, hoping to refocus his thoughts on another man who had blurred into the background of life. His one desire left unspoken to the world was to find that man before it was too late.

CHAPTER 28

—◆—

FRANK LOOKED OUT over the cityscape from his office window, fear etching lines on his face. His last conversation with Matt was harrowing as well as informative. He learned more about Matt in those few minutes than he had working on him as a patient. And for some sick reason he'd felt relaxed enough to open up to this man he hardly knew, connected by the fact that they were both addicts who had nearly lost everything they owned and loved. He was closer to becoming a Matt Collins than he cared to admit.

He sat down at his desk and put his head in his hands. This next drug drop was going to be a dynamic positioning of his place with the kingpin. Even though deep inside he wanted out, he knew this one drop was more money than he'd make in a lifetime. He wanted his family safe and he wanted to have his life back. If they made it through this transfer, he'd be done. That is, if the kingpin would let him out.

The door to his office opened and Matt stood there staring at Frank. He had a half smile on his face but his eyes looked worried. Frank had mixed emotions about this meeting they were about to have. He wasn't sure what side of the fence he was on when he greeted Matt.

"Hey, man. Come on in. Was just getting things ready for our talk."

"Yeah, I been thinking about it too much. My stomach is in a knot if, you want to know the truth of the matter."

Frank gave a nervous chuckle. "Let's get started, Matt. Tell me what's on your mind."

Matt sat down and cleared his throat. "I been thinking about our last conversation, Frank. We covered a lot of ground and I feel like I know you better. I hope you feel the same way."

Frank nodded. "Yep, it was good. But what's on your mind?"

"Well, I didn't share with you that I want tell the cops about this drug deal. Don't freak out, because we need them on our side. It's the only way to go, but I need you behind me. This is your life, too. I want to put this kingpin down. He killed Tommy. We have to face the reality that we all could lose our lives if this thing goes South. And having the law on our side could come in real handy. I don't see another way for this to turn out well. If we keep the police out of the loop and get caught, we will all go to prison. I think we have a good chance if we include them on the front end. They want the kingpin, not the small guy."

Frank stood up and went over to his window. He was hurting inside but also scared to death. "Matt, I hear you. I know how you want to avenge Tommy's death. But you don't realize who you're dealing with. This kingpin is a friggin' nightmare. Your worst nightmare. He's not gonna do the drop if he feels anything at all unusual."

Matt tried to change directions. "Okay, Frank. Let's go over what the plan is. I want to focus on this thing because lots of lives are at stake. I'm all ears."

Frank raised his eyebrows as if to question Matt's sincerity. "I hope you realize just how dangerous this is. You know the harbor? Well, that's the designated drop off point as of now. It could change at any moment. As for now, the kingpin will have his man pull a boat into the harbor at slot twenty-two, at around 2:00 in the morning on February 19. But everything is subject to change."

Matt listened, looking straight at Frank as he continued. "There is a new drive-through that nearly sits on the docks right behind the shopping mall near the harbor. We'll pull in there and park, driving a black SUV. I've got one already picked out for us. We will be wearing black and have gloves on. There can be no room for error, Matt."

"Will we have guns on us, Frank? Just asking."

"Concealed. They know we'll be loaded, but so will they. We're not dealing with stupidity here. But nobody will make a move unless it all goes wrong. And the kingpin doesn't want that to happen any more than we do. He's got a lot at stake here. His whole reputation is on the line."

"Okay, so we pull up. Then what happens."

"I will make the call to the kingpin. He'll be in the area somewhere. This is too big a deal and the last drug deal went to hell in a handbasket. He doesn't want this one to go wrong, so he'll be somewhere in close vicinity. Perhaps on a boat out in the Gulf. The goons unload about five bags of coffee, which will contain the snow. We carry them to the SUV immediately and by the time the fifth one has been handed over, we transfer the money and they pull out. It will happen smoothly but quickly. We can't do anything too fast or someone on the docks will suspect something."

"Do we check the stash ourselves, on the spot?"

"No way. We can't show that we don't trust him. He's killed for less than that."

"I see. So we get the goods, jump in the SUV and leave. Slowly."

"Right. There will be some people on the docks. Always are. We keep our eyes open and our mouths shut. This guy is sharp and he'll pick up on the slightest thing gone wrong. We'll be dead before we even think about pulling out our guns."

"Dang. You trying to scare me or something?"

Frank shook his head. "Nope. But I'm trying to prepare you for the worst here. As you saw during the drug swap, things do go wrong. That is the norm, actually. Death is imminent. I don't want that to happen with us, Matt. We both have plans for our lives. But we have to do this just like the kingpin wants or we are dead meat."

"I'm prepared to follow the plan. But I have to know if you're in this with me or not. Because it isn't gonna go down well if you're not in it all the way. I don't want you to go to prison for the rest of your life. That's a long time away from your wife and child. Think about it, Frank. I'm offering you freedom for standing on my side of the line. We got to get the police and FBI involved."

Frank was quiet for a few minutes. "I need to think about this. I'm afraid if I say yes, then we're gonna get shot as soon as the kingpin senses something. And he's real good at smelling a rat. But if I don't stand with you, I'm probably going to prison for a long time. That isn't a very appealing choice."

"Come on, Frank. Use your head, man. There isn't another choice. Just be a man and stand up and do the right thing. Let's get this behind us. You and I could do something really neat together instead of dropping drugs that we know kids are gonna use."

Frank nodded again. "I know. I hear you loud and clear. I love my work and would hate to give that up for money I won't be around to enjoy. That's nuts. I'm sweating just thinking about it."

Matt laughed but it wasn't a real laugh. "I've seen enough of the operation that you're involved in and I know it's a powerful thing run by the bottom dwellers of society. The number of people whose lives will be ruined is monumental compared to losing a few lives to stop the ring."

He continued. "We gotta do this, Frank. I'm not kidding. Think of the deaths we'll stop, the marriages we'll save, and the children we'll spare from this addiction. It's worth risking our lives for that, isn't it? Man, we can't go through with this without getting this kingpin nailed. It's time, Frank. We gotta do it now!"Matt got up and shook his hand. "What do ya say, buddy? You with me?"

Frank felt the proverbial fence between his legs. The pull was strong to make the money. Big money. But he knew Matt was right. And he yearned to have his marriage back and his career safe. He was playing Russian roulette and his time was probably about up. "Okay, Matt. I'll do it. But damn, let's do this right or we're gonna get ourselves shot up good."

Matt grinned and walked to the door. "Relax, man. Yeah, it's a risk. But we can manage it. And the FBI will be hanging around like monkeys in the trees. They're good at this kind of stuff. I'll take a drive to the police station now and get it set up. I'm sure they'll be in touch with us. Stay close, dude. I'm gonna need you when they call."

CHAPTER 29

⁜

I WALKED INTO the Okaloosa County Sheriff's Department looking for Jim Davis. He'd been sheriff for at least ten years and was known for his tough exterior. The building was large but nondescript; it had green walls and the standard metal chairs along the wall as you entered the building. A man with a badge that gave his name as "Sgt. Dick Johnson" was sitting at the front desk looking at me with a frown.

"Can I help you, sir?"

I cleared my throat. I felt guilty just standing there. "Sure. I'm looking for Sheriff Davis. Is he around?"

"And what do you need to see him about?"

I didn't know what to say. "It's personal. Is he busy? I can come back another time."

"No. Just have a seat and I'll get him for you."

My stomach was up in my throat. I was trying to think of a good way to say "We're fixin' to have a drug drop and I need your help" when Sheriff Davis walked through the doorway and smiled at me. My fears dropped away one clink at a time and hit the floor. I shook his hand and we walked back to his office. His desk was slightly cluttered in an 'I'm too busy to be interrupted' sort of way. But his smile said otherwise, and I was grateful. I swallowed the lump in my throat and tried to pull my thoughts together.

"How can I help you, Mr —?"

"Oh, I'm sorry. Matt Collins. I really appreciate your seeing me, Sheriff."

"That's my job, Mr. Collins. What can I do for you today?"

I wiped the small beads of sweat from my brow and smiled. "I need your help in a big way, Sheriff. You see, I have information concerning a drug drop in Destin and I would like to come forward with information at this time. Can we talk a minute?"

Sheriff Davis sat straight up in his chair. His demeanor changed from friendly to serious in a nanosecond. "What's going on, Mr. Collins? Let's cut to the chase here. You know of a drug deal that's coming down in Destin? And how would you know that?"

"Well, it's a long story. I'll try to shorten it for you. You see, I've been homeless for some time. Someone has stepped in to help me get my life back on track and I also took a small job at RT's doing a gig with some band members I knew. The drummer in the band was using cocaine pretty heavily and died recently from an overdose or some bad snow."

Davis was all ears. He was slowly doodling on a pad in front of him but I knew he was on red alert.

"Go ahead. I want you to give me the details."

"I saw some things at RT's that made me think something bigger was going on. I mean, I used to use the white stuff, so I know how it all works. I had also been in the hospital recently from a heart attack and noticed something funny going on with my doctor. I put two and two together and bingo; I've uncovered the drug ring. Now I got wind of a deal coming down the pike that's gonna be big. You'd be able to get the kingpin, which is who you really want, right?"

"Oh, yeah. We want to stop the big guys. I don't really care about the users as much as the ones who are selling the stuff."

"Well, if I relay this information to you, you have to promise that you'll not touch the source of this information. We need to be in a safe zone while we work this thing out. I mean, we don't wanna have to do time or anything. Is that possible?"

Davis pushed his chair back. "How much snow are we talking here? How many kilos?"

"Maybe thirty kilos. A lot of money is about to change hands here."

"So who is the other informant? You and who else? I can sense you are trying to protect someone, am I correct?"

"Can I be completely honest here, Sheriff?"

"There's no other way to be, man. Just lay it on the line."

I took a deep breath. This was new to me, talking to the cops. Usually I was hiding from them. "I have a doctor friend who's willing to help set this up. He's the only one who can set up this drug drop. Actually the kingpin sets it up, but you already know that. So you have me and the doc working this deal. We need the DEA involved. It's too big for the local deputies, don't you agree? I mean, we're putting our lives on the line so that you can catch this kingpin."

"Well, it's not quite that simple, Mr. Collins. But yeah, I'll see what I can do. So lay out the setup. Where is it gonna happen, and when?"

"It's happening on February 19, at 2:00 in the morning. Down on the harbor. It's gonna be dark and it's gonna happen fast. The doc is going make a quick phone call to the kingpin; he'll be expecting that call. However, the doctor will keep him on the phone long enough for you to track him down. He'll be in the area somewhere. Probably out in the Gulf. At the same time, a boat's gonna pull into slip number twenty-two at exactly 2:00 a.m. The doc and I are going to have two goons with us who will load the kilos into our vehicle. When the last bag is handed over the money exchange will happen. I'm sure you know how these things go down. One tiny hair moves on our heads and guns will go off. That kingpin will be so tense sitting in the harbor with only one way out, that if he even senses any tension or danger, the whole thing will blow up. People will get hurt. You got the picture, Sheriff?"

Davis pushed away from his desk and chewed on a toothpick. "Oh, yeah, these things are hair-triggered, for sure. In fact, they rarely ever go off like planned. I need to make some phone calls. You got a number where I can reach you?"

I wrote down my cell number on a pad I saw on the front of the desk and handed it to the sheriff. "If you call me and I'm with some dudes connected to this drug raid, I'm not gonna talk to you. Just so ya know, Sheriff. I want you to promise protection for me and the doc. We both want to get our lives back on track. I'm just trying to help him out and also get rid of the source that took Tommy down. Can you agree to any protection now?"

Davis shook his head. "It's not me who decides about your fate. The judge decides that. You will have to be taken in when this whole things comes down, but you probably will be released with something like parole with time served. I can't say, really. It all depends on the judge. But you're doing the right thing by coming to me, Mr. Collins. I'm sure glad you decided to talk. We're sick of the drugs coming in on the boats that enter the harbor. We've already had several drug rings nailed in the last couple years. But it's gotten worse. Kids are using it like it's sugar. And it's in the corporate world in Destin. Everywhere. Your brother, your neighbor, your insurance salesman."

"Tell me about it. I was a surgeon. So is my friend. We want our lives back, Sheriff. Hope you will help us out. I don't have anything else to lose, but the doc here has a wife and children."

"He didn't seem concerned about all that earlier, it seems. I can't promise you anything. I'll get back to you in the next couple of days. We got plenty of time to work this out, Matt. Thanks again for coming in."

I got up and walked out, dialing Frank's number. The phone rang six times. No answer. This couldn't be good. He swore he'd answer even if he was in surgery. I called the hospital to see if he was there and they said he was not working today. That he'd taken the day off. He failed to mention that to me this morning. I raced to the bus stop and rode to Madison Drive and got off. I was heading to Frank's office as fast as I could get there. Something wasn't right. I could feel it in my gut. He should've answered his phone.

I raced down the street in the direction of the hospital. Frank's office was on the second floor of the medical building so I took the stairs two at a time, a decision I momentarily regretted after feeling some chest pains. The stents in my chest were holding, I hoped, but I felt the stress building up. The door to his office was cracked open and I came through the door fast, slamming it against the wall.

What I saw brought me to my knees. Frank was sitting on the floor leaning against the wall, with his head in his hands. There was a dusting of snow on the coffee table and a straw leaning against his cell phone. He was geeked.

"What in the world have you done, man? Are you crazy? With all we've got coming down the pike, you pick now to get stoned?"

Frank looked dazed but ashamed. "I know, dude. My wife just left me. Leslie's gone with the twins. And she says she's not coming back."

"So your answer to that problem is to get stupid? Are you serious? Come on, Frank. You're past that. We got something good about to happen in our lives. We're finally doing something right. And you want to mess that up now? How is that gonna help your marriage?"

"Hey, I got a headache the size of Nebraska. Could you talk any louder? I'll get a grip. Just give me a minute."

I walked across the room looking for the coffee pot. I spotted it near the sink and made a strong pot of coffee. "Here, drink this and pull yourself together. I'm gonna get a call in the morning from the DEA and we will be expected to meet with them to set up the drug drop scene. You think you can be ready for that?"

Frank looked at me with drug-glazed eyes. "I'll be ready, man. I just need a good night's sleep is all. Don't get in a wad about this. I'm cool. I know we gotta pull this thing off, Matt. I'm not totally stupid."

I laughed. "That doesn't sound too good coming out of your mouth right now. Your wife will be pleased that you are doing something right for a change. Changing your ways, if you hold it together long enough. This is your chance to get your marriage back on track. But you cannot turn to blow every time things don't go your way. Life isn't gonna go our way all the time, Frank."

"Oh I'm perfectly aware of that. I've had plenty of practice making the wrong decisions in a fit of panic or depression. I'm more than ready for a change. But tonight, well, I just crashed. I fell apart. Can you give me a break?"

I wiped my face and shook my head. "No. I can't give you any more breaks. Not today or any other day. We've done enough to last a lifetime, Frank. We need to clean up our act and lead the life we were meant to live. Whatever that is, it's not sniffing snow up our noses. Let's get ready for tomorrow. I need you crisp when we talk to the DEA. There is no room for error, Frank. Zip."

"I understand, man. I get it already. Just call me and I'll be there."

I left his office with the worst headache I'd had in years. But I also had a desire of epic proportions not to return to my old ways. That bench haunted me enough as it was. I wanted to put some space between my old life and the idiotic choices I'd made. If Frank couldn't do that, then I would have to leave him behind. There was no compromising anymore. I was excited to see how things would go down on this bust, and I was thrilled to be a part of it. I only hoped Frank and I would get a reprieve from doing time.

I suddenly had a yearning to talk to Brother Joe. It'd been too long, so I walked to the apartment Joe had offered me, using the time to lay out what we were going to tell the DEA. Step by step in my mind, I set up each marker. But I knew the kingpin could change things as the time neared. We would all have to remain flexible. And fearless. By the time I reached the apartment my brain was fried, so I hit the bed and was asleep in two seconds. No supper. And Joe was going to have to wait until morning.

CHAPTER 30

———— ⚜ ————

JOE WAS BENT over his desk writing a sermon when Matt knocked on the door. He raised his head up and strained to see out the side panels of the door. *No car in the driveway. It must be Matt*, he thought.

"Come on in."

Matt strode in with a slow smile, looking a little tense. "Morning, Joe."

Joe got up from his desk and walked up to Matt, sticking out his hand. "You been a little scarce lately, Son."

"I know. Just busy. You got a minute, Joe?"

"Always have a minute for you. Sit down. You want some coffee?"

"Sounds perfect."

Joe hustled up some coffee and sat back down at his desk; the steam from the coffee curling around his head. "Okay, Matt. I'm all yours. What's up?"

Matt cleared his throat and sat back in his chair, wondering how to start. "I said I'd been busy but I need to talk to you about something. We briefly hit on it a while ago. My wanting revenge for Tommy's death. You recall that conversation, Joe?"

Joe nodded quietly.

"After that first drug deal that you and I were involved in, I met with Dr. Harrison and returned the money, right? And later he set up a drug drop and I agreed because I wanted to turn the whole gang in."

Joe nodded, chewing on his pencil. He was noticing the stress on Matt's face.

"Well, now it's time to face the music. The drug drop is going down on the February 19 at 2:00 in the morning. Right on the harbor, Joe. I'm nervous as a cat but excited in a way I can't explain. The sheriff has called the DEA in and we will meet with them tomorrow morning. Frank and I, that is. But here's the thing: I just left Frank's office and he'd just taken a snort of cocaine to cope with his wife moving out. What a train wreck."

"He's gonna mess up the meeting tomorrow, Matt. Can he come out of this and be sharp?"

"I hope so. I jumped his case and he seemed to get it. I'll find out later, I guess. I just wanted you to know it was going down. Don't you dare show up. The DEA are a mean group; they don't want something to happen that is off the plan sheet. Guns are huge and they're gonna go off. You can count on it. But I don't want you to be the one they're aiming at."

"It sounds pretty dangerous, Matt. Not what I wanted you to be involved in while you were trying to get your life back on track. How in the world did you find your way into this mess? I know you were trying to avenge Tommy's death, but now what are you going do? This is a life threatening situation."

"I know, Joe. It's not what I expected when I moved into the apartment you've so kindly allowed me to use. I'm sorry if I've disappointed you. It's not that I don't appreciate what you've done for me. I mean, I couldn't have made it out there with my health issues and all. But this thing had to be done. These guys have been moving drugs in and out of here way too long. In the middle of the night when the town is sleeping."

"I see it on the streets, Matt. You forget I walk this town in the middle of the night. Many of those men who are lying in places normal people wouldn't walk have allowed themselves to fall into addiction. It's a dark place. I'm proud of you for turning these guys in. But don't let yourself be fooled. This drug raid is massive if the sheriff has called in the DEA, for heaven's sake. You are playing ball with the big boys now. Last time you nearly got shot. It was nothing short of a miracle that you escaped unharmed."

"And then you got involved. What in the world were you thinking, Joe? You have a parish to look after. I didn't even know you knew how to shoot a gun!"

"That's because you don't know what I was like before I went into seminary. God called me when I was at my worst place. I had plenty of guns. I've done everything you've done and maybe more. But when God put a call on my life, after much sweat and blood, I caved and allowed him in. But that doesn't mean I've forgotten how to use a gun. I was one mean dude in my youth."

Matt couldn't help but grin, looking at the older man. "I bet you were, Joe. No doubt about it. I wish I could've seen you in action."

Now it was Joe's turn to laugh. "You didn't miss much. But back to the subject; what's gonna happen after the bust? What are your plans?"

"Well, first of all, I don't know how this thing's gonna turn out. I mean, they've said we could get off with a light sentence, time served or immunity. But there are no promises. A judge has been called in to take care of all of this. They want no loose ends. These guys are serious. I mean there will be no room for error and we're talking big guns here, Joe. They're using AR-15 automatics. You know how powerful that gun is?"

"That's a powerful weapon, all right. But I know these men will take that kingpin down before he knows what hit him. Just stay low. Watch your back. Most of what's gonna happen will take place immediately after they unload the snow. Don't start the shooting, Matt. Let the goons in that boat start it. They'll feel the electricity in the air and that's what usually sets them off. They panic because they know they're going down first. The kingpin is off somewhere safe and sound."

"That's exactly how it's gonna go down, Joe. You hit the nail on the head."

"So you gonna hear from them today?"

"Yep. The sheriff will call and set up a meeting with Frank, me and the DEA. They'll want to know what the layout is. Frank will give them the details. He's the only one talking to the kingpin."

"I'll be praying, Matt. Let's go in the kitchen and I'll fix us some eggs. I'm starving."

The aroma of bacon cooking always brought Matt back to his childhood, waking up in the mornings and knowing his father was fixing his own breakfast. He let their mother sleep in for a few more minutes before getting up to take care of the kids. He was usually out the door before Matt got his clothes on. But the bacon smell remained in the kitchen all day long.

Joe was a good cook and the eggs were always perfect. Fresh biscuits and strawberry preserves. Today he'd made some black-eyed peas and pan fried potatoes. It was a Southern meal and Matt was hungry.

"Okay, now that we're both eating, let's talk about your future, Matt. Where are you headed?"

Matt scratched his head and looked out the window at the bare trees lining the driveway. "I'm not sure. I would love to get back into medicine in some form or fashion. I even joked with Frank about doing something together. But that has not yet taken form in my mind."

"Well, it's a direction of sorts. I'm happy to hear that you want to go forward with your career. I know it may seem like a stretch, Matt. But give it some time. Things may just shape up to where you see a path back to helping people. Did you enjoy your work as a doctor?"

"I breathed, slept, and ate being a doctor. I've had my head in the sand for so long now that I've forgotten how much I loved it. But it would come back. I know it would. I still have it in me to diagnose and find the solution. It's a challenge that I crave in my life."

"You gotta get through this period and then you can focus on getting your life back on track. Matt, promise me this will be the last time you stray from that path. We never know how long we're gonna live. Do it soon. Not later."

Matt swallowed a huge bite of biscuit and savored the preserves that were dripping onto his plate. "I'll try to move forward as soon as I can breathe. Right now, I'm nervous about tomorrow. I'll meet with these guys and help in any way I can to take out this kingpin. But after this, I'm done with life threatening situations."

Joe put his hand on Matt's hand. "I've gotten fond of you, Son. I don't want anything to happen to you now. Let me know how things are going. Don't leave me out of the loop. I'll do whatever I need to do to help you, but after this drug raid, no more substance in your life or I'll have to ask you to leave the apartment. And it would kill me to do that. I have rules. And using would really step over those rules."

Matt had abused the gift that Joe had given to him. He also knew too well how fragile trust was to get back. It had taken Matt a long time to trust him. Not that it was that big a stretch to believe in a pastor. But to allow him all the way into his world was huge.

"I'll be where you want me to be, after this is all over. Give me that chance, Joe. I apologize for putting your life at risk. And also for bringing this drug raid so close to your world. It'll never happen again."

Matt got up and pushed his chair back under the table. His stomach was full and he was anxious for his phone to ring. Joe walked him to the door and slapped him on the back. He had a big grin on his face.

"I've got your back, Matt. Just like I did before. If you need an extra gun, or a good shot, I'm your man. Don't forget that. I may be old, but I'm still good with a gun. I may wear a robe on Sunday, but that old Joe is still in there. You can count on it."

Matt laughed and gave him a bear hug. "It's good to know you're on my side. I wouldn't want to go to war against you, man. I'll call you as soon as I talk to the DEA. Just so you know what's going down."

As Matt walked out of the house he had an uneasy feeling. An odd sensation, like this might be the last time he'd see Brother Joe again. He shook it off and ignored the queasiness in his stomach. Wrote it up to nerves. But it churned inside him as he headed back to his apartment. Had to be a throwback from the fear of this drug raid. Had to be. Joe was in good health and there was no reason to think he'd die. So what was that feeling? He dodged a black cat running across the yard and laughed. *Just what I need.* He felt the heaviness of what was ahead of him. He entered his apartment and checked his guns, found his bullets, and awaited the call. *This isn't the time for me to be squirrely. I am going to need every nerve I have to pull this thing off. And then maybe, just maybe, I can live my life.*

CHAPTER 31

THE BLACK SHINY Cadillac Escalade had been rolling for about an hour, heading out of Pensacola to Destin, carrying a team of men who would carry out the sting. Jeff Rawlings surveyed the landscape. He was always behind the wheel on these jobs and could feel the tension in the car.

"Our ETA is about 30 minutes."

As if by remote control the three passengers checked their respective watches. This team had seen a lot of action. But the report from the Destin sheriff sounded like this one was going to be the kind of bust that made headlines. These men knew better than most the money that thirty kilos would generate, the greed it would ignite, and the body bags it could fill if they were not on top of their game. Their combined experience had taken tons of product off the street. When they got an assignment they had one objective—to own the theater of engagement. Each man knew he had a job to do with precision and excellence or there would be an empty seat or two on the way home. There was a steady focus in their eyes as they neared Destin on the task that was about to be undertaken.

As soon as Agent Drake Howard heard the time of arrival he produced a blackberry and dialed the local sheriff. He took his job as the communications chief very seriously. He was the glue that would hold this whole caper together. Their objectives were uncomplicated. Stop the flow of harmful drugs on the ground, and take down the bad guys. A distant third was the goal of returning home alive.

"Sheriff, this is Drake Howard of the DEA. We will be pulling up to your front door in twenty-nine minutes. Please secure an office for us to establish a command post. We look forward to working with your team."

"It'll be ready." The sheriff was tense. It was obvious in his tone.

Drakes's words were concise and brief. The call ended as quickly as it began. As Drake spoke, Agent Fenton Carlyle was studying a map of the area and making cryptic notes on a note pad. He already had a working knowledge of the access roads and possible escape routes in the harbor/beach town that was about to become ground zero in the war on drugs. He was the tactical brains of the outfit and was already embracing the challenges that this beautiful fishing village presented. Next to him in the back seat of the caddy was Agent Max Santoni. He was the "go-to guy" for weapons and explosives. And he was enjoying the intel he was getting first hand from Fenton. Max leaned over and glanced at the map.

"Fenton, locate a spot for a nest for the Barrett M107. The right spot with that weapon will allow us to increase our effectiveness for a little over a mile if things began to get dicey."

"I got it covered, man." Fenton nodded without looking up from his laptop screen as they crossed the last bridge into town.

The depth of the water impressed Captain Jeff. "We're probably going amphibious on this mission." He looked up in his rearview mirror at Max.

"Do they make wet suits in your size, big guy?"

"Affirmative." He grinned at his wheel man. It was the closest thing to humor they had shared thus far on the trip.

Max was a big man in every sense of the word. His six-foot six-inch height, barrel chest, and massive forearms gave him a lethal look even when he was unarmed. But he never was. He was called "Treetop" in his early days of guarding the border and was transferred to DEA when the coyotes had put a bounty on his head. He had earned a fierce reputation among those who crossed the border who were smuggling flesh as well as drugs. The border might be crossed but you'd never get past Max. Max couldn't remember encountering an obstacle that couldn't be eliminated by shooting, beating up, or blowing up something or somebody. His bald head and even tan made it impossible for you to determine his age, and his black Oakley wrap sunglasses matched his almost sinister smile.

The three other passengers were glad Max was on their side, as he was their man when it came to finding the right equipment. That kept a lethal edge on their operation. Fenton sat on Max's right. He had a more studious look that complemented his iron-like physique. The youngest of the group, he had gone straight into the agency after two tours in Afghanistan. As a forward observer for the army intelligence his experience at interfacing with air force and CIA operatives made him the perfect candidate for the job they were now being saddled with.

The Cadillac SUV pulled into the sheriff's station. Jim Davis had seen them pull in and had stepped outside to greet the DEA agents. To Jim they resembled the cavalry. Jeff warmly greeted the sheriff with a handshake. Jim held the door as Jeff and Drake headed in with Max and Fenton, taking in as much detail as they could absorb. The five men funneled down a narrow hallway as Jim opened a door to a small room. At Fenton's prior insistence maps were already in place.

"I assure you, gentlemen, that my team has outfitted the room in a hurry but there is plenty of coffee. Next to the coffeemaker are menus from most of the takeout restaurants in town." Jim paused, looking at the men, wanting to appear on top of things. "Are any of you hungry?"

"No. We'll pass on that." Jeff answered for everyone.

Three deputies filed into the room and introductions were made. Jeff jumped up at the head of the conference table.

"Okay, listen up! We got way more cocaine coming in than we have time. So I'm gonna say 'sorry' right up front if I step on any toes. When this all goes down like clockwork, and I trust it will, we'll have plenty of time to soothe any hurt feelings. 'Til then let's all suck it up and act like men."

"Jim, I need you to have Captain Pauley of the Coast Guard on hand as we debrief our insiders," Jeff directed. "Give us a read on these guys. Tell me again how we got such priceless information from a citizen. Do we trust this snitch? And if so, why?"

"I spoke to citizen Matt Collins myself, and he seems to be motivated by the death of a friend of his, a coworker who died as a direct result of the cocaine that slipped through our notice. He has another contact deep inside who is a doctor. No local arrest records, and they only want amnesty if they flip on the king-pin. They have been cooperative to date. And I've given no direct promise to overlook any of their misdeeds. I did give them personal assurance that I would do my best."

"Thanks, Jim." Jeff picked up the conversation. "Get our citizens in here ASAP and have Captain Pauley and the highest magistrate we can get over here. I want him on site to help with warrants and plea deals as well as personal exposure to our snitches. There will be no loose ends here. Get back to me and get the insider down to the harbor to size up the drop." Jeff paused to take a sip of the hot coffee that Jim had placed before him.

"I need someone on the phone with the FBI in Jacksonville as soon as we talk to our snitches. I want jackets pulled on everyone named inside the organization to assist us in obtaining any last minute warrants we may need." His voice dropped an octave when he spoke again. "And if all hell breaks loose, those jackets will help identify a few bodies if it turns ugly. Any questions?"

The room had taken on what Sheriff Davis could only describe as an electric silence.

"Okay, guys, thanks for listening. I know there will be questions as we go. Let's talk this up a lot. But only with the people you see present in this room. No wives, girlfriends, or barroom buddies are gonna hear about this 'til it's over. Let's keep it quiet in the department, as well—no leaks, no bloodshed. That is our hope. Get those snitches in here and get the ball rolling!"

With that Jeff sat down and Drake handed him a large mug filled with coffee.

"Man, Drake, this is looking like it's gonna be as tricky as that drop that went down in Gainesville. Let's hope it ends up a heck of a lot cleaner." Drake agreed as they glanced at Sheriff Davis talking on his cell phone.

Matt's cell phone rang. "Hey, this is Matt." He knew immediately it was Jim Davis.

He was a bit uneasy about answering the phone after everything he'd been through. He was really hoping Frank was gonna keep it together for the big dance. They had a lot riding on this. And Frank had proven to have feet of clay at all the wrong times.

"Matt, the DEA is in town. We'd like to get you both in here to be debriefed tomorrow morning early."

"We'll be there at 8:00 tomorrow. This time of year there won't be much going on at the harbor and that might make us more noticeable walking around if we're going there to check things out."

"I assure you that a judge will be on hand to clarify our legal hassles. That will help put you and Frank at ease."

As they walked into the sheriff's office the next morning, Matt thought Frank looked a little shaky but he also was confident this was probably Frank's best morning in a long time. They were quickly ushered back to Jim's office. As the door closed, a slender, clean-cut guy introduced himself as a DEA agent. He was flanked by a local judge and the district attorney. Sheriff Davis was also standing with Captain Jeff, who did all of the talking. He introduced Fenton, who stepped forward at the mention of his name.

"Fenton is gonna drive you two to the harbor and you're gonna tell him everything you know about the drop. He's gonna leave you at the Coffee House when you're done. We'll get your vehicle over to you by the time you get there. We will have no contact with you 'til the deal goes down."

Fenton and Max accompanied them to the harbor and Frank pointed to the spot that was rented for the drop.

"Keep your hands below the dash as you point," Max instructed. "You never know who's looking." Matt glanced at Frank again and thought, the information is not doing much to calm Frank down.

"Frank, is there any way we can lure the kingpin onto the boat where the swap is going down?"

Frank looked at the DEA guy. "Would you give up the comfort of a yacht the size of a semi for the potential of badges and bullets?"

"I know," said Max. "Just looking to make it easy. What kind of boat is the kingpin gonna be on?

"It's a 74-foot Hatteras. Hard to miss."

Max groaned. "Yeah, even harder to board and impossible to sneak up on. But that is our worry, Frank. You just keep talking to the kingpin. Keep him as calm as you can. The calmer he is, the less likely you and Matt are to get hurt if this goes south."

"I'll do what I can. But I warn you this guy is a hair trigger. He's got some weird built-in radar and if he even thinks someone is off key, he's gonna split. Someone is gonna die and I don't want to be that someone. And neither does Matt. Who will be covering us?"

"Don't give it a thought, man. When you arrive we'll be all over this place. You may not see all of us, but there'll be guns aimed at the drop boat and anything that breathes. Just keep your eyes wide open."

"I don't think you'll have to worry about that, dude. Frank and I haven't had tons of experience like you guys have, but we do want to live. We're not coming out here without a firearm. So don't ask us to do that. It would feel too naked to just walk out here with no weapon." Matt sounded tense.

"Pack one on, but don't let it show. And don't be the first one to fire. We can't cover you fast enough if you fire your weapon."

Max paused and looked around. "Look, guys, this thing is gonna happen fast and smooth. If you do your part, we'll get the kingpin. What you don't know is that we've got men who'll go amphibious to get that kingpin. So get ready for the action. You'll never see this again in your lifetime. And that might be a good thing."

CHAPTER 32

— ⚜ —

NOTHING LIKE A phone call to turn things around. Paco suddenly had renewed hope that the invisible Matt Collins might be found. He wouldn't dare phone Hunter but his appetite was whetted again to continue the search for his father.

The information obtained from Blake had thrown Paco into a new quandary. Blake had said Matt had recently been to Biloxi. He'd been selling timeshares and was getting back on his feet. Conversations with Matt that Blake had told him about had confirmed that Matt had, indeed, resurfaced in Mississippi. Paco shuffled the new information around in his mind as he walked away from the phone call. He shook his head as he walked. The trail was warm in Mississippi, but there was no way he was going to get Hunter's hopes back up 'til he saw the whites of Matt's eyes.

The wind was picking up and Paco's coffee meter was on full. And he decided to take refuge in a news stand he had passed on his way to get coffee. Newsome's News was a great place to get out of the wind. Paco stomped the snow off his feet as he entered a wonderful world of cigars and ink. Newsome's had been a family run business since the '20s and it had ninety-one years of selling newspapers from around the world under its belt along with cigars of every kind and flavor. The company had provided the Newsome family with a modest income despite the rise of the dot-com competition. Humidors lined the walls and the smell of fresh cigars was thick. Rows of newspapers and magazines crowded the floor. The place was unchanged since the early days of the last century, yet the inventory was new every day.

The refugee from the cold was looking for a Biloxi newspaper. After asking the clerk nicely, he was handed a *Sun Herald*, and any reservations he had had about heading down there disappeared when he saw the temperature was sixty-four degrees.

While reaching in his pocket, a cough burst from his chest. Then two more in rapid succession. Paco covered his mouth and quickly ducked outside to revive himself. He thought little of the small specks of blood in a tiny spray pattern in his palm. He quickly pulled his collar up and headed into the wind toward the truck stop to begin another interstate trek. He thought the change of weather might do him some good as he carefully trudged the sidewalk in his thinly soled shoes.

Today the truck stop seemed a million miles away and Paco was happy when it came into view. Rows of tractor trailers lined the parking lot and he paid extra attention to the big oil tankers that he saw, wishing fancifully that he would see Roy's easy smile. He entered the dining area and ordered a Coke as he sat down. As soon as the waitress turned her back, he wedged the glass between his legs and stealthily retrieved his bottle from his vest pocket and blended himself a cocktail. In his usual manner he struck up a conversation with an equipment hauler from Rhode Island, bound for Minnesota but he quickly lost interest in the conversation. The southbound hobo looked up and down the lunch counter for a friendly face that might be headed to Biloxi.

The day faded into night and Paco had refilled his undercover cocktail three times. Drowsiness threatened to overtake him when a man walked up to him.

"Hey, buddy, you looking for a little road work? "

Paco's face brightened and he stood up, reaching out his hand to introduce himself. "I'm Paco. Whatcha got?"

"I'm Jim Waverly. Look, Paco, I'm headed to Tampa with a load of softener salt. It's in eighty-pound bags and I need a lumper."

"A lumper?" Paco asked.

"Yeah, I need a guy who'll ride along and stack my load onto pallets at the other end. Its hard work but I will get you as far as Tampa and pay you one hundred fifty bucks to unload my truck."

"When do we leave?"

"Soon as I pay my check. Is that bundle all your stuff?"

"It's all I'm gonna need for this trip," Paco said.

Minutes later the two walked out to Jim's truck, a plain white trailer pulled by a cabover Peterbilt that had to be twenty years old. But the passenger seat was soft and Paco was happy to be on his way. Jim was a gaunt man, tall and skinny. Long stringy brown hair came out from under his dirty ball cap, which disguised the fact that he was mostly bald on top. He ground the gears as the engine droned into the night. The headlights lit up the highway as Paco's head began to bob, fighting sleep. The warmth in the cab, the streetlights passing overhead, and the endless variety of exit signs were more than Paco's consciousness could handle. He fell into a deep sleep. The next twelve hours were a blur of sleep, shallow conversation, hot coffee, and country music.

"Well, my friend, at least you got plenty of rest for the unloading." Jim laughed after watching Paco doze in and out of sleep.

As they backed onto a loading dock in Clay Camp, Florida, just outside of Tampa, Jim began to talk earnestly.

"I'm sure glad you came along. It woulda taken me a couple of extra hours to find a couple loaders down here who spoke enough English to do the job right. The tow motor guy will tell ya how to stack each pallet and he'll wait at the tailgate for you to load each one. Then he'll stack the full pallets up. Once we get 'er empty I'll pay you up and take you to the nearest truck stop. Hey, I tell you what, Paco, you get this unloaded in five hours or less and I'll throw in a case of beer and a pint of whiskey for your extra effort."

Paco's eyes lit up at the prospect of happy hour at the end of his labor. Two hours had passed and he staggered to the rear of the truck with a hand cart stacked eight high with eighty pound bags of salt. The cart came to an abrupt halt as it tilted forward. Then he carefully stacked each of the heavy bags on an endless supply of pallets. Paco only had breaks as the tow motor disappeared into the warehouse, returning with another empty pallet for Paco to fill. Sweat poured into his eyes and burned as he tried to rub them with salty fingers and the pain was unbearable for moments at a time, but Paco pushed himself harder than he had in a long time. Jim poked his head in to check on his labor force.

"How ya doin', buddy?"

"Man, that beer is gonna go down good 'cause I'm gonna beat that clock if it kills me."

"If ya need some water, they got a fountain by the men's room."

"Thanks, I'm gonna git 'er done."

After four hours and forty-eight minutes, an exhausted Paco eased between the rear of the trailer and the building and jumped out onto the parking lot. His eyes beamed from a sweaty and exhausted face. Jim greeted Paco as he caught his balance.

"Man, you beat the clock, buddy. What flavor beer you gonna ask for at the truck stop?"

"Bud, man, I need a cold Bud."

"Well you're gonna get plenty. Get some water now while I go get my load sheet signed and I'll be right back."

Paco crept to the water fountain. Every muscle in his body burned. He was sore and tired but he was gonna be one hundred fifty dollars richer and have plenty of beer for the night. Jim strutted back with the clipboard in hand smiling at Paco.

"Man, you look a sight. Sure did love watching you work. Boy, you're a tough old hombre. Wait right here. I'm gonna roll forward to that guard shack over there and go in. When I come out, jump in the truck and I'll pay you. We gonna head for the coldest beer in town."

Paco smiled an exhausted smile, and though he was out of breath he answered in a raspy voice, "Cool, man, I'm dyin' for a beer."

"Well, won't be long now." Jim assured him. "As soon as you jump in my truck you'll be paid and we are on our way."

"Okay," Paco repeated, his back now slumping from overwork. Jim pointed at the guard shack and jumped in the truck.

Paco watched as the engine sprang to life and eased away from the dock, and then headed towards the guard shack. He began his tired walk to rejoin his new friend. His steps were labored and he looked on as the truck passed the guard shack and neared the highway. Paco picked up his pace, confused by the sudden development. The truck eased onto the highway and to Paco's shock, he saw his backpack stuffed through the open window, and he watched it tumble down the road. The truck rolled out of sight. Paco had no time to be astonished because everything he owned was tumbling around between passing cars. With each car his pack became more battered. He dragged his tired body and for a moment watched helplessly as all of his possessions were scattered on the road. His knees burned with exhaustion as he dodged cars, collecting his things.

Cars zoomed by him in an impersonal and almost degrading fashion as he tried to stuff his belongings back into his pack. Tears streamed from his face, distorted from insanity and fatigue. The crazy chase of his belongings took more than a half hour. No one even slowed for him. Teenagers laughed as they passed him and the old man ducked in and out of traffic to get a shirt and a pair of jeans. His world was full of cruel and unrelenting pain and he felt humiliated, tired, and defeated. A new reality sunk into Paco's tormented skull; he was alone in a strange town with seven dollars left in his worn out pockets. No place to sleep, nowhere to go. Hunger no longer troubled him. The world grew dark and mean, and as the sun began to fade, his own mind seemed to torment him with every mistake. Every false step. He was a mess now. Violence clenched every fiber of his being.

Paco had become a lonely crazed man by the side of the road with nowhere to go, and caught up in the grip of more self-loathing than even he was accustomed to. He kicked his backpack into a dry ditch by the side of the busy road. With no one to be mad at but himself, he looked to the sky in sheer torment, screaming out loud to the air, "Damn you, Matt Collins, and damn your son, Hunter!" Paco hated the sound of his own voice. He knew that he loved Hunter and had no one to blame but himself. He caught up to his pack again and sat on it, head bowed, eyes nearly blinded with tears. "I quit! I quit!" he yelled through his tears. He had broken, but there was still a thread of survival inside. Another moment passed and Paco had collected himself. He stood on his wobbly legs and hoisted his pack onto his worn out back. *I've been in worse spots,* he reminded himself. The dusty worn out bum dragged himself down the lonely highway, his mind empties of anything but exhaustion. With his body full of pain, Paco coughed again and even more pain gripped his chest. He felt a warm moist spot in the palm of his hand. Instinctively he wiped it on his already filthy jeans. A red stain smeared across the faded indigo fabric. As if Paco could stand even more shock, he looked at his palm and saw blood.

Sick, broke, and lost, Paco was determined to make this trip pay off. Like a man who just came in second in a gunfight, he wandered down the unfamiliar highway, not knowing if he was getting closer or farther from town. He was filthy from working in the back of the trailer. Sweat continued dripping down his brow and he was growing weary from lack of food. His single-minded pursuit of Matt Collins was all he had to crowd out the angry thoughts of being robbed by that skinny trucker. Paco was so full of pain and anguish from the wasted day's work that he nearly forgot he had traded the frosty streets of Philadelphia for the sandy warm streets of Florida. Putting one foot in front of the other, he had a feeling that his luck had run out. And inside he knew he couldn't take much more. His body was wearing out fast.

CHAPTER 33

A FRONT HAD moved in across the Gulf, bringing with it a thick wet fog that floated above the water covering everything in its path. The sky had no moon and no stars. It was quiet and the water was still. Almost like a lake. It was the middle of February and an usually warm night for winter. The docks were pretty much empty of the usual drifters looking for work. There were a few men checking lines, making sure their boats were secure for the night. A few were bedding down for a short sleep after drinking too many warm beers at a local bar. Boat slip number twenty-two was empty, which was unusual. The Lucy Lou was normally moored by this time of night, but this particular night she was nowhere to be found. There was music floating up in the air from one of the small bars that stayed open late for the dock workers or heavier drinkers, and the sound of drums echoed across the water.

Frank was in constant contact with the kingpin, rechecking positions and reassuring him that his demands would be met. He had to remain calm and the pressure was building inside his body. His thoughts were racing ahead, knowing things would take off suddenly and then there was no turning back. He had spoken to Max one more time before trying to grab a few hours of sleep. But he was kidding himself about sleep. There was no way he was gonna be able to sleep with the pressure he was feeling. He decided to ring Matt. He knew his phone might be tapped but this call was necessary.

"Hey, man. Just had to call you before this thing goes down. You ready for this?"

Matt yawned and stood up, walking to the apartment window. "No. If you want to know the truth, I'm not ready. But no one is, except those guys who've done this for years. Even then, nerves get set off like fireworks. I'm ready to get it over with."

"No kidding. I'm trying to sound calm to the kingpin. He keeps calling me to make sure something's not changed. He's uneasy. I don't like the way he sounds but I'm acting like I don't even notice. Maybe because the drop off boat will be in the harbor and there's only one way out. That would freak out any drug dealer." Frank laughed, but it was a little strained.

"I just hope these guys know what they're dealing with. The guns that are available now are ridiculous. We don't stand a chance if anything goes wrong. You know that, Frank?"

"Yep. I do. Nothing we can do about it now, buddy. We brought this on ourselves. We decided to turn this dude in and now we're gonna have to see it through. We better get off the phone. I was just checking to make sure you hadn't run out on me or something!"

Matt smiled. "No way am I gonna let you have all the fun, man. Pick me up before 2:00. We don't want to be late, ya know."

"I'll be early. Don't worry."

Four men filed out of the sheriff's office and got into their SUV. They were talking amongst themselves about the maneuver they were about to pull off. Jeff was on the phone talking to headquarters, who had agreed to send ten men down to head off the dock. Those ten men were undercover and were already on location when the SUV pulled up in the parking lot above the harbor walk. All men had Glocks and additional firearms and were trained to handle any situation that might arise. Each man had a microphone as thin as a human hair that came out from their ear two inches. They could hear a pin drop through the device. They had designed a code language so they could communicate easily without using so many words.

Jeff was driving and turned his earpiece on. His heart rate was up a little and the adrenalin was kicking in. The men were prepared. He was ready. But all of the men felt the tension in the air. "This is closer quarters than we're used to," Jeff remarked to the back seat.

Fenton answered, sounding hoarse. "It's tight, man. But we got a lot of dogs on the scene. Nothin's gonna get through the line tonight. You wait and see."

"Are you serious? We got more ammo than a friggin' platoon. The goons on that boat will freak out if they raise an eyebrow." Max laughed, shaking the whole car.

"Well, even though we've done this hundreds of times, we still have to stay sharp. Because Matt and Frank are sophomores at this, it can go against us if things get critical. Know what I mean?" Jeff was sipping his coffee and wishing he was home in bed.

"Yeah Jeff, you're right. We'll just have to watch them closely. Nobody drops on our side, ya hear? Nobody. Our heads will roll if Frank and Matt die. It's 1:30. Time's short."

"All joking aside, we're about to take that kingpin out. But the goons will fire if they see anything happening on the water. When we get to the harbor, I'm pulling in behind Lagoons Restaurant. All our men will be on the docks working on boats and floating in the air. Don't look anywhere. Just relax and blend in. We don't want any hairs raised on their arms while that drop boat is moving into the harbor. It's foggy so that's gonna play in our favor. Stay ready, men."

While the ten additional DEA agents were covering the docks, there were five men underwater in the Gulf waiting for a signal that the yacht carrying the kingpin had pulled into location. These men were carrying CAR-A4 carbines. They were the elite who had trained for amphibious assault and were prepared at a moment's notice to attack. The water was still, which worked two ways in the raid. It was easy to see everything from underneath the water, but it was also easy to be seen. The darkness helped, but any stirring would be noticed. The kingpin would not enter the Gulf waters alone in his yacht; he would have men on board watching the area with night goggles and guns aimed at every direction. The fog was worsening, which reduced the field of vision to just short of twenty feet.

When Jeff and the other agents arrived, they dispersed in different directions to their separate covers. Other than the occasional noise of a wire cable clanking against a mast there wasn't much noise on the harbor. The stillness in the air increased the tension as the men waited for the boat to pull into slip number twenty-two. It would be easy to hear a motor on the water, but they wouldn't see the boat until it was right in front of them. All sides were at a great disadvantage during this phase of the raid.

When Matt and Frank pulled up behind Pelican's Roost, just past Lagoons Restaurant, they could've heard a pin drop on the harbor. It didn't seem like a night for a drug raid. The boats were gently rocking to and fro against the slips and there were only a few men about, tending to their boats.

"It's early yet, Frank. Let's just stay put. Get back in the car so we don't attract attention."

"Just checking out the scenery, man. A little nervous energy on my part, I'll admit it."

"This is serious, Frank. We can't afford to mess up. You can count on the fact that we're being watched already. Those agents have sur-rounded this area and know everything that's going on. If a fly moves they know it."

Frank chuckled. "Relax, Matt. I get the picture. We'll sit here until we get the signal from Jeff. Make sure your ear piece is turned on now."

Matt checked his piece and sat back, waiting. His gun was loaded and he could feel it in his pocket. He'd used a gun a long time ago. Or at least it felt like a long time. His mind ran ahead to a time in his life when drugs were used on a regular basis. The word *drugs* drew a picture in his mind of guns and deals being made in the dark places of cities and small towns. Matt had been involved with that dirty part of life right in the middle of his medical career. The people he had dealt with were sleazy drug dealers and goons who sold drugs for the kingpin. He had always kept a pistol around "just in case."

Tonight he would have to set aside his feelings about the past and his fear of using his gun again. This was a different time. A different situation. He was actually gonna help nail one of the biggest drug dealers in the South. Life on the street had changed him into a hard-shelled skeptic. He had problems with trust and kept to himself. He wasn't proud of his background but he had had little hope for his future until he'd met Brother Joe. Just thinking of his name made Matt smile. The timing of that meeting was incredible. Otherworldly. And it pretty much felt otherworldly at the docks with all the thick fog surrounding everything.

Frank's thoughts were racing as he remembered one decision after another that he'd made, only to experience the consequences of an empty home. His wife gone. His children gone. He had no choice but to follow Matt's suggestion and end this merry-go-round he'd been on for years. Greedy, selfish and unrealistic. If tonight did nothing else for him it would open his eyes to what was important in life and also give him the chance to give back. The kingpin was gonna be surprised. More shocked than he'd ever imagined. His worst nightmare was about to happen and Frank was thankful to be a part of it. The giant would fall.

CHAPTER 34

———— ⚜ ————

THE FOG WAS getting worse and it was nearly impossible to see anything. Matt and Frank were sitting on pins and needles waiting for some signal from Jeff that the boat was arriving. Louis and Mickey drove up in a black sedan and sat waiting on Frank to give them a signal. The tension was tight and Frank was getting edgy.

"Damn, when is that boat coming in?"

"Hang in there, Frank. We gotta keep cool. It's too risky for us to be uptight."

"I've done this before, Matt. But I don't trust that kingpin tonight. "

"I know, man. We've covered that before. We're gonna get that signal any minute and then things are gonna happen quickly. Just don't sit here giving off negative vibes. I want to live."

Frank laughed. "You're right. I just want this thing over, dude. I don't usually have so many people around when I take a drop."

"You got the friggin' DEA here. How much help do ya need?"

"In the past, I didn't need any help, buddy. But tonight we've ratted and we're taking the giant down. I'm just nervous, is all. If this thing goes awry, we'll all die."

"Just remember not to touch your gun unless you get a signal from Jeff. They've got bigger guns and will have us covered. They're pros. We're sophomores here. We know nothing, Frank."

"I think I've got some knowledge of drug deliveries. But I'll shut up and do what I'm told. I've instructed Louis and Mickey. And we were briefed by Jeff and Max. This thing should go off just fine."

It was one minute until two a.m. when Jeff spoke quietly into Frank's earpiece.

"I can vaguely hear a muffled engine. Don't know how far he is away from the slip."

"Okay. We're sitting here on ready."

"May be farther away than we think. Sound carries in the fog and he's gonna be going pretty slow."

The news didn't make it any easier to wait. But both men had no choice but to sit back and take a deep breath. It seemed like hours but it was about fifteen minutes and Jeff was in Frank's ear again.

"Okay, boys. There's a boat coming in right now. I can barely make out the name. Looks like *Royal Flush*. It's headed for slip number twenty-two. Here's our man."

"What's the first move, Jeff?"

"Just wait until he's pulled in and slowly get out of the van and walk towards the boat. Keep your hands visible at all times. We don't want to cause any doubt."

"Ten four."

Matt took a deep breath and the two men touched fists together. This was their chance to do something good for a change.

Frank was sitting, still tapping his leg with his hand. Suddenly Jeff was in his ear again.

"Okay, men. This is it. Get outta your vehicle and start walking towards the boat. Don't act nervous. Don't draw attention to yourselves or anything around you. You can talk to each other and smile. Do everything you can to put these goons at ease on the boat."

"We're out now."

Matt and Frank stepped out of the van and closed the door. The noise the door made echoed through the dock area. They waved at Louis and Mickey and the two men got out of their car and walked behind them a few steps back.

"Wonder how heavy these bags are gonna be, Matt?"

"Heavy. And we got a lot to unload. That's why we got Mickey. He's a brute of a guy. But we gotta keep him cool. He could blow this whole thing."

"I thought of that. He does have a hair trigger."

"Just talk calmly to him. He'll be fine."

"We gotta believe that, Matt."

As they approached the boat the goons appeared on the edge of it, directing the other thugs on the boat to help tie it off at the dock. They waved at Matt and Frank to come forward. The two doctors walked slowly up to the boat and stopped, looking up at the goons.

"You guys ready to do this?" The goons were sneering a little. Cocky, Matt thought.

"Yeah, we're ready. You ready to unload?" Frank sounded cool.

One of the goons yelled at the crew to start unloading. "You got the money?"

"Yep. It's right here in this briefcase."

"The kingpin wants no mistakes. Or you'll be dead, ya hear?"

"Too late for mistakes, man. Let's get this thing going."

The crew began to bring up the bags labeled "coffee" and bend down to open the string at the top for Frank to test. Frank was surprised at this show of vulnerability, but he took some cocaine out of one of the bags and put it in a test tube. When he was satisfied that it was pure he motioned for the goons to unload the huge sacks. Mickey and Louise grabbed two dollies and began loading them. The bags were heavy and awkward to handle but Mickey was stout. There were six one-hundred pound bags and the two men stacked a couple of bags and headed up the hill to the van to unload them. Then they walked back down the hill and loaded up three more. When the last bag was loaded the goons demanded the money. Tension was in the air because the last of the bags was sitting on top of the stack on the dolly and Mickey was ready to carry it up the hill to the van. Frank and Matt avoided eye contact with the goons and stayed calm.

"Dude, show me the money."

"It's here in the briefcase, man. Check it out for yourself."

The goon thumbed through the stacks of money and nodded. "You did good, dude. Wouldn't have been too smart to mess with the money."

Frank nodded and stepped back. Jeff took that as a cue and just when he was about to signal, Louis and Mickey moved away from the boat and headed up the hill. As Jeff gave his prearranged signal for his agents to move in, all hell broke loose. Men came out from the shadows in every direction and covered the boat in slip number twenty-two. The agents moved powerfully and quickly and the goons were caught by surprise. They had lost themselves in the chore of unloading. When they looked around, there were six men with guns aimed at their heads. You could hear a pin drop.

"Keep your hands up, buddy. You're under arrest. Now don't move or we'll shoot. And these guys don't miss." Jeff's voice was strong and intimidating. "Names?" he ordered them.

Frank spoke up. "Pete and Joey," he said, pointing to each of them in turn.

The two thugs had worked for the kingpin for seven years. They knew he wouldn't be happy. Pete reached for his gun and four shots were fired right into his legs. He screamed and fell on his face, writhing in pain. Joey froze, shaking.

"Don't shoot! Don't shoot! Look what you've done to Pete!"

"I told ya not to move! Put the cuffs on 'em. Call an ambulance. We gotta get these guys to Crestview. They're gonna spend the night in jail. And Max, get the briefcase."

Max grabbed the briefcase and aimed his gun at Joey. His face was like stone. "You move, buddy, and you're history. Food for the fish. I'll say you fell overboard and we couldn't find ya. Just dare me."

Joey stood still with his head down, shaking his head. "We're dead, anyways. If the kingpin finds out we'll be dead, anyways."

"You won't have to worry 'bout that kingpin. He'll be dead in about two seconds," Max replied with a smirk on his face.

Pete lay on the floor moaning, rocking back and forth. Joey whispered words to soothe his friend. "We shoulda known better than to trust these guys, Pete. After all these years of doin' this stuff, we shoulda known betta. We're dead meat now. Either way, we're dead meat."

Seconds later, six frogmen came over the top of the kingpin's yacht. He'd anchored out about two hundred yards from shore, not too far from the mouth of the harbor. He'd been more nervous this time than before because the drop boat was boxed in with only one way out. His instincts told him this wasn't a smart move but his greed took over and pushed common sense out the window. He'd done this a million times and only lost a few men in the worst raids. His confidence was high but there were moments of hesitation that he suspected he should have paid closer attention to. He'd heard the shots and commanded the three crew men on board to have their guns out, ready for action. When the frogmen entered the yacht they had their firearms already in position. Their guns were aimed at the kingpin just about the time he turned around and started to raise his arm to fire.

"I don't think I'd do that, Snowman. Now put your arm down slowly and drop your weapon. All of you! You're under arrest!"

Two of the crewmen hesitated only a moment and then fired their rifles. All six frogmen pulled their triggers. They had perfect aim and the two crewmen went down like flies, which left one crew member and Suarez, the kingpin. Suarez had been selling coke for years and not once had he ever come close to getting killed. This time he had been blindsided. Trusted too easily. Now he was gonna pay with his life.

He decided to go for broke. He had nothing to lose at this point. He was going to lose his life either way. The drug lord wouldn't put up with any excuses or accidents. It was all or nothing to him. He turned and aimed one more time and pulled the trigger. Before the bullet left his gun the six guns aimed at his head went off and hit their target, leaving blood, tissue, and bone fragments everywhere.

The game was over. The noise had echoed across the water and Jeff and Max had heard the explosion. Jeff signaled the frogmen. The

Snowman was down. All the preparation, and the game was won in less than fifteen minutes.

"You got it under control out there?" Jeff spoke out loud.

A deep voice answered. It was Marshall Duncan.

"We got three bodies here and one live one. A crewman. Suarez is down. Need the Coast Guard here to pick up the crew man, have a medic with the Coast Guard to bag the dead, and a helicopter to pick up the bodies."

"They've already been notified and are on their way. Let me know when they arrive."

Matt and Frank were staying out of the way, letting the DEA take care of the technicalities. Sheriff Davis walked up and slapped Frank on the back.

"Ya did well, man. Your nightmare is over. But you and Matt will have to go to the sheriff's office. There's a judge there who wants to talk to you. Glad that you didn't get wounded in this raid; it could have been a lot more bloody."

"I was worried at first, but your men were on top of it. I was impressed. It couldn't have gone any smoother. Pete and Joey seemed pretty surprised."

"Oddly, they were unprepared. Not expecting anything like this to happen. I think they got too comfortable in their skin. You can't do that when you're handling drugs. Stupid move on their part, but lucky for us. We're dealing with a certain mentality here driven by greed and addiction. Tempers fly, and it never takes much to blow the whole deal," Jeff said, smiling broadly.

Matt stood up and stretched. "I'm just glad it's over and that the kingpin is dead. I bet he was shocked to see those frogmen on the boat."

Frank laughed. "No kidding. Who wouldn't be with six barrels aimed at them?"

"Those men were on that boat before anyone ever saw 'em. They work silently; it's scary to watch. The training is rigorous and not many make it. I wouldn't want to meet those guys in a dark alley." Jeff said.

"I don't want to know what that'd be like, frankly. But you guys are nice to have around," Matt remarked, chuckling. His knees felt weak. He'd done some stupid things in the past and now that he was on a better path, seeing this in real time was an eye opener to what could've happened in his own life.

Suddenly a chopper was heard in the air. The fog had lifted some, but it was still risky. Jeff got a report that the Coast Guard had arrived and the one crew man was taken aboard. They were on their way to the harbor to pick up Joey and an ambulance had been called for Pete. Deputies were on the scene and would escort Pete in handcuffs to the hospital.

The chopper lowered down slowly and dropped a long cable with a bed attached to it. The wind was calm so it was easier to load the bodies and lift them into the chopper. There was an ominous feeling in the air as Marshall and his men helped load one body at a time until all the bodies were loaded.

Matt watched it all unfold, thinking about Suarez, who had had the world at his fingertips; all the money he could ever want to spend. But it was never enough. They always wanted more. The yacht was taped off with yellow tape and the Coast Guard prepared to tow it in. The lights of the Coast Guard boat striped the water as they slowly pulled away from the site. It was an eerie sight to see the large yacht being pulled in to shore. A bloody scene and a bitter end for the kingpin.

Matt and Frank arrived at the sheriff's office escorted by a deputy. They were met by the district attorney and Judge Wilford Higgins.

"Mr. Collins, Mr. Harrison, this is Judge Higgins and the DA, Charles Minton."

Matt and Frank shook their hands and sat down, wondering what their fate would be after how the raid turned out.

"It's customary to press charges, gentlemen, considering your background in drugs. Because this is a huge breakthrough in the endeavor to eliminate drugs on the Gulf Coast of Florida, I have taken into consideration the risk you took bringing in that kingpin, who has delivered drugs in this area for a long time." Attorney Charles paced the floor, looking down and taking his glasses on and off.

Matt and Frank sat there in silence. They'd agreed on the ride over to the sheriff's office that saying as little as possible would be their best bet.

The DA continued, enjoying the floor time. "You got dangerously close to a life sentence. I hope you are aware of that. If you hadn't broken up such a large drug ring you would be in big trouble, given your history. There's a part of me that wants to charge you with selling an illegal substance and slapping you in prison for a long, long time." He cleared his throat and raised an eyebrow.

Sweat was pouring down Frank's face. He had so much at stake here. His family, his career. Matt wanted to start his life over. But he was really dragged into this catastrophe by wanting to avenge Tommy's death. Both men were trying to look honest and sincere.

"What do you want to do, Charles? Let's get this thing cleaned up as quickly as possible. You know how I hate dragging things out this time of night." Judge Higgins frowned, wiping sweat from his brow.

"I know, I know. You don't have to remind me." Charles cleared his throat again and picked up his pacing.

"You've dodged a bullet, Mr. Collins, and Mr. Harrison. I don't know what you were thinking, getting involved in something as serious as this, but if I catch you doing this again, I'll put you in the slammer and never look back. We're sick of the drugs flowing in and out of here like maple syrup dripping off pancakes. It's nuts. And to think you are a doctor, Mr. Harrison. It's horrendous."

Frank nodded and didn't dare to look up.

"I'm gonna let you off this time, but it's against my better judgment. Judge Higgins is more lenient than I am, but I'm putting a lot of weight on the fact that we did get our man. So let's look at community service for the both of you. Two years. And I mean I want to see something done beyond picking up litter on the road. Make a difference around here. You started it with the drug raid. Keep your noses clean. I'll be watching you both."

The Judge took his turn. "Dr. Collins and Dr. Harrison, take this as a warning. This was a serious crime you got yourselves involved in, and had it turned out any other way, you two would be looking at a prison sentence. I did a little digging on you, Matt Collins, and you're well-known as a cardiologist, Frank Harrison. I see you, Dr. Collins, were also a doctor once. Hopefully you'll get your life back on track and carry on with your career. Now get out of here. The community service is volunteer on your part. There'll be no record of a crime here for both of you. But like Charles said, you dodged a bullet that had your name on it. Don't let that happen again."

Both men stood up took a deep breath. Matt spoke up first. "Thank you, Judge Minton. I do appreciate your consideration in this matter. I won't disappoint you."

Frank was sweating so badly that his shirt was soaking. He stood up and shook Judge Minton's hand, trying to find a smile on his guilt-ridden face. "You don't know what this means to me, sir. I can have my life back, if it's not already too late. I really appreciate your leniency. I sincerely say that I hope we never meet again, at least under these circumstances."

The sheriff walked into the room and spoke up. "You both may be contacted about information on this case. We have a report filed and have your contact numbers. Please cooperate with us fully so that we can stop this crime from happening on our harbor. This is a family destination and we don't need smugglers coming in to our shores selling cocaine and other illegal drugs. You've been very fortunate here today. Don't blow it."

Matt and Frank walked out of the office and saw a black sedan parked at the curb. The engine was still running. Matt leaned over and poked his head in the driver's window.

"What in the world are you doing here, Brother Joe?"

Joe laughed his deep laugh and smiled back at Matt. "Get in, Son. It's time to head home."

Matt waved at Frank to get in with him, and Joe pulled away from the curb and headed towards Frank's house.

"You guys come out all right in this deal?"

Matt couldn't wait to reply. "Oh, yeah. We got off with community service. But I tell you what, Brother Joe. I've about had enough of the drug business for a lifetime!"

Frank laughed. His face was just now getting some color in it. "You have no idea how relieved I am, Matt."

Joe chuckled.. "I'm also thankful you boys got off with such a light reprimand. I know you have to be worn out and hungry. Anyone for the Coffee House?"

Both men nodded eagerly and Joe pulled quickly into the parking lot and shut the engine down. "Man, I'm glad this is over with. I've been kept up too many nights worrying about you, Matt. It's time for things to settle down, don't ya think?"

Matt nodded as they walked into the coffee shop and sat down at the only table open. The place was packed with truckers and campers. They all got caught up in the atmosphere of conversation that had taken over the shop. The relief that was felt by the two doctors was indescribable. They knew it was nothing short of a miracle that they were sitting in a coffee shop eating a small meal with Brother Joe, recovering from the horrific experience of a drug raid right in Destin's harbor.

"I tell you what, Matt. This is the start of a new beginning for my life. I'm never going back to the way I was. And I owe all of that to you, man." The relief on his face made Frank look younger than he was.

"No way, buddy. We just worked together as a team to get this guy taken out. What a cool way to end the drug addiction in our own lives. I had it for a while. You allowed it to nearly ruin your marriage. But it's over now. And we perhaps saved some kids from being sucked into the Snowman's dream." Matt sipped on his coffee and grinned.

"I'm grateful for this night. We could be on our way to prison, Matt. For years. Do you know what that would do to us? They'd turn us into meat. It's a meat market in there."

"Don't give it another thought, man. We're headed down a new road. May not know where we're going but it's gonna be better than where we've been."

CHAPTER 35

❧

NIGHT WAS COMING fast and Paco's steps were labored and heavy as he saw a gas station. He remembered movies from his childhood and wondered if mirages had a lit Texaco sign in front of them. He washed his face as best as he could with a broken soap dispenser and glanced in the mirror. He viewed his reflection with disdain for being so stupid as to be taken in so easily.

As he rinsed his hair, water soaked the collar of his shirt and a puddle formed beneath his shoes. Paco was too tired and sore to care. He walked into the convenience store and spotted the forty-ounce bottles of malt liquor. He removed two bottles of Steele Reserve and walked to the counter. His stomach was growling so he also grabbed a bag of corn chips.

He found a shady spot between the dumpster and the building that shielded him from view of the highway. Eighty ounces of beer and eight ounces of chips was a fine meal for a man in his position. He unscrewed the lid and guzzled the cold liquid. The foul tasting beverage overflowed from his mouth and streamed from his cheeks. It blended with the moisture left from his wash up, on the upper portion of his shirt.

He opened the bag of chips and began eating the contents. His first night in Florida promised to be a long one. He was going to have to sleep under the stars and began to worry about alligators, and bugs he hadn't had to contend with in the frosty Pennsylvania nights.

Wandering about after his meal, Paco found a park and headed towards a bench. He used his pack as his pillow and draped his legs over the back of the bench. The sky was so beautiful that Paco admired the handiwork that an unknown creator had taken the time to decorate. The moments were brief as Paco quickly succumbed to his exhaustion.

Pain rudely awakened him without warning. The source of his pain was the tapping of a nightstick on his left boot. It was the local sheriff prodding him. "Hey! No sleeping here!" The officer insisted to the bewildered Paco.

"Oh, yeah, sorry, man." Paco said, as he struggled to find his feet and balance. "I must have dozed off. I'm meeting a friend here. We been unloading a truck at the feed store up the highway and he's coming right back. We're gonna leave immediately."

The officer could tell the vagrant had been working hard. "You been drinking?"

"Just a beer with dinner, officer."

"Well, that's a school over there and you can't be sleeping in a school zone."

"Oh, I understand. I wasn't camping; just dozed off waiting for my friend."

"You got any ID?"

Paco's heart fell as he dug through his beat-up wallet to produce a tattered Pennsylvania ID card, only to have the cop raise an eyebrow at its condition.

"I'm just in town for the day. Me and my friend came from Philly with a load of salt. My friend has papers and everything on his truck and we're leaving when he comes back."

"Well, wait here while I run you for warrants."

"Yessir. I'm gonna sit right here."

"Make sure you don't fall asleep."

After about ten minutes the officer returned with Paco's ID card.

"No recent warrants, sir. I'm just gonna have to ask you to keep moving."

"Yessir," Paco replied. Heaving his backpack onto his shoulders he wandered down the road. His radar was sharpened to the presence of the officer. To him the ordeal wasn't really over 'til the cop was out of sight. Got to find the closest truck stop and head for Biloxi, he realized.

It took six hours but Paco finally bummed a ride with a driver headed to New Orleans. About to give up, Paco was elated to have a ride. The driver's name was Verne. He was a heavy guy whose belly barely got under the wheel of his Kenworth diesel. It was a cab-over model so Paco felt like he was hovering over the road as they sped along. The CB radio was breaking in and out, making it even tougher on Paco to get any sleep on the trip. Verne was a real chatterbox on the CB and Paco could scarcely get a conversation started. But Verne knew where every cop weigh station and DOT car was before he got within a quarter mile of them.

Paco's head was nodding as the CB emitted its static laden messages. Soon Paco's chin was resting on his chest. Then suddenly, as if in a dream, Paco heard an announcement on the radio.

"Breaker one nine, breaker one nine. You got the Soul Tanker lookin' for a weather check on I-10."

Surely it was Roy, his old friend from Pennsylvania.

"Let me have the mike, Verne." Verne looked at Paco like he'd lost his mind.

"Okay, dude. Hang on a minute."

Paco keyed the microphone. "Hey! How 'bout it, Soul Tanker!"

"This here is the Soul Tanker."

"Come on, Roy! Is that you?" Paco momentarily threw radio protocol out the window.

"This is Soul Tanker. Who that talkin' at me?"

"It's me, Paco, from Philly."

A long silence followed. "Paco, you old wanderin' fool, where are you? Uh, what's yer 20?"

Paco checked with Verne. "What's my 20?"

"You're westbound headed for New Orleans."

Paco keyed the mike. "I'm westbound on I-10, headed for New Orleans."

Another long silence. Roy finally responded. The voice crackled back on the CB.

"I'm in Live Oak bound for Miami."

"Can we stop? I'd like to see the old coot. Maybe spend some time with him and then head back to Biloxi. I got some time and I need the rest. My search for Matt can wait while I catch my breath." Paco asked Verne and he quickly agreed.

"Yeah, there's a truck stop in Live Oak. I can drop you there in about ten minutes. Paco's excitement was now explosive.

"Hey, I can be at the truck stop in ten minutes. Can you meet me, Roy? I'll ride to Miami with ya."

"Affirmative, Paco, my friend. I'll be here when you drop."

Paco handed the mike back to Verne and threw himself back in the seat.

"How about that? My buddy Roy down here in the Sunshine State! I never would have believed it."

After saying thanks to Verne, Paco jumped out of the Kenworth and walked the parking lot of the truck stop looking for the friendly face of his friend Roy. He was getting very familiar with these lots with the endless rows of trucks and the sleepy looking drivers milling about. The smell of exhaust and raw diesel burned his eyes as he searched for his comrade. The heat radiating from the big rigs intermittent with the cool breezes that swept between the trucks created an invigorating mix as he continued his search.

Suddenly Paco heard a shrill whistle from behind. He turned around and Roy was walking fast to catch up with him. The two men slapped each other on the back.

"What are you doing down here in gator country, Mr. Soul Tanker?" Paco laughed as he asked.

"You just don't know where I'm gonna turn up next. Now you're the same! When I heard you on my radio, I nearly dropped the mike."

"Yeah, it's been a rough trip. But man, I'm happy to see you."

"You ever find that dude you were after?"

"Well I got a fresh trail in Biloxi and I'm on my way there. You know anyone going there?"

"No, I'm heading for Miami. That's the other way but we can find a connection for you on the way back up. What do you say Paco, my man? Wanna be my copilot?"

"Dude, you look like you could use some sleep."

"Look, man, when I heard you were gonna meet me I cruised in and got a couple of burgers. Let's eat in the truck."

"I ran into some trouble on the road. I can't pay for the burger."

"Don't want to hear nothin' 'bout the money, Paco. The food's on me 'til we get you a ride to Biloxi."

The two climbed back into Roy's truck and they took turns eating and talking. Roy looked at his log sheet for a minute and they pulled back on the highway. He turned off the CB, fished around for an R&B radio station, and the highway just seemed to smooth out for the duo.

"Paco, I dig seeing you but ya look like ten miles of bad road. Why don't you climb up in the top bunk and get some shut eye?"

Paco didn't have the energy to defend the argument. And the truck was cool and it felt so good to be with Roy again. Verne had been nice enough, but he felt at home with Roy.

"Go ahead, my friend, push that stuff to the back and crash for a while. I won't let nothin' bad happen."

Paco turned around and was shuffling through stuff to make a nest for himself in the queen sized sleeper. He climbed in and was taken by the softness of the mattress. He couldn't remember when he'd been able to stretch out flat. The whine of the engine and the music had a hypnotic quality. As Paco lay in the bunk, he mused at the fact that the last time he was in Roy's truck he enjoyed the warmth. Tonight he was enjoying the air conditioning. *Man, living inside sure has its comforts*, he thought, as sleep closed in around him.

Roy drove a while and got sleepy so he pulled off at a rest stop and left the truck running. Before he dozed off in the lower birth, he grabbed Paco's backpack and stuffed a hundred dollar bill in one of the pockets. He knew that would be a nice surprise out there on the road. He slept awhile and woke up wanting coffee.

Paco felt the cabin pressure change as Roy jumped into the truck.

"I got two big old coffees here, Paco. You ready, or you want to sleep some more?" Paco roused himself. His muscles had stiffened in the night from over work. His hair was matted to his forehead as the world spun in his conscious mind.

"The coffee sounds good, my friend." Paco climbed back into the copilot seat, wincing with each move he made. He lifted the coffee to his lips and the hot liquid found its mark. "Did you get any sleep, Roy?"

"Yeah, dude, I got as much as I could with you snoring so much up there! You were sawin' some lumber." Roy had an easy, deep laugh.

"I put on my head phones and you were a million miles away. How did you get so beat up, Paco? Man, ya got me worried, dude."

Paco laughed and looked out the window for a moment. "I took a ride with a guy who said he needed a lumper. I unloaded twenty-two pallets of rock salt and the guy left me flat. Didn't pay me a dime."

"Damn, that's cold. It ain't even legal. They should take that dude's driver's license for pulling that stuff. Bad business." Paco was so beat up he let Roy rant on his behalf.

"You hungry? Let's go in and get some eggs, Paco."

"Nah, man, you go in, Roy. I'm just gonna rest. I'm too tired to eat."

"Look, Paco. You got to come home with me. We'll find you a place to stay. You got to get well, man. Don't be killin' yourself for a man you don't know. You got to get that old fire back. You're really hurting and it shows."

"Thanks, Roy. I hear what you're saying, but I'm gonna be sick whether I'm in Biloxi or Philly. I would rather keep moving. Hell, neither place is home, ya know?"

"Yeah, Paco, I hear ya, but dude, you gotta grow up sometime. You just can't survive out there anymore. You gotta find somewhere to live."

"I'll be all right. It's all I know, Roy. It's all I know."

Roy could see his friend wasn't in a frame of mind to be persuaded.

The two continued their happy journey to Miami and made the turn north. Roy was using his laptop and sending emails to get Paco a connecting load into Biloxi. Finally an email came in and it was a trucker that was interested in lending a hand. The email contained a phone number and Paco made the call to a Mr. Rob Steele. Over the phone the two men arranged to meet at Rob's farm on the outskirts of Lakeland.

Roy obtained a lot of information in one phone call. Rob raised ostriches and alpacas. Nine hours later Roy and Paco made the turn off the dirt road to the farm. The big tanker stopped at the end of the driveway and Roy shut down his big rig. He turned in his seat to give Paco his undivided attention.

"Paco, this guy is gonna give you a ride all the way to Biloxi. My friend, when you step out of his truck you'll be no farther ahead than you are right now. You're my partner and I really dig ya, man. Look, this whole thing's tearing me up. You're sick, you're worn out, and you look like you've been run over by a train. Brother, I've seen guys like you over the years but very few were at this stage of the game. It's not too late. Let's get you set up. The street is a mean place and you're no spring chicken. Please Paco, let's go home and get well." Roy paused and wiped his brow. "Dude, I'll help you find the kid's dad after you get back on your feet."

"Roy, you been great to me. I love riding with you. Wish we could do it forever. I been sick before and I'll be sick again. I know better than anyone just how mean the streets can be. But this is the life I have chosen and very little is gonna happen from now on that I can brag about. I want to find Matt Collins and that'll probably be my last contribution to society. The streets are my home and the streets in Mississippi are no worse than the ones in Philly. I'll be all right, bro, you take care."

Paco shook his friend's hand, knowing he might not ever see him again. It brought a tear to his wrinkled, worn out eyes as he climbed out of the rig. But he had a job to do, and he knew that he'd better be doing it as fast as he could. He knew his days were numbered. He just didn't know when the clock would stop.

Roy pulled away shaking his head and looking in his rear view mirror at Paco walking away. He thought Paco was a very interesting man, but Roy knew he'd seen his best days. The world would be a better place if there were more people like Paco. He waved out of the window but Paco never saw it. His eyes were on the day ahead of him and his feet were on solid ground.

CHAPTER 36

———— ✦ ————

HUNTER WAS TIRED of school and burnt out with the schedule. It was ruthless. He was told it would be, but now that he was burning the candle at both ends he believed it. Every single word. He'd hardly seen Holly at all. And she was partially what kept him in medical school. She was studying to be a surgeon and so was he. So they took a lot of the same classes. When he did run into her at school he couldn't think for looking at her beauty. She took his breath away like the first time he saw her. He was going to marry her. But he sure couldn't share that thought with her yet.

It was the end of March, and spring was all over the place. When Hunter walked outside his dorm room and into the fresh air, he smelled freshly cut grass. It brought back memories of home. Which brought back memories of his mother. And then he was back thinking about his father, who he was dying to meet. He must've been pretty good doctor to have his photo up on a wall at a free clinic. Hunter was rushing to anatomy class when he ran right into Holly.

"Hey, girl! Where ya been lately? I've been missing you."

Holly blushed. She was still not used to Hunter's attentions. "Hey, yourself. I've been studying. Like you need to do! Where you headed?"

"Anatomy."

"Ugh. Let's skip class and go eat an 'all you can eat' breakfast at the Pancake House. They're serving breakfast now and I've heard it's killer."

Hunter rolled his eyes. "Are you serious? You know how much I love to eat. How could you do that to me?"

Holly laughed. Her hair was like silk and shone in the sunlight. Like pure gold. "Oh, come on. Don't be a party pooper. Can't you skip just one class?"

"No way. It'll ruin my reputation. One thing I've learned in this university is that skipping class is not cool. And I need all the help I can get. I'm not like you, Holly. I have to cram for everything. You don't even crack a book and you ace the tests. It's not reasonable."

Suddenly Holly got serious. "You're one of the smartest guys I know. Maybe because you do study so hard. So don't ever make excuses for that. You have a determination that I don't have. Not sure why. But don't change it, dude."

Hunter watched her race off to class and he stood there like a high school kid, staring at her hair flowing behind her. He loved how her feet hit the pavement. He craved her smile. The way her front teeth touched her upper lip. The way she furrowed her brows if she was really listening. He pulled himself away as she entered the science building, laughing at how sick in love he was with her.

It felt good to have someone in his world that he could care about. His mother was gone and he didn't see Aunt Jenny very often. He would never admit it to anyone, but he was lonely. It was tough growing up without a father in his life. He had no man to identify with. No father to help him forge ahead in his life. His mother had worked all the time as a secretary so that they would have food on their table and had also waitressed in the evenings at a diner down the street from their house. So there were many days and nights that he spent alone in his room, wondering about his father.

When he was through with his last class, Hunter decided to text Holly and ask her to dinner. He was typing the message when a text came through his phone. It was her, asking him to eat pizza with her. His legs were like butter as he walked to his car. He had a lot to talk about with her tonight. They'd been dating for a short time but he knew she was the one. She had a way of dodging his questions. Of avoiding anything personal. So tonight was his moment to grab her and get her to open up.

He picked her up at her dorm and sped down the street.

"So, you have a good day, doc?"

She laughed her perfect laugh. "Sure did. Almost changed my mind about being a surgeon, though."

"Why? Had to work on a cadaver?"

She grimaced. "Yeah. Not the first one but this time it was a woman and that was harder for me. Don't know why."

"What bothered you about it? You've got a pretty strong stomach, as I recall."

She shrugged and looked out the window.

"Holly? What's up? You okay?"

He looked closer and saw a tear running down her porcelain face. Her chin was quivering.

"It's nothing, really. I just got emotional when I saw that. Wasn't expecting it, is all."

"I know something's wrong, honey. You don't have a squeamish stomach. You've seen worse than that. Why does that bother you so much?" Hunter took her hand and rubbed it. He pulled over and parked in the Pizza Shop parking lot. "Talk to me, honey. What's going on."

Holly turned slowly and looked Hunter straight in the eye. "If I tell you, will you still love me?"

"Of course. Don't be silly. I can see you're upset. You know you can tell me anything. I've sure dumped enough on you."

"This is different. No one knows this. I shouldn't even be telling you, Hunter."

He pulled her close to him and kissed her cheek. "Holly, I had something to talk to you about, too. But I want you to go first. Now come on, just say it. I'm not going anywhere."

"Well, when I was examining the body today, I saw some damage in the genital area. A lot of bruising. The rectum was torn. There were signs of trauma all over the place. I—"

"Go ahead. What's upsetting you about that? The woman was dead. She's not feeling anything anymore. We're not supposed to be thinking about the person or getting emotional about them. It's for research and knowledge. They've given their bodies for that reason."

"I know all that stuff. But this was different. It hit home. It was way too familiar to me."

Hunter sat up straight and felt the hairs on his arms stand up. *What was she saying?*

She faced Hunter again. "Will you promise not to ever say anything to anyone about this? I mean, no one, Hunter. Forever."

"That's an easy promise, Holly. Of course I won't say anything."

"Well, I was raped when I was fourteen. It was real bad. I've told no one. The cops weren't called. No one was notified. My mother didn't want anyone to know. So she washed me up and took care of any wounds. She was afraid of what the neighbors would think. That it might ruin my reputation. So I shoved it inside and acted like it never happened. But it did. It was real."

Hunter was shocked. He didn't show it on his face, but on the inside he was screaming. His precious girlfriend had been raped. The words echoed in his brain. They ripped deep ruts into his heart. He pulled her close to him and held her, whispering softly into her ear.

"Honey, it's okay. I'm glad you told me. You don't need to hold that inside of you the rest of your life. I'm glad this happened because that could affect you in so many ways in the future. When we have children. You needed to get that out."

She turned and looked at him with tears streaming down her face. Her eyes never left his face.

"What did you say? 'When we have children'?"

"Uh, yeah. Remember I wanted to talk to you tonight. It may seem a bit early to you, but I wanted to know if you and I could possibly talk about getting married one day soon. I mean, not right this second. But in the near future, when we both can agree on a time that's good for us."

Holly laughed but he could tell it was a nervous laugh. She was in shock. "Are you serious? After what I just told you, and you are talking about us getting married?"

"Why is that a surprise? I have told you I love you. What you have shared has nothing to do with that love. Do you believe me?"

She shook her head. "No, I'm not clean, Hunter. I've been ruined. I don't want you to have to live with that."

"Holly, stop it! You have no idea what you're saying to me. I don't think you have a clue about how I feel about you. About us. You mean the world to me and I need you in my life. I've waited a long time to really love and it feels fantastic. I want you in my life for as long as I live. And I don't care what you've been through in your past, I love you."

Holly was in tears as she laid her head on Hunter's shoulder. She'd never met anyone like him, and she had taken a huge risk in telling him about the rape. He could have walked away in disgust. But he didn't. He only moved in closer.

"I don't deserve that kind of love, Hunter. But I will tell you one thing. I love being with you and I don't think I've ever known anyone quite so open.

Hunter raised her face up to his and kissed her soft, pink mouth. "You have no idea that you've just made me the happiest guy in the world, do you?"

She smiled and shook her head. "You don't know how difficult it was for me to share that. Your reaction is such a relief. And now I feel better because I don't have anymore secrets that I am afraid you will discover."

Hunter went home after their date, listening to his favorite song on the radio in his car. The stereo wasn't all that good but it was rocking tonight. He was happy about his talk with Holly. He was broken inside because of her pain. But he knew one thing for sure; he'd never be lonely again.

CHAPTER 37

———— ✦ ————

FRANK PULLED IN the driveway of his modest home on Yacht Club Lane. He recalled the look in Leslie's eyes when they had purchased it. The home that had now become a house of lies. He paused in his car as if he were viewing the scene for the very first time. Leslie's car was there, in its old place. Frank noticed how she'd let the car get dirty since she and the kids had left. He'd asked for this meeting with her.

The past couple years were a snarl of secrets and lies, half truths, omitted facts, missing days, and lost weekends. The sordid mess that only unbridled addiction could create. Frank rested his head on his steering wheel. *Can anything undo the hurt I've caused this family?* Tears came to his weary eyes. *Will she ever take me back? Will she believe that this time we're gonna make it?*

Frank drew in his breath and released it as he slowly opened the door to his car. Just as his hand embraced the handle on the car his cell phone alerted him that there was a text message. Closer inspection proved the text had come from Matt Collins. The text simply read; "No matter what, Frank, don't use. I'm with you, buddy. Just do the next right thing." Frank paused as he read the encouraging words. As he eased up the driveway to his home, he stepped out of his car with a humility he hadn't felt since his finals at med school. Bracing for the worst while hoping for the best.

Leslie was in the other room as Frank entered the living room, walking past the waist-high bar set that had been his usual stop for as long as he could remember. A dry feeling swept over his throat. He was operating without a net tonight, wondering if Leslie would catch him or let him splatter on the concrete below.

211

Leslie entered the room and as their eyes met, a chill fell on the room as heavy as the fog on the harbor. Anguish and unspoken hardship between them was so vivid he could have cut it with a knife. As Frank took in her presence he felt clumsy and awkward. He was awash with the overwhelming desire to hold her and kiss her. At the same time he wanted to order her out of the house and leave him once and for all. As if her leaving would take away the pain and humiliation of the miserable mistakes he had made in the past.

Franks voice sounded almost frail as he spoke. "Hello, Leslie! Thanks for coming over."

Leslie's voice filled his heart when she answered. "Frank, I'm here, but I don't know for how long. You said you wanted to talk and you look sober, but I don't know how much I can take tonight. The kids have school tomorrow and . . ."

Leslie was making excuses to leave before the conversation had even begun. The house no longer felt like home to her. It had become a museum of disappointments and broken promises. She caught herself rambling and took a deep breath.

"Please sit down at least for a second."

They sat at either end of the leather sofa. They couldn't sit far enough apart. The strain between them was palpable. Both had so much to say, but neither knew where to start. Leslie broke the uncomfortable silence.

"Frank, you said you had some news for me. And you don't look like you've been drinking. So what's the story? Another shipment, another loan from God knows where?"

"Honey, that's all behind me now."

Leslie's face was like stone. She'd heard it so many times. But Frank continued. "You know I was in over my head. The kingpin had me by the short hairs, Les. A couple weeks ago some guy came to me. A patient. Seemed to be a real nobody. I tried to rope him into the organization, but he wasn't budging. His name was Matt Collins and he was a recovered alcoholic and drug addict. I had treated him after a massive heart attack. I wouldn't have bet he would even be around this long."

He paused and looked at Leslie. "I know I'm talking too much, but bear with me. At one point this Collins guy had his hands on a ton of money. He could have blown town and resurfaced anywhere. But he did the right thing; he came back and returned the money. Something odd happened when he confronted me. I felt like I could confide in him, so I did. We agreed to do a huge drug run with the cops and FBI involved, and now the kingpin is dead and the police are busting up the entire ring. For some crazy reason, I have been given a second chance. I know it's hard to believe, Leslie, but I like this Matt guy. I feel like he can help me stay clean. Honey, I'm telling you, no more cocaine for me. No more drinking. Whatever time I have left I'll use to help people. Not hurt them. And it starts with you and the twins."

"Frank, the twins have names. Ashley and Avery. They've been here and you haven't even said 'hello' to them. I bet you can't tell me who their teachers are, what their favorite color is, or what really scares them in the night. We've all become furniture in this house. We all walk on eggshells hoping not to upset Daddy or he'll get drunk and break things."

Leslie's eyes burned into Frank's. "Frank, there's been a hell of a lot more damage here than just your precious reputation. Your children need a dad. And I need a husband." Leslie began to cry. It was the longest Frank had stood still for a conversation in years. "Frank, I'm just not sure this can be fixed."

Frank glided to her end of the sofa. He reached over and held her as she cried. Her sobbing worked his heart over like a jackhammer and they rocked back and forth in each other's arms, both knowing it was going to take more than a hug to fix all of the brokenness. Frank knew it was his turn to speak. He knelt in front of his wife and clenched her hand.

"Honey, you have no reason to trust me. I'll earn that back. I have to do this with or without you. I'm begging you to do this with me, but I understand if you can't. But you give me this chance and together we'll find the love we had back in school. I know the kids need time to heal, as well. It's gonna be different; were going to get back every smile, every laugh, every precious moment that white dragon stole. Honey, I hate what I've become. It's going take time to get this right. I'm gonna make mistakes. But if we do this together, I believe I can be the husband you always wanted and the father every kid deserves."

"Frank, I so want to believe you. But I feel like we've been up and down so many times that I'm numb."

"I know you need some time to process this. I'm not asking you to move home tonight. I'm asking you to stay close so that when your heart tells you to come home, I'll be here waiting for you. No more games from me. I won't have any secrets. If you need some time for you, just leave the kids for me to take care of. Our household will get mended the same way I broke it, one day at a time."

"I see a change in you. What happened?" She stopped crying, looking puzzled at what she was hearing.

"That powder I loved so much kills people. I sold it to people who sold it to people, and people died. Lives were ruined. I should have gone to jail. This judge has shown me mercy and I don't want him to regret it. I've been watching Matt, and he's growing every day. His health's coming back and his stamina. He's been staying with this preacher in Destin and I'm telling you he's not the same man they wheeled in on that gurney. He was confused, had no plan and no hope. And it's as if he's being brought back to life with each passing day. I like this guy and whatever it is that can change a man, well, he seems to possess it. We've been ordered to do public service work and I think he has the background to pull this off. And together we can build something good for this area. I just feel it. I just need a chance to give to the community. We've made a good living here and it's time I gave something back."

Leslie spoke softly. "Somewhere inside I still love you. I just can't reach it right now. I'm full of fear. You need to be surrounded by people who have confidence in you, and right now that's not me. I need time to think. I need time to see if this is all real."

Franks shoulders fell. He'd really hoped she would come home. But she seemed set to have made up her mind. Leslie stood up and yelled for Ashley and Avery. The girls showed no emotion as they entered the room.

"Kids, kiss Daddy goodbye! We may visit him this weekend."

"Mommy, can't we stay here? I don't want to leave." Avery turned and pleaded with her mom.

"Avery, please honey, let's get in the car. We'll talk on the way back to the apartment. We'll visit Daddy again soon. I promise."

Ashley was stoic as she robotically hugged her dad's leg and gracefully walked to the door while Avery stomped her feet in protest. Leslie turned at the door with a frown on her face.

"Frank. I don't know what it's gonna take to mend this marriage. But if you don't fix yourself there's no fixing us."

Frank stood in the empty house staring at the front door where his whole life had walked out. He deserved everything she'd said. But he wanted a chance to prove he was changing. His heart ached for the first time and he realized he really did love her. He wanted more than anything to hold her in his arms but she hadn't seen the reality in Matt's life or the drama on the docks. Frank had to let go and trust some unseen force to save the marriage that he'd destroyed.

As soon as her headlights left the driveway Frank was on the phone with Matt.

"Hi, Frank! So glad you called! I've been thinking a lot about you. And picking up the phone was a lot smarter than picking up a drink or popping a pill. You didn't take any pills, did ya, Frank?"

"No, man. I'm shaky but I've got to see this through. Matt, I'm glad you're here for me. I really miss that woman."

"Frank, listen to me. When I got out of your hospital I had nowhere to go. Man, I needed a drink about as bad as you need one now. I can't say when the miracle happened for me, but I do believe this; you keep using and that miracle will pass you by. And let's face it, if you don't change, she is better off at a safe distance. I know it hurts, Frank, but if you pick up that powder it's gonna hurt worse tomorrow. Let's focus on moving forward so we can reverse some of the damage that white crap has inflicted on the world."

"Matt, I need your strength tonight."

"I know, Frank and tomorrow I'll need yours. We're a team, brother, we can do this."

CHAPTER 38

———— ⚜ ————

IT WAS A regular night at Ruby's and the juke box was roaring the classic sounds of the '70s. Chic turned around and wiped the bar clean and glanced at the end where he saw his old friend Blake. He smiled and walked slowly towards his friend, laughing at this unexpected pleasure.

"So what do I owe this visit to?" Chic stuck out his hand.

"Hey, man. Just got off work and decided to stop by and have a drink with ya."

"How ya been, Blake? Things going okay?"

"Yeah, man. Doing fine. Weather's holding up mighty good and I got plenty of work. Had a few health issues but it's all under control now."

"Health issues? What you talking 'bout, man?"

Blake cleared his throat. "Had a small heart attack is all. Nothing serious, ya know."

"Nothing serious? You only got one heart, dude."

"Yeah, tell me about it. Just have to clean up my act. But funny thing is, the doc said I could have one drink a day. I was relieved, to say the least."

"Well, I'm just glad you're okay. "

Chic got his drink and came around the other side of the bar to sit by his friend. Business was slow so he took a few minutes to catch up. Blake smelled like smoke and too much cologne but Chic wasn't about to bring up the smoking issue."

"So, Chic, I been thinking about that dude who called me not too long ago. What was his name?"

"You mean Paco?"

"Yeah, that's him. You heard anything from him?"

"Not since you talked to him. I hope he has found that guy Matt Collins by now."

"Well, I was thinking about our conversation on my way to Ruby's. I told the guy that Matt had headed to Biloxi, but it was Destin. I told him wrong."

Chic jumped off his stool and pounded on the bar with his palm. "You're joking, right?"

"No, sorry to say, I'm not. Can you get in touch with him?"

"I have no idea how to find the guy now. He headed to Biloxi but I don't know where he is."

"I hate that I made that kind of mistake, but maybe you can hunt him down. Sorry, man."

Chic slapped him on the back. "No problem, man. Good to see ya. I better get back to work. Got some people coming in here. You need another drink?"

"No way. Can only have one, remember? I'm heading outta here. Good to see you. I'll be back soon."

Chic walked behind the bar thunderstruck. *How could he make that kind of mistake? Paco is homeless. He doesn't have the means to travel around like we do. How in the world am I gonna find him?*

He finished out the night working the bar and then headed home to figure out how to get in touch with Paco. His worry was that even if he put something in the paper in Biloxi, Paco might not even read the local papers. When he walked into his house he threw his keys on the counter and pulled a beer out of the fridge. The kitchen still smelled like the spaghetti he had cooked last night and the dishes were piled in the sink.

He sat at his computer, opened Google, and searched for the local paper in Biloxi as he sipped on his beer, hoping it would wash away the stress of the day. One of the searches brought up the *Sun Herald*. He clicked on it and searched under "Help Wanted." There were rows and rows of jobs listed. He shook his head, wondering how in the world Paco would ever find an ad listed in that section. It would be one chance in a million that he'd ever see an ad. He got up and paced the room, stopping to look out the window at the haze around the moon. The streetlights looked like stationary fireflies in the fog that had floated in for the night.

His only choice was to write an ad in the "Help Wanted" section of the *Sun Herald* and hope against all odds that somehow, some way, Paco would see the ad. He made up his mind to call in the morning and discuss this with someone on the editorial staff. He just had to find a way to let Paco know that he was in the wrong town. He shook his head in frustration remembering Paco's deep desire to locate this stranger. How in the world did a doctor get from Philadelphia to Destin and what in the heck was he doing there?

His arthritis was acting up from standing so long at the bar for years, getting cases in and out of the cooler. It was really taking its toll on his body. He collapsed on his bed and turned the television on, not really able to focus on the anchorman talking about the price of oil going up. As he allowed his mind to wander, it settled on thoughts of his daughter Miranda, whom he hadn't heard from in years. He was worried about her but had no phone number to call her. She had disappeared into the woodwork several years ago and he had no idea where she was. Or who she was with. What if she was homeless like Paco? He couldn't see her lasting out there for long. But somehow people did. His heart ached for her. He fell asleep wishing he could hear her voice in the loneliness of the night. But soon sleep took over and he slept through the night, waking only to hear a salesman on television trying to sell the newest invention.

The sun was coming through the bedroom windows, glaring into his eyes as he shoved the covers off and rolled out of bed. He still had his clothes on from last night. He stumbled into the kitchen, fixed some strong coffee, and pulled up the *Sun Herald* again on the computer. He grabbed a pen on the counter and jotted down the numbers given for the editorial department. Before he dialed the number, he wrote a short note to Paco. It simply read: *Paco, if you see this ad, call Chic at 215-770-5589.* He picked up the phone and dialed one of the numbers and waited. Finally a human being got on the phone and he gave her the ad. She asked if he wanted to place the ad in the personals, but he adamantly said no. He wanted it to go in Help Wanted. She took his credit card and asked how long he wanted it to run. "Two weeks," he said. "If I want to continue it after that, I'll have to call you back."

He got up and tackled cleaning his kitchen and then switched to washing clothes. By the time it was time to head in to the bar, he had a clean house and had placed the ad for Paco. He prayed it would be seen. That was all he could hope for. The old man had a way of getting under his skin. It was ridiculous. He'd only seen him twice. But there was something different about him; for one thing, he was intelligent. Secondly, he didn't fit the mold of homelessness, whatever that was. He had a history that would raise eyebrows of the elite in Philadelphia. But he just couldn't stay in the race. He'd apparently met this young man in college who had never known his father, and now it was in his gut to find this man. And Chic knew he wouldn't stop until he found him. But it would help if he was looking in the right place. That burned into Chic's mind on his way in to work. He was wasting valuable time in Biloxi. And how much time did Paco have left on this earth to continue that search? Only God knew.

CHAPTER 39

———— ⚜ ————

IT WAS RAINING cats and dogs when the semi pulled into Biloxi. Paco was worn out and ready to get out of the cab. He was grateful for the ride and thanked Rob. But the guy had smoked a cigar the whole way and it was getting old. The whole cab was filled with smoke. He stepped down, waved to Rob, and watched the big semi pull away.

Paco walked into the truck stop and headed for the showers. It was going to feel good to take a hot shower and he needed to get cleaned up so he could find another job. He had a little money in his pocket but he needed to stay in Biloxi long enough to track down Matt. So his main focus was hunting down a short term-job opportunity that wouldn't tax his broken-down body too much.

It's amazing what a hot shower can do to a tired body. He stood naked and alone in the showers and let his mind go. He washed what was left of his gray hair, cleaned his beard, and used soap on his teeth. He started digging in his backpack to see how much change he had left and his hand hit a folded piece of paper. When he lifted it out of the pocket he saw it was a hundred dollar bill. *What?* He looked around puzzled and then it hit him. Roy had put that in there when he was sleeping! It had to be Roy! He needed a tooth brush and decided to look for one in the small shop. It was a miracle he even had any teeth left. When he got dressed, he headed out to the counter and purchased a travel size tooth-paste and toothbrush and went back into the shower area to brush his teeth. It hurt his gums and they bled. But he didn't want to look home-less. And bad teeth were a dead giveaway.

Cleaned and fresh, he took his backpack and sleeping bag and started walking. He had put on a rain parka with a hood and that kept him

221

pretty dry. But the pickings were slim at the moment on where he could stay that was out of the rain. He spotted a man leaning against a building with a backpack beside his leg. He took a chance and walked up to him.

"Hey, man. You got any idea where I could keep dry for the night?"

The stranger looked at him like he was crazy. "Ya kiddin' me, buddy? If I did, I'd be there right now, wouldn't I?"

"Yea, I suppose you would. Just thought I'd ask. I wondered if there was a cheap motel anywhere around?"

The man shook his head. "Used to be a motel down on Ninth Street. Not sure if it's still open. The druggies got it shut down. But check it out."

"Thanks, dude. Take care of yourself."

Paco headed to Ninth Street and walked right up to The Sundowner. It was a broken down motel sitting on the corner of Ninth and Macabee Street. The motel was L-shaped and all the rooms were on the front. He went into the office and there was a little old lady sitting behind the counter knitting a scarf. She had her front teeth out and was smoking a cigarette.

"Evening, ma'am. You got a room I can rent for the night? I might need it for a couple nights, if it's open."

Pauline looked up and grinned a toothless grin. "I gotcha a room all right, mister. Cost ya about thirty bucks, though. You got that kinda money?"

"I sure do. I could use a bed to sleep in tonight."

She reached up and pulled a key down for Room 3 and handed Paco the key. He pulled out thirty dollars and grabbed the key from her hand.

"Thanks. Name is Paco. What's yours?"

"Pauline. And don't ask nothin' else cause you're gonna get nothin' if ya do."

"'Night."

Paco walked to his room and unlocked the door. It was stuffy in there and dark. He cut on the lamp, which had a broken shade, and the bulb was only about forty watts. He sat down on the bed and it was so soft he nearly fell into the middle of the mattress. But it was still better than sleeping on the ground, so he laid his backpack on the other side of the bed and pulled down the covers. Then he laid his sleeping bag on the bottom sheet and pulled the covers over it. He was gonna be warm tonight. And safe. He silently thanked Roy for the extra money. He'd already showered, so he locked the room up and went looking for some supper. He was hungry and all he saw on both sides of the street was a diner. It was an old airstream and had a large neon sign out that was flashing in red: "Rosie's Diner." Paco walked in and grabbed a stool at the counter. Two young girls with white aprons on came over to take his order. They were giggling and whispering to each other.

"Guess I look a mess to you girls. Sorry. Been a long day."

The one with "Julie" on her badge looked at Paco and grinned. She had freckles and a great smile. "No matter. What can we get for you?"

"Well, I'm pretty hungry. How 'bout a hamburger and fries and a milkshake?"

"We can do that. I'll get your shake and the hamburger will be ready in a few minutes."

Paco nodded and watched as they skipped back into the kitchen. He could see a tall, strong-looking man with a shaved head back there. He decided right then to be on his best behavior. What he didn't need was a fight.

He grabbed the local paper off the end of the counter and read the front page, waiting on his burger. He scanned the paper looking for the want ads but they weren't in the paper for some reason. So he read the local news and put the paper back on the counter. He was tired, but the hunger kept him paying attention to what was happening in the kitchen. He took a moment to look around the diner and saw a man and woman sitting in a booth near the end of the row on the left of the front door. They obviously were lovers because they were hanging all over each other. The next booth had an older man and his wife. They were watching the young couple but pretending not to see anything. On the other side was a young girl who sat alone eating her dinner. Paco tried not to stare but he was curious about this girl. She seemed fragile for some reason. He decided to move so he got closer to her booth and sat down where he could see her. He had a hat on so his eyes were not so easily seen. But he could see her clearly. He studied her face and wondered what she was doing out alone. She was so thin.

His hamburger came and he tried to eat slowly so he could keep an eye on the young woman. He thought he saw a tear running down her face and he felt a quick tug in his heart. She looked at him for a second and he looked down, not wanting her to think he was watching her. He ate his food and drank the chocolate shake, feeling the cold ice cream as it moved down into his stomach. He shivered but it was good.

Just when he was looking out the window getting lost in his thoughts, the girl got up and went to the ladies' room. When he looked back her way, he noticed that she was gone. He craned his neck to see if he could find her in the diner, but she simply was gone. He was saddened because she seemed so distressed, but he finished his food and went up to the cashier to pay. He told the woman he wanted to pay for the girl's supper, so the cashier added it to his tab and took his money. He turned to walk out, looking one more time for the girl. He still didn't see her so he moseyed out the door and took a seat on a bench not far from the diner. He sat quietly watching the crowds of people walk by and felt himself getting sleepy. He was just about to head back to the Sundowner Motel when she walked right out of the diner and past his bench. She took a bench a little farther down the sidewalk, so Paco sat there a little longer to make sure she was okay.

As Paco watched her out of the corner of his eye, he saw a tall man sit down next to her. They began to argue and he stormed off, yelling at her. She seemed upset and began to cry. Paco had seen enough so he decided to approach her carefully to make sure the man hadn't hurt her. It was out of character for him to speak to anyone on the street unless it was another homeless person. But something about this girl was haunting him. He walked up to her slowly.

"Ma'am, I could see you were distressed. You okay?"

The girl nodded and wiped her tears. "I'm fine. Don't worry."

"Well, you got some mighty big tears there if you're fine. I don't think I've ever seen such big tears."

A smile started from the thin small corners of her mouth and he saw a little lift of her eyebrow. He was making ground but he had to be careful now.

"What are ya upset about? You're too young to be that upset."

"Aw, nothing. Really. Thanks for asking, though."

Paco shook his head and smiled. He pulled on the bill of his hat and turned to walk away. He heard her call him back.

"You wouldn't have a few quarters, would ya? I need to make a phone call."

Paco stopped in his tracks and turned to face her. "I bet I do. Lemme check."

He found six quarters in his backpack and handed them to her. "Here, young lady. That should be enough for your call."

She nodded. "Thanks."

Paco stood there a moment. He wanted to ask her more questions. "You got any family? Anyone you could talk to?"

"Yea, got a dad. But haven't talked to him in ages. He probably wouldn't even recognize my voice."

"Oh, I bet you're wrong there. Give him a shot. Bet he'll know you straight away."

She looked at him and smiled. "Maybe I will. Thanks for the quarters. That was nice of you."

"You take care, sweetie. What's your name, anyway?"

"Name is Miranda. What's yours?"

"I'm too old to have a name. You just take care and if you need anything, I'll be around for a few weeks. Looking for work around here. I'll keep my eye out for ya."

"Thanks. See ya."

CHAPTER 40

✦

IT WAS LATE for a phone call. Especially for Chic. He didn't have too many people who even knew his phone number, so he felt a little nervous about who it was. Usually calls in the middle of the night meant trouble. And that was something he didn't need more of.

"Hello?" His voice was a little raspy and he yawned nervously.

"Dad?" A small female voice was on the other end of the line. Chic's breath slowed to a stop. He pressed the phone to his ear to hear better.

"Hello? I can hardly hear you."

"Dad?" Her voice sounded shaky and weak.

Chic heard her this time. His heart started racing. "Miranda? Is that you, honey?"

"Dad? Can we—" She started crying hard and could barely speak.

"What's the matter, honey? Are you in trouble? Are you okay?"

She caught her breath and tried one more time. "Dad. I need to talk to someone. Do you have a second?"

"Of course I have all the time in the world for you, honey. What's going on? Where are you?"

"I'm in Biloxi. I'm okay, Dad. Just tired and not feeling too good. I'm tired of being alone, Dad."

"What's the matter, Miranda? You with someone now?"

"No. Just had a horrendous argument with Josh. He just doesn't get me, Dad. It's been this way for about a year now. He actually walked away from me just a few minutes ago . . ." Her voice trailed off.

"Honey, do you want to come home? I'll fly you home in a New York minute. I'd love to have you here with me for awhile."

Miranda pulled back. "No, Dad. I'm not coming home. But I just needed to hear your voice."

"You got any money? I can send you some money."

"Actually, I'm pretty broke. But the strangest thing just happened. I was eating at Rosie's Diner just a few minutes ago and there was an older man sitting in the booth near mine. I could feel him watching me and it was awkward because I kept crying. Didn't want anyone to notice, you know?"

"Yeah, I been there. So what about this old man?"

"Well I went to the restroom and he must have paid for my meal because when I walked out he was gone and the waitress said my meal was already paid for."

"That was a nice thing for him to do. I owe him one." Chic smiled but was a little concerned about this guy.

"That's not all, Dad. When I walked out of the place I went to one of the benches on the sidewalk to just sit and think about me and Josh. Suddenly Josh came out of nowhere and started yelling at me again and then walked off. I was furious."

"You need to ditch this guy. Want me to come up there and take care of him for you?"

Miranda laughed. "No, Dad. Relax. He's gotta calm down is all. But listen. This guy I'm telling you about, he noticed I was sitting there crying and upset. He walked up and asked if I was okay. I chatted with him a moment and he asked if I had any family. I told him I had a dad that I hadn't talked to in a long time. He gave me six quarters out of his backpack and told me to give you a call. That I needed to stay in touch with you better."

Chic's mind was running in ten directions, trying to piece everything together. "So who was this guy? You get a name or anything?"

"No. He asked my name but he said he was too old to have a name. I laughed because it was so funny, but he really was a nice old man. He—"

"Wait, Miranda. Did I hear you say he had a backpack? Was he a homeless guy?"

"Yeah, I think he was, Dad. But he wasn't dirty or anything. He just looked like he had been through a lot. He was very polite and I wasn't afraid of him."

Chic froze in his seat. It would just be too much of a coincidence for it to be Paco.

"So he wouldn't say his name? Did he have a beard? Was his hair gray?"

"No on the name, but he did have a beard. And his hair was gray. About 5'10" tall. Wore a ball cap. Why are you asking these questions, Dad?"

"Oh. Nothing, really. Except I'm trying to get in touch with a homeless guy that's down there in your area. It's pretty important that I find him. I wish you had found out that guy's name."

"Well, he did say he was doing some work in this area for a while and I would be able to track him down. You want me to get in touch with him if I can?"

Chic was sweating. "Oh, man, honey. If that's my guy, I would owe you big time if you found him. What can I do for you tonight? What do you need, angel?"

"Just to know you're there, Dad. How are you? What have you been doing? Still working at that bar?"

"Yeah, still working at Ruby's. It's something to do and I've met a lot of people."

"I miss you, Dad. I really want to see you soon."

"I miss you. I've been worried sick about you, Miranda. It's been such a long time since we've spoken. Are you and Josh living together? Does he love you?"

"Well, he did. I'm not sure about now. And yes, we're living together, Dad. I know you don't approve. But this is now, Dad. Everyone is living together."

Chic paused, trying to decide how to handle it. "So how's that working for you, girl? He gets what he needs from you. No reason to commit." He felt her attitude change on the other end of the phone.

"I'm the one who doesn't want to commit, Dad. Because my parents didn't last, it occurred to me that it might be best if I just didn't get married. That way, we really can't break up. We're just trying things out. It takes the pressure off."

"Oh, really? Look, Miranda. I did my best as a father and husband. I've apologized many times for the fact that it didn't work out with your mother. But don't let that keep you from marrying. There are plenty of marriages that work, you know. Come and see me. Let me fly you here. We need a good visit, don't you think?"

Miranda stood there with the phone in her hand. She felt so far apart from her father. Miles away. "Sure, Dad. I'll come up soon. Listen, if I find that guy again, I'll call you. Take care and thanks so much for being there for me. It was so wonderful to hear your voice." She paused again and then said, "I gotta run, Dad. I'll call you back if I find your man."

Chic sighed. Somehow he kept failing her. "I'm sorry, honey. I'm so happy you called me. I mean it, Miranda. Don't wait so long to call next time. I've been worried sick about you out there."

"I'm fine, Dad. Really."

"You do have a place to live, don't you? You're not on the street somewhere—"

She cut him off hurriedly. "Bye, Dad. I'll talk to you soon. I'm fine. Really."

Chic hung up the phone with a lump in his throat. Why *couldn't I have a decent conversation with her? After all this time I really needed to connect with her. She is all I have. Damn. I didn't even get her address.* He checked the phone for a number but it said *out of area.* And to think that she may have spoken to Paco. He sat there thinking of the odds of that scenario happening and shook his head. His life had been a mess up until now. He'd overreacted to an affair Doris had had and the divorce was ugly. She had begged for them to try again, but he had held on to his pride. And oddly, that was all he had left now. His pride. That wasn't much comfort on lonely nights.

He walked away from the phone and sat in his chair in the quiet of his house. All the lights were off but the light by his bed. He heard the wind kick up outside and remembered it was supposed to rain. The thought occurred to him that she might be homeless, too. Maybe that was why Paco felt so comfortable approaching her. And that thought made him sick. He felt his chest tighten. He almost panicked. The urgency he felt to get in touch with Paco went up about ten notches.

CHAPTER 41

My alarm went off and jarred me awake. I looked at the time and pushed back the covers, knowing I would miss breakfast with Brother Joe if I didn't hustle. I'd missed eating with him for a week and I knew he would be checking in on me if I didn't show up soon. He was a stickler about keeping promises and I had made that agreement when I moved into my apartment. This wasn't the time for me to ruin this arrangement, right when my life might be settling down to some shade of normalcy. I showered, shaved, brushed my teeth, jumped into my clothes, and headed out the door. Men were already up mowing the lawn at the parsonage so the smell of freshly cut grass followed me into the door as I greeted my favorite pastor.

"'Mornin', Joe. How's it going?"

"Do I hear a familiar voice out there today? And to what do I owe this pleasure?"

"Uh, sorry, Joe. I been pretty busy lately."

"You don't have to apologize. But I would like you checking in a little more often. How are things going?"

"Good now. But it's been a harrowing experience. You know I was determined to get that kingpin nailed, and we did. But could've gotten myself killed several times. Wish in a way you'd been there. It was your kind of action, Joe!"

"I would've, but you told me to stay away, remember?"

"I'm grateful for getting off as easy as we did. But the community service thing has got to be nailed down, Joe. I want to run some ideas by you."

"Well let's sit down and eat. I've fixed a great breakfast this morning and I want you to enjoy it with me. What have you been eating? You look thin."

"Oh forget it, Joe. I'm fine. But this looks great. I didn't realize how hungry I was until I smelled your cooking. I've missed this time with you."

"Are you okay, Matt? You staying out of trouble?"

"Clean as a whistle, Brother Joe. "

Brother Joe took a huge bite of biscuit and strawberry preserves and wiped his mouth. "So what have you been thinking, Matt? You've got something on your mind."

"I do. But I'm not sure how we'll pull it off. I've been talking to Frank and we know we need to come up with something that'll help people in the community. What I'd like to do, and I know it may sound impossible, would be to set up a clinic on the street that the poor could come to. The homeless. There's a segment of society that falls through the cracks. I was in that segment not so long ago. Remember?"

His eyebrow raised. "I do seem to recall something like that."

Matt finished his eggs and pushed the plate away. "So what do you think? Frank thinks it would be too hard to pull off. But it's something I think would make a difference. I'm ready to do something like that."

"It would be a nonprofit clinic. How hard would that be?"

"I would have to check. But it's needed. We've got to try."

"I'll do anything I can to help you, Matt. But that's a big endeavor for you to take on. It'll take a lot of research. That Dr. Harrison should be able to help in that area. Don't you think?"

"I am counting on it. But I got to get him on board with the idea first."

"Eat your breakfast and we'll talk later. Keep me posted on how things are going. And don't give up if that is what you feel you should be doing."

"You're always straight with me, Joe. Do you think I'm reaching too high?"

"You may not be reaching high enough."

I left Joe's house and walked to RT's, wanting to touch base with Paul. It seemed like a year since I'd seen him. Tommy's death had changed everything. I was anxious to see if they had found a new drummer and I kind of missed my harmonica. When I got there, the front doors were locked so I went around the building to see if the back entrance was unlocked. The rusty lock was hanging open on the door so I walked in and waded through some empty crates. Paul was sitting at the bar talking to the manager. I sat down and waited until they were finished and then I stepped out of the shadows.

"Hey, man. Been a long time since I saw you!"

Paul looked shocked to see me and he grabbed my arm. "Man! Where ya been so long? I been worried about you! Sit down. Let's talk a sec."

I sat down and propped my feet on a chair next to mine. It felt good to see Paul.

"I don't know where to start, dude. Just got through with a drug bust and I couldn't wait to tell you that the kingpin is dead. We got him, man. He's done for."

Paul laughed but I could tell he was relieved. Tommy's death wasn't for nothing.

"It went down smooth and fast. I just had to stay outta the way of the bullets. Wish you could've seen it, Paul. It was amazing."

"I bet it was. And wouldn't you know you'd be right in the thick of things. It's a wonder you didn't get yourself killed."

"Close. It was close. But Dr. Harrison and I worked it out and actually got off with community service. You should have seen the guns the DEA used! They were freakin' deadly, man. You talk about some trained agents. I was amazed at how they handled themselves. You wouldn't ever dream of being right in the middle of a drug bust like that, Paul. Even though it was dangerous as hell, I'd do it all over again just to see those goons get shot up. And the kingpin had to be shocked out of his gourd when those frogmen came over the side of his yacht."

"Hold on a sec, Matt. You're goin' too fast. What frogmen? So the kingpin wasn't on the delivery boat?"

"No way! He came in the Gulf on a huge yacht. Like a sitting duck! A chopper swooped in and hovered over him and the frogmen came up over the side. He didn't have a chance in hell to get away. I wish I could've seen his face. Think of all the kids we saved by putting him down."

Paul was silent for a moment. "Yeah, pretty amazing stuff there, Matt. Wish we could've saved Tommy. That was a waste, letting him die like that. Friggin' waste."

"Did you find another drummer?"

"Yep. We did. Johnny Granger. He's amazing and very talented. A beast on the drums. You've gotta hear him. Can you hang around and sit in tonight? We'd love to have you back on the harmonica!"

"Sure. I got nothing to do tonight. I'd love it. Man, I've missed you, Paul. You look good. How're things going?"

"Smooth. We're bringing in lots of folks, so the owner is happy. We get paid. So what's to gripe about? It's all good."

"Glad to hear it, man. Can't wait to hear the band again. How's Ginger doing?"

"She always has her issues. But she's playing great and if she can keep her mind off her problems, she does a great backup with me and Derek. Mac's doing good. Drinking a little too much but we all have that from time to time. Hell, we work in a bar."

"Yeah. But watch it, Paul. That's what put me on that bench, ya know."

"Let's get that harmonica so you can be warming up. The gang will come in later. You and I can go grab some lunch and hang out a while before we have to be back here."

I felt excited to see Paul again and get back with the band for a night. It took my mind off of the drug raid and the life-threatening situations I'd been through in the last few months. I could always count on Paul to come through as a friend. I just hoped I would be there for him if he ever needed me. I walked around the bar, checking out the guitars that were leaning against the stage door. I couldn't take the life of a musician, but it sure was nice to step into those shoes every once in a while and get off the merry-go-round of life. My eyes were scanning the photos on the back wall of the bar and I suddenly thought again of my parents, who I had failed to call during all of this mess. I grabbed a piece of paper from the bar and made a note to call them when I got home. No matter how late it was. If they'd even speak to me. I wasn't exactly on their good list. I was betting my name was in some black book they had tucked away in a drawer, or at least in their minds. And I wouldn't have blamed them for one second.

CHAPTER 42

———— ✤ ————

THE PHONE RANG in Pittsburg at eleven o'clock. I could still picture the small house with all the lights off but one single lamp. Mother had a habit of reading at night when my father was asleep. On the bedside table was a photo of me and my brother, Les. Short for Lester. He was a design engineer for Boeing in Seattle. A brilliant man who had never drank or smoked. A perfect son. And then there was me. The aspiring doctor who became a neurosurgeon and achieved great things. And blew it all on drugs and alcohol. I just knew she'd be thrilled to hear from me at this late hour. But I knew if I didn't call now, it probably wasn't going to happen.

Mother was sixty-nine years old. We hadn't been on good terms for a long time. She always saw me as the black sheep of the family. I never really knew why. So I knew she wasn't sitting up at night waiting for me to call. She'd been through all my addictions and had had enough. But now that I was on my way up, I thought it'd be nice if I took the time to share it with her. I was nervous, though. If I was honest, I hated living at home. Even though he was a good father, he could be a jerk sometimes. But since I didn't turn out so well, how could I judge him so harshly?

"Mom? It's Matt. You doing okay?"

Silence on the other end of the phone. "Matt?"

"Mother, it's so good to hear your voice! How are you?"

"Where have you been, Matt? We've been worried. Are you okay?"

"I'm good, Mom. That's why I'm calling. To tell you how I am."

"It's been so long! What have you been doing? You left here and we heard nothing. How can you do that to us?"

I swallowed. This wasn't going too well. "Mom, please. I know I've been gone a while and no, I didn't call you. But it wasn't easy leaving town the way I did. I—"

She cut me off. "Like you did? You left without talking to us. We were scared for your life and you walked away from a career for the alcohol."

I could tell she was getting upset. I didn't know how to make this better. "I take full responsibility for what I did, Mom. I admit I drank way too much and it got the best of me. I want to apologize for leaving you with no explanation. But frankly, I wasn't capable of explaining back then."

She was quiet for a moment. I could hear her breathing. "Son, we love you. But you have hurt us with your actions. Your irresponsibility. Where are you now?"

"I'm in Destin, Florida. I've been through hell, Mother. I've even experienced a heart attack. But I want you to know I'm okay now. Sober. And about to take on a wonderful project that I'll share with you later. I really wanted to hear your voice and Dad's and say that I'm sorry. I'm trying to get my life back on track and need your and Dad's support. How is Les?"

"Well, if you called him now and then you'd know how he was. We talked to him tonight. He was doing great. He used to ask if we'd heard from you, but he gave up. We all gave up, Matt. And now you pop back in and we're supposed to just jump for joy?"

"Gosh, Mom. Give me a break, will you? I know I drank too much and it nearly ruined my career. But I'm getting straightened out. I've met some great people here who are helping me figure this out."

"We're happy for you, Matt. Of course I want you to get your life on course again. That's all we ever wanted. But you are almost fifty years old. How could you have let your career slide like that after all those years in med school?"

"Addiction is a wicked thing, Mother. There's no explanation except that the addiction owns you."

"Guess I can't relate on that issue. I never drank. Your father's sitting here. Do you want to talk to him?"

"Might as well, Mom. Sorry I hurt you. I didn't mean to."

"Just get your life back, Matt. That will make me happy. I love you."

At least she said that. But the overall conversation was awful. And now Dad was going to get on the phone.

"Matt? How in the hell are ya?"

"Good, Dad. How are you?"

"Still trying to shoot my age. What's going on? You haven't called in ages."

"I'm in Destin, Florida, Dad. Trying to get my life back on track. I'm sober. It's been months since I had a drink. But I've also had a bad heart attack, so that is a great deterrent, ya know?"

"Sorry to hear that, Matt. Real sorry. You okay now?"

"Yeah, good as new. But I have to watch myself now. I'll be calling you back real soon, Dad, to share a wonderful opportunity I may have to get back into my career. Just tell Mom that I am getting my life back together, will ya, Dad?"

"Sure, Son. Take care of yourself. Don't slip back into that alcoholism. It'll kill ya, Matt. We love you. Call us soon."

"Thanks, Dad. You take care of yourself. Tell Mom I love her. Bye."

I sat there in my chair just looking at the wall. Well, that didn't go too well. Mother didn't want to even talk to me at first. Was she that angry at me? I realized that I had a long way to go in getting my life back. I loved my parents but I hadn't been too good at showing it. Now I had my chance to live in a way that would make them proud. And I couldn't wait to do it. I got up and went to the kitchen to make some coffee. I picked up my cell and found my brother's number. *What the heck! I'm gonna call Les.* Hopefully this would turn out better than the last phone call.

"Les? It's Matt! Your long lost brother!"

Silence. I could feel the shock rolling over him. "Matt? What in the hell are you doing calling me out of the blue?"

"Well, thought I'd risk it, Les. We haven't talked in a long time."

Les seemed to pause too long. I heard a deep sigh. "You okay, Matt?"

"Yeah. You?"

"Yeah. I'm good. Working hard. What are you doing these days?"

"I'm in Destin, Florida. I'm sober. Been that way for months now. Had a bad heart attack. Just wanted to hear your voice, Les. Talked to Mom just a minute ago and it didn't go too well."

"Shoulda called me first. I'd a told you not to make that call this late at night."

"Well, it's over now. But man, she was angry at me."

"You kinda deserved it, Matt. You walked outta her life without a word. We were worried. You sound better. What are ya doing with yourself now?"

I avoided the truth again. I could tell he was not too pleased and I didn't blame him. "Been through a lot, Les. Wish I could share it, but I'm not too fond of talking about it. Some other time maybe. I'm about to launch a great idea that might help a lot of people. I've met some terrific people here in Destin who can make this happen. I'm gonna team up with another doctor. I'll let ya know more later."

"Well, from what little you have decided to share with me, it sounds cool. But you're still hiding yourself. How long can that go on, brother?"

"I'm sorry, Les. It's just difficult for me to open up and share my failures. My whole life's been a failure since I left Philly. Can you understand that? I'm trying to tell you that I'm getting my life back together. It'll be more exciting to talk to you when things are in place."

"Guess I get it, Matt. Thanks for calling. Glad to know your okay. Been a long time, that's for sure. "

I knew he was sore at me. It hurt to hear it in his voice. "Sure. Thanks, Les. Talk to you soon."

I was glad I had called my parents and my brother but I was even more glad those calls were over with. I had dreaded them for so long that I was almost paralyzed. Now I could focus on what I wanted to do with the free clinic. It wouldn't make me tons of money, but I would get a salary. So would Frank. It would be fine. And we'd be giving back for a change because I was getting tired of taking. Now I had to call Frank tomorrow. We needed to have a long conversation about what we wanted in life. What we wanted in our careers. I was hoping we were on the same page because I really didn't have another option at this point.

I lay down in my bed and closed my eyes, thinking I'd fall asleep momentarily. Wrong. I was up for two hours looking at the ceiling. I finally got up and cleaned my kitchen. Watched a little television. Then I jumped under the covers and fell into a sound sleep.

In my dream I was fishing with my brother and my uncle. We were in a small fishing boat and it was cold. We fished for hours, all bundled up, drinking a beer and laughing. My uncle stood up and fell in. Les and I were young. Maybe nine or so. He shouldn't have allowed us to drink. But he did. That was the way Uncle Jed was. But this time it was a friggin' nightmare. He fell in and we couldn't get him out. We screamed and cried and tried to find him in the murky water. But he just sank like a chunk of concrete to the bottom. There was no getting him back. We were frozen in our boat, sitting there shaking. We didn't know what to do. If we left the site we wouldn't know where to look for him. If we didn't leave, no one would know we were in trouble. We decided to try to set our eyes on two markers on land to tell where the location of our boat was. Then we turned on the motor and headed to shore.

The dream was so real. We found a man on shore and he called for the Coast Guard. They came but it was too late. We showed them our location and they searched and searched. His body was never found.

I woke up sweating and feeling nauseous. I went to the bathroom and rinsed my face off with cold water. I looked in the mirror and I was white as a sheet. Suddenly it occurred to me that I had forgotten this event in my life. This wasn't a dream. It was real. I grabbed my cell and dialed Les's number. It rang and rang. I had to know if he remembered it. He didn't answer. Probably had turned his phone off. I didn't blame him; he had an important job with a lot of responsibility. But it would have been nice to be able to run the dream by Les.

I got up and fixed a cup of coffee and sat down at the kitchen table. I was older than Les by two years. Mom would have expected me to watch out for him. The fact that Uncle Jed had allowed us to drink beer seemed weird now that I was older, looking back. But Mom would've expected me to protect Les from that slip up. And the fact the Uncle Jed drowned on my watch would make her dislike me even more. Because for some reason I couldn't remember now for the life of me, every single time I did anything at all with Les, something bad always happened. It was like I was cursed. My father and I got along pretty well. But Mom was always blaming me for anything that happened. Even with the neighbor's children. I resented it and left home immediately after high school. I chose a college away from home and never went back.

I needed to find my way back to her. Somehow. I was hoping my finding a new position in my field would excite her. But maybe this time she would have to see that it really was going to stick. That I was clean and sober for a long time. It wasn't a good feeling to know one of my parents didn't approve of me. Or my life. But I also came to the realization that I had to do this for me. Not for anyone else.

I shook off the dream and decided to talk to Les some other time. I'd already woken him up once. I didn't want to risk our shaky relationship again by trying to get him to remember a nightmare from our youth. If he had forgotten it, good for him. I almost had. I climbed back in bed and tried to grab a few winks before dawn. And at last sleep came and along with it a much needed respite from life itself.

CHAPTER 43

———— ⚜ ————

THE SUN SEEMED to explode as it sank over the Gulf waters. Frank fought the five o'clock traffic all the way back to 77 Yacht Club Lane. Tonight was going to be a happy night for him. Leslie had found a support group for wives and ex-wives of cocaine addicts. Tonight she'd leave the girls with him while she attended her first meeting. Frank was determined to make the night a success so he ordered the girls' favorite pizza. Ashley loved pepperoni and Avery loved hers piled with cheese, mushrooms and sausage. Frank left nothing to chance and ordered one of each to head off a fight. He hurried in and threw on his old shorts and a polo shirt and slipped a pair of loafers over his bare feet. He ran about the house taking care of all of the last minute details, setting the large TV in the family room to the Disney channel. He took out a stack of the kids' favorite DVDs. He was anxious to share his enthusiasm about his newfound sober life with the family he wanted back more than anything.

Gosh, how'd they get to be eight? He thought, smiling. Seemed like only yesterday Leslie returned from the doctor with the ultrasound pictures that confirmed she was carrying twins. How they had laughed when they studied the blurry images that clearly showed the outline of two tiny little heads. She had been so worried about the enormity of the task—twice the diapers, twice the formula. Frank had reassured her that his practice would more than adequately provide for the sudden family. They had begun to feel a sense of confidence about facing the challenges twins would pose. Frank grunted, remembering his overconfidence at what life could dish out to a family that was just beginning.

From the night they were born the girls had a special connection. They were hungry at the same time and even wet at the same time, often making Leslie's job twice as difficult. Then came the ordeal with Stevie which brought on the wave of addiction that washed over Frank's life. He was distant on their fourth birthday. Slept off a drunk on their first day of school. And he was comatose when they lost their first tooth. His face grew dark as he viewed the progression that had made him a stranger to the children he had been so blessed with.

Franks chest heaved with a slight resolve as he set the table with the girls' favorite glasses. He was determined to win their young hearts back. He was determined to study them and learn all he could about two of the girls who somehow got lost in his whirlwind of addiction. It created such turmoil with him trying to hold down a budding medical career while leaving Mom to contend with the chicken pox, measles, and the unending parade of colds. Not to mention the fights getting them ready for school and the stacks of valentines and Christmas cards that had to be filled out for parties. Avery was born first by one minute. And she loved to tell everyone. She was sugar and spice and everything nice, while Ashley was a little more rough and tumble.

Frank's cell phone interrupted his memories. Matt asked, "Hey, Frank, how's it going?"

"Oh, hi, Matt. I wish the girls would get here! I ordered pizza and got some movies. It's gonna be a special night."

Matt could feel the excitement in his new friend's voice. "That's all swell, Frank. But don't try to fix it all tonight. Relax a little. Let the twins set the pace. Just have fun with them and remember, Frank, those girls need their dad as much as you need them. Don't try and force the conversation but let it be real and natural."

Matt caught himself. "I sound like 'Dear Abby.' Shoot, man, who am I to give advice?" He laughed into the phone and said, "I just don't want you to set yourself up for disappointment, Frank. You've been great for a few weeks now. It'll all come back. I mean, holy cow, neither of us made this mess overnight. But we're gonna get it all back one day at a time."

"Matt, I couldn't have done it without you. You've been there every step of the way."

"You and I are a team. I just feel like we can do something great once we get past this community service thing."

"I agree," Frank concurred. "I felt that way when you first confronted me in my office."

"Well, brother, it's all forward motion now. If you keep it all together your family will be back together in no time. And then it'll be worth the hassle you're going through now."

"How did you get so smart?"

"I don't know. Must be from hanging around Brother Joe."

"How is he?" Frank asked.

"He's all right."

"Matt, I hated to see him dragged into that mess after the bad drug drop but everything felt so desperate. It's good to be out of that web."

"You can never underestimate old Joe. He seemed to get a rush out of being in the action."

"Hey, Matt, I gotta go! Leslie will be here any minute!"

It was growing dark as Frank wheeled a bike from the garage for the girls to ride in the driveway. He stopped and surveyed his street. *What a great neighborhood*, he thought as he took a moment to picture his whole family together again. He promised himself to work twice as hard. To keep it all together this time. Leslie's door opened and when she got out, Frank's heart almost leaped out of his chest. She had really dressed up for the meeting and in Frank's estimation, she looked like a million bucks. She wore a smart skirt suit and it showed off her legs.

She walked up, smiling. "Hi, Frank. How was your week?" Her tone was mellow.

Frank opened his arms and welcomed her with a hug. "Hey, lady! You look marvelous!"

Leslie leaned in for a kiss on the cheek. Avery and Ashley darted for the bike. The girls barely acknowledged their father as he and Leslie spoke. The squabbling over the bike was punctuated by Leslie's correction.

"Girls, stop it! There's another bike in the garage."

Tonight both girls wanted the same bike and weren't going to give in. Finally Avery relented. Ashley rolled around both her parents' cars.

Avery yelled. "My turn! Come on Ashley, it's my turn."

They're acting out, probably because they're uneasy staying with me, Frank realized.

Leslie looked at Frank and he saw the beginning of a question on her lovely face. "Are you sure you're up to this?"

"Up to it? Man, I've been looking forward to it all week. After the meeting you should come in and have pizza with us. I ordered plenty. Should be here any minute."

As if on cue, the pizza delivery guy rolled into the driveway just as Ashley was emerging from between the two cars. Avery was behind her, yelling for her turn. Ashley turned quick to avoid the pizza guy's antiquated Grand Prix but she didn't slow down for fear that Avery would catch her to claim her turn. She jerked the handlebars to the left and passed the sidewalk with her sister in pursuit. Frank gently took Leslie's hand.

"Thank you for going to this meeting tonight."

"Well, Frank, I hate going. I mean after all, you were the one with the problem. Why should I have to go—"

Before another word left her mouth there was the sound of a horn, a metallic crash, a sick thud, and the shriek of a petrified Avery. Brakes squealed and a pickup truck rolled to a quick stop. Frank's world fell silent. Everything moved in slow motion. The scenery seemed to jerk with every step as he ran to the end of the driveway. Neighbors emerged. Avery ran toward her father with her face contorted in horror. Frank jumped over the tangled metal that used to be a bike. He couldn't get to Ashley fast enough. Leslie grabbed Avery, holding her. As Frank ran closer he saw a skinny truck driver bent over the lifeless form that he didn't dare believe was his daughter. He crumpled to his knees, inches from his baby girl's bloody form. In moments Frank's world went from high hopes to horrendous tragedy. Sound slowly came back into his world and he wailed in emotional anguish as he scooped up his daughter and ran to his lawn, tripping over the curb. The two fell together. He held her steadily as they fell prostrate on the fresh cut grass.

He had been trained to act swiftly, but he felt sluggish and inept as he worked over his precious patient. Her breathing was restored but her adorable face was covered in blood. Frank alternated between putting air in her lungs and kissing her forehead, sobbing over his silent daughter. Her eyes fluttered momentarily, as Ashley sleepily whispered to him.

"Daddy, I'm hurting. Where is Avery? I want to see Avery." Her voice was a mere whisper.

Her eyelids closed again and her face, which was almost angelic, became peaceful under a thin flowing coat of blood.

"Hold on, Ashley, just hold on. Daddy is here."

His voice became desperate and mean sounding, yelling at the anonymous faces about him.

"My God, where is the ambulance? Did someone call an ambulance?"

His voice trailed off and sirens in the distance hinted that help might be on its way.

Avery was hysterical, in the arms of a horrified Leslie. She seemed to fade into the huddle of mortified onlookers as Dr. Frank Harrison worked over his precious daughter. His polo shirt was covered in blood as he continued to yell for an ambulance. Chaos ruled the moments. And for the rest of the hour, Frank and Leslie's world was a blur of sirens, white coats, and people rushing around mindlessly. All the while, Ashley's life hung in the balance. The ambulance shot down the street and the EMTs lifted the limp body onto a stretcher. Frank watched as a feeling of panic set it. He rode in the back of the ambulance, unable to forget the look on Leslie's face as he climbed in beside Ashley.

A helicopter was waiting at Fort Walton Beach Medical Center to carry Ashley to Pensacola. The chopper lifted off the ground in seconds and Frank looked out over the city of Fort Walton wishing he'd paid more attention to his daughters in the driveway. It was every parent's nightmare and he was living it in color. His heart was racing and he couldn't get his breath. He kept his eye on Ashley and kept looking at his watch. Time was of the essence but it almost felt like he was going in slow motion.

The physician in him kicked in after a few minutes and he was grateful for the professionalism that all the EMTs had shown. But he was worried that Ashley might have serious head trauma. The flight only took thirty minutes but it felt like forever to Frank. Deputies were on the scene talking to the truck driver, taking notes and writing down all the information. It was an accident. Not the driver's fault. But he would have to live with the sound of that thud for the rest of his life. Frank felt sorry for the guy but right now he was worried about his daughter's life.

The news hit Matt hard when he got the call. His face looked pale to Joe as they raced between Destin and Pensacola.

"You okay, Matt?"

"Yeah, man, I just hate it when kids get hurt. That girl's got to be okay, Joe. She has to be."

Joe looked through the windshield at the road speeding by them as Matt drove.

"Joe, not long ago I was racing down this road in an ambulance, and Frank saved my life. Now I just want to be there to support him."

"Well you two have an incredible history going in a very short time."

"We sure do. Sorta like you and me."

"You didn't have to speak up for him with the police. You could've fed Frank to the DEA, but you didn't. You two have a way of bailing each other out, but this sounds like it's a bit over both your heads."

"Well, no one likes to admit that, but you're right. But right now it's all about that little girl. Frank didn't give me any details; just that he needed a shirt. It's a doctor's worst nightmare to see his own family hurt in a manner that is outside of your own expertise."

Joe gave Matt a bemused look. " No parent is prepared for the loss of a child. Didn't you tell me they had lost another child?"

"Yeah, Frank lost a boy named Stevie years ago, and from what I gathered from Frank, it was a tipping point in his coke habit."

Joe looked at his new protégé. "Matt, we're walking into a real pressure cooker here. It's important that you put your thoughts of the future aside and let's just be there for this family."

"You're right again, Brother Joe. I just want to be there for Frank."

The conversation remained reflective as they rolled into the parking lot. Joe took the wheel and parked the car as Matt dashed into the emergency entrance. For a moment he felt like he was back in Philadelphia. When he saw attendants and nurses, he just wanted to seize control, but kept himself in check as he sought Frank's whereabouts. He got the room number from the desk and was walking as fast as he could. He located the waiting room and found Leslie seated and clutching Avery's hand. Matt knelt in front of her.

"Hi, Leslie. I'm Matt Collins, a friend of Frank's. How is Ashley?"

"Nice to meet you, Matt. Frank's in the room now and he'll be out in a minute, so I can go in. Matt, she has been unconscious since we left Fort Walton. They airlifted her."

Matt put his hand on Leslie's. "My friend Joe is on his way in. Let us watch Avery so you can go see Ashley."

As Joe entered from the parking lot, Frank and Dr. Seth Billings, a neurologist, emerged from Room 106 in the intensive care unit. Leslie and Frank fell into each other's arms as Matt and Joe looked on helplessly. Then Dr. Billings addressed the parents.

"We are doing all we can. I won't lead you folks on. The situation is very serious. We won't know for the next twenty-four hours what the full extent of the injuries are. The good news is that she is stable. But pressure continues to build around her temporal lobes. We have not located the source of the bleeding. There may be damage to the medulla but we can't be certain 'til we do more tests. She does have a broken arm and some broken ribs. A few bruises and cuts. You folks have a place to stay nearby?"

"Well, we'll get a room at the Holiday Inn." Frank spoke up, looking the doctor in the eye.

Dr. Billings pulled Frank towards two chairs and they sat down. "Dr. Harrison, we have to work together here, this is serious."

Frank knew where this was headed. The two doctors looked each other in the eyes. "Are you asking what I think you're asking?"

"Yes, I am. There could be quality of life issues very soon. If you have to discontinue treatment, this is gonna be a decision you both need to make."

"I'll decide if it comes to that. Dammit, Seth, you better do all you can to avoid that situation."

"I'll do the best I can but you two get some sleep tonight. We have a lot of work to do in the morning. Dr. Singh will be here through the night. I'll see you tomorrow."

Frank turned to Leslie and they embraced Avery between them.

"She's in a coma, Leslie. They don't know if she will ever wake up." He whispered low in her ear. Tears streamed down Leslie's face as she thought of her daughter lying there. So frail and still.

"We have to bring her back, Frank. Think of Avery. She won't be able to take it if her sister doesn't make it. You have to do something. Get the best doctors in. Please Frank, keep our daughter alive."

Frank felt the weight of responsibility hanging on him like a heavy yoke around his neck. His heart was heavy as lead in his chest. It was a grave situation but not impossible to overcome. He had a hope that came from somewhere else that his daughter would survive this accident. But he didn't know how just yet. He prayed to a God that he had ignored for years. And he whispered quietly to his wife to soothe her.

"I'll do everything I can to save her, Leslie. But we need to pray like we've never prayed before. The knowledge of doctors only goes so far."

CHAPTER 44

— ⚜ —

IT WAS A starry night and the air was clear and a little cool. After being in the hospital with Frank and his family, it felt good to me to be outside in the night air and take a break from the tension. The prognosis didn't look good for Ashley and I felt heaviness in my heart for that family.

The trip back to Destin had been pretty quiet. Joe had gone back to the parsonage after dropping me off at the beach. I really needed some time alone to think. It had been a tough day and my mind felt exhausted. I took some deep breaths and looked around the park. It was getting late but I noticed that the night life was flourishing. Tourists were taking over the city and spring breakers had arrived in full force. All the hotels were full, and most of the rental cottages on the beach had families in them. Restaurants were busy and bars were full every night. This was money making time for the businesses on the coastline and I enjoyed watching Destin come to life again. It was different watching it happen from the street. I walked slowly back to the bench I'd lived on for many months and propped my head against the back of it. I looked around and saw a few men sitting under a tree. They had beer bottles lined up around their feet and I knew from doing it myself that they were getting drunk. It was the only way they were going to be able to sleep.

Life had taken flight and I found it difficult to piece it all together. From Joe finding me in that Coffee House to landing a drug bust with Frank. And now this horrific accident that had nearly taken the life of one of Frank's daughters. My head was in a spin. I mulled over the injuries and tried to come up with a solution. Frank would not accept "no" for an answer. He was a perfectionist in his work, just like I was, and I knew as sure as I was sitting there that he would be lying awake trying to figure it all out. I owed it to him in a way to help Ashley. She was yoo young to die. I decided to search some medical journals as soon as I got home. Maybe I would dig up something that wasn't coming to mind at the moment.

My thoughts ran along the edge of what the judge had said to us after the raid had been completed. *Community service.* I really liked the idea of a free clinic but didn't quite know all the ins and outs of setting up a small clinic like that. My vision was to allow the homeless and poor in at no charge. So the funds had to be in place. We would need an attorney to draw up the 501-C paperwork. That wouldn't be an issue. But I knew the fundraising was huge and it would be ongoing. It excited me to even think I'd be back in my career, my first love. I had missed it and even when I was in the hospital with Frank; the smell drew me in. I had sat by too long and let life pass me by. I had spent way too many nights drunk and stupid. I was more than ready to jump back on the merry-go-round and give back to society. A lot of the men on the street that I'd met were tired of the boring, mundane life outside. They were invisible to most people and moved around the city on back roads and at night. If you asked most residents if Destin had many homeless people, they would answer no. Because they hardly ever saw the people in ragged clothes. But if the truth be known, the numbers of homeless in Destin and Fort Walton would be staggering to the rest of the population. I wanted to make a dent in their lives. To offer them medical care would make a huge impact on their futures.

All of my future hopes seemed far away at the moment as I sat and looked out at the ocean. It was too dark to see the waves, but the sound of them crashing to shore was deafening. The wind had kicked up and there was quite a surf out there. I headed back home to get some sleep, because I knew tomorrow would be filled with questions about Ashley and many doctors trying to find answers. Frank would need my support. It was a long walk home and when I finally made it to my apartment, I hit the shower and just stood there letting the hot water run over my head. I dried off, walked over to my bed, pulled the covers back, and fell into the pile of pillows. I was asleep before I'd had time to give any thought to Ashley's injuries.

A loud knock on the door awakened me. I took a quick glance at the clock on my end table and noted that it was already seven. I pulled on a pair of jeans and headed to the door, running my fingers through my crazy hair.

"Mornin', Joe. Sorry. I must've overslept."

"You probably needed it, Matt. I'm just being sure that you didn't sleep too long. Breakfast is in the oven and I brought you a hot cup of coffee. You got a rough day ahead. How do you feel?"

"Confused. And very concerned about Ashley. I'm going hit the computer for a few minutes to see what I can drum up about head injuries. I have a feeling we're going to discuss her injuries this morning and I want to be visit a few sites to see if I can refresh my memories about the brain. Even if it doesn't help Ashley, it'll make me feel more prepared."

"Sounds like a great idea to me. See you shortly, Matt."

I showered again, put on a fresh shirt and pants, loafers, and ran a brush through my hair. I needed a hair cut badly but it'd have to wait. I dove into the Internet and researched what I could about Ashely's injuries, then zipped across to Joe's to grab a quick bite. He was waiting at the table, drinking a cup of coffee and reading the morning paper.

He was also coughing when I walked in and I didn't like the sound of it. "Nasty cough there, Joe. You need to see somebody about that cough."

"Oh, hey, Matt! No. It's nothing. I'll be fine. Just a little drainage is all. Here, sit down and let's eat before the food gets cold. I've made us a breakfast fit for a king."

"I see that. And I'm starved. But you do need to get that cough checked out. I don't want you getting pneumonia on me. Anything in the paper of interest?"

"Nothing much. Just the usual murders and businesses closing. This economy is crashing before our eyes. You know?"

"I've been out of the loop so long, Joe, that I don't really have a grasp of what's going on. I've got to get back to Pensacola this morning. You feel like heading that direction again?"

"I wouldn't want to be anywhere else. Wish there was more I could do, Matt. That family is in real crisis."

"Yeah, they are. Let's finish breakfast and head that way as quickly as possible. I'd love to catch that Dr. Billings before he leaves. I want to hear what he has to say about Ashley's injuries. Remember, the first twenty-four hours are the most critical."

Joe grinned. It was nice to see the doctor coming out in Matt. If he ever wondered what Matt would do with his life, he wasn't wondering now. The boy was a doctor to the bone. You could almost smell it.

CHAPTER 45

———— ⚜ ————

FRANK WOKE TO the sound of the intercom calling a doctor. Sleep was impossible in the hospital and he knew that professionally, but this was the first time he'd experienced it personally. His eyes were bloodshot and his arm was asleep from propping himself up on the sofa arm in the waiting room outside ICU.

His daughter was lying in ICU fighting for her life, and Frank was getting worried. Dr. Billings hadn't stuck his head outside the doors to inform him of any changes, good or bad. He got up and started looking for some hot coffee. He needed something to wake him up because this was going to be a one of the most stressful days of his life, besides watching his daughter get hit by a truck. He decided to head down to the cafeteria and grab a quick bite of breakfast so he'd have the energy to get through the day. Leslie and Avery were in the Holiday Inn across the street, and he was hoping she'd had a better night's sleep than he did.

He was just finishing up when he saw Matt and Brother Joe walking past the windows of the cafeteria. He jumped up and went after them. "Hey, Matt! Wait! I'm in here eating breakfast. Let me pay and I'll go up with you."

Matt and Joe stopped and waved. They could see the tiredness in Frank's face.

"You guys are here early. Really nice of you to show up. I'm waiting now to see the doctor. I'm a little worried, Matt. I'm not sure what to expect this morning. Her injuries are bad but we don't know how bad."

"I know, Frank. I've been looking at some medical sites on brain injuries, especially temporal lobe trauma. Did you have a chance to look that up?"

"I've not had access to a computer since I got here. But I am aware of the swelling issues. That's what I want to see Dr. Billings about."

"Let's get up there now. Maybe we'll catch him doing his rounds. They are keeping a close eye on her, I'm sure. We got to hope for the best, Frank."

The three men caught an elevator to the fifth floor and walked straight to ICU. They asked a nurse if Dr. Billings was in and she remarked that he'd been looking for Dr. Harrison. They found a seat not too far from the door and waited for the doctor to arrive. Frank was visibly shaken.

"Look, man. I know you're worried sick about Ashley. I would be, too. But this guy seems to know his stuff. Let's hope things are a lot better right now. It's been just long enough to where her brain may have released some of that fluid."

"I'm counting on it, Matt. I—"

"Good morning, gentlemen. I've been looking for you, Dr. Harrison." Dr. Billings spoke with a strong voice. His face gave away nothing.

"I've been waiting to see you all morning, Doctor. How is she today? Any change?"

"Why don't we come into this room down the hall? I'd like you to see the MRI and CT scan."

Matt and Frank walked with the doctor while Joe sat down and grabbed a newspaper.

"I'm assuming you'll allow Matt to come, seeing as how he's a surgeon. I know I'd sure feel better if he was in this room."

"I'm aware of Matt Collins. I looked you up on the Internet last night because your name was vaguely familiar. My search confirmed that you were who I thought you were. I remembered you from that Westbury Clinic in Philadelphia. I headed up that project at the very beginning and kept up with the progress over the years. Was impressed with the work you did."

Matt froze in his tracks. *What are the odds of running into someone who knows about that clinic?*

"Yeah, that was a great time in my life. It's been a while since I thought about that clinic but it really serviced a lot of people who wouldn't ordinarily have received medical care."

"That's what I liked about it. We need one in this area."

Matt was stunned at that statement. He wanted to talk to Dr. Billings longer and share his new ideas about a free clinic in Destin, but Ashley's life was at stake and he knew this wasn't the time or the place.

Seth Billings sat down at a desk that had several lit windows. He pulled up Ashley's MRI and CT scans and asked Frank and Matt to join him.

"Doctors, these are the two films we have on Ashley. Both show a swelling in her temporal lobe. There was great trauma to that side of the brain. It's been twenty-four hours and the swelling has subsided some, but we are going to place holes in the skull to give the brain room to drain and also ease the pressure. I want to see how she does in the next twenty-four hours. We'll keep her in the coma another day to make sure her brain gets rest and has time to heal a little from the trauma."

Matt rolled his chair closer and looked at the scan. His hands ran across the glass, his brain racing. They spent forty-five minutes in the room discussing all the possibilities and then headed back to the ICU to check on Ashley. The procedure would take place at 11:00 and then it would just be a matter of waiting. Frank and Matt walked back to the elevator, discussing what they saw on the X-rays.

"Did you see the swelling, Matt? It doesn't look good at all."

"Well, don't jump to conclusions, Frank. A lot of things can happen in the next twenty-four hours. The edema could diminish and Ashley could escape with minimal effects from the injury. She is young and that is in her favor. Children can heal very rapidly. Let's wait before we allow panic to set in."

Frank sighed and shook his head. "It's easy for you to say that, Matt. It's not your daughter lying in there. But I know you're right. I imagine Leslie and Avery are in the waiting room by now. Let's go see if we can catch them. I know Leslie has to be at her wits' end with worry."

They got off the elevator and turned the corner and Avery came running up to her father.

"Hey, baby. How's my girl?"

"Daddy! Where's Ashley? I want her to come back home with us. Mommy says we might be leaving soon."

Frank looked at Leslie and she shrugged her shoulders. Tears were forming in her eyes and he knew she'd just told Avery that to calm her down.

"Sure, honey. Ashley will be fine. We'll see her soon. The doctors are taking care of her right now."

Leslie stood up and Frank gave her a hug. "Honey, I know it won't help you to know this, but Dr. Billings is going to relieve the pressure on her brain at 11:00 and then it's a matter of time before we'll know how she will respond. We can't see her right now, Leslie. Visitation is every three hours. And only one of us can go in at a time. She needs complete rest."

Leslie shook her head and sat back down. Frank could tell she was exhausted from putting up a front for Avery.

"I don't think I can take much more, Frank. She's so small. So helpless. What if she doesn't make it? What if she dies, like Stevie did?"

Frank instinctively drew back but caught himself. Stevie's death was still haunting him. "Leslie, we can't compare this to Stevie's death. You know that. There is a good chance she'll recover and have no side effects of this injury. We have to believe that."

Leslie looked at Frank with tears running down her face. "I remember what his death did to you, Frank. It was the downfall of our marriage. You turned to cocaine and just sank deeper and deeper. We can't live through that again. It was almost impossible to overcome the first time. Do you understand the gravity of that statement?"

Frank nodded sadly. "Honey, more now than ever. I can see what I did to our marriage. I'm trying to start over and I need you to believe in me even when your gut tells you not to. For some reason, Matt and I feel she's going to be okay. Now we have to hang on to that until there's a good reason not to."

Leslie wiped her tears and nodded. "I'll do my best, Frank. But if you slip back into that same routine of lying and hiding your addiction, I'll leave this time. And I'll never come back. You will lose the girls forever."

Frank looked sadly at her and saw the color draining from her face. "Let's concentrate on Ashley right now. She needs our support. Brother Joe has been kind enough to come here to pray for her. Matt is here. We need to combine forces here, Leslie. She's got to make it through this."

Matt and Joe and Frank sat at a table in the lunchroom. The tension was high. Leslie had taken Avery to McDonalds and then back to the Holiday Inn for a break from the hospital, so it was a good time to talk about the technical issues facing Avery.

"Matt, what do you think her chances are? I mean, she hasn't gotten worse during the first twenty-four hours. There is still swelling, but they'll relieve the pressure now."

"It just depends on how much damage was done to her brain. We don't know that right now. Some of it we won't know until the swelling goes down and they bring her out of the coma. It's a guess right now, Frank. We're stabbing in the dark here."

"I have a good feeling about it, but I know it's mostly because I want her to live. I'm almost willing her to overcome this."

"Dr. Billings seems like he's on top of things. I know everything is being done. It's no fun sitting here while your daughter's life is hanging in the balance. I've handled many cases where people's lives were at risk. There's nothing to do but pray, wait, and see how her body is going to deal with the trauma."

"Leslie is really hurting. It's ripping her apart. I mean, we lost a son already. We couldn't handle losing a daughter."

"She came down on you pretty hard. It's difficult to sit and listen to that and face just how much damage you caused. I was fortunate to have been single when I went through the worst of my addiction. Of course, I probably wouldn't have stopped drinking or using cocaine if I hadn't had a heart attack. That pretty much put a plug in it."

"I don't want to have to go through that, Matt. I've got a lot on the line here. You could have lost your license. Thank God you didn't." He paused and finished his sandwich.

Joe took the last bite of his meatloaf and wiped his mouth. "Matt, have you and Frank talked at all about what you want to do with your lives? I don't know how you feel about the future, Frank, but I think you could use something positive to focus on right now."

Matt looked at Frank and shrugged. "No, I really haven't had a chance to nail anything down, Joe. But Frank, did you hear what Dr. Billings said in the film room?"

Frank nodded and smiled, which felt foreign to his face at this point. "I sure did. Don't think I didn't catch that about the free clinic. I was freaked out that he knew who you were."

Joe butted in. "What's up with that? Talk to me."

Matt was smiling from ear to ear. "Joe, it was so strange. We were just about to go over the MRI and CT scan with Dr. Billings when he said that he'd looked me up on the Internet to see if he knew me. Apparently he was one of the founding contributors in that Westbury Clinic that I worked at for years. I was astonished that he even knew me. Knew my work there. What are the odds of that?"

Joe laughed. "At this point nothing is going to surprise me, Matt. Absolutely nothing."

Frank smiled. "You must've been a pretty damn good surgeon, buddy. I don't think Seth Billings would've brought that up if you hadn't had a pristine reputation as a surgeon."

"I have to say it did make me feel good for a few minutes until I looked at what an idiot I was to drink myself right out of the medical world. Do you realize what I left behind when I left Philadelphia and headed south? At that point, I didn't even care where I was going."

"Well, I am glad you're here now. You've been such support for me and you've made me face up to my addiction. So what are you thinking about, Matt, about our new venture together? Got any cool ideas?"

Matt cleared his throat. He wasn't sure how this would sit with Frank but he knew Joe loved the idea.

"It's just an idea, Frank. I haven't nailed down the how-to's yet. But my idea was that we would open a free clinic here in Destin. That's why I looked so shocked when Seth mentioned that we needed one in Destin. That was exactly what my plan was. You and I could get a 501-C for the clinic and have the opportunity to service all the homeless and poor people who live in the surrounding area. There's more homeless out there than you can imagine. No one can see them but that doesn't mean that they're not there."

Frank pushed away from the table and stuck his hands in his pockets. "I like the idea at first glance, Matt. It sounds pretty solid. Do you think we could pull off the fundraising it would take to finance a venture like that? Could we get any government grants? I admit the need is there. But you would know more about that than I would. As far as the home-less goes."

"True. We'd have to get a lawyer who does 501-C's. No biggie. And I bet Seth would help us with a lot of this. We need to make an appoint-ment to see him or ask him to dinner one night after Ashley recovers and you can focus on something else besides keeping your daughter alive!"

They all laughed. "Yeah, I guess that's a priority now. But I could get excited about this, Matt. We wouldn't get rich. But man, it would be sat-isfying to help people like that. Let's check into it after we get through this crisis with Ashley."

Joe interrupted. "I think it's a good time for a prayer, don't ya think?"

The two men got quiet and looked at each other and smiled. Joe knew how to own a room.

CHAPTER 46

———— ⚜ ————

THE REMNANTS OF winter were digging their claws into the beginning of spring. The temperature had warmed up enough for the snow to melt, but there were areas that remained hidden from the sun's warm rays that still had small piles of dirty snow tucked away. Hunter was walking back to his dorm, enjoying the brief warmer temperatures that wouldn't stay long. It made him want to take the week off and play hooky. He was getting closer and closer to Holly. She had really opened up to him and they were spending loads of time together. It was almost too good to be true.

Just as he walked through the door his cell rang. "Uh, Hunter? I hate to say it, but I won't be able to make the art exhibit tonight. I've evidently caught Lonnie's cold. I feel so bad." Holly sounded terrible.

Hunter sighed. "Darn. Are you serious? I hate that! What can I do?"

"I don't want you to catch this. It's grungy and I feel awful."

"I feel so bad for you. What can I do, honey?"

"Well . . . I could use some chicken noodle soup. Could you drop that by?"

Hunter grinned. She was worth getting sick for. "Sure, baby. I'll be right over. Anything else?"

"Ice cream. Peach ice cream. That might feel good to my sore throat."

"I'll be there in about an hour. Stay warm. You got any Echinacea?"

"No. But I'll take anything to get better."

"See you soon."

Hunter put his books down and checked his email. A message from Aunt Jenny.

Hunter, hope this finds you well. It's still cold but I see the beginnings of spring in small ways. I know we have another month before anything even remotely turns green around here, but it's something to look forward to. I'm doing okay, but have a cold right now. I think it's going around. You stay warm and wash your hands a lot. Ha! I know you're in medical school but I can still tell you what to do!

I want to hear all about your classes and if you have anyone special in your life. Please drop me a line and catch me up on your life. Any luck on finding information about Matt? I know you really wanted to find him, honey. Wishing you all the luck and sending a few prayers up for you. Write soon. Love you.

Aunt J.

He hit reply and wrote her a short note.

Hey Aunt J.

Thanks for the note. Sorry you are sick and yeah it's going around here big time. I'm ducking around corners to keep well. Holly, my girlfriend, is sick with the crud that's going around. You stay indoors and get well.

As far as my finding Matt, I've had no luck. I have someone looking for him for me and he's run into some neat information. Matt was a doctor at a free clinic called Westbury Clinic. We've not found anything else out. But that gave me some hope. I'll keep you posted.

School is tough but I knew it would be. Gotta run and take soup to Holly. Wish I could see you, but I'll visit soon. Take care and get well fast.

Hunter.

Hunter dashed out the door and got in his car. The streets were busy, and he weaved in and out of traffic and pulled into the grocery store parking lot. He parked and a girl pulled up beside him in a BMW sports car. When she got out he realized she was a girl from his anatomy class. Sandy Moore.

"Hey, Hunter! What you doing at the grocery? How come you're not in class?"

"My girlfriend's sick. Gotta pick up some chicken soup and ice cream!"

"Oh, man, sorry to hear that. Holly . . . that's her name, right?"

"Yeah. She must be pretty sick."

"Hey, you want to hit that art exhibit that's going on at Seybert Hall?"

Hunter winced. He really wanted to go. "I've got to take her this soup first. I was gonna hit the exhibit afterwards, if it's not too late."

"I'll be looking for you. It's supposed to be good."

"Okay, Sandy. See you there."

Hunter walked into the grocery store wiping the sweat off his face. He grabbed some chicken soup, crackers, peach ice cream, and echinacea, which he found in the vitamin row. On a whim he hit the florist section for some roses. That would win him some points he was going to need later in the week. He got in line, paid for the groceries, and rushed to his car. The afternoon warmth was fading as he pulled into Holly's driveway. He put his leather jacket on and zipped it up, grabbed the grocery sack and flowers, and walked up to her door. He tried the knob only to find it locked, so he rang the bell. After a few rings, Holly showed up at the door wearing flannel pajama pants and a long sleeved tee that was ripped at the elbow. Her hair was wadded up in a ball on top of her head and there were loose strands hanging down in her face. Her nose was red from blowing it too much and her eyes were bloodshot.

"Man, you look rough, Holly! You must feel awful!"

Holly coughed and moved aside so he could get inside fast. Cold air rushed in through the open door.

"Sorry I look so bad. It's the worst flu I've ever had. Chills and fever. Thought it was just a cold but now I've got fever. Ugh."

"I brought you some roses, sweetie. Hope they make you feel better. You got a vase?"

"Yeah, above the sink. Just sit them on the counter and I'll get it later."

"No way! I'll fix them for you. You go sit down; you need to rest."

Holly laughed watching him fix the flowers. "That was sweet of you to bring those flowers and the soup. I love roses. How did you know?"

Hunter laughed. "What girl doesn't like roses, huh?"

They walked into the living room where Holly piled on the sofa with three blankets and her favorite quilt that her mother had made. Hunter sat at the end of the sofa near her feet.

"So what was it you wanted to talk to me about, Hunter? You mentioned earlier today that you had something you wanted to discuss with me."

"Oh, it's not that important. I mean, we can wait until you feel better." Hunter suddenly felt nervous.

"Oh, come on. Now that you've gotten me out of bed and dragged me into the living room and brought me flowers, you have to tell me what's on your mind."

"I . . . uh, well . . . I was wondering . . . It's not the place, Holly, I'm not going to talk about it while you're sick. That's just stupid. We'll go out to dinner one night when you're feeling better, okay?"

Holly laughed at his awkwardness. "Hunter, you are hilarious. So you going back to the dorm?"

"No, I was thinking I would still go to that art exhibit at Seybert Hall. Remember?"

"Yeah, darn! I wanted to see that, too. What time was it?"

Hunter looked at his watch. "I can go right now and see it. But I hate to leave you here alone."

"Don't be silly! Go for it, dude. And report back to me because I'll want to hear all about it."

"Okay, if you're sure. I can stay here with you for a while and watch a movie or something."

"No way! You get out of here and check it out. One of us needs to go."

Hunter stood up and walked to the door, looking back at Holly. She was so cute sitting on the sofa all messy and sleepy. "I'll call you when I get home. Now you get to feeling better. Love you, baby."

Holly grinned. "Love you, too! Now go!"

Hunter zipped over to Seybert Hall and parked the car on a side street. Cars were lined up all around the block and the parking lot was full. He ran up the steps looking for Sandy and her friends. The room was crowded and noisy and it was nearly impossible to see anyone. Hunter moved along the outside of the room, catching a glimpse now and then of a painting on the wall, grabbing a drink from the hostess. He ran into some friends of his who were in his chemistry class, but they disappeared in the crowd, leaving Hunter to fend for himself.

Wandering through the two major rooms, he saw Sandy in the far corner and yelled at her. She somehow heard him over the noisy talking and moved towards him. She was with five of her friends and they were all drinking. Hunter noticed that they'd all had too much to drink and the night had just begun. He looked around the room and realized that with all the people in the hall, he felt totally alone without Holly. There was no point in staying any longer, so he politely excused himself and headed out the door, looking back once to see a frown on Sandy's face. He waved at her and ran to his car.

He'd seen enough. It wasn't what he thought it was going to be, and he had one lady on his mind who was taking up all his energy. He climbed into his car and drove back slowly back to Holly's apartment. He walked up the steps and put his hand on the door latch and it opened. He walked in quietly, noticing the quilt had fallen to the floor beside his sleeping beauty. The room was dark except for a dim light in the kitchen. There was a slight aroma of chicken soup in the air mixed with cough syrup, and a pile of Kleenex on the floor by the quilt. He slowly walked up to her and stood, looking down at her face. Her hair was loose now and spilling out over the pillow. Her mouth was slightly open and her arms were stretched up over her head. She looked relaxed and he didn't want to wake her. But he wanted so much to tell her what was in his heart. It was so hard for him to open up to her and let her know how he felt. He knew she was waiting for it. He longed to tell her. He wanted more than anything to have someone to belong to.

He took a deep breath a leaned down over her. Without waking her he touched her hair. His heart was beating fast and he wanted to kiss her so badly. Instead he carefully whispered in her ear.

"Baby, I just wanted to tell you I'm so in love with you. I can't do anything without thinking of you. I know we're young and we have a lot of school left, but I want you for my wife. I want to wake up with you beside me. I want you to spend the rest of your life with me, Holly. I love you so much We've talked about this before, but I guess I am asking this time. Will you marry me?"

She stirred slightly and turned over with her face towards the back of the sofa. He stepped back and watched her for a moment and then turned and walked to the front door. He looked back once, grinning, and then opened the door and stepped out, closing the door behind him quietly.

Holly jumped off the couch and shouted, "Yes!" He did love her! She'd stayed quiet so he would talk to her without hesitating, like he usually did. It was beautiful. His words took her breath away. But now she had to act like she didn't know. She didn't think she could contain the feelings. She lay back down, pulling the quilt back over her, smiling. Then on a whim, she picked up her cell phone and texted Hunter, laughing wildly, which sent her into a fit of coughing.

"The answer is yes."

Hunter got the text when he was just about home. He nearly ran off the road when he read her words. So the deal was done. They were going to be together for life! Later he couldn't even remember driving the rest of the way home. They had talked about it before briefly, but had never really nailed it down. Now it was really going to happen. His mind was snapped back to attention when his roommate yelled at him when he came through the door.

"Did you forget we have an exam in physics tomorrow? A hundred questions. And we have to ace this test!"

CHAPTER 47

———— ⚜ ————

THE MORNING LIGHT invaded Paco's eyes with as much subtlety as an air raid siren. Sun flooded the nearly half century old room. Paco sat on the edge of his mattress as he gathered his thoughts. He was fighting a gloom that was settling on him. He had to snap out of it and find some work. He was craving a cup of coffee but chose to forgo the trip to the lobby to avoid facing Pauline and having to explain the absence of rent money.

His room had been home for nearly a week and his money had dwindled. He looked around but it did little to lift his spirits. The brown and tan shag carpet with the black highlights was matted and faded, and the paneling was dark mahogany that had no shine left after years of tobacco smoke. The door to the bathroom had a six-inch hole in it where it was clear someone had tried to kick it in at one time. The fixtures in the bathroom were avocado green and the faucet dripped continuously. The whole room creaked as Paco lumbered across it. He so desperately wanted to be in stealth mode and every click and clatter seemed to reverberate, making it impossible for Paco to be silent.

He quickly dressed and rushed through the door. The driveway was littered with cigarette butts and empty potato chip bags as sunlight bathed the courtyard and revealed every bit of waste that had blown across the blacktop. He made his way to the road but not before Pauline came out from behind the counter and stepped onto the broken sidewalk.

"Hey, stranger! You can't leave without coffee!"

Paco felt like a roach caught in the beam of a cheap flashlight. He did a loop and found himself face to face with the very lady he was hoping to avoid.

"Hey, Pauline, it's a beautiful day."

"Come in and get some coffee, Paco. It was fresh an hour and a half ago."

Paco grinned. "Yeah ? Well ma'am, your coffee looks like me; still got color, but a bit past my prime."

"I bet you say that to all the ladies you owe rent."

"Well, Pauline, you're the first one I've tried it on."

The two laughed as they headed for the coffee pot. Pauline smiled as she poured his coffee.

"I wasn't sure I would see you this morning. But I'm glad I did. We get so many wealthy tourists in here; not all of them as distinguished as you." Pauline's banter continued.

Paco took the cup and smiled. "Much obliged for the coffee. I'm hoping to find some work today so I can come back tonight with a little more than an excuse."

"What kind of work you looking for ?"

"Anything that will pay." Paco grinned as his back pushed open the door and he spun out. Pauline followed him out.

"Seriously, Paco, you got to get something. I can't carry you here."

"Don't worry, I'll cover this. Pauline, you been very good to me. I'm okay on the street but the way I been feeling lately, I wanted to stay here a little longer. That is, if I can make ends meet. You asked what kind of work I wanted to do. I prefer carpentry but since I don't have tools with me, I'll do custodian work."

"I can see you're not in the greatest of health. And I hate to put you out. But I got responsibilities, you know?"

"Yeah, I know. I don't want no special treatment."

"Hey! I got an idea! There was a guy here named Matt had some remodel work at the Golden Eye."

Paco's jaw dropped. "Matt Collins?"

Pauline strained her memory. "Maybe, but I'm not really sure. I know it was Matt and he was from up north somewhere. I think he might have some work for you."

"Wow! Where is this guy?"

"Well, the Golden Eye is down on the strip. Why don't you rest 'til lunch and I'll give you a ride. Hate to see you making a first impression after a sweaty walk."

"Aw, thanks, Pauline, but I've been walking for years."

"Paco, you've been doing a lot of things for years that have to stop. Go clean up your room, take it easy, and I'll run you over at lunch. I'm going to look after my investment in you."

Paco grinned. It had been a long time since anyone had ever called him an investment. He felt like a bad risk as he returned to his room and began picking up the assortment of clothes that he had scattered around the room. He washed out some of his shirts and jeans and hung them around the room to dry. Noon found him reclining on his bed doing the crossword puzzle in the newspaper.

A sudden knock at the door was quickly followed by Pauline's apologetic entrance. She stopped and surveyed the view in Paco's room. "Very nice, Sonny! Who's your decorator? Levi Strauss?"

Paco laughed as he jolted upright in the bed and discarded his crossword puzzle in the wastebasket. The oral recommendation had made Paco not want to read the want ads. As the two left the room, the folded copy of the *Sun Herald* hung halfway out of the basket. In the third column from the right, six ads from the top, read the unnoticed ad Chic had placed in the paper.

"Pauline I have to tell you again how grateful I am for the ride. I really hope this is the guy I been tracking."

Pauline chimed in. "Even if it's not, you get this job and I'll work with you on the rent as long as you don't get to drinking and out of hand."

The two climbed into Pauline's old Dodge pickup and headed out. As they talked, she took Paco to the grand entrance of the Golden Eye. Pauline's pickup looked out of place as it turned around the parking circle. The valets were unmoved by her presence in the circle, and their conversation was uninterrupted by the beat up Dodge that they simply assumed was just another underpaid employee of the casino. Pauline was still giving Paco last minute coaching as he piled out. He turned toward the exit after two steps she called his name.

"Paco!"

He turned around to speak but she interrupted.

"Fix your collar!"

He grinned as he adjusted the fabric folded around the top of his shirt, bending slightly so their eyes would line up through the windows. "Thanks, Mom!" He blurted, followed by his trademark chuckle. Turning back around, he entered the posh surroundings like he owned the place. For a split second he was the only one who was unaware of the difference between his clothes and those of the patrons who decorated the ornate lobby.

The sun was just beginning to set as Paco wandered back from his interview. Matt Collins was still eluding him. What he did have was a job. And Matt turned out to be Matthew Hamilton; he was doing updating work for the casino. His crew would go in a vacant room, restore it, and then move to the next. The job required a lot of cleanup work and Paco had the fortune of coming in just as the previous employee had quit.

Paco was anxious to tell Pauline of his good fortune but when he arrived back at the motel he didn't see her pickup. So he headed for his room hoping to watch TV and call it a night early. As he opened the door, to his surprise, the clothing that had been drying was gone. He stood in shock, momentarily thinking he had been robbed. Looking closer, he found instead that his clothes were folded and neatly put away. As he walked around admiring his room, the old Dodge pulled up outside his door. Pauline came in with two bags of groceries. She walked straight to his small kitchen and began stacking the contents on the counter.

"How'd it go with Matt?"

Paco shook off his surprise and began to answer her while watching the grocery items stack up.

"I found Matt and got the job. I start tomorrow."

He was studying Pauline's face as best as he could. She showed little expression as she opened a plastic container filled with rotisserie chicken.

Then she retrieved two paper plates and began arranging chicken pieces, potatoes, and macaroni salad on both of the plates. Paco's eyes were drawn to the six-pack of 16-ounce beers she had lugged in with the rest of the groceries and his mouth watered. She handed him a plate and watched him smile sheepishly.

"Well, then, tonight we'll celebrate your new job. And we should toast to a long gainful time of employment."

"I'll drink to that!" Paco said, as the aluminum can burst into life with the flip of the tab.

The two of them sat in chairs outside of Paco's room with a small wicker table between them. Words seemed kind of scarce between them as Paco sought not to gobble his food too quickly. He couldn't remember the last time he'd eaten in the company of a lady, and the two of them just silently enjoyed one another as they strained to make polite conversation. When the food was gone Paco bolted to his feet and picked up after Pauline, adding to her discomfort. Both felt out of place as the makeshift bus boy returned with two fresh beers. They quietly sipped their respective beverages. Pauline broke the burgeoning silence.

"You enjoy your meal?"

"Oh, yes, but I like the company even more." The old vagrant hadn't lost his charm, and he was feeling quite relaxed as the night closed in around them.

"How long you been on your own, Paco?"

The question stirred the dusty tramp's memory. "Well, most of my life, to tell you the truth. I don't get a lot of dinner invitations. Why do you ask?" He smiled at her kindly.

"You ever get tired of life on the road?"

The question hit Paco with all of the subtlety of an electric chair. He thought for a moment. Then he smiled and responded with a question. "You ever hear of an old dog that don't want to come in when it rains?"

"I've never let an old dog in without waking up with the fleas," Pauline stated rather reflectively.

Paco's face revealed a mild shock, and he cocked his face to the left in a gesture that demanded clarification. Pauline continued to talk, her tongue loosened by the few beers they had shared.

"Guys like you are a real challenge. I've met a few drifters and got my hopes up only to have them dashed. My heart has been broken so many times that it no longer works like most."

Paco stared in rapt attention, feeling uneasiness creep in.

"I like you, Paco. You're funny. I think you're a hard worker. You're honest and you seem to really like people. That's got me thinking. You are a good risk."

"Pauline, the road is not just my home, it's what I do. It's part of my life now. I don't think I could ever make it in the mainstream."

Pauline frowned. "Mainstream? Nothing here is mainstream. This is an out-of-the-way motel in an out-of-the-way town. I gave up on 'Ozzie and Harriet' years ago. Normal ain't normal anymore. And I just don't want to be alone any longer."

"Well, tonight you're not alone."

Paco's hand rested on hers as he looked up at the stars. Sipping his beer, the silence around them gave way to the sound of big trucks in the distance that became a serenade of sorts to the couple as they sat in the darkness. Paco's attention focused on a patch of stars in the northwest sky. He soon was lost in his thoughts. He gazed, knowing that under that canopy Matt and Hunter were completely unaware of each other.

He felt the comfort of the touch of her hand under his hand. He reflected on his quest for Matt Collins, momentarily taking comfort in the fact that his chest seemed to be better. It had been a few days since he had coughed blood up, which led him to think he might be getting better. He was aware of nothing but the stars and his companion and he felt more relaxed than he had in a long time. He was also aware that Pauline was wishing for something more than he had to give. He didn't want to hurt her, but he knew himself too well. And it just wasn't in the cards for him to settle down with Pauline. He appreciated her kindness cloaked in the gruffness of her voice. But there was no way he was going to stop searching for Matt. He owed that to Hunter, and as long as his body would hold out, he was on the move.

That thought began to show up on his face, or so it seemed to Pauline. She looked closely at him while he was watching the sky, and a tear formed in her eyes that at some point found its way down her wrinkled dry skin and dropped unnoticed on her chest. She wiped it briskly and pulled her hand away to finish her food. She was kidding herself to think that there was even a slight chance Paco would ever love her. It hurt her to resign herself to the fact that this part of her life was over. She had allowed some silly notion to plant a seed in her heart that maybe, just maybe, he would see how much she cared. And that it was time he settle down and take care of the tiny amount of time he had left in this world. But as she watched Paco, with his weathered face and beard, his gnarly hands and bent stature, she realized that what he said was true. He was a traveling man who lived for the road. And no woman, not even her, would be able to tie him down to any kind of normal life. She decided to just enjoy his presence for this one night and not allow that small crack in her heart to show ever again. She would remember one thing for the rest of her life, though—the touch of that worn out hand on hers.

CHAPTER 48

---✦---

THE PRESSURE WAS on for Frank to stay sober. He sat in his hotel room with his television on, sipping a glass of wine and nibbling on some nuts he'd picked up at the front desk. He wasn't used to being the one who was worried sick about a loved one. He could handle the stress of being a doctor, but he was falling apart sitting in the hotel room waiting for a call from Seth Billings.

Matt had been a tremendous help and support. In a way, he wished Matt could've been the one working on Ashley. But it wasn't going to happen so he had to trust the man on board. Seth seemed to know what he was doing and didn't seem overly concerned about Ashley's symptoms. The swelling needed to come down so she could be brought out of the coma. Then he would see what damage had occurred in her brain. The fear was building but he knew how to handle that. He drank the rest of his glass of wine and leaned his head back against the headboard. He needed a good stiff drink but he'd promised Leslie that he wouldn't go there. But she was on another floor of the hotel. She'd never know.

It was 11:00 and he was tired. He got up and hit the shower, letting the hot water run down his back. He felt so tense and nervous inside. He stayed in the shower for ten minutes and got out, dried off, and lay in bed thinking again. He reached for his phone to dial Matt's number and the phone rang.

"Hey, man. Just thinking of you. I know it's tough right now, Frank. But don't let it get the best of you. We'll know something in the morning and I don't want you up all night worrying. You need to me to come up and hang out with you for a while?"

"This is tough duty, Matt. Thought I'd handle it better than I am. I'm sipping on a glass of wine, watching some old movie. But my mind is on Ashley. How do you feel about it all? Any gut feelings?"

"Funny you should say that. I feel good about Seth Billings. I think the guy's sound and knows what he's doing. But a lot depends on how Ashley's brain takes the trauma. We just gotta wait through this night and there's no good way to do it."

"I'm finding that out, Matt. Believe me. Thanks for the call. I'll be up early if you want to meet me for breakfast in the cafeteria at the hospital. Say around 7:00?"

"I'll be there, friend. See you then! And Frank, put the wine up. Don't do it, man. Come on. This is the time for you to show Leslie you meant what you said to her."

Frank knew he was right. He sat on the edge of the bed rubbing his face. What a long night this was going to be. He decided to call Leslie's room to see if she was still awake. She answered on the second ring.

"Hello, Frank. I'm whispering because Avery's asleep."

"Sorry, honey. I was just checking to see if you were okay. I'm having a tough time tonight."

"That's putting it mildly. I don't know if I can sleep, Frank. I'm worried sick about Ashley. She's so small lying up there in that hospital bed alone. Wish I could have stayed with her."

"She doesn't know, honey. She doesn't know anything. That's a blessing, you know?"

"Yeah, I do. But it doesn't make it any easier."

"You want me to come down and stay with you tonight?" Maybe he was pushing it too far.

She hesitated. "Well, Avery is already asleep in my bed. I sure don't want to wake her up. She was crying the whole time she was taking a bath. Hard to explain to her what's going on in that room."

"I know, honey. It was just a thought. I'll be up early if you want to meet me in the hospital cafeteria. Matt's gonna be there early, too."

"I'll see how Avery's doing. I'm not gonna push her right now. If she sleeps in, then I'll hang around here until she wakes up. So don't wait on me, okay?"

"Okay, honey. Try and get some sleep."

"You do the same."

Frank walked into the bathroom and splashed cold water on his face. He looked at his reflection in the mirror and shook his head. He needed to get a grip. He moved into the bedroom and grabbed the bottle of wine. It felt so good in his hand. He smelled the wine and inhaled it deep into his body. It would be so easy to drink the whole bottle and slip into a deep sleep. That's exactly what he needed. To pass out and sleep until morning. No one would blame him. He'd have the perfect excuse. He picked up the wine glass and sat down on the bed. He poured a full glass and sat back against a pillow, leaning his head back against the bed. His hand was shaking. He wanted the wine so badly that he could hardly stand it. For a few minutes he just about talked himself into drinking it. His mouth was watering with the memory of how it burned going down his throat. He took one sip and suddenly he jumped up and ran to the sink and spit it out. He slung the glass against the wall and wine went everywhere. He grabbed the bottle and poured the rest of it down the bathroom sink and ran water to rinse it down.

He was sweating and his hands were shaking. He'd almost ruined what he and Matt hoped to accomplish. He had nearly lost the one chance he had to get Leslie and the girls back. What was he thinking? It wasn't worth losing everything he stood for.

He climbed into bed, drank a sip of cold water, and turned out the light. He turned the television off and pulled the covers up to his neck. It was going to be a long night, but he decided that he would face it like a man. It was time that he grew up and stopped the selfishness. He had to want a life more than he wanted the alcohol and drugs.

New to his body, the realization felt good to his heart. He gritted his teeth and tried to close his eyes. Sleep was elusive so he decided not to fight it. He just lay there in the dark listening to his heartbeat. But even though he would be worn out in the morning from the lack of sleep, at least he would be sober. His wife needed to see that more than anything else in the world. And his daughter who lay in a room alone, sleeping so deeply she wouldn't remember anything, deserved to have a sober father who could offer her the best life possible. The best care possible.

At 4:00 a.m. he finally fell into a fitful sleep. He dreamed crazy dreams and woke up sweating. But he was the happiest man alive when he stepped out of his shower. He'd shown himself he could beat the dragon that had such a hold on his life. It felt good but he knew he'd have to face it again and again until it left him alone. He was so ready for that change in his life. And he was going to do it if it killed him.

It was 8:00 a.m. and Seth Billings was riding the elevator to ICU. He could hear his shoes squishing on the recently waxed floors and could almost hear his own heart beating when he walked into Ashley's room. He had seen the results of the most recent MRI and CT scans and they had shown that the swelling was down and there was no bleeding at this time. Her brain had certainly had sufficient time to rest and start recovering from the extreme trauma. He wanted to bring her out of the coma but could not project any results on damage at this time. Her memory might be affected or her speech. There was no guarantee about anything at this point.

Frank, Matt, and Joe were sitting at the table in the cafeteria going over what they knew about Ashley's injuries and the test results. It seemed like things were improving as the hours passed.

"Man, what a rotten night's sleep! All I could think about was my sweet Ashley. Wondering how she's gonna be when they bring her out of that coma."

"I was the same way, Frank. Nothing's worse than waiting. Let's head upstairs to ICU and see what Seth says. I'm as anxious as you are to see how she is when she wakes up. Don't expect her to be a hundred percent. She's going have to come out of it in her own way. We just don't know what damage there might be. Have you prepared Leslie for that?"

"I tried to. But it's going be tough on her as a mother. No mother wants to see her child suffering. No parent does. This has really been a wakeup call for me, Matt. I've got to get my life on track and move forward in a big way for my family."

"I agree. This is the time and I'm as ready as you are for that. We're on a great journey, Frank. I can't wait to see what we do with this clinic I want us to open. We'll talk to Seth about it today if we get that kind of time with him."

When they walked into the Ashley's room it was dead quiet. Dr. Billings was standing at the foot of her bed looking at her chart and going over things with a nurse. He turned and saw Frank standing there, and just as he was about to speak, Leslie and Avery walked into the room. Brother Joe grabbed Avery and talked her into heading towards the newborn area of the hospital. She went reluctantly, but Joe knew it would be a good distraction for her while her sister was being taken care of.

"Good morning, guys. Glad you came up early. I was just about to bring Ashley out of her coma, but was trying to give you time to get up here. I want to preface this with a word to you, Frank, and Leslie. There are no promises of what we'll find when she wakes up. I want you to be prepared for anything, because that's exactly what we could face. With this kind of brain injury, we don't know what she'll be like when she wakes up. She may see you and cry, or talk. We just don't know. But be prepared in case she doesn't recognize you right off. It's not that uncommon."

Frank and Leslie nodded. "We've discussed this, Dr. Billings, for that very reason. It's not going to be easy seeing her like that, but we have tried to prepare ourselves for the worst. "

Frank hugged Leslie, who had tears running down her face.

"You guys stay back from the bed. I know you want to be near her, but we need to have some room to move around her. I'll let you get close to her once she has adjusted to being awake. It's going to take a little while so just relax. I don't want her to feel any tension in the room or see worried looks on your faces. Just smile and relax."

Seth started decreasing the amount of sedative and slowly brought it down to zero. Frank and Leslie sat down in chairs near the window and Matt sat on the window sill. The only sounds in the room were the nurse's shoes on the clean floor and all the machines monitoring Ashley. Seth was quiet but fully in charge. He was watching everything closely for any change, any reaction. After about twenty-five minutes she began to stir a little.

"Ashley, wake up, honey. It's Dr. Billings. I want you to try to open your eyes if you can. I know you are sleepy, but try to open your eyes."

Ashley didn't respond but lay there occasionally moving her hand or one foot. Her eyes fluttered a couple of times and Frank could tell she was trying to wake up. She was pretty drugged so it would take some time for her to become fully awake. Frank knew Leslie wanted her to just start talking but he had warned her against such hopes. Her waking up would come slowly. Every few minutes Seth would talk to Ashley, encouraging her to wake up. He rubbed her arms and legs and touched her face. Twenty more minutes went by and she finally began to stir. Her head went side to side as she struggled to wake up. She put her hand on her eyes and rubbed them.

"Watch her closely, Frank. We want to see some eye movement and when she opens her eyes, we are looking for recognition. She is not going to know where she is at first. She may not even remember the accident. Probably won't. So there will be some fear involved." Matt tried to reassure him so there wouldn't be an overreaction.

Frank nodded. He was watching closely, knowing this was a critical time. "Yeah, I am trying not to expect much when she first sees us."

Leslie was crying but kept it quiet. Seth had made it clear that he didn't want a lot of noise. He had moved to the other side of the bed as Ashley had turned her head towards the window. She opened her eyes for a moment and stared at Matt, and then she closed them again. It was minutes before she opened them up again. A tear rolled down her face and suddenly she began to cry. Her sobs were loud and agonizing to hear and Leslie jumped up to run towards her. Seth stopped her by grabbing her arms.

"Leslie, you have to keep it quiet. I know this upsets you but she's fine. We have to allow her to wake up and adjust. Some of the crying is from the sedative. Let's give her a few more minutes. Just relax."

Leslie sat back down and Frank put his arm around her. This was a tough time and they both needed to listen to Seth. Ashley opened her eyes again and stared at Matt. She smiled and then turned her head to Dr. Billings.

"Ashley, it's okay. You're in the hospital. You were in an accident but you are fine. Can you see me?" He asked her.

She slowly nodded. She looked at Matt again and smiled, opening her mouth to speak, but nothing came out. Matt got up and walked towards her slowly. He sat at the edge of the bed and put his hand on her forehead, smoothing her hair. Frank was at the foot of the bed with Leslie. She never took her eyes off Matt.

"Hey, sweet girl, are you feeling okay? It's good to see you smiling. You have a beautiful smile."

Ashley moved her hand to his and smiled again. Matt knew she thought he was Frank but he went along with it until she woke up completely. He didn't want to scare her. Seth moved Frank and Leslie out of the room with a quick explanation.

"Let's let her take this slowly. For some reason she is allowing Matt in, so let's go with that for a few minutes. I know this is tough on you, but she will come around. You have to be patient."

"Okay, Seth. But let us know when we can come back in. We are dying to hold her and comfort her. This is killing us." Frank was beside himself but was thankful.

It wasn't long before Matt came out. "Seth has suggested that we take a break and go eat something. She's fragile right now and needs to rest. He'll let us know when we can return to see her. Let's go eat something at the cafeteria and wait for his call."

Frank was sweating but he knew Seth was right. He glanced over at the closed door to Ashley's room. It took all of his strength to keep from running to her.

CHAPTER 49

———— ⚜ ————

Time felt like it was moving too slowly. I was sick of waiting, like Frank and Leslie. Without even really knowing the twins, I was feeling a lot of emotions sitting in the waiting room. We were hoping to hear from Seth Billings soon. I was more than ready to see Ashley again so we could work with her to get her to talk and get a better grasp on reality. I could see that she was struggling to remember. I had worked with adults before who'd had severe brain trauma. But this was only the second child I'd seen with this type of injury. Frank was beside himself and Leslie was about to lose it totally. The only thing holding her sanity was Avery, who seemed untouched by all the events.

We were sitting in a side room that had toys and coloring books in the corner for children. Avery was sitting across the room by herself, lost in her own world. She had her iPad and was playing games quietly. Frank and I were going over Ashley's injuries with Leslie. We were pretty lost in our own conversation, as Ashley had been the center of our conversation since the accident.

Avery had been pretty good about taking care of herself and seemed calm enough. I was wondering if she felt anything, being a twin. They were identical twins but with their own personalities. Both had beautiful long brown hair and features much like Leslie's. But they had Frank's black eyes. They were really brown but they were so dark they looked black. Sometimes twins are connected in a wonderful way. I would've loved to have gotten inside her head to see what she was thinking—how she was processing all of this.

Seth had not called so we were trying to be patient. I kept checking my watch and pacing back and forth. Finally Frank sat me down and we started going over our plans for the free clinic just to get our minds off of Ashley. Leslie excused herself and went to the bathroom so we just dove into our conversation, excited about the distraction. Ashley's door was not too far away and occasionally we glanced over at the door and checked the hallway to make sure we hadn't missed Seth. An hour passed with nothing consequential happening, and we were beginning to wonder what was taking so long. I was just about to get up and check Ashley's room when we heard laughter coming from the hallway. Leslie jumped up and looked at Frank.

"Did you hear that, honey? I just heard someone laughing."

"So did I! Who in the world would be laughing on this floor? The nurses are pretty quiet. The patients are too sick to laugh. Or near death."

"So what's going on? Matt, did you hear it?"

"Yeah, I sure did. Let's see what's going on."

We got up and walked into the hallway and stood outside Ashley's door. We heard some talking and pushed the door open slowly. Frank, Leslie and I were speechless. There sitting on Ashley's bed was Avery. They were both laughing. Laughing. We couldn't believe our eyes! Frank and Leslie rushed up to the bedside and Ashley looked at them and smiled.

"Hey, Mommy! Avery brought me the iPad to play some games! But I'm not too good at it right now."

Leslie hugged her daughter. "I'm so glad you know who I am, honey. How do you feel?"

"I'm sore, Momma. I want to go home. How did I break my arm? And where did I get all these cuts and bruises?"

"Honey, you were in a bad accident and—"

Seth walked in and interrupted us all. "What in the world is this? How did you get by the nurses' station?" But he smiled as he scolded us.

"Seth! She's awake. She knows what we're saying!"

I moved in to soften the blow. "Seth, we're sorry. But we were in the waiting room and heard laughter and came running in here to find Avery sitting on the bed talking to Ashley. How could we interrupt that?"

Seth laughed and scratched his head. "This is crazy! So, young lady, how do you feel? Do you know who everyone is in the room?"

Ashley was quiet. "Well, I know Mommy and Daddy. I'm not sure who he is." She pointed to Matt.

"I'm Matt, honey. Don't worry about me. You haven't known me very long."

"This is amazing! You look great. I'm so glad you feel better. Let's everyone get back from the bed and let me check her out."

We all moved back and watched the miracle happen. Ashley slowly sat up, but she was sore. Very sore. He laid her back down and asked her to count, spell her name, and a few other questions. It was amazing to see her come back to life. Seth was obviously blown away, but Avery just sat there and grinned.

"I knew she'd be all right, Mommy. I knew it. I told her last night to wake up. And she did!"

"Honey, we all are so thankful. But we need to let her rest." Leslie smiled at her two daughters.

"Your mother is right, Avery. We need to let Ashley rest. This is supposed to be a place for very sick people. I think Ashley is on the wrong floor!"

Frank and Leslie both were crying tears of joy. They were sitting on Ashley's bed watching in amazement. Seth broke the spell and hurried them out of the room.

"We need to allow her to rest now. I hate to break up the party and I'm thrilled with what I see. But we will need to run tests tomorrow to check her out thoroughly. Things are looking great, but we have to allow her plenty of time to rest."

I walked Avery out of the room and Frank and Leslie said goodnight to Ashley. It had been a long day and we all were pretty tired from the stress. When Frank walked out he knelt down and spoke to Avery.

"What did you say to her, honey, to bring her back? What made you go into the room alone?"

"I could feel her waking up. So I went in there and we looked at each other and started laughing. It was that simple. She just needed to see me."

Frank scratched his head. "That's amazing, honey. She loves you so much."

He stood up and looked at Leslie. "Can you believe it? She said she felt her waking up."

Leslie smiled and shook her head. "Frank. You got it all wrong. She said that to me last night. She said. 'Mommy, Ashley's waking up.'"

Seth was standing at the door of Ashley's room shaking his head. This was nothing short of a miracle. But those girls somehow communicated even when they were apart. I knew then that something remarkable had taken place that we couldn't explain. But another thought kept running through my worn out brain. It wouldn't be long before Frank and I would open a free clinic and I could be a doctor again. I was happy for Frank and his family. His daughter's life had been pulled back from the edge of death. I could relate. And my life was about to take a turn I never thought I would take again.

"Dr. Matt Collins." It had a nice ring to it. I hoped I could pull it off one more time.

On the day that Ashley came home from the hospital, we were all watchful as she adjusted to daily life again. There were blank spots in her memory that Leslie had to work on. Therapists were scheduled to come to the house for months to try to get her back to a normal level of understanding. She had gone through physical therapy and speech therapy to make sure all of those areas were right. There were only a few bandages remaining as a result of the injury. Her hair still had to grow back in where it was cut from the surgery. But she was young and bounced back quickly.

Frank and Leslie were awkward at first, not used to seeing each other under the same roof in a while. "Frank, I'm taking the upstairs bedroom so I can be near the girls. You have any objections?"

He smiled. "No, not at all. I'm just glad to have you all under the same roof again."

She couldn't help but smile. But it was a tiny one that I might have missed. Frank did not. I saw him breathe a small sigh of relief to see anything remotely close to a smile on her face. The strain between them was obvious. The barrier was like the Great Wall of China. I waited in the living room as Frank and Leslie took the girls upstairs and Leslie started their baths. Frank came down and fixed us both some fresh coffee, sitting in a chair next to the fireplace. He looked like he'd aged ten years since the accident.

"Frank, this has been an extremely stressful time for you and Leslie. I'm not going to stay long tonight. I just wanted to see Ashley's face when she walked into this house. It had to feel good to her to come back home."

"It's been helpful to me for you to be around, Matt. I really appreciate it and want you to know that. We've come a long way, buddy. When I look back to when you were in the hospital and I was working on your heart, it blows my mind what all has taken place since then. And now we're even talking about going into business together. It's nuts. It makes no sense but it feels so right."

I laughed. "I know what you mean, Frank. I want to give you plenty of time to get over Ashley's injury and recovery. You and I have a lot to discuss concerning this new venture, but we have to wait until you have the mental energy to give it your full attention. I do think, however, that it's something we both can sink our teeth into."

"I've already been thinking about it, believe it or not. I was skeptical when you first mentioned it, but now I'm looking forward to the planning stage. It might just be the change I need in my life. You know as well as I do that being a cardiologist carries a lot of stress. I love my patients, but it is nearly impossible to deal with the costs of malpractice insurance; not to mention that I'm still paying off my loans from medical school."

I couldn't help but laugh. "How well I remember those debts! This would be a totally different angle in our fields. We would be able to use our knowledge in this clinic and help those who are needy, or homeless. I want us to look at how we want to set the clinic up and what it would take to raise the money. Just what we talked about the other day at the hospital."

"I haven't been able to focus as much as I've wanted to on it, Matt. Now that things have a chance to settle down in my household, I'll have mental energy to put into helping you work this out. Nothing like this is being done in Destin and it's exciting to be pioneering such an endeavor. The need is obviously there. I'm behind it a hundred percent, Matt."

"That sounds good to me. As soon as you feel comfortable, let's get together and discuss all the ins and outs. We might also bring in Seth Billings to see if he's even remotely interested. I like that guy and we just might be surprised at his answer. He was involved with Westbury Clinic. And that was small scale compared to what I want us to do here."

"Just let me get on my feet here and I'll be able to dig in with you on this project. Thanks so much for coming home with us tonight. The girls are going to need some extra attention, so I'm going to cut this visit short, Matt. But you have been wonderful and I really appreciate it. Do you have a ride home?"

"Yeah, Joe is picking me up. He had some errands he had to take care of, and I bet he's sitting in your driveway now, waiting on me."

"Well, don't keep the man waiting. We need him to be on our side!"

"Talk to you soon, Frank. Tell the girls 'bye' for me."

I walked away feeling really good about the free clinic. And I also had an assuredness that Ashley was going to fully recover from her injuries. She was an amazing little girl and stronger than we had realized.

As I headed out the door I saw Joe sitting in the driveway with his head leaned back against the headrest. He was fast asleep. Worn out. The sight grabbed me a little as I realized again that Brother Joe was getting older. His hair was completely gray and he had developed some health issues that I was concerned about. He was still going out many nights feeding the homeless and covering those sleeping giants with coats and blankets. I owed him big time and felt good about developing this idea of the free clinic. I knew it would make him proud. It was also something I could write home about, which I planned to do as soon as I got back to my apartment. It would be refreshing to be able to share with my parents something positive about my life. I felt like they'd given up on my finding my life back. But this time I was going to prove them wrong.

Even though I was impressed with Ashley's remarkable recovery, I knew there would be things that would show up as time went on that were ramifications of the injury. Little things that might not be obvious at the moment. Frank was smart enough to figure them out. But it didn't hurt to have a neurologist as a good friend and it was about time for me to come back to life. All the training I had was bursting to get out. To be used again. My heart had come full circle and now it was time for me to busy myself with the healing of others. That was a huge part of my love for this free clinic. Frank was on board. Now I had to get Seth Billings to come alongside. This was going to be a day of redemption for us all when we opened the clinic. Especially for Frank and me.

I really needed to collect my thoughts before talking to Frank in detail about the clinic. It seemed to be a perfect fit for us, but there were some huge hurdles to cross. The fundraising seemed insurmountable. I knew nothing about that.

Yet if I looked back on my life, I felt like I had been heading toward this direction all along. All the experiences I'd come through, including living on a bench near the ocean, had set the stage for this free clinic. That's how sure I was about it. It was going to be difficult for Frank and Seth both to let go of their high paying jobs and take a lower salary to help so many people. It was a different mindset.

I decided to call Seth when I got back to my apartment. It wouldn't hurt to feel him out to see if I could get a read on how he was going to react to the idea of a free clinic. He might be so dug into his job that he would never dream of letting go. I had to find that out. Because if both doctors were not into this like I was, it wouldn't fly. There was power in the three of us. Singly, I would drown trying to accomplish it.

It had been a long day. Saying goodbye to Joe, I walked in, sat down on my sofa, and dialed the hospital number. After asking for Seth Billings I was suddenly talking to an answering machine. I left a short message for Seth and hung up, feeling a little let down. He'd call back soon enough. I guess I was anxious to get some reaction that would show me I was doing the right thing. It made sense to me, but I couldn't always count on that. But my gut was telling me it was right. And in medical school I was told by an old professor to always listen to my gut. This one time, no matter what hurdles I ran into, I was going to push through until something told me it was time to let it go.

It was too early to go to bed, but my head hit the pillow and I fell into a deep sleep. I dreamed I heard the clanking of a cleat against the mast of a large sailboat. I was jarred awake just in time to hear my cell phone ringing in the kitchen on the counter. I jumped up to answer it, nearly tripping on my shoes. I grabbed it off the counter and hit the green button.

"Hello? Hello?"

"Matt? It's Seth Billings. Sorry I missed your call! Everything okay?"

I felt like I had slept for hours and it had only been half an hour. My voice was deep. "Hey, Seth! Thanks for calling back, man. I just wanted to set up a time to talk to you whenever it's best for you. Is that possible? I know you're busy."

Seth laughed. "Sure, Matt. Sure. What's up? Anything I can help you with?"

"It's not a medical problem, which seems ironic, I'm sure. It's something bigger than that. Maybe lunch tomorrow, or dinner? Or you could come here to my apartment. Whichever is easiest for you."

"I'm off tomorrow night. I'll head your way around 7:00. How's that sound?"

"Perfect. My apartment is to the right of the parsonage near St. Luke's Presbyterian Church."

"I'll find you. See you at 7:00."

I hung up the phone, smiling, and went to the kitchen table with a pad and pen and wrote a long letter to my parents. I tried to explain in detail my hopes for the free clinic and the men I wanted to get involved with in this endeavor. My mind was racing and it was difficult for me to stay focused and tell it in a manner that would highlight what I was trying to accomplish. I so wanted them to be proud of me and excited about this vision. I knew not to hope too much, but it was something I was becoming very passionate about.

After finishing the letter, I sealed it in an envelope, addressed it, and headed out the door. I saw a light on at Joe's and knew we could have a bite together and discuss the day's adventures. He had never turned me down yet. When he opened the door we both smiled.

"It's not like you haven't seen me enough lately. How about a little bite of something and a good discussion on this free clinic before we hit the sack?"

"Sounds like a winner! I'll get the bread and make us a few sandwiches, and you pull up a chair and tell me what's on your mind. I was hoping you'd stop in for a talk before bed. I'm a bit wound up over Ashley and Avery's connection. That was a miracle if I ever saw one."

I smiled but didn't say a word. I was soaking up this old man I had grown to love, knowing my time with him was going to end at some point. It would not be the same when I moved out of that apartment. But at the same time, I was going to make him proud of me or die trying.

CHAPTER 50

⚜

Spring was a time for love. It was a time for new beginnings. Birds were singing and flowers were blooming. People were out cutting their grass, sending that fragrance through the air that brought back memories of childhood and long summer days.

Hunter was taking Holly to a local fair where vendors of a wide variety of gifts and accessories were selling their wares. Holly was excited because she was looking for a purse. Something not too expensive. Hunter was hoping for some jewelry, a ring, in particular. But Holly didn't know that. She'd agreed to marry him, but he wanted her to have an engagement ring. He was sort of old-fashioned and would like to see that on her hand. To know that she belonged to him. When she came out of her dorm her long auburn hair was blowing in the wind and there was lightness in her step.

"Hey, girl! You excited about today?"

"I couldn't wait! It's a toss-up because I would love to spend time outside, but I really need a purse. You are so sweet to take me to this. I know this type of thing isn't your fave."

Hunter laughed and brushed his thick brown hair back off his face. A haircut was warranted. But today he just didn't care.

"I'm looking forward to it, Holly. I have some things I'll be looking for, too, so I promise you I'm not dreading it at all. And I get to spend an afternoon with you. How bad could that be?"

She blushed. His love was so obvious. "Are Jake and Paula going with us?"

"No, they backed out at the last minute. It would've been nice to have them around, but you and I do fine alone. Don't ya think?"

"Oh yeah. Like we don't spend enough time together. We nearly failed that last bone test. And I needed an A fiercely."

"You're doing fine. Don't give it a second thought. Anatomy isn't that difficult; nothing compared to physics and chemistry. My brain is fried over those tests."

"Do you realize how many tests we have ahead of us? It's mind boggling. Okay. Where are we going first? Which building?"

"Let's head for the art center. I want to look for a few things before we look for purses. Do you mind, Holly?"

"No! I'm going to enjoy this no matter what we're shopping for. Man, it's crowded. I had no idea it was going to be such a big deal. Did you see the cars lined up around the buildings? Both parking lots were slammed."

"Sure did. Amazing. This should be good. Let's get some coffee and get started."

An hour later, wading through the crowds, Hunter located a jeweler who had some magnificent diamond rings. He didn't have a lot of money but he could finance it if they would agree. Holly had meandered across the room and they promised to text when they were ready to change buildings. He studied the ring and listened as he was told about the platinum over silver band and prongs. He was impressed with the clarity of the stone and he was already leaning towards one of the rings that had a simple setting. Holly didn't like a lot of bling so this one ring would be perfect. He'd brought some money his mother had left him and hoped it was enough to buy something decent for her. After about twenty minutes of negotiating the shop owner came down enough for Hunter to pay cash for the ring. He was so excited he could hardly breathe. He had just purchased an engagement ring.

His phone vibrated in his pocket and he looked across the room to see if he could find Holly. That was not easy because there were at least three hundred people in this huge center. They were like ants on an ant hill. In fact, once he moved out of his spot near the table, there were fifty people waiting to get it. He could feel his blood pressure rising as he tried to get to her. She'd texted that she was by the Louis Vuitton purses but he had no idea where that was. It took another twenty minutes to push his way over to the other side of the room. Suddenly he caught a glimpse of her hair. When he spotted her he yelled her name out above all the noise and she looked his way and smiled the biggest grin he'd ever seen. He waved and pointed towards the door. She nodded and started pushing her way through the crowd.

Hunter moved outside the door and waited for her to arrive. When she came out she was sweating and flustered. She'd seen a purse she wanted but there were a hundred other women grabbing for it. "It was a joke!" She told him. She was miserable so he suggested that they head towards an eatery and order something they could eat outside.

"I know you're frustrated, honey; there were a lot more people in that building than I ever thought would be here today. Good gosh! I've never seen so many people grabbing at things in my life! Are you okay?"

"Yeah. I agree with you. Too many people. But I did like that purse." She winked at him and looked at the menu.

"Let's get our meal ordered and head over to those tables under the trees in the shade. It's lovely outside and we could use some fresh air."

They carried their lunch over to a table underneath some trees. There was a gentle breeze blowing and it was a perfect day to be outside. He was excited about the ring, but wanted to wait a little bit before he gave it to her.

"Have you found out anything more about your father?"

"What made you ask that now?"

"Oh, I was just thinking about my family; how much they mean to me. Your mom is gone. All you have is your Aunt Jenny."

"Well, I've found nothing, but Paco did run into a few important clues. I shared with you about the Westbury Clinic where he found my father's photo on the wall. That was exciting to me and it made him more real. But I want to meet him face to face. That is something I think about a lot."

"I can see why. I'd like to meet him, too. Have you heard from Paco in a while?"

"No. I was hoping I would hear something pretty soon. He's no spring chicken, you know? I sure hope he finds something before it's too late. I have no idea where Matt Collins is. But somehow I feel we'll meet him one day. Maybe because I want it so badly."

They both ate quietly for a few minutes and then Hunter pulled out a box and sat it on the table. He was grinning but tried to hold it back. She raised her eyebrow and stared at him.

"What have you done?"

Hunter swallowed a huge bite of brownie. "What? I'm not doing anything."

"You did so! What is that box?"

"It's nothing. Just relax."

"How can I relax when you put that right in front of me! Do I get to open it?"

"I guess so. That is, if you want to." He was really making her fidget.

"Okay. I'm gonna open it, but you weren't supposed to buy me anything. We promised each other that we would not spend any money on gifts for a while. We overdid it at Christmas. Remember?"

"This is different, Holly." His voice was steady.

Holly sat up and looked at him squarely. "What do you mean 'different'?"

"You'll see. Open the box."

Holly reached over and touched the box. She picked it up and her stomach went into her throat. It was a small box. She knew it had to be something small. Like a ring. She opened it and screamed. Some people near them looked around, staring.

"Oh, my gosh! Look what you did! I can't believe this, Hunter. It's beautiful."

Hunter scooted over next to her and wrapped his arms around her. He pulled her close and whispered in her ear.

"Will you be my wife? Will you marry me someday soon?"

Tears streamed down her face. "I'll marry you, baby. I love you. You have to absolutely be the sweetest man in the world. How did you pick this out?"

Hunter was grinning like a cat. "I'm so excited that you like it. One of the jewelers here sold it to me. It seemed perfect for you."

"I love the setting and look, it fits!"

"That's a relief! It was a guess. But I heard you talking to your sister about rings and I thought I remembered you saying you wore a five."

"So you heard that, huh? I think your hearing is selective!"

Hunter laughed. "That's a guy thing, I think." He paused to look at her eyes. "You about through eating?"

"Yeah. Let's get outta here."

It was getting late and Hunter knew he needed to get back to his room. They were piled up on the sofa watching an old movie, eating popcorn and drinking a beer. The room was a mess and it looked like they'd eaten everything in the kitchen. Holly's favorite quilt was pulled up over the two of them, and Hunter was yawning every ten seconds.

"Man, don't know why I'm so tired, but I've sure enjoyed our day. We need to talk, though, Holly. That is, if you can stop eating."

She hit him over the head with a pillow and laughed. "Hush! What do we need to talk about? And by the way, I love my ring."

Hunter smiled. "We need to talk about our wedding. Where we want to go. How we want it to be."

"Not too soon for that?"

"No. Not one bit. Don't you have some ideas of how you want it to be? Any dreams of a wedding?"

"Not really. Didn't plan on it happening at this point. Wanted to get through medical school, you know?"

"Me. too. But then I saw you."

"Stop. You're being silly."

"No. It's true. I saw you and I fell in love. It was sick."

Holly blushed. "Hunter, that just doesn't happen. I've read about such things but it doesn't happen in real life."

"Bingo. It just did. Hello?"

"I know you say that, but you don't just love someone without knowing them."

"I did. First time in my life, ever. But it came fast and hard. I knew you were the one."

"How could you know that? Huh? Tell me!"

"I knew by looking at your hair, how it blows in the wind. How it shines. Your eyes. Man, I'm embarrassing myself. You don't want to hear this."

"Yes, I do. Did you really love me that quick? 'Cause it took me about a month to grab who you were inside. I liked you right off. But I didn't get you until after about a month. Then it was easy to fall in love with you."

"A month? Damn! Well, I wasn't looking for it. I never knew how it would feel and sure didn't think it would happen like it did. You're amazing. I knew we would be a perfect fit."

She snuggled up to him and laid her head on his shoulder. He felt so strong but he really had a very sensitive side. "I think you're pretty amazing, too. Except in anatomy. You really need to get a grip."

He pushed her away and fell out laughing. "Oh, you talk big. Now tell me where you'd like to go on your honeymoon. Let's daydream a little."

"Well, for one thing, we won't have a lot of money so we can't go too far. I love the mountains. What do you think about the mountains?"

Hunter frowned. "Well, I was sort of thinking about the ocean. Sorry, Holly. I've always wanted to go to the coast."

She scrunched up her nose but when she saw the look in his eyes, she nodded. "That's perfect, baby. The coast it is. Where exactly were you thinking? New Orleans? I've heard a lot about that place. Sounded pretty rough."

"Nah. Not New Orleans. I was really thinking about Destin or Pensacola. I've read that the beaches are white as snow."

"Sounds lovely. Let's get some brochures and start looking. Won't hurt to look. It sort of makes it more real, you know?"

"Yeah. We will have to find a place to stay. But that won't be difficult. I'm getting excited now. This will be fun, Holly. If we can ever figure out how to get away from school long enough for a long weekend."

"Yeah, it will. But we can do it. We got plenty of time to plan. Honey, you better head back to your dorm. It's getting really late and we both have to get up early."

Hunter frowned but got up, throwing the quilt on the floor. "It's been so nice today. I hate to end it. But I need a hug before I leave."

She stood up on her tiptoes and wrapped her arms around his neck. "Baby, I love you. Thank you so much for the beautiful ring. I will never take it off. See you tomorrow, okay?"

He kissed her and held her tight. It felt good to almost be a family. He had a dream about their wedding but he decided not to voice it now. It might ruin the moment.

"Night, babe. See you in the morning. Sleep well."

CHAPTER 51

※

As SETH BILLINGS crossed the Bridge into Destin, the view of the Emerald Coast presented itself to Seth's work-fatigued eyes like a post-card from a tropical paradise. He had forgotten how great it felt to be in a town where beach and harbor combined into the perfect vacation spot. The fishing village sign at the start of the bridge hit his heart like a tiny javelin. Checking the time on his Rolex watch, he saw he was just going to make his appointment with Matt Collins on time.

His SL500 made the trip in from Pensacola a real pleasure. Seth enjoyed the finer things in life. His career had been calculated every step of the way to allow his talents to maximize the lifestyle he had always wanted. The kind his dad would be proud of. Seth came from a wealthy family and was now generating wealth of his own. However, there was a difference between him and his father; he actually had a heart.

He was taken aback when he saw the tiny apartment to the right of the parsonage. He climbed the steps and rang the bell. Matt greeted him warmly and walked him into the living room. Matt had made fresh cof-fee and the aroma grabbed Seth as he looked quickly around the small apartment.

He took the leather chair next to the sofa and the two men wrestled through some small talk.

"Frank is permitting me to speak on his behalf for the remainder of this meeting. He is very busy at home these days. Ashley, as you know, continues to recover nicely from the near tragedy. And he is working feverishly to reunite his family. We are intent on opening a clinic in this area, which is one of the things I want to discuss with you, Seth. It's a new kind of clinic for this area and I want to model it after Westbury

Clinic, where I did some work early in my career. I think you recalled that clinic the other day when we first met. I was surprised that you had a part in it. The need here is great and trends indicate the need will continue to grow well into the next decade." Matt paused, taking another sip of coffee. He was watching for Seth's reaction.

"I do remember Westbury Clinic, Matt, and was impressed with your work there, as I mentioned the other day. This sounds exciting!"

"The fee schedule will be free for homeless patients and services will be offered on a sliding scale to poor families in the area. Our funding will be largely from private contributors as well as funds that the government will allocate to us. The pharmaceutical companies will also cover any shortfalls we experience in the beginning. One of the primary missions has to be providing medical care for homeless people."

"I know there must be a great need for that. I live in another world. But every city has a lower end of society that struggles with basic needs."

"They are not a target group for any major facility in the area for obvious reasons, but I can tell you from experience the need is great. Frank and I are committed to its success and would love to have you on board with us. I might add that the work will be quite thankless and it is not the kind of lucrative venture you're accustomed to. It is my intention to assemble a team of highly trained and respected clinicians, all of them committed to healing and ministering to the needs of the people who have already fallen through the cracks of society. They have no resources, no voice. No voting power. Most will never again know the love of their families. Their days are filled with humiliation, and the load they carry is the daily reminder of every mistake they have ever made. They are unpredictable and not capable of genuine gratitude. In short, it's a very low pay, very thankless job. Your only reward for a job well done will be the reflection you see in the mirror at night and the knowledge that your day was spent helping those who are incapable of helping themselves."

Seth nodded, realizing that this conversation wasn't quite what he expected, but he was impressed with Matt's proposal and was curiously enjoying the knowledge this man had not just of the medical world but of the many homeless in the Emerald Coast area.

Matt continued. "I picked you because I saw something in your eyes when you worked on Ashley. Our profession has made cynics out of the best of us. We are all so careful navigating fee schedules and insurance plans, keeping up with the growing market created by the drug companies who advertise in a way that is aimed directly at patients. What I'm offering is a return to the fundamental care that once marked our profession. We will be asked to perform procedures knowing the pay won't be there. But we'll be helping people. No one can ever again accuse us of selling out for money. We'll be in a position to do research not fettered by the political views of the party in power. Man, I want to take you out to where these men live. They walk between public showers and soup kitchens. The lucky ones have bikes and tents. The street's a terrible place to get sick! You can't go home and soak your feet after a bug bite; the police keep you moving."

Seth was overwhelmed with all this information. "Matt, you have a lot of passion for this project. It's obvious this is something you've given a lot of thought. And I know what you're saying is true."

"You may ask yourself who could get into a position like that? Or who could be so dumb as to lose everything? You may wonder what kind of man lives in a condition that is not much better than an animal? I'll tell you what kind of man gets into a spot like that. Because that kind of man just welcomed you into his home and poured your coffee!"

Seth stared at Matt, shaking his head, trying to grasp what he'd just said. "You mean you? You were homeless?"

"Yes, it's true! Until a few weeks ago I was that man! Had it not been for the kindness of a man by the name of Joseph Mason, I might still be out there. Or worse yet, perhaps even dead. I got myself so far out there I thought I was never coming back. My friends and people who went to the same church couldn't even help because I didn't have the courage to be honest about my predicament."

Matt handed him a copy of a Sunday paper and pointed to an editorial column. Seth put on his glasses and read the column, shaking his head in disbelief. "*We need to clean our streets of the homeless and vagrants before the tourists arrive.*" He removed his Cazal-framed glasses and put one earpiece between his teeth, chewing on it nervously. His stare told Matt that there was a lot of action going on inside his head.

"Matt, I . . ." He paused, choking with emotion. "I had no idea."

"No one did, no one at all. Not even my family. Seth, we live in a place so profoundly prosperous that being poor feels like you committed a crime, being broke feels like a misdemeanor, and losing the power to take care of yourself feels like a felony."

Seth stood up as if he could take no more. "Matt, you have presented a very compelling case. I'm speechless hearing of your own personal suffering and I'm trying to grasp that you're on your way back up as we speak. I hope that you and Frank are successful in this endeavor. As for me, I have so much to think about. I have a life, a mortgage. This would require such a . . . ." His words halted and his voice trailed as his eyes teared up.

Matt spoke up again. "Is the word you're looking for 'sacrifice'?"

"Why, yes, Matt. I would have to uproot my family; my kids would share in the price tag of this venture. My wife has a lifestyle that needs maintenance."

Matt was hoping for a more immediate positive response from Seth. But he knew how large a sacrifice Seth would have to make. He extended his hand to Seth with a smile.

"Can I ask you to simply think about it? Maybe you could support us in a conciliatory fashion, or as an investor? All I ask is that you follow your heart. It's something you would be able to sink your teeth into, Seth. It reminds me of the oath we took when we became doctors."

Matt walked Seth to the door. "Thanks for coming by, Seth. It meant a lot to me."

Seth paused at the door and turned to Matt, smiling. "I assure you that I will, indeed, think about it. Even though the whole concept seems foreign to me, Matt, I want you to know that if I come in, I can only come in with both barrels blazing. If you receive any support from me it will be my full support or none at all. I assure you of that; it's just the way I am. I can't sit back and offer a check on occasion. The need is simply too great. But if my answer is no, I will work day and night to find the man who can say yes. Agreed?"

"Agreed! Thanks again for your time."

"Thank you, Matt, for your offer. And thanks for sharing your story."

The two shook hands for a final time and mutually promised to revisit the issue at a later date.

Matt returned to his leather chair and dropped into it a little frustrated. He had hoped that Seth would have been more receptive to his cry for help. He stood up, went to his closet, and threw on his leather coat. He headed towards the street as he looked back and peeked into Joe's window. As he peered in, he saw Joe seated at his kitchen table, his hands folded and head bowed. Matt realized he was probably praying, so he turned and headed for the highway on foot. He dodged a little traffic and crossed over and walked down the sidewalk. He soon arrived near his old familiar bench.

The overlook by the harbor was almost a sacred spot. Matt reached in his pocket and took out a piece of gum, his new favorite thing to do. Smoking cigarettes, like the booze, was simply a habit he could no longer accept. As the minty freshness filled his mouth he began to wonder why the heart attack hadn't taken his life. He wondered if the world would be different had he succumbed to his failing heart. How had he made a difference? While Matt was lost in thought, a shadow drew up the walkway to his hideout. He could tell from the sound of the tennis shoes and the pace of the steps that it was Joe on his nightly rounds. As Joe turned the corner near the decking he seemed almost startled to see his younger friend on the old familiar bench.

"Son! What are you doing out here? You surprised me. Is everything okay?"

Matt looked up at Joe and smiled a slow smile. "Sure, Joe. Have a seat. Just sitting here thinking about life."

"Bet you did plenty of that all those nights you were out here in the dark."

"Yeah, I did. I just hope I can pull off this clinic, Joe. I really want it to happen. Haven't wanted anything to happen like this in a long time. It feels good, you know?"

"I can see why it would, Matt. You would be getting your feet wet again in the area of work that you love. You would feel alive again. I want that for you."

"I want it, too. Seth Billings didn't jump on board like I thought he would. But he does have to think about making a sacrifice like that. To me it is a step up. It's a different ball game for him and Frank. They both would take huge cuts in salaries and they have families to take care of. I am being selfish to think they would want this as much as I do. I'm not making any sacrifice at all. Do I need to rethink this whole thing, Joe?"

"I'm not sure, Matt. It is a sacrifice for them, but also a lot more rewarding than the practices they have now. It depends on what they call 'rewarding'. And where their heart is. Remember you were on a park bench drinking your life away less than a year ago. You didn't care whether you lived or died. Now you want to save the other sleeping giants out here. That's quite a jump."

"I would like to make a difference in some way. Just have to figure out how."

Joe got up and walked to the end of the decking and pointed towards the sea. "Matt, there is one huge body of water out there. When you look out to sea, it almost seems like there is no beginning and no end."

Matt smiled. Joe tried to be so subtle in his delivery. But Matt knew exactly what he was getting at. He waved goodbye to his dear friend and sat back down on his bench. He had a lot of thinking left to do. And the night was young. The decision to open a free clinic was a noble thing, but it went beyond that for Matt. He knew what it was like to sit outside alone with unending days ahead and no hope, no chance of moving up. He sighed and thought about the two men he wanted to include in this endeavor. He hoped they had a difficult time letting this idea go. He hoped it ripped at their heart. And he hoped the free clinic would rise up and help those men that most people pass without a thought. Liked they used to pass him.

CHAPTER 52

⚜

MATTHEW HAMILTON WAS a short, stocky, suntanned, hot-tempered man who always wore a hat with a small brim and a white t-shirt with the sleeves cut out. His jeans were torn and baggy, and he had a slight limp. He was known around town as one of the toughest men to work for, but somehow when he interviewed Paco, they hit it off immediately. The work was steady and the pay was acceptable. Paco was ready to dig in for a few weeks and make some good money. He had no idea where he was headed next in his search for Matt. But he knew he would need some money if he wanted to continue his travels. He was tired and his chest felt tight most of the time. But he never let on to Matthew that he had any health issues at all. That wouldn't do on a construction job.

The rooms they worked on were decked out to the nines. The first one Paco saw took his breath away, and at first glance he didn't see anything wrong. But after he stepped inside the bathroom he saw how the tile floor had cracked in too many places. Matthew was a perfectionist and was told that he had an open line of credit to use to put the room back to its original condition. There were new drapes to hang in the bedroom, new tile to lay, new carpet to put down, and a lot of painting. Matthew was a man of few words, so Paco had plenty of time to think while he was on the job. They worked all morning and took thirty minutes for lunch.

"You been here long, Paco?"

Paco swallowed half his water before answering. He never wanted to appear like he was in a hurry to answer. "Nah. Just about a week, really. Heading down the coast but I needed a good job for a while. Kinda like it here. How long you been here?"

"Twenty years. And I've seen a lot of people come and go. So don't ya get too settled 'cause it's tough makin' a living."

Paco chuckled. The guy was pretty tight with his words. "I don't plan on settlin' down here or nuthin'. Just want to make a little money. I been lookin' for a fella and I'm havin' a heck of a time locating him."

"What's his name?"

"Matt Collins. A doctor."

Matthew laughed loudly and swallowed a huge bite of his second sandwich. "Like the name."

"I bet you do. He's got a son he doesn't know about. Sure would like to tell him about it."

"Whoa. That's news you might not want to be carrying around. No tellling what kind of reaction you might get."

"Not too worried 'bout that. But the boy needs to know who his dad is. He's dyin' to know. All I want to do is bring the information to Matt Collins. He can do with it what he wants."

Matthew rubbed his beard. "Careful, dude. You're no spring chicken. Let's get back to work."

Paco swallowed his last bite, threw away his trash, and headed towards the bathroom to start laying the tile. By three o'clock he was covered in dust and his back was hurting. He just kept on going because Matthew was not going to stop until the bathroom was done. There wasn't room for both of them, so Matthew cut the smaller tiles for Paco and helped finish the shoe mold. Paco spotted a crack in the bathtub but Matthew said it wasn't bad enough to replace.

"How long you been out on the road, Paco?" That question came out of thin air.

"Oh, 'bout twenty years, I think. I lose track of time, ya know. Don't even have a watch, but I do have a cell phone, so I guess there's no excuse for not knowin' what day it is."

"I can't imagine not having a roof over my head, man. What do you do when it rains?"

"I get out of the rain." Paco laughed.

The question reminded him of Pauline, but he kept working until both men were outside of the bathroom admiring the new tile floor. Paco spotted what appeared to be a white thread and he bent over, reaching as far as he could to retrieve the thread without stepping on the tile. He grunted and groaned as he pulled the offensive oversight from the grout and eyeballed the grout to make sure he hadn't displaced any. When he stood up, dust billowed around him like a cloud.

"Well let's call it a day! Should dry overnight and you can sponge it down when you get here in the morning. Wanna grab a beer?"

"No! I got to be gettin' back to my room; it's been a long day." The dusty vagabond walked down the elevator to head home.

As the elevator descended Paco shook his head and the white powder from the grout fell from his hair. *Why was I saying no to a beer after working all day?* He had been dragging lately and really wasn't himself. As the elevator opened, Paco wandered through the sliding elevator doors. He had his hand in his pockets and felt two quarters tucked away with some lint. As he passed the slot machines he'd gotten familiar with each day after work, he put a quarter in one of the machines and it bleeped and binged. The monitor read "Sorry, not a winner! Try again!" Without thinking he put another quarter in and hit the spin button. There was a loud metallic crack, a series of loud bells, and a red light that looked like it was off a cop car from the '60s started spinning. Paco felt like he'd stolen something and the quarters started flooding out before he even realized what happened.

The big red "jackpot" sign was flashing and the quarters now filled the tray at the bottom of the machine and were still flowing. Paco quickly looked around for a bucket that would hold his winnings and grabbed one by his chair. He'd never seen so much money in his life. The money began bouncing off the multi-colored carpet in the lobby. Paco knelt in front of the machine and threw handfuls of quarters into a bucket. Glancing up, he noticed a security guard who at first looked like he was going to help him retrieve his winnings. The security guard was tall and lanky with hair that looked wet. It was plastered to his head and he had a receding hairline that made him look older than he was. He wore a maroon sport coat with the casino emblem on the breast pocket. He was taller than Paco by about four inches but thin as a reed. He had deep brown eyes that stood out from his well-tanned skin. He carried a two-way radio in his left hand the way a man would brandish a weapon.

Paco was bubbling with excitement as he stood up to greet the security man while surveying the carpet for stray quarters.

"Hey, man. Guess you saw me win this thing. First time for me!"

Jerry Stone spoke with robot clarity. "Congratulations on your win!"

The two men faced each other and then Jerry put the radio to his mouth and pressed the button to speak.

"This is Officer Stone and I have a possible 11-49 by the quarter slots."

Time stood on end as Paco was feverishly dreaming of the ways he would spend his new windfall. But he wondered what an 11-49 was. The two were soon joined by a heavyset guy named Al Peterson who was wearing the same jacket as Jerry.

"Watcha got, Jerry?

"This gentleman just hit the jackpot. And from the looks of things he's an employee of the casino."

Al reached over and offered to take the bucket of quarters from Paco's hands and Paco resisted the temptation to surrender his new-found wealth to the heavy set guy. At this point Matthew was making his way through the casino to the parking lot and noticed some commotion between Paco and the security guard. He slowly sauntered over.

"What's going on over here?" Matthew was worried that his new employee was making a fuss that could ruin their job opportunity.

Jerry spoke first. "This man just hit the jackpot and he's dressed in work clothes."

"So is there a dress code for winning?" Matthew asked in a matter-of-fact tone.

The short guard interrupted. "This casino has a rule that no employee of the casino is allowed to gamble."

Matthew smiled, relieved. "Gentlemen, this man is a friend of mine working for me on the remodel job upstairs. I'm an independent contractor; I'm not a casino employee and neither is Paco."

Paco didn't dare breathe. His tiny fortune hung in the balance as the men debated. The two guards looked at each other and stepped back a few steps conferring about the matter. Jerry talked on his radio then shrugged and listened to the garbled response. He stepped forward and stretched out his hand.

"Congratulations, sir! You've hit the jackpot today! May I cash out your quarters for you?"

Paco hugged the bucket and frowned. "No, I'm all right. I'll take them just like this."

Matthew encouraged Paco to cash out at a nearby window but he was intent on getting out of there with his money and wanted to leave before someone else threatened his winnings. So he carried the heavy bucket to the entrance, where he jumped in the first cab and headed for the Sundowner Motel. Later that night he and Pauline sat in his room and stacked quarters all over the room. After the taxi ride his winnings totaled seven hundred eighty-three dollars. More money than he'd had in his possession for as long as he could remember.

Paco grinned as he looked over at Pauline. "All in a day's work."

The two laughed and Pauline opened a beer and took a sip. "Paco, what are you going to do with all this loot?"

Paco sat back in his chair dreamily. "I'm gonna take you out for a big steak dinner. Then I'm gonna set aside a couple hundred dollars for findin' Matt Collins."

"I think you're obsessed with finding that guy. You talk about finding him every day, yet you're not really looking."

Pauline's words stung Paco yet he continued to listen. "If you really want to find this guy you need to have a plan. Then you need to work your plan. I'll be happy to help you but I'm also a little surprised you won't use any of that money toward improving your health. You need a doctor. Sweetie, I been cleaning up after you for over a week now and I know you been coughing up blood, and it's getting hard for you to hide from everyone just how sick you are."

Paco looked at Pauline. "You know, you're right. I have to make a plan and stick to it. I know what I've got to do."

"What is that, honey?"

"I'm gonna put an ad in the paper and have Matt Collins call me here."

"What about your health?"

Paco got up and patted Pauline on the back and went and retrieved his first beer. "It will pass darlin', it always does."

Pauline could hardly believe her ears. She rolled her eyes and simply dropped the subject, as she saw that he had a brick wall around him that wasn't coming down any time soon. Men like him came and went; they were out on the street for life and nothing was going to change that. Paco was intelligent and she liked that about him. But he didn't want to use his knowledge to keep himself alive. She knew he was a sick man, but if he wanted to pretend that everything was hunky dory then that was his prerogative.

As she headed towards the kitchen to make some hot coffee she glanced at him counting his win. *It would have been nice to reel him in. He'd have made a great dance partner. But my dance card has been empty for so many years I've forgotten where I put it. I would've liked that chance just one more time.* She'd always loved fishing, but she faced the glaring fact that this one fish was going to become that great fish that got away.

CHAPTER 53

⚜

I WAS GETTING ready to head over to RT's to pick up a little money doing a quick gig when the phone rang. I looked at my watch. It was early yet and I had plenty of time before we played. I was broke and needed the money badly, and Paul was really patient about my coming and going. He knew I wouldn't be there long so he was just allowing us to enjoy our friendship and play together. I owed him big time.

"Hello?"

"Matt? Les here. Hope I didn't catch you at a bad time."

I was surprised but smiling. "No way. Going to work shortly but we have plenty of time to talk. What's up?"

"Nothing really. But after you called the other night I got to thinking about you and thought I'd call and see how you were. Really."

I felt my heartbeat pick up. "I'm okay, Les. Been through a pretty tough time in my life but am coming out of it slowly."

"I sensed that when we talked earlier, and I just need to know you're really okay. We are brothers, ya know. Even though we haven't talked that much over the years I do care about you. Are you okay, Matt? What's going on in your life?"

Now I had a lump in my throat that wouldn't go down if I drank the ocean. "Well, where do I start? No one really knows what I've been through, Les. I've kept it to myself pretty much. Not something I really want out. I'm not too proud of this time in my life."

"You know I'll keep it quiet. Mom and Dad will never hear about this conversation. I give you my word."

I paused, wondering if I should just keep things surface. I knew he meant well, but what I had to tell him wasn't going to be easy to take. Unless he already guessed my situation.

"Les, you were around when I left Philadelphia. You knew then that I was in trouble. My life was spiraling downhill fast. I had nowhere to turn so I left town as fast as I could. I meandered around and lived on the streets for quite a while. This may come as a shock to you but my drinking got worse after I left there."

Quiet on the other end of the line. "That is upsetting to hear, Matt. I had surmised this but had no way of confirming that my feelings were correct. Why didn't you call me?"

"What was I going to say, Les? 'Come and get me, I've turned into a drunk'? I was ashamed about my addiction and didn't know how to get out of it. I also fought the urge to drink and after awhile just gave in to it. I lived to drink. That pretty much sums it up."

"So you headed south and ended up in Destin?"

"Yeah, pretty much. It's been a wild ride here. Living on the street was no piece of cake, Les. I have a whole new opinion of the homeless now. I've been one of them, and it's one of the toughest things I've ever done. Even after making it through medical school."

"It hurts me to think you've lived outside all this time."

"Well, I met someone quite a few months ago and he changed the direction of my life. After my heart attack I went back to the park bench. I could've died out there, Les. Easily. But this man is a pastor and went out at night to help the homeless. I was one of those men. He finally met me face to face at the Coffee House and we had breakfast together. He asked me if I needed a place to stay and after lying to him, I finally agreed that I was homeless. It was a hard thing to admit. I now have an apartment to live in and every morning I eat breakfast with this wonderful gentleman. His name is Brother Joe."

"Wow, sounds like a cool guy. So how is your health now?"

"I'm better. Avoided open heart surgery. But I got a long way to go, brother. I'm digging my way back to a life. I've met up with a cardio doctor who is going to open a free clinic with me. We haven't worked out the details but we are both in this together. I've tried recently to pull in another surgeon, and he is giving it some thought. Pretty exciting stuff."

"It sounds like it. Need any help with the fundraising? I'm pretty savvy at that."

I was astounded by that news. "What? That's crazy. Of course I need your help! Never thought I would be talking about this to you in the first place. I had no idea you were good at fundraising, Les."

"There's a lot you don't know about me. But we can catch up on me later. I am glad to hear that your health is improving. Probably helped just to have a roof over your head. It removed a lot of stress, right?"

"Yeah, and spending time with Brother Joe is amazing. You'd love this guy. He's very real and knows more than most men I know."

Les fell out laughing. It was great to hear his laugh again. "I got ya. You need to let me know more about this free clinic so I can put together a proposal for the fundraising. I'd really like to help you, Matt."

"Thanks, Les. Say, I have something else to talk to you about. Do you need to go or do you have time to discuss something else?"

"Shoot it by me, brother. Since I haven't talked to you in years, what are a few more minutes!"

I wasn't quite sure how to bring it up. It occurred to me that Les might be offended by my bringing up something from the past that was so ugly. So frightening.

"I've got something to talk to you about and you have to be honest with me. I had a dream the other night and it was very disturbing. After I woke up I realized it was not just a dream, but reality. Do you remember when we went out fishing with Uncle Jed?"

Silence on the other end. Then Les cleared his throat. "Uh, yeah. I remember that clear as day. How could I forget, man?"

"It was so weird, Les. I mean, I guess I'd shoved this event out of my mind completely until I had this awful dream. He was drinking and fell over the side of the boat. You and I tried so hard to see where he was and to get to him, but we couldn't. It was a nightmare. I dreamed mother blamed me for you having a beer and for his death, actually. Is that how you recall it, Les?"

"Matt, it does us no good to rehash this horrible event. But yes, that's what happened. I never understood why you got blamed for it. Mother was always blaming you. Maybe because you were a lot like Dad, and they had a tumultuous relationship. There is no other explanation. But Uncle Jed was an alcoholic. Maybe that's who you inherited it from! He drank all the time. And why they allowed us to go out on the water with him, I'll never know. He was already drinking when we started out. His death haunted me for years and I still don't enjoy going out on a lake fishing."

"I'm so glad you shared that with me, because I'm not fond of that, either. But the disdainful way his funeral was handled and the looks on all the faces. I felt guilty and I didn't do anything wrong. It was a pretty large lake. Did they ever find his body? All I remember is that the casket was empty and it felt creepy standing at the gravesite. I remember us throwing a rock into the hole. Do you?"

Les let go of a deep laugh and it grabbed my heart. I had missed this guy a lot in the last couple of years. It felt good to listen to his voice.

"I remember tossing those rocks into the hole. We weren't particularly fond of Uncle Jed. He was loud and boisterous and always making jokes that weren't funny. A little off color. But mother defended him; she really loved him. He was older than her and probably protected her when she was younger. Who knows. I'm sorry you had such a nightmare, Matt. It's not a pleasant memory."

"No, it was terrible to have that flashback. But I'm glad I talked to you about it. You were pretty young when that happened, Les."

"Yeah. We both were just kids. Say, Matt. I hope you get to do this free clinic. It sounds like a great idea and I know you would love to get back into your field again. Keep me posted, will you? I meant what I said about helping with the fundraising. It would be neat to be involved somehow in this new endeavor of yours. It might connect us again, like old times."

"I'd like nothing more. Say hello to Mom and Dad. I'll keep you posted on things here."

"One more thing, Matt. Will this heart thing flare up again? Do you think you have it under control?"

"I'm better now. Much better."

"Come on, Matt. Don't avoid my question. Why can't you just open up and talk to me?"

"I did have a heart attack, Les. I told Mom and Dad that. It scared me to death, if you want to know the truth. But I do have a good doctor. He's the one I'm going into business with, if this thing works out. I have cleaned up my act and gotten stronger. But I need to earn a living. If it weren't for Brother Joe I wouldn't eat at all during the day. We eat a big breakfast and then I am hungry the rest of the day unless someone asks me for lunch to talk about a business issue. I am ready to jump back into society and become an active citizen. My time on the bench is over but it wouldn't take much for me to be back there again. That is a fear I have to live with."

"Matt, you know I would help you. Do you need some money?"

"No way. I'll get my act together. I just wanted you to know how it is for me. Don't say a word to Mom and Dad. They don't need to worry. Sometime you and I will have a heart to heart about how society treats the homeless. Believe me, I know firsthand. And it's not a pretty picture."

"I can only imagine. I would love to hear about it. I'll let you go for now. But promise you will let me know about the free clinic and how I can help or be a part of its birth."

"That is more than I would have thought I would ever hear in a conversation with you. I would be thrilled to have you on board with this. I am so glad to have had this talk with you. Thanks so much and I hope I didn't keep you too long."

"No way. I'll call you soon. Take care of yourself and watch your heart. It's good to have you back, Matt. Seriously."

I hung up the phone feeling connected to my family for the first time in a long time. Les was a great guy and had a good heart. I had forgotten how unusual our connection was. We really did get along well and complement each other. Checking my watch, I realized I needed to get going. Paul was being kind to remain so flexible about my moving in and out of the band. I didn't want to push it because I really needed the money. Walking all the way to RT's was getting old. I needed a bike desperately and decided to buy one with my next paycheck. I knew Joe wouldn't allow me to go hungry, but I needed to find transportation and eventually buy a car. I couldn't imagine owning a car again, but that needed to happen.

RT's was a bustling place around 7:00 that night. I loved seeing the band warming up and hearing the conversation floating in the air. Paul was walking towards me with a grin. He looked like he hadn't slept in a week.

"Hey, dude. Glad you decided to show up!"

"I've missed you guys. How's it going?"

"Not bad. The new drummer, Kevin, is rad. Seriously."

"Can't wait to hear him again. It's been awhile since I've played the harp but I'm gonna practice a second before we start. What are the songs? You got a list?"

"Yeah, I'll bring it to you in a sec. Get it back to me, dude. We need you tonight. Gonna be a big crowd."

"I'll be ready. Looking forward to it, man."

When Paul walked away I wiped the sweat off my brow. I had a long way to go before I was going to be good enough to play with this band. I don't know how he was tolerating me. But I was glad for the friendship that seemed to have lasted through a lot of rough times. Paul and this band were good for me now, especially when I needed quick money. But there was no way I could do this for a living. Paul was aging and this was not a big money maker. I don't know what he was thinking when he started this band. He had majored in math and science. His mind was like a steel trap. But the call of the band was so strong in him. He could've been a professor, which made me laugh when I looked at his long hair and torn jeans.

The night started with a bang as the college kids started roaming in. They were big drinkers so this was going to be a wild night. It felt good to disappear behind the other band members until I got warmed up. As the night went on, I found myself playing louder and being bolder in my runs. I would get a look from Paul from time to time, but mostly I remained in the background. There were tons of girls in the crowd and they were screaming and having a great time.

I noticed one lady in the back of the bar who was especially beautiful. It'd been a long time since I had even thought about women, because I knew I had nothing to offer. I was still out of the game. I couldn't even pay for dinner. But she was gorgeous. I had to concentrate and that was a good thing, because I might have gotten lost in her beauty. Paul glanced at me a couple of times and raised his eyebrows. He probably caught me looking. Busted.

When the gig was over, it was about 1:00 in the morning. I was worn out but had a ball playing with the guys. My mind occasionally wandered to the free clinic and how that would come about. But mostly I thought about the woman in the back of the room. It was fun to let my mind go for a change. Paul came over to me and had a smirk on his face.

"Dude, could you be any more obvious? You really liked that lady, didn't ya?"

"She was a keeper, I'm telling you."

"How'd you enjoy the gig?"

"I loved it. It felt good to be with you guys again. I've been under a lot of stress and this was a great way to release it. I needed the money, too. I'm going to purchase a good bike to get around town. This walking's for the birds. Know what I mean?"

"Sure is, buddy. Don't know how you've done it this long. I'd go nuts without my car. Say, you need a ride home?"

"Nah. I'm walking tonight. But thanks, man, for everything. It was real tonight."

"We're playing tomorrow night for a shorter gig. Nine to twelve. Come on in if you want to play. The door's always open."

"I'll be here. Need to pick up as much as I can so I can buy a good bike and some other things I need. See you tomorrow, Paul."

As I left RT's I noticed the lovely woman I'd seen earlier in the night walking to her car. I wasn't surprised to see she was driving a BMW roadster. I was almost tempted to call out to her, but thought better of it. What I would have given to have spent some time with a female! How long had it been since I kissed a girl? I couldn't remember. But as I watched her get into her car my heart flipped a little. I wasn't ready for anyone yet. But I sure had something to aim for. I had a smile on my face as I walked along the beach road to the parsonage. My apartment was waiting for me instead of the bench. That was the best news of the night. Along with that pretty woman that pulled away in her fast roadster. One day. One day.

CHAPTER 54

———— ⚜ ————

FRANK AND LESLIE were getting more and more comfortable with the fact that they were back living under the same roof. Leslie had moved into their bedroom and Frank was smiling again. The girls were playing in their bedroom; Ashley had made huge progress in her recovery and she and Avery were getting ready for bed. It had been a stormy night with torrential rain and heavy winds. The television had cut off several times and the lights had gone off twice. It had been rather dry for the last couple months so the rain was welcomed. But the girls were afraid of the wind so they had stayed close to Frank and Leslie until the storm passed.

"Okay, girls. Let's get you two in bed. The storm has gone and I don't want to hear any more excuses!"

Leslie took the girls upstairs and got them tucked in. She went to her room and changed clothes, more than ready to get comfortable. As she passed by the mirror she took a long look at her reflection. Frowning, she brushed her hair away from her face, looking at the collection of small wrinkles that had formed around her eyes. *This ordeal with Ashley has aged me ten years. I look old. But thank God she's alive, wrinkles or no wrinkles. I couldn't have lived without her.* She walked into the living room and sat down beside Frank, who was reading the local paper.

"Honey, how are you feeling? How was the hospital today?"

"It was fine. A lot of work today. A lot of patients. Leslie, we need to talk."

"What about, dear? You sound so serious."

"I am serious. We need to talk about something that Matt and I have discussed. I know you are slightly aware of the new venture we are discussing, but I wanted to run it by you so that I can get an idea as to whether you are going to be behind this or not."

"Are you talking about the free clinic?"

"Yeah. I am."

"I don't know that much about it, but I can't imagine not encouraging you. You'll still work at the hospital, right?"

Frank sighed. This was the tough part. "Honey, if I get on board with Matt on this thing, I'll be resigning or slowing down at the hospital. I know that's a shock to you, but I can't do this halfway. It's all or nothing. The need is too great; Matt can't do this alone. And it would give me a chance to give back to the community—"

Leslie cut him off at the pass. "You'd quit the hospital? Are you serious? After all these years? How would we make it? What kind of money would you make? Do you realize we have two daughters who have to go to private school, not to mention college?"

"Calm down, Leslie. Relax. We are in the talking stages in this thing, but I am leaning towards being a partner in it. I really like the concept and know how great the need is. I know you have a lot of questions and I will answer them as best I can. But I want you to promise not to overreact to this idea until you've heard all the facts. We need to get all the information down so you have that to look at and study. I want us to make a sound decision soon so I can tell Matt I'm all in or out."

Leslie sat back on the sofa and crossed her arms. Her body language wasn't reflecting anything good. She looked at Frank and frowned. "Do you actually think that you can change careers in midstream? I know you would use your medical knowledge in the clinic and I'm all for helping people. But we have extended ourselves to live on a much greater salary. How will we scale it back, Frank? We have to think about it."

"I am thinking. The girls may have to go to public school. We started the private school because they were not getting the attention they needed at the public school. But they are older now and it might not even be an issue anymore."

"I'm really not too happy with the public schools and you know that. But what else do we cut? It will be a huge sacrifice to us. Can you not keep your current job and add this to it, or do it on weekends?"

"I need to talk to Matt more and find out what the options are. I really want to do this, Leslie. I've never been as excited about anything as I am this free clinic. I've practiced for a long time and was getting burned out until Matt came along with this great idea."

Leslie shook her head. "I just don't see how you'll do it. Or what you expect me to say. But I'll give you time to find out all you can about it. I know the salary won't be enough for us to live on, Frank."

"I'll look into it. I know what it takes for us to have a good life and I'm not about to compromise the girls' lives. Or yours, for that matter. I love you, Leslie, and I adore those girls. You know that. Matt doesn't expect me to work for nothing. He has to make a living, too."

"Do what your heart tells you to do; I realize you are overworked at the hospital. I just wish you could find a happy medium between the two. Think about it, Frank."

Leslie got up and walked into their bedroom and smiled. Frank nodded, catching the alluring grin.

"I'll be in shortly. I want to make a phone call first."

Matt was lying in bed thinking about his conversation with Seth when his phone rang. The loud ring was jarring and when he looked to see who it was, he was worried. Why would Frank call him so late at night?

"Frank?"

"Yeah. You asleep?"

"I'm not now. What's up? Everything okay with the kids?"

"Yeah, Ashley is improving slowly. That's not why I called. It's about the clinic. Leslie's not on board with it right now. She's worried about how much our lifestyle's going to be affected."

Matt winced. "Knew that was coming."

"Yeah, I did, too. But I haven't changed in my desire to join up with you, man. It's just that we need to work out the details. I was thinking I could work at the hospital enough to bring in some good money. Not sure what you and I would make at the clinic. You have any idea?"

"Not until we see where the funding comes from. I'm sure the pharmaceutical companies will help fund it. They'll make good profits from a clinic of this type. However, it'll take an ongoing influx of money to keep this thing going. Some patients will pay depending on their income; I'm sure you know better than me how these clinics are run. I'll get more information about all of this before too long. It's not going to be easy. And Seth wants to get involved but he's going to have to speak to his wife, too. I think it would make a difference with him if he could continue working at the hospital and just donate time to the clinic. You can do the same thing, Frank. It doesn't have to affect your lifestyle dramatically. I'm the one who'll be there one hundred percent of the time. I'm looking forward to it; it's my way of giving back."

"This clinic will be tremendous, Matt. It will change so many lives in Destin. Not only the homeless, but a lot of families who can't afford good insurance. I heard there were over five hundred children going to school hungry. It just doesn't stop. I'm on board with it and you can count on me to do anything I can to make this happen."

"Just relieve Leslie's mind about the pay. Your life won't really change that much on the outside. But inside, you'll know you'll be helping people who wouldn't normally get this kind of care."

"You want me to talk to Seth? I'll share with him just what you told me. Coming from another doctor who's working for the same hospital, it might put things in perspective. It sounds like it could take more of our time than we're willing to give, but what'll happen is that we'll find ourselves wanting to stay at the clinic more and more because of how it makes us feel."

"It's gonna change our lives. I guarantee you this time next year, after we open this clinic, we won't be the same three men that we are today. Please call and let me know how your talk goes with Seth. I really like that guy. I want him on our team."

"He'll be there if I have anything to do with it."

"You're the man, Frank. I'm counting on you to pull this off."

"And you're not homeless, Matt. You just ain't paying yet."

Matt laughed as he hung up the phone. He didn't feel homeless in his bed. But he had no checking account, no credit cards, and no money except for what he earned at RT's. That was pretty near homeless. Everything except the tent and sleeping bag. Or the hardness of that damn bench.

CHAPTER 55

DESTIN WAS HEATING up quickly as spring was about to turn into summer. Tourists were sleeping in after their late nights, and the streets were quiet. As I left my apartment I looked around for the zillionth time, acknowledging that I lived in paradise. On the outside looking in, this was a postcard come to life. A perfect place to live. But from where I had been, it was a tough place to make a living.

I was going to Dan's Bike Shop on the main highway to buy my first bicycle. I felt like a kid but this bike was going to change my life. No more walking everywhere. My legs were like iron from walking for the last few years and I had developed a long stride. I'd worked enough at RT's to purchase a good bicycle and Dan's was the place to go. He always had deals and everyone in town went there first.

As I headed down the highway 98, I noticed a lot of litter on the sides of the road. One detriment of tourism. But tourists brought a lot of money into the area and everybody was always in a good mood. Restaurants that served breakfast were packed and the car wash was full.

It took me about twenty minutes but when I got to the bike shop there were already people inside shopping for a bicycle. I knew which one I wanted; I'd been in there many times to check out the newest styles. Dan came over and smiled. He had such a great spirit about him, but his eyes were always what caught me. They were as blue as an April sky.

"Hey, man. You finally gonna fork over for a bike? You been looking at this one for almost six months now. Can't believe you're here."

I laughed. He was right. It'd taken me forever to save up for this thing. "Hey, dude. Yeah, I'm finally here to buy this bike. Took me long enough, huh?"

"Seriously! But you picked out a good one. I have that one myself. It's smooth as silk and the power is there when you need it."

"I just need to get around town some way other than my own two feet. I'm sick of walking everywhere. Can't wait to sit on this thing and feel the wind on my face."

Dan smiled. "I'll ring you up right now. You've waited long enough to have this bike and I'm glad you're getting it today. Four people have been looking at it and I was afraid one of them would buy it before you got back here. I can order another one but it takes a while to get it in."

"My name's all over this bike. I'm ready to pedal my way to RT's and work! You have no idea what this means to me."

"I think I have some idea. Here's your change. Now I want to see you ride off. It'd make my day!"

I hopped on the bike and pedaled out of the parking lot. Dan shouted to me as I rode away, and I laughed like a child. It felt so good to be moving at a good pace as I headed to Main Street. I was hoping to catch Paul before he went into a meeting with the owner. I wanted to run by him all the things I spoke to Frank and Seth about the clinic.

Just as I turned the corner and pulled up into the parking lot of RT's, I saw a white BMW roadster sitting in the parking lot. My heart skipped a beat. *What in the world is that girl doing here at this time of day?* I knew that was her car. What I didn't know was her name. Pretty car. The owner wasn't bad, either. In fact I'd had a difficult time getting her out of my mind ever since I laid eyes on her. I locked my bike on the corner of a post and walked in through the back door. Paul was sitting on a bar stool talking to the pretty woman who owned the sports car. I was jealous immediately. As I approached Paul, he turned and smiled.

"Hey, dude. You're here early. I was just talking with Celeste Rutherford. She's looking for a job and I was going to put in a good word for her with McKenzie. He is going to hire an assistant manager so I thought I'd set her up a meeting with him. You two met?"

I had lost my ability to speak. I merely shook my head no.

"Matt? This is Celeste Rutherford. Celeste, this is Matt Collins. He plays in the band with us from time to time."

Celeste nodded and put out her hand. It was hard for me to take it. "Hello, Matt. Nice to meet you. I think I saw you playing the other night. I'm sure that's a lot of fun."

She made it sound trite. Maybe because it was. I found my voice again. "Thanks. I think I did see you in the crowd. Nice to meet you."

Paul got up, raised his eyebrow at me, and headed towards the back. "I'm going to try to catch McKenzie before he leaves. You two talk a minute and I'll be right back."

I sat down on a bar stool two seats down from her and smiled. At least I tried to smile. My stomach was in a knot and I had no idea why. It couldn't have been because she was so beautiful. It couldn't have been because I hadn't talked to a woman in so long I didn't know how to form the words. I had nothing to say. What was I going to talk about? My career? Oh, yes. The clinic.

"You live here full time?"

She nodded, sipping a Coke. "Yeah. Been here about six months and decided I wanted to make this home. How about you?" She flashed her green eyes at me and I was gone. I realized how out of practice I was.

"I've lived here quite a while. Surprised we haven't run into each other before RT's. Do you have family here?"

"No. My parents are both dead. But my brother lives in Orlando, so it will be much easier for us to see each other since I used to live in Baltimore." She studied me and then dropped her eyes. I couldn't tell if I'd passed inspection or not.

"So you need a job? You looking for full-time work?" I just had a brain storm.

"I need work. I can't stay home all the time and do nothing. Why? You got any ideas? I don't know much about this area and I really don't know where else to apply."

I was going for broke here. "Well, I've got a great idea. But I need to fill you in on everything. Can we walk next door and eat some brunch? I'd like to share what I'm doing and see if you're the least bit interested."

Her green eyes bore right through me. Surely she couldn't read my mind. Her face had grown serious and I was worried she wouldn't hear me out. So I broke the silence.

"Hold on. That's not a pickup line. I really have something I want to talk to you about. It might appeal to you and it might not. Would you give me a chance?"

"Okay. Will you tell Paul we're going next door? Just in case I don't like what you're doing, I need to talk to McKenzie about a job!"

I got up and walked to the back and found Paul sitting in McKenzie's office. "Dude, I'm going to take Celeste next door for brunch. I'll be back in about forty-five minutes. That won't hurt her chances of getting a job here, will it?"

McKenzie spoke up. "No way. She's too pretty not to hire. You better sway her first chance you get, 'cause I'm gonna offer her something she can't refuse."

I smiled confidently but inside I was worried. I had nothing to offer her yet. But I was going to try to reel her in. If she was interested in the clinic, then I'd try to hire her for the front office. We walked next door and sat down at a table in the back. It wasn't crowded so our timing was perfect. I knew I had no business talking to Celeste before I even got the clinic going, but I couldn't help myself. It gave me a unique opportunity to get to know her without it being a date. We ordered our drinks and picked out something to eat and then I got enough nerve to ask her some questions. She beat me to the punch.

"So, Matt. What do you do?"

I felt cornered. Didn't want to share my homeless situation just yet so I tried to walk around that question. "Right now I'm playing at RT's several nights a week. But ultimately I want to open a free medical clinic here in Destin. That's what I want to talk to you about."

"Sounds interesting. So you're a doctor?"

"Yes, I am."

"So why aren't you practicing now?"

"Long story."

"Oh. Sorry. Didn't mean to pry."

I winced. This wasn't going like I wanted it to. "You're not prying, Celeste. Just a little tough for me to talk about right now. Tell me about you. What have you been doing with your life? What do you like to do?"

Celeste blushed and smiled at me. "You're good at turning the attention away from yourself! I've been a legal secretary, a stay-at-home mom, and I've worked on a cattle ranch that my parents owned." She saw me raise my eyebrows. "Okay, I know that sounds weird. But I loved it."

"What exactly did you do on that ranch?"

"Actually, I worked in the lab mostly, or did whatever needed to be done."

"Sounds interesting. So what do you want to do now? Waitress?"

"Not really. But I need some income and wanted to find something quick."

"Would you be interested in getting back into the medical world again? Only this time, no cows?"

She laughed and I loved the sound echoing across the room. "I might. What were you thinking about, Matt?"

I sighed. "I would love for you to work at the clinic in some capacity. We are in the beginning stages of getting this thing going. But I saw you the other night and thought about you when I was going over the plans. We would need someone to make appointments and run the front office. A lot of insurance headaches and also dealing with the homeless. That's really where my heart is. With the homeless."

She studied me for a while and ate slowly. I kept quiet. I wasn't quite ready to share about my own life. Or lack of it. Suddenly the question came out of nowhere and hit me in the face. I nearly choked on my egg sandwich.

"You been homeless, Matt?"

I swallowed my food and drank a sip of Sprite. *Did I look homeless?* I cleared my throat and looked at her square in the eyes. "I really don't like talking about it, but to be honest with you, yes, I've been homeless. I have a place to live right now, but I'm still finding my way back."

A tear had formed in one of her eyes. I watched it run down her perfect face. "Are you serious? You are a doctor and you were homeless? How in the world did that happen?"

"It wasn't easy. But I managed to do it in record time."

"That had to be rough, Matt. What a fall. How long were you outside?"

"Longer than I wanted to be. I had a heart attack and that kind of woke me up." The conversation had just gotten a little heavy. I really wanted to lighten things up before we ended our meal.

"How are you now? Your health better?"

"I'm fine. Back to fighting weight. But let's get back to the clinic and you. Would you consider working for me there? I think you would enjoy being in a clinic. It's a lot more personable than a huge hospital. I'm really excited about providing treatment for the homeless because they are falling through the cracks in society. I should know."

She smiled. "Yeah, you should. I'll give it some thought. When do you think this thing will get off the ground?"

"I'm working on that now. I'll give you my phone number and I would like yours, if you're interested in the job. It will be a little while before I am ready to hire you, so you might want to take this job RT's is offering you until I am ready."

"You seem awful sure about hiring me. What makes you so certain that I'm the right person for the job?"

I looked in her beautiful eyes and studied what I saw. "Some things you just know, Celeste. Some things you know in your gut."

A tiny smile started at the corner of her lovely mouth. I had a difficult time not staring at her mouth, but I managed to ask for our check and pay the bill without making a total fool of myself.

"I hope that you've enjoyed this chat as much as I have. I don't remember when I've even had a conversation with a woman. It's been too long. I'm sorry if I was too forward, Celeste. I noticed you at RT's and when I saw you leave I almost yelled at you to make you stop. But you were headed towards your car and I didn't want to scare you."

"I saw you in the band and wondered who you were. I've been to RT's before and you weren't in the band then. You should have talked to me. I might have had a drink with you."

"Well, that's another thing. I don't drink. I'm a recovered alcoholic."

She looked down and nodded. "I really don't drink that much, either. So will you let me know how things are progressing so I will know when to stop by the clinic?"

"I hope I'll talk to you many times before I get that clinic open!" I watched her closely for signs of pulling back. I saw none.

"Of course I will, silly. Let's get together soon. I would love to have a few friends here; it gets quite lonely in a new town when you don't know anyone."

"I'll make sure you don't feel lonely. I know how that feels. I've been pretty much trying to survive lately so I haven't dated at all. You take care of yourself and I'm certain we'll be talking soon. I'm going back to RT's to talk to Paul. You coming along?"

"Yeah, I need to nail that job. Thanks for the chat. And the job offer! I'll look forward to seeing what you're going to do with the free clinic. Sounds very interesting and philanthropic."

"It's just a way for me to give back. Someone has been pretty good to me. I need to spread that around a little bit. Don't ya think?"

"Sounds like a powerful way to do it."

As I walked behind her towards RT's, it felt so natural being with her. I had to remind myself that we'd only just met. I wanted more than anything to get to know her. I loved her spirit already. But I had nothing to offer a woman so I had held back a little, hoping she found something about me that was interesting enough for her to want to see me again. My heart was warm and I grabbed one last glimpse of her before she headed towards the office to see McKenzie. In my mind, I had a feeling that I'd just met my wife. It was a stretch. But everything about my life after meeting Brother Joe was a stretch. Just in case I was correct in my assumption, I was going to be on my best behavior with her.

CHAPTER 56

McKenzie's office was cluttered with papers and books stacked to the window sill, and it was hot even with the ceiling fan whirling at high speed. His hair and clothing were messy just like his office, and McKenzie was into so many things that no one but him could find anything on his desk. RT's was not that busy. It was the other ninety things he had his hands in that caused bedlam in his life. He needed a secretary to keep things in order. He'd lived this way for years and didn't know if he could change. But he was hoping against hope that Celeste would be the woman who would accomplish what he couldn't on his own.

Celeste winced as she tried to find an uncovered chair to sit in. Paul saw her frustration and cleared a chair near the desk.

"So did you have a nice chat with Matt?" McKenzie glared over his glasses at her, raising a furry eyebrow.

"I did. Very interesting man."

"Oh, don't get too caught up in him, Celeste. I need you to work for me. As you can see, my desk is a mess. I need someone to organize my desk and my entire life."

Celeste shuddered. Something about this man was really getting to her. "I see. You do have a lot of papers on your desk. And you must love to read."

"Actually I live to read. If you came to my house you would see that almost every wall is lined with books."

Paul stepped in with a laugh. "Don't let him get to you, Celeste. He's really a nice guy. A little eccentric, maybe. The good news is that he is hardly ever here. So you would have the run of the office. He spends his time in Europe, California, and New York. I'll help you any way I can. Really."

McKenzie excused himself and took a phone call on his cell, walking outside the door. Celeste sat there looking at Paul with so many questions running through her mind. "If you don't mind, tell me about Matt, Paul. Do you two know him well?"

McKenzie poked his head back in and glared at her. "You still thinking about Matt? Why, he's nothing. He's not even working! You don't need to get mixed up with him right now. He's got to get his act together, lady."

Celeste looked at Paul and raised her hands up. "Paul? Any comments?"

"I've known Matt for many years. You couldn't find a better man. Yes, he's had his struggles like all of us. I'm sure he told you he was homeless for a while. But he's on his way back. He was a notable surgeon in Philadelphia and alcohol took him down. But he's coming back full swing. Was he talking to you about the free clinic?"

"Yeah, we spent some time on that. I was very impressed with his ideas. Do you think it's possible to open a free clinic here? Will the city of Destin support that?"

"Are you kidding? It's badly needed. And people will come from Walton County to this clinic. It's genius. And that's what Matt is. Genius."

"He was very nice to me. Offered me a job when the clinic opens."

McKenzie had plopped back down in his chair and was halfway listening to her talk. "McKenzie, you are in a mess right now, so I'll help you out. I'll get you organized and make your life easier. But when the clinic opens up, I will probably want to support Matt in this endeavor. I haven't talked to him for very long, but my heart is telling me that Matt really has his eye on the poor, the struggling, and the homeless. I want to be a part of that. Can you hire me with those stipulations?"

McKenzie frowned. He nearly growled. "I suppose I don't have a choice, now do I? If I want you, I have to swallow the fact that a skinny has-been doctor will take you away at some God-forsaken date in the future. How am I supposed to deal with that?"

Paul couldn't help but laugh. "Hang on, McKenzie. She'll be around long enough to make your world better. That's all you need. You're never here, anyway. I practically run this place. So just let it happen. Celeste is willing to do the work and is self motivated. You can take off and travel and not worry about anything."

"How long have you known her, Paul?"

"About two hours now. But I can read people very quickly. And I like her. I like her a lot."

Celeste blushed. They were talking like she wasn't sitting there in the flesh. "I like you, too, Paul." She smiled at him and winked.

"Well let's get out of here. I've got a gig to play and Matt does, too. It's time for practice."

Celeste and McKenzie agreed on a salary and shook hands. She turned and walked out of the room, hoping to see Matt waiting outside for Paul. He wasn't around so she sat down at a table and watched the band getting ready to play. Her mind was running in ten different directions, sorting through the information Paul had shared with her about Matt and the job she had in front of her, getting McKenzie's office in order. She was lost in her own thoughts when Matt showed up.

Matt saw her sitting at a table across the room and his heart skipped a beat. He pulled back because his mind needed to be on the gig and not on a woman he hardly knew. He waved at her and climbed up on the stage. But he was aware that her eyes were following him. He walked up to Paul and whispered low.

"Hey. How did the interview go with McKenzie?"

"Went great. She got hired. But your ears had to be burning, buddy. We talked about you most of the time."

"Oh, great. I'm sure McKenzie loved that. What in the world were you talking about?"

"Dude. I was in your corner. I told her all about you! The homeless thing, the free clinic. Well, I only touched base on it. After all, she was in there applying for a job."

Matt shook his head. "I wasn't going to make too big a deal about my being homeless. I told her a little but you need to chill on that, man. I'm not exactly proud of that part of my life."

"Sorry, dude. I didn't mean to make you uncomfortable. Let's get started practicing. You're cold on that harp and I want you to warm up those lips."

Matt grinned and hopped up on his stool. The night went by without too many mistakes. His were slight and he hoped Celeste hadn't heard them. He'd gotten so involved with the songs that he failed to notice that she had walked out halfway through the show. His heart sank when he looked around for her. Paul noticed that he was glancing around and waved at him.

"Dude. She's gone. Sorry, I hope you aren't too disappointed. You did a great job tonight, especially since you've been out for a while. You gonna play with us regularly?"

"Yeah, until I get this darn clinic up and running. I need the cash, man. You mind?"

"You kidding? I love it. We hardly see each other and this just gives us some common ground again."

"Exactly. I owe you, man. Big time. Do you realize how far I have to go to just be at the minimum level of existence?"

Paul frowned. "What are you talking about, dude? You were on a bench and now you're talking about opening a free clinic. Come on. Give yourself a break."

"What I need is a kick in the pants. I did this to myself and I know I'm paying the consequences. I have no business going after Celeste for anything other than as an employee. What do I have to offer her? Besides, I'm probably not ready to date, anyway. Where was my head?"

"Take it easy, Matt. She's gonna be working at RT's for a while. You have a lot of work to do to get that clinic open. And you need Frank and

Seth on board to make this work. I'm proud of you. But enough of this emotional stuff. You up for something to eat?"

Matt laughed. "Always hungry."

"Let's get outta here and find some food."

Matt walked outside and checked the lock on his bike. He was still thinking about Celeste when he turned around and saw her car pulling up. His damaged heart started beating fast but he tried not to show it on the outside.

"Hey, lady. What's going on?"

"Hey, Matt. Just wanted to say thank you for such a nice interview this afternoon. I really appreciate being treated like a lady and also for your belief in me. I am very interested in what you are envisioning and hope I can be a part of that at some point. But mainly, I just wanted to say thanks."

"I heard the interview went well with McKenzie."

"Yeah. It was fine. Thank heavens Paul was there. It might not have gone so well without his intervention."

Matt laughed. "I don't even want to imagine that. I'm glad you enjoyed our talk because I sure did. Say, Paul and I are gonna grab a bite to eat. You care to join us?"

Celeste looked down and then glanced back at Matt. "No. I better not. But thanks. Listen, you have a good night and I'll catch you later. And by the way, you sounded pretty tight up there on stage. I love the sound you guys have. Really good."

"Shoot. I was barely holding my own. But thanks. Hope to see you soon, Celeste. Keep me posted on how things are going, and I'll keep you updated on the clinic."

She drove away and he went back in to grab Paul, who immediately saw the fallen look on his face.

"Come on, dude. Let's go. I don't even want to ask what happened out there in the parking lot. You look like you just lost your best friend. Let's eat. I'm starving."

Matt followed Paul outside and they got into the car and headed to Moe's Diner. It was an old Airstream-type trailer that had been turned into an old fashioned-diner. The landscaping was killer with huge palms and plenty of lights. People loved it and the food was fairly good. Paul ordered and excused himself to take a call on his cell. Matt sat and looked out the window, hoping against the odds that he'd see Celeste's BMW roadster pull up. But what he really wanted was a life, which seemed to be coming at the pace of a sloth. An animal that moves so slow a person can hardly track its progress.

Suddenly, out of nowhere, two cars crashed right outside the diner. Paul came running in, waving frantically at Matt.

"Dude. Get out here! There's been a terrible collision!"

Matt hopped up and ran out the door, nearly knocking Paul down. He ran toward the cars and picked the one with the most front end damage. Inside was a woman who had a severe head injury. She was unconscious. He did CPR on her as Paul dialed 911.

Matt was in his element. And the hunger he had for being a doctor surged through his veins. This was what he was born for. And this was what he was going to do, he promised himself, kneeling there in his ragged, bloody clothes.

CHAPTER 57

⚜

JEFFREY BULINGER PEERED out of his office window as the last bit of daylight faded on the horizon, giving way to a dazzling array of stars. Each one perfectly mounted in the jet black canvas of the night sky over Biloxi. The view helped to distract him from the papers on his desk from his day job at the Van Cleave Middle School over on Bulldog Avenue. Jeffrey had taken a job as the night clerk at the *Sun Herald* to supplement his income. His chair swiveled from side to side as he sipped his third cup of coffee.

"Jeff," as his friends called him, was wearing corduroy slacks and an Oxford-collar white shirt with his trademark knit tie. At age thirty eight he'd been saddled with the job of bringing Van Cleave's history program up to the standard that was so highly touted in the science, math, and language arts departments. His unkempt blond hair gave him a boyish look that belied his determination to be a great teacher and the experience he brought to the table when it came to enriching the minds of future generations. He loved his craft yet his students seemed less impressed by his knowledge than they were his oddities. He was easily the butt of a lot of jokes at Van Cleave. His heart was that of a teacher but his bank account dictated that he hold a night position at the *Sun Herald*.

His job there was quite mundane to him; he had to answer the phones and write classified ads. His work was often chopped up and corrected by the day staff. The job provided an extra paycheck and an opportunity to grade papers. But his mind for dates and times and a nearly photographic memory were largely unappreciated.

This night, like so many before it, held no bright prospects. He had asked his students to prepare book reports on the events leading up to the

Revolutionary War. He liked the way this project allowed him insight as to how much the kids had learned as they headed into their final quarter. Though on the *Sun*'s payroll, his thoughts were largely consumed by the class of students he was currently charged with.

The office was brightly lit by an abundance of florescent bulbs. The phone rang and he quickly answered it. In a cheerful voice he lifted the receiver and spoke clearly.

"*Sun Herald*, this is Jeff speaking, how may I help you?"

Paco's crusty old voice carried in a manner that showed no professional eloquence but a sincerity that kind of drew Jeff in from the start of the conversation.

"Hi, my name's Paco and my girlfriend suggested I call and see if I could take out an ad in the classifieds."

Jeff's eyes narrowed in curiosity as he listened to each word.

"Well, sir, what is it you're trying to do?"

"I'm trying to locate a guy who's a doctor that landed here in Biloxi. He has a son, see, and he don't even know it. The boy is a real nice kid and he's in medical school at Seton Hall, and his dad doesn't even know he's alive. His mom died, so the poor kid can't even find his dad."

Jeff jotted notes on a yellow legal pad as he listened carefully, slowly becoming aware that this was not the kind of call he got every day. His voice was quizzical.

"So, ah, 'Mr. Paco,' is it?"

"Just 'Paco,' man."

"Okay, I'm not sure what you're asking me to do."

"Well I figured we could place an ad and hope this doctor just might read it."

Jeff seemed unimpressed with the plan, but tried to clarify. "So you want me to put an ad in the paper that says, 'Hey Matt, you got a son.'"

"No, man! I just want the guy to find me. And I'll tell him he has a son and how to get in touch with him. I have a couple hundred bucks to pay for the ad."

"So you think this Matt guy is now a doctor here in Biloxi?"

"Yes, I've tracked him this far. It's been a real trip; you wouldn't believe what I've been through, especially in Florida."

The call was interrupted by a burst of coughing from Paco. He caught his breath and excused himself.

"So we gonna put an ad in or just sit here talking?"

Jeff frowned. He was touched by the story but he wasn't convinced that an ad was the correct way to get the attention of a doctor.

"Mr. Paco, why don't you give me your number. Lemme check around and see if I can find this guy and then I'll call you back and let you know where he is. Maybe we can tell him together; it would make a great human interest story for the paper and it would give me a chance at writing something besides ad copy for the *Sun Herald*. We have an extensive data base here at the paper and I might even get a reporter to help track this guy down."

"Wow! We might find this guy in a week's time."

"Well, don't get your hopes up too high." He looked down at his pad. "Where do I find you, Mr. Paco?"

"You can find me at the Sundowner Motel."

"Oh, I know the place. It's a little out of my way but I can stop on my way in from Bulldog Street." Jeffrey made a face and rubbed his chin, remembering how bad the motel was.

The two exchanged numbers and Jeff agreed that he would call Paco as soon as he heard anything.

Paco hung up the phone breathing deeply, as if fresh air had been blown into his lungs. He was elated at the offer to get a reporter on the search. Surely a reporter could find Matt Collins after all of the experience he would have had in finding missing people.

He looked at the clock and was annoyed that Pauline still had not returned with the beer that he sent her out to get. He paced around the room for a bit, processing the information from the conversation with Jeff, wondering what was taking Pauline so long.

Jeff was at the *Sun Herald* busily tapping the keys of the computer on his desk, researching. He sat back in his chair sipping his coffee, thinking. *He called himself 'Paco'.* Why did the name haunt him? Working the night desk, he'd grown accustomed to thinking aloud. "I've heard that name." He returned to his computer screen and began to review the ads he'd written over the past weeks. And boom, there it was! *Paco, if you see this ad, call Chic at 215-770-5589.* A couple more clicks of the mouse confirmed it was a Philadelphia area code. *Could it be?* Grabbing the phone he dialed quickly. Sure enough, the voice on the other end answered, "Chic here."

"Hi, this is Jeff Bulinger from the Biloxi *Sun Herald*. I was hoping you might have a moment to speak with me."

Chic was off duty at Ruby's and was sitting at his desk wondering what in the world this guy wanted. "Sure Jeff, what's up?"

"I been talking with a man who calls himself 'Paco'." That got Chic's attention immediately. He sat up straight, his heart skipping a beat.

"No kidding! The guy made it all the way to Mississippi?"

"He sure did. And found his way to my office to place an ad for a Matt Collins."

"I been dying to talk to that guy! I have something I need to tell him. Can you get me in touch with him? Is there any way I could call him?"

"All he gave me was a broken down motel he was staying at. The Sundowner Motel. You can try that if you want to. Can't promise he'll be there, though. This guy's pretty rough."

Chic laughed. "Yeah, he is. But you'd be surprised at what's behind those ragged clothes and rough exterior."

"You know anything about this Matt character he's obsessed with finding? He's willing to spend his last dollar on an ad to locate that man. Who the heck is this guy, anyway?"

"Paco's on a journey to find this doctor because he met Matt's son and felt sorry for him. Turns out the boy's never met his dad. It's quite a story, really. You should write that one up in the newspaper."

"What's the son's name? You got that info?"

"I think I recall his first name was Hunter. But that's all I heard. Thanks for the call. I believe I'll try calling the Sundowner Motel. Sure would like to catch that hobo if I can."

"So where is this Matt Collins? You know any other info on the guy?"

"He's supposed to be in Destin, Florida now. That was what I wanted to tell Paco."

"Well, I sure hope you find the old guy because he's not sounding too healthy and he's dying to know where Matt Collins is."

"I'll do my best. Thanks again, Jeff."

On the other side of town, Paco had been pacing back and forth, growing more impatient by the minute. He'd sent Pauline to get some beer and she was late. He'd painted a million pictures in his mind as to why she was taking so long. None of them fit Pauline's profile, but he had rehearsed them 'til he'd gotten himself into a full-blown tizzy.

She came in, slamming the door shut and sat the beer down on the kitchen counter in Paco's room. Her face was red from the heat but she didn't miss the tension in the room.

"What took you so long?" Paco blurted with a scowl. There was an intensity in Paco's tone that Pauline hadn't braced for as she looked at him in disbelief. "Well? It's never taken you this long to get beer before."

The accusing tone was cutting the air like a shiny dagger. Pauline was holding the money he'd won at the casino. Ironically, it had been awhile since he had had any money at all, not to mention the million years since he had had a friend. There was no trace of a smile on his face as he waited for an answer.

Pauline's voice started softly. "I'm not used to being talked to with such suspicion." She looked at him and continued. "I thought I'd surprise you with a new pair of sneakers so I stopped at the store to get you a pair. They were on sale. Here are the rest of your precious winnings. I don't want to touch your money."

Paco couldn't believe what he was hearing. His entire state of mind was pointless and dead wrong. Years on the street had dulled all of his social skills and the pack he usually ran with just didn't do nice things for each other. Every foul thought, every out of line word he'd spoken, sort of fell flat on the floor. Paco couldn't even tell what color his new tennis shoes were for the shame of having spoken sharply to his one and only friend.

He was still lost for words as he reached over and twisted the beer out of the stretchy plastic rings that held the six pack together. The silence in the room was deafening. He knew very little about being close to someone and even less about making apologies. He walked to the counter, poured a glass of whiskey, and drank it up. Ironically, the magic elixir that had pulled him from so many scrapes did little to help him find the words his mind so franticly searched for. The unfounded anger now mixed with a growing feeling of gratitude that was more than he was used to. He retreated to the bathroom were he drenched his face with cold water. Glancing up, he didn't like the image looking back at him from the medicine chest mirror. He emerged from the bathroom and spoke as humbly as possible. His voice was hoarse from the harshness of the drink.

"Look, I'm sorry, I really like the shoes. You were trying to be nice and I blew it out of the water. Don't know what got into me, Pauline. Just feeling edgy is all."

Pauline seemed numb to his remarks. He was certain it wasn't the apology she'd expected but she was as lost for words as her accuser. "Did you call the paper?"

"Yeah, I did. I talked to a guy named Jeff and he seemed eager to help. I think we're gonna find this Matt Collins real soon. If he's in town, Jeff will find him."

The news was shared without the triumphant feelings he had expected to feel. Somehow his outburst of anger had blown out the flame of hope that had built up inside of him.

"Happy to hear it, Paco. What happens after you find this guy? Will you move along ? Find a new town with another lost doctor?"

Her tone was pretty flat. He knew it belied the heavy heart and sadness she felt inside. As she looked at Paco, he was aware that she realized that he was not coming towards her. He was moving farther away.

The question hung in the air like a bad odor. Paco had not expected that question, nor had he really thought about it. The suggestion suddenly made Paco feel as though he had tricked Pauline in some way. And there was little in Pauline's face that would alter that feeling.

As the night progressed, there were a lot of quiet spaces unfilled in their time together sitting at the kitchen table. Pauline seemed lost in a world that she wasn't going to share, and Paco was simply feeling the warm burn of the liquor as it slid down his throat. For some reason, the night had turned sour. Perhaps the true colors of their relationship were coming through the momentary joy of winning at the casino. The simple dinner shared between the two. The excitement of counting the money. Paco never said he would stay. He never promised her anything. But somewhere in her old maid's heart perhaps she was holding onto a small flicker of hope that he would decide to hang around a little longer.

A couple hours later the lights were all out at the Sundowner, yet Paco was wide awake. His mind was racing like the cars at an Indy racetrack. Without much thought he got out of bed and dressed quietly. He looked around his room one last time, watching Pauline, who was curled up on the sofa, fast asleep. He pulled out two hundred dollars and put it on the night stand; more than he owed her on paper, yet somehow so much less than the debt of gratitude he felt toward his dear friend. He had treated her badly on this last night; he'd had no intentions of leaving yet. But somehow, he got a restless spirit in him and the hunt for Matt drew back in the shadows of importance. He had no thoughts of Hunter or his desire to bring about a reunion. All he could think about was getting back on the road. Sleeping outside.

He knew he was taking a risk carrying the money with him. But once that feeling of restlessness got him and the call of the road was in his head, he told himself he was no longer was responsible for his actions. He no longer cared about anything or anyone. It was what had kept him going all these years, moving from place to place. He was attached to nothing. He had not allowed himself to care about anyone. Hunter had crept in by sheer luck. That young boy had snagged his heart and realizing that almost got him angry as he slung his backpack over his shoulder and slipped into the night. He could feel the humidity in his hair as he walked out into the lonely darkness that had come to feel like home. He had money in his pocket but had no idea where he was headed.

All he knew was that he had a craving to sleep in the woods somewhere. His torn sleeping bag would be a welcome friend as he allowed the liquor to erase any feelings of guilt that he had inside his old weathered heart.

Pauline lay like a spurned lover, knowing something was wrong but unaware yet that Paco had walked out of her life. She was getting old and gray and was hard of hearing. Her false teeth were yellow and her nails cracked and uncared for. But for one fleeting moment, when her body felt youthful once more, she dreamed of her knight in shining armor; an old homeless tramp who came to her in her dreams and took her hand to dance.

She would wake later in the night to discover she was alone. And a tear would fall before she got up and made herself a cup of hot tea. What could have been was gone. Like two ships passing in the night. But the difference was that she was heartbroken and she realized Paco had already moved on with only a spit of feeling left behind.

Burning the midnight oil, Jeff was feverishly writing on his big yellow pad at a desk in his living room. Throwing his pen on top of the desk, he decided he would go to the Sundowner in the morning and deliver the news to Paco in person. Matt Collins was actually in Destin and not in Biloxi at all. He had jotted down contact numbers for Paco of people who would know how to locate Matt if he were still in practice. He looked forward to seeing the old guy face to face. His conversation with Chic had given him a little more background and that made the old tramp even more intriguing.

As Jeff settled down to sleep in a king-size bed with piles of covers and the air conditioner on low, Paco found a place to fall sleep deep in the woods on the outskirts of town. The eagerness of the reporter to find Paco wouldn't be a match for the rambling tramp. For he was a master at being invisible. And he wouldn't be found until he chose to be. He had plenty of liquor in his backpack and money tucked away. He could stay hidden for days and not miss the companionship of society. In fact, when he was like this, he rather preferred the solitude.

Lying in his old ragged sleeping bag, Paco dreamed of Hunter, a young man who was dying to meet a father he'd lived without. But it would be days before he would climb out of his camouflaged hideout and face what he'd done. The hurt he'd caused Pauline and the unfinished efforts of seeking to get in touch with Matt would only harden his cracked heart even more. His body was wearing out and his lungs were carrying a dangerous amount of fluid. But somewhere in there a determination would arise, and once again the old man would start his journey. But for now, he would be a disappointment to several people. Jeffrey Bulinger would be one of them. But he would get over the frustration of the near miss. It was the raspy-voiced old woman at the Sundowner who would go to her grave with a love for the elusive hobo who had vanished in the night.

CHAPTER 58

———— ✦ ————

THE RAIN WAS coming down in buckets. Joe had not seen rain like that for twenty years. The ground was soaked and water was building fast on the roads. It was a good summer type rain where the air smells strongly of rainwater and the sky was a dark gray, shooting sheets of water down to the earth. Pools of water were collecting quickly at every dip in the road or ground. And the forecast didn't look good; rain all day and into the night.

Joe was fixing a good breakfast in hopes that Matt would stop by. He'd reneged on his promise to stop in each morning and Joe had ignored it because he knew Matt was trying hard to get things going on the clinic. But today, with the rain coming down, Joe had an inkling that Matt was in the mood for one of his buffet breakfasts, so he put a plate at the table for Matt and sat and drank his coffee, giving Matt plenty of time to wake up.

As he read the paper, his mind wandered to all the parish members that had died recently. There were a lot of elderly in his congregation and they were all getting sick or were very frail. He needed to attract some younger people and had spoken with the minister of music about changing the service to appeal to the youth. The older members were staunch Presbyterians and enjoyed the old way of doing things. But Joe knew that the church would die out if things didn't change. His eyes scanned the obit column and found another homeless man had died. No family, a pauper's funeral. The only name he had was Lobo. Joe remembered him well and teared up at the thought of his death. It didn't surprise him because Lobo was quite the drinker. But the personality that man had when he was sober was something to be admired. The other homeless men would miss him, as the laughter he created in their lives was badly needed.

Just as Joe was about to start breakfast there was a gentle knock on the door. He called out loudly across the room. "Come in! The door's unlocked."

"It's me, Joe. Sorry I haven't been around a lot lately."

Joe smiled warmly. He loved the sound of Matt's voice. He'd grown very fond of the man and really looked forward to their talks. With Matt getting busier, those talks were less and less.

"Hey, buddy. Good to see you. I've missed you coming through that door. How've you been?"

"I've missed you too, believe me. I've been busy trying to put a deal together with Frank and Seth. I'm starving! What are you trying to do to me, man? The smell when you walk into this house is mouth watering."

Joe laughed. "Sit down, Son. We've got a lot of catching up to do, and I'm hungry, too. Go ahead and serve your plate and we'll say a quick blessing."

After they'd prayed, the two men ate in silence. But nothing got past Joe. He knew Matt was worried about the free clinic, but there was something else bothering him this morning and he couldn't put his finger on it yet.

"How are the talks going between Frank and Seth? They on board, yet?"

"Boy, Joe, you really get to the point of things. They are discussing it with their wives. I'm the only single one of the group. Money is an issue. But they can still work at the hospital and make good money. The clinic won't pay much but I know they'll get so much reward from helping people who are in need. You know how you are about the homeless. You can hardly stay in at night for wanting to go out among them to give them blankets or sleeping bags, or water. It's almost addictive for you. And I've been on the receiving end. Pretty powerful stuff, man."

"It is powerful. I'm here to tell you that it changes me more than it changes them. I'm not the same man I was ten years ago. That's how long I've been walking among those sleeping giants at night. I have loved it from the start but the things they have whispered in my ear have rocked my world. They have made me laugh and cry in the same visit. They are good men who are broken. Just like you and me."

"You don't have to convince me, man. I was one of them. But Frank and Seth will come around. I can feel it. They just have to work through it. It won't really change their quality of life that much, except for the fact that they will donate some time to the clinic instead of just working at the hospital. It will be a needed challenge in their lives."

"Wives are giving them a hard time?"

"Yep. The wives. But they are afraid of a radical change in lifestyle. I'm hoping to reassure them that the change will be minimal, if any."

"I have done some studying about the financing of this clinic. The pharmaceutical companies will most likely pay for the clinic, because they know they'll make a lot of money from the prescriptions you write. They want you in business, Matt. It means more money for them."

"You're right, Joe. It's new to me and that's why I'm feeling insecure about it. But if I get these men on board, I'll find an attorney to help me do some of this. I'm going to need some money to pay an attorney so I will ask Frank and Seth to donate some and I'll work at RT's as many nights a week as I can to get a decent paycheck. First I need the state of Florida to recognize that my education meets their standard for practicing in Florida. Florida is very protective of the elderly and the laws are slanted towards that demographic. I'll have to apply for a business license and get the other two working on the pharmaceutical companies."

"You've got your plate full, Matt. I have a feeling Frank and Seth will be great assets to the clinic. You seem to think highly of these guys and that is critical for this thing to be a success. How's Paul doing? What's going on at RT's?"

Matt swallowed too quickly and choked on his biscuit. Joe didn't miss the nuance. "Oh, things are as usual at the bar. Paul's always great. Don't know what I'd do without him. He's so supportive in everything I'm doing and loves having me hanging with the band. I'm learning a lot about the harp and am getting stronger in my playing. The other members rib me but I like it. It's challenging but in a different way than getting the clinic up and going. There's not much stress for me there and I get so much enjoyment out of playing with those guys."

"Anything else going on?"

Matt kept his head low. "Nope. Why do you ask?"

"Oh, I don't know. Something like a girl in your life? I was just thinking—"

"Are you serious? Were you were at RT's yesterday? Please don't tell me you were sitting in the lounge in the shadows! You are like living next door to the FBI!"

"Relax. Of course I wasn't there. But I just sensed something. Is that a crime?" Joe was holding back a smile.

"No it isn't. But I just don't know how you figure things out so quickly. I did meet someone and want to hire her for the clinic. She's an intelligent woman and it just may work out. Right now she'll work for RT's; actually for McKenzie, the owner. You know that guy?"

"Yeah. Ran into him a time or two. He's rather eccentric; dresses rather sloppy with his shirt halfway out of his trousers. Glasses on the end of his nose. Bushy eyebrows."

"You got him, all right. Anyway, her name is Celeste Rutherford and I met her through Paul. Actually, he was sort of interviewing her when I walked into the bar yesterday early. Very nice. I liked her a lot. But I hardly know her. We sat and talked over brunch and I shared with her about the clinic. She was actually very interested. I was impressed. So who knows? It may work out or it may not. I'm just ready to get this thing going."

"I'm happy for you, Matt. Just let me know when the wedding is." Joe got up and laughed all the way into the kitchen.

Matt sat there scratching his head. *How does that man get inside my head?* He stood up and carried his dishes into the kitchen. He was beyond comfortably full. He was stuffed.

"I'm done here, Joe. I think that either your cooking is improving or I was terribly hungry. I'm headed over to RT's. We play tonight and Paul wanted to go over the new songs with me. I'll come back home and get some of the legwork done on this clinic, like finding a building, for starters. Hope you have a great day."

Still puzzled by Joe's remarks, Matt started out on his bike with a location in mind for the clinic. As he was meandering in and out of streets, he passed Bennington Drive and noticed a beautiful three story office building that would make a perfect clinic. It was up for sale or lease. He turned in and parked his bike, walking around the building. He pulled out his cell phone and dialed Frank's number. His gut told him that this was the place.

"Frank? Matt here. Guess where I am."

"The Caribbean? Hell, I don't know. Where are you?"

"I'm at the corner of Bennington Drive and highway 98. There's the most beautiful building standing here empty, just waiting for us to grab it. Can you get away for a few minutes and see this thing?"

"Sure. Be right down."

Matt hung up the phone and finished walking around the building. Fifteen minutes later, Frank drove up. He was grinning from ear to ear. "I had no idea this building was empty. It was built several years ago and I've always liked it. What a perfect location for a free clinic! The guys on the street can access it easily. We'd have walk-in traffic. And it's easy to be seen. I love the idea. Any number on that sign we can call to make an appointment to see the inside of this beauty?"

"I've got the number. Let's dial now and see if we can get in." Matt punched in the number and a sleepy-sounding agent answered the phone. "Hello?"

"Good morning. Didn't mean to wake you, but I am standing in front of the office building at the corner of Bennington and—"

"Highway 98. Right. What can I do for you?"

"Well, I would like to check out the inside. Any way for you to let us in right now? I know you just woke up, but we really are interested."

"You looking for an office building?"

"I want to open a free clinic. Is it for sale or . . . ?"

Frank was laughing, listening to the tough guy on the phone. "Get 'em, Matt. Does he want to lease this thing or not?"

"Doesn't appear to be that interested. But he's coming over. I think he's skeptical, but I really don't care. I'm pumped about finding this gem right off the bat. I had no idea we'd be so lucky as to nail something so quickly. There really aren't that many places that this clinic would work. I thought about Airport Road, but this is so much more accessible. You agree?"

Frank was walking around the side of the building making mental notes. "Of course I agree. This is perfect for us. I really like the place. It's big enough but not too big. Plenty of office space."

"Yeah. We need to get right on these pharmaceutical companies, Frank. We need the funding and they are hungry wolves. We should make a great pair."

"I'm on it. Leslie has changed her tune since hearing I don't have to quit the hospital. That did it for her. So I'm on board, Matt. Hey! Here comes that character you spoke with on the phone! He's awake now."

Matt chuckled. The red-haired man got out of the car and walked over to Matt.

"Morning. I'm Jason Barnes, and you are?" He stuck out his hand.

"Matt Collins. Dr. Matt Collins. And this is Dr. Frank Harrison. We're interested in getting into the building so we can check it out. How long has the sign been up?"

"A year. Just got the listing last week. You guys from here?"

"Yep. Both of us. So can we do a walk-through ?"

"Sure. Come on in. This is quite a building. Were you guys looking to use this as a medical building? It would be great for doctors' offices. Let me show you around."

Matt could tell the guy was not fully awake. But they had to move quickly because this was too good a location to sit long. "We are going to use it as a free clinic. We would like to check out the bottom floors to see if there are large enough spaces for surgery and examination rooms. The upper floors might be used as offices for doctors."

Jason started showing the rooms one by one, and Frank and Matt took inventory. The building was perfect for what they wanted. Each room was decked out with wide rich molding. It was a masterpiece of a building and would make a great clinic. The presence on Highway 98 was powerful. There were hardwood floors in the reception area and plenty of space for surgery. When they'd researched the whole building including the closets, they ended up back at the front reception area.

"You think this will work for you?"

"It's perfect. But we need to discuss some options. I know it's up for sale, but we really want to lease it first. Is there a possibility of a lease/purchase?"

"I'm going to have to talk to the seller. It has been on the market for a year so they may consider a lease option. Can I have your contact information so I can get in touch with you after I speak with the seller?"

"Sure. We'll give you our cell numbers. Feel free to contact us at any time. We are in a hurry to get this done, so I hope it won't be a problem. I don't want this building to get away from us. The location couldn't be better."

Jason grinned. "I understand, sir. I'll get in touch with you as soon as I get an answer. You guys have a nice day and I'll be talking to you soon."

Matt looked at Frank and they slapped hands. "Man, this would be too perfect for us. I can't believe I rode right up on this building. Don't you just love it?"

"I do! It really pumps me to see the work done in there—the molding, the floors. It looks brand new."

"I've got to run, Frank. Thanks for coming out on such short notice. I'll let you know if I hear anything. In the meantime, talk to the pharmaceutical companies and tell me if you get any results. We are on our way, man. This clinic is gonna happen."

"Your vision will stand, Matt. And many lives will be saved. Forgotten lives."

Those words echoed in Matt's head. Forgotten lives. He could remember feeling forgotten not so long ago. Until old Joe found him. He pedaled over to RT's, looking forward to a good solid practice. But in the back of his mind was the word *forgotten*. He never wanted to hear that word again in relation to human beings. And if he had any life left in him at all, he would make sure those men outside in Destin would be treated like human beings instead of animals.

He walked into RT's and stood still, listening to the band warming up. The sound was music to his ears. He laughed and headed for the stage. His stool was sitting there waiting for him, and on top of the stool was his harmonica. He had a place to be. His life mattered. That was what Joe had whispered to him on the bench. But he'd thought it was a dream.

CHAPTER 59

✣

It was a perfect day in April. The sun had risen bright and early and all of Jenny's flowers were in bloom. She stood on her porch looking with pride at the roses that were against the white fence. Everyone who saw them couldn't believe how large they were. She washed the dirt off her hands and took her shoes off and headed into the house. There was a roast in the oven, vegetables on the stove, and a potato casserole baking. She even had yeast rolls rising in the window. The aroma was wafting through the rooms, making her hungry. This was the first day in a long time that she hadn't felt the depression that had crept into her life like a dark shadow, covering her world gray. She'd never fought depression before and worked hard to overcome it. But today, of all days, Hunter was coming to see her and he was bringing the girl he was going to marry.

Walking into her house was like stepping back in time. She'd put off spending the money to update everything and it was painfully obvious. Suddenly she saw how drab things were. How out of date. Her heart fell as she walked through the hallway and looked into the bedrooms. What was wrong with her? What was she saving her money for?

Jenny walked back into the kitchen to check on the meal, shaking her head in disgust. *Can't I do anything right? I need to get a grip. Hunter is all I have and I live like Benjamin Franklin never invented the light bulb. I hope he isn't embarrassed to bring Holly here.* She looked in the mirror in the living room and decided to change her dress. She'd picked out a flowered dress she bought five years ago. She loved the soft colors and it was comfortable. She was older now and she dressed for comfort. But since Holly was coming, it might be nice if she tried a little harder to look like she was up with the times. A little more hip. She laughed at herself. No man would want her. She was too stuck in the '70s. Hunter never said a word when he came to see her. He was probably used to it. But today she wanted Hunter to be proud of her. So she pulled out a red dress and sandals and put on more makeup than she normally wore. Red lipstick. He wouldn't recognize her when he came through the door.

Hunter had talked the whole way up to Aunt Jenny's. Holly was amazed at how much he talked. She felt like he was nervous and that made her laugh. She was really looking forward to meeting his aunt and sat back to listen more closely about his life.

"I really don't have any relatives except for a few distant cousins, other than my Aunt Jenny. She means the world to me because she was close to my mother. But when I see her now, it makes me so sad. I think she's aged ten years since my mother died. And so have I."

"Oh, you are fine, Hunter. It just took something out of you initially. It does everyone. You'll be fine. I really look forward to seeing your aunt. You've spoken so highly of her that I know I'm going to love her. She is important to you so she will be important to me, too. Does she live alone?"

"Yeah. She never remarried after her husband died. I wasn't close to Charles, but I heard he was a good man. He died young and she was so brokenhearted that she couldn't remarry. Now it's too late. I think she's pretty lonely, if you want to know the truth. She goes all out when I come to see her. It makes it difficult to leave, you know?"

"I can see why. You have such a caring heart, Hunter. Hope she likes me."

"Are you serious? She'll love you."

"Hope so. She'll be protective of you. I would be, too, if I was her."

"She's like a pit bull when she is in her protective mode. But since I've gotten older, she's slacked off some. Especially since my mom died."

"I'm excited about our engagement. We need to talk about where we want to get married. And when."

355

"I'm thinking about a beach wedding. I'd love to stay in a beach house near the ocean and wake up every morning looking at the water. Does that sound romantic to you?"

"I'd love that. You mentioned that earlier and I know it would feel good to get away from here and be in a more tropical surrounding."

"My thoughts exactly. Can you imagine living like that? With a bedroom that faced the ocean? I'd be ruined. I wouldn't want to leave the house!"

"It would certainly put an edge on the day. Nice place to have a honeymoon. Let's check it out on the Internet and see if we can find a rental company for a nice beach cottage."

"Hey! We're here. There's Aunt Jenny's house! Now, don't be nervous. She's easy to love."

Holly waited for Hunter to pull into the driveway and then she opened her door and got out. Hunter came around and they walked up the steps to the porch and knocked on the door. Jenny was inside running around getting things ready. She really liked the dress she had on and hoped Hunter noticed the upgrade. She walked to the door and opened it and smiled her best smile.

"Well, you must be Holly! Come on in. Hey, Hunter! Come here and give me a hug."

Hunter was smiling at her, surprised to see her so dressed up. "Hey, Aunt Jenny. This is Holly, the girl I told you about the other night."

Holly hugged Jenny and smiled. "Aunt Jenny, it's so good to finally meet you. I've heard so much about you! Thank you so much for having me over."

"Well, if my nephew has proposed to you, I need to know who you are! Come on in. Dinner is about ready. It's so good to see both of you. Hunter, you know where the tea is. Could you get the glasses from the table and pour us some tea?"

Hunter was so excited about Holly meeting his aunt that he was a little preoccupied in watching Holly. "Huh? Oh, yeah. The tea. Sure, I'll pour it."

Holly laughed. "Don't pay any attention to him, Aunt Jenny. He's been up for weeks studying. You'd be proud of him. But it's a ruthless schedule for us both."

"Sit down, you two, and let's have a good dinner. I want to hear all about what you're doing."

Hunter smiled at his aunt. She'd done good. This was his favorite meal. "I know you've worked all day in the kitchen. This looks so good. I'm starving."

"I know what you like. I should. I've heard you complain for years."

Hunter raised his eyebrows. She continued. "Holly, tell me about yourself. Are you going to be a doctor, too?"

"Oh, yes. That's what has drawn us together so quickly. We both love the medical field. I'm not sure yet what direction I'm going in, but I definitely want my own practice. I don't want to just work in a hospital."

"Holly and I both want that. I cannot wait to have my own practice. But if I decide to be a surgeon, then that all will change. Aunt Jenny, it's tough to know what to specialize in. Used to be you could just be a good doctor and you did a multiple of things. Not anymore."

"I understand that. Things have gotten so specialized now that you have to see ten doctors just to take care of your health. It's annoying. Was hoping you could change that, Hunter!"

"Oh, I wish I could. But it's a tough world out there. And malpractice insurance is killer. Almost cost prohibitive."

"Aunt Jenny, we'll spend the rest of our lives paying for medical school and malpractice insurance. It's enough to make you change your major!"

"So what's going on in your lives? What about this wedding? I was happy to hear you'd proposed to her, Hunter. Where is the wedding going to be? You decided yet, Holly?"

"We were talking just now on the way here that we'd kind of like a beach wedding. I was thinking Destin, Florida. We'd like to stay in a beachfront cottage. What do you think?"

Jenny smiled and looked at Holly. "This guy's a romantic, isn't he? Hunter, that sounds amazing. What woman wouldn't want to wake up and see the ocean?"

"Well, we need to get away from here and see something different. We'll be so busy when we get back to school that our heads will swim. We really don't have time for a honeymoon, but we'll go over a long weekend. I'm excited."

"What do your parents think?"

"They don't know yet. They were out of town when he proposed to me. So I'm going to tell them soon. We aren't going to get married until fall."

Jenny grinned. "Hunter, are you ready for that? Marriage? That's a big step."

Hunter smiled and winked at Holly. "You only find the right woman once in your life. Why would I wait? She's perfect for me. We've given this a lot of thought and we both want the same things in life. So to answer your question, yes, I'm ready. I want a family. And Holly does, too."

"I'm happy for you, Hunter. You're all the family I have left. And I am so happy to meet Holly and know you are in love with her. She has to be a special girl for you to love her like you do. Holly, I want to welcome you to our family. Wish there were more people to greet you today."

"If I ever find my father, she'll get to meet him. That would mean the world to me, you know, Aunt Jenny?"

Jenny stared at her nephew and tears welled up in her eyes. "Yeah, I do know, Son. Let's eat and I've got some homemade chocolate chip cookies waiting for you with some vanilla ice cream and strawberries. How does that sound?"

"Good thing I haven't gotten my dress yet! I'm going to gain ten pounds on this one meal alone." Holly laughed and took the last bite of her roast and potatoes.

"Aunt Jenny, can we go downstairs and look through mother's things again? I wanted to show Holly some of them."

"Sure you can. It's your stuff, Hunter. You can do whatever you want to with it."

"Good. I want her to see photographs of my mom and stuff. But first I want that dessert you promised us!"

Jenny walked into the kitchen shaking her head. He was still a kid. Just a kid.

The basement was cooler and a little damp. Holly came down the steps after Hunter, curious about the trunk and things that were left to him by his mother. She was dying to know what his mother was like.

"Honey, are you sure you feel like looking at this stuff again? Is it going to be difficult for you?"

"Nah. I'm ready to show you some things. It's time, don't ya think?"

"Yeah. I want to know everything about you. And I want you to see my family, too."

Hunter kissed her and looked up the stairs to see if Aunt Jenny was watching. "I want to see who your parents are. I want to know the people who brought you into this world. I owe them big time. I lived a long time without you and now I cannot imagine living any more of my life without you, sweet girl."

Holly smiled and saw again that romantic side of Hunter. She adored him. "Well let's dig in here and see what we can find. I look forward to seeing her face. To see if I see you in her."

They dug into the trunk and Hunter found several photographs of his mother. Holly stared at the face for a long time trying to see the resemblance. It was there, but vaguely. That made her wonder about his father.

"Do you have any photos of Matt? Just curious?"

"Yeah. Let me look."

Hunter dug around and found some of Matt and his mom. "Here, look at him. He's not too bad looking."

Holly took one look and shouted. "You look a lot like him, Matt. A lot. Do you see the resemblance?"

Hunter shook his head. "Not really. But you see me differently than I do. Is there a good resemblance?"

"Yes there is. I can see it better in his face than I do your mom."

"Wow, that's cool. But Aunt Jenny wouldn't want to hear that. It seems Matt was quite the drinker. And she fears that will show up in me at some point."

"It doesn't have to. But you have to be aware of the tendencies. You already know that, of course."

"I could go forever without a drink. I just needed one to get the nerve up to ask you out. And then to ask you to marry me! So I'm done now. Don't need it anymore."

They laughed and spent the afternoon looking through the letters and photos that were in the trunk. Holly began to form a better picture of Hunter's family and life. She was even more anxious to have him meet her parents. Then it would feel like they were really family.

When they were about ready to go upstairs, Holly stopped Hunter at the foot of the stairs and whispered low, so Jenny would not hear.

"Hunter, wouldn't it be neat to have photos of your parents and mine at our wedding? Maybe on one of the tables? It would feel like your parents were there with us. I think that would be special, don't you?"

"I would love that. I know Mom would want to be here if she could. It would feel good to look over and see her face. Her smile. As far as my father, I don't know the guy. I wish I did. One day I hope to run up on him. But it's cool to have his face there with Mom's. She did love him. I can tell by the letters. Wish he'd stayed around but he doesn't even know I exist. What a surprise when I find him. I just hope he sees it as good news, like I do."

"I'm sure he'll be proud of you, Hunter."

"I want to find him before our wedding. I am going to do it, Holly. Just hope he's still alive. Aunt Jenny insinuated that he might be dead because of the drinking. That would kill me if he was. I want that chance to see his face. To hear him talk. To watch him laugh. I want to know what he does for a living. How good a doctor he is or was. So many questions."

"I'll be here the whole way, baby. We'll find out the answers soon enough. Now let's go tell you aunt goodbye. It's been a great visit but we do need to head back to school."

"One more kiss before we get upstairs."

They ran up the stairs laughing, and found Jenny sitting at the table smiling.

"Thanks for such a wonderful meal, Aunt Jenny! We better get going. We both have a lot of studying to do for tomorrow. It's getting tougher by the day, now."

Jenny got up and walked them to the door. "You don't know how much this meant to me. Thanks so much for bringing Holly by, Hunter."

"I loved meeting you, Aunt Jenny. Take care of yourself and we will see you soon. We'll also get back to you about the date of our wedding!"

"You are as beautiful as he said you were. Thanks for coming. You guys drive safely."

Hunter hugged his aunt and kissed her cheek. A tear was in her eyes but she wiped it away. He knew she was lonely and it hurt for a moment to leave her. But he needed time with Holly in the car and he was looking forward to it.

"I'll talk to you soon, Aunt Jenny. Thanks for the great meal. She's a great girl, huh?"

"Your mother would approve. She would've loved her."

"That's what I needed to hear. Love you. See you soon."

Jenny watched as they pulled away. Her heart was beating fast. *He's looking more like Matt every day. Lara would die if she could see how much they resemble each other. And they both are doctors.*

She stood there and watched the car disappear from view as the dust rolled around and settled in the road. Maybe he would find his father. Maybe Matt wasn't drinking anymore. Maybe Hunter would have the relationship he'd wanted since he was a kid. Maybe.

CHAPTER 60

— ⚜ —

A LIGHT RAIN had started up and the wipers were putting Hunter to sleep. He shook his head and glanced over at Holly. She was so beautiful and her eyes looked sleepy. He was so thankful she'd met his aunt and wondered what she thought. It was a lazy late afternoon and a quick trip back to the school. He wished he could slow time down so they could enjoy this time together. His mind drifted off to when they would be married. Her words pushed through the fog and brought him back to reality.

"Hunter! You were drifting off the road! Wake up."

"Sorry, babe. Was daydreaming. Did you have a good time today?"

"You know I did. I loved meeting your favorite aunt."

"And seeing pictures of my mom? And even Matt?"

"Yeah, that was very cool. I long for you to meet my parents. Not because they are anything special but I want you to know where I came from. You know?"

Hunter got quiet. "Yeah. I know that feeling. Wish you could meet my father. Heck, I wish I could meet him. "

"I know that weighs heavy on your mind. What would you say if you did meet him? Have you thought about that?"

"I sure have. Nothing else but that." He paused and took a sip of Coke. "I'd ask him where he's been all these years. Well, I'd like to ask him that. But of course he didn't know I was alive. So it's not his fault I was raised without him. But I would want to go over his life so I could understand my mother's decision to withhold such important information."

"She had her reasons, obviously. But we can't second guess her decision now. She's not here to defend it."

"I know. I've thought of that, too. But it does seem strange. She really loved him. Looking at the pictures of them together, they appeared to be very happy. It had to be tough when she broke it off with him. Especially after she found herself pregnant. That's such an emotional time and she handled that all alone."

"For a woman, that's really tough. Your body and emotions are changing at the speed of light. I don't know how she held back telling him."

"Well, she felt like he didn't want kids. He was drinking a lot. Maybe she didn't want me around that. Or was afraid he would marry her out of guilt. That happens too many times, and the marriage doesn't last."

"Yeah. I have known couples like that. But wonder what Matt thought about the abrupt breakup?"

"That makes no sense. How would he just let her go? I cannot wait to ask him that one day."

"Is there a lot of anger inside about this, Hunter?"

"I wouldn't call it anger. Mostly curiosity. I wasn't aware there was even a small chance that I'd get to meet my real father. But for some reason I really believe he's still alive somewhere. I think I'll get to see him one day."

"I hope you do, baby. It means so much to you."

"He has no idea how many nights I've spent thinking about our first meeting. How much I want to see his face and listen to him talk. It's silly but I do think about him a lot."

"That's normal, honey. I just don't want you to be disappointed when you do get to see him. Don't have a lot of expectations."

"No, I won't. I know we both don't even know each other. The chances of him wanting me in his life are slim and none. He may be married with kids of his own. That part does bother me a bit."

"What part?"

"The part that he might not want me in his life. It could complicate things for him. He just may say that it's nice to meet me but he's not interested in having a relationship. That would be tough to handle."

"Don't go that far into it, Hunter. You will drive yourself nuts. The main thing is that you get to see him in person and talk. That would be good for starters. If anything develops after that, it would be sheer icing on the cake. Don't you agree?"

"Yeah. You're right, honey. I need to chill. I haven't heard from Paco in ages. Don't even know if the old man is still alive. That worries me a little. I wish I had a way to get in touch with him. He calls me from pay phones. No way to call him back."

Holly laid her head back on the seat and was lost in thought as they pulled into the school parking lot. Hunter sat and looked at her for a few moments. His heart was beating fast just thinking about Matt. He closed his eyes and just sat there holding her hand.

"Hunter, we have a long journey to go through together." She turned and looked at him. He sat up. He could tell she was serious.

"We do, honey. And I'm so glad I have you."

"But we don't know what's ahead. We're new at this, Hunter. I just want you to know I'll be there for you not matter what. With this Matt guy. I'll be there for you."

"You are all I have, Holly. I need you in my life. My mother is gone and all I have is Aunt Jenny. I need you so much, because you get me. You understand things. We're going to have fun and learn and grow. Both of us will end up doctors. But I know the tough times are ahead and it could take a toll on our relationship. I don't want that to happen, girl. We have to be set in stone."

Holly smiled at him, tears running down her face. "You get to me, Mr. Romantic. I love you and I know we'll pull through. Now I'd better run inside before it really storms. I've loved our day. Thank you so much for sharing part of your world with me. Call me!"

She was gone. Running to her apartment through the pouring rain. For a moment Hunter was afraid he would never see her again. But then he smiled. They were in stone. Nothing would separate them.

Lonnie was reading a thesis he'd written about the many chemicals and hormones in food and their effect on the immune system. He was bent over his desk with several half empty glasses of Coke, a beer, and an unfinished pizza in a box right beside his papers. The room reeked of uneaten food that had sat out too long, and stale beer. There was a light on above his head, but the rest of the apartment was dark. And Lonnie was meeting a deadline on this paper. He'd postponed it, procrastinated until it was down to the hour. He was do glad to see Hunter so he could take a short break.

"Hey, dude! Where ya been? Here I am slaving over this paper and you're out gallivanting around with Holly!"

Hunter laughed and walked over the mess on the desk. "It's obvious what you've been doing. What a mess!"

"I know. Give me a break. I've got a deadline. Would you please take a look at what I've written and let me know if you think it's any good?"

Hunter took of his lightweight jacket and laid it across a chair in the kitchen. "Sure, I'll check it out."

He took the paper and read it quickly, making notes on the side margin and grunting now and then about what he was reading. Lonnie was watching closely, knowing Hunter would be a tough critic.

After what seemed like ages, he broke down and asked Hunter what he thought. "Okay, man. Don't keep me in the dark. What do you think?"

Hunter laid the papers down and shook his head.

"I'm dreading what you're going to say," Lonnie said.

"Man, it's perfect. How in the world did you write this stuff with all this mess around you? How did you do it, man?"

Lonnie looked pleasantly shocked. "Good, huh? You like it?"

"Like it? I love it. You did a great job on this. Did your research, didn't you? I mean, the wording is fantastic. It's awesome. You outdid yourself, dude. I bet you get an A on this thing."

"Oh, come on, Hunter. It's not that good. I'm stretching it a bit because the FDA has approved all of the chemicals. But they have a tendency to discover a year later that these same chemicals cause cancer. The tests conducted should have been done earlier. It always happens. They did it with the scare about eating eggs. First we can't eat them. Then we can. That's what provoked this paper, really. I love eggs more than chocolate. And you know how much I love chocolate!"

"I sure do. I think it's got a good angle and I like the way you presented it. Go for it, dude. It's good."

Lonnie grinned and grabbed a cold piece of pizza. "So how was your day?"

"It went better than I thought. We ate a good meal with Aunt Jenny. She said to tell you 'hi,' by the way. And then Holly and I went to the basement and I showed her a lot of photographs of my mom and also of Matt Collins."

"You still determined to find this guy, Hunter?"

"Yeah, don't know how else to go about it. I haven't gotten a call from that guy Paco, have I?"

"No way. Not while I've been here."

"You wouldn't forget about that, would you, Lonnie?"

"Are you serious? I know what that means to you, man. I wouldn't do that to you."

"Well, actually I was hoping you did. That would mean he called. Now all I can do is wait. I have no way to find him."

"He'll call if he's got something to tell you, Hunter. I know it sucks to sit here and wait. But he has been pretty good about keeping you posted. This is the longest you've had to wait."

"I know. But I'm dying to know where he is and where he's looking for Matt now."

"Hunter, you've got to get a life. You can't live your life waiting for this invisible man to come out of the mist. I know you want to meet your father, and I want that to happen for you. But the odds are so slim that he'll be found. You have no idea where he is. Where to look. How in the world is that hobo going to find him?"

Hunter thought for a moment. "He's getting old. And I don't think he's in that good of health. That cough of his sounds serious. I wish he'd call so I could get a better grasp on what I'm dealing with here."

"He's tramping across the country with no money and really no idea where Matt is. He's gotten some tips here and there but he's walking blindly. I just want you to face reality, Hunter. We got a lot of studying to do and you need to have your mind crisp. Can you let it go for a while and just wait on Paco to call?"

Hunter nodded. "I know you're right. I have a lot on my plate. Not to mention that Holly and I are planning a wedding. I have a lot to focus on and I know what you are saying. Paco really seemed to want to help me but he has no phone. No way of communication unless he uses a pay phone. It's so primitive. Doesn't give me much hope of ever finding Matt."

"Let it go for a while. If he calls, you can ask him all the questions you want. But for now, you have to let this go. Holly has her plate full, too. We all do. If we make it through medical school it'll be nothing short of a miracle. Internship is ahead of us. It's going to be ruthless. And the debt is mounting. So we have to make it, Hunter. We have no choice."

"I'll get my head together, dude. I've got to. Thanks for the talk. I needed it, apparently. I'm going to hit the books and study a little. But you did a great job on that paper; I'm proud of you!"

Hunter headed back to his room and sat on the edge of his bed. Maybe he had spent too many hours daydreaming about Matt. Wishing. He had better get his head on straight and work hard. This was his one and only chance to make a good living and have a life. And he wasn't about to let Holly graduate without him. His dreams of meeting his father would have to be put on hold for a few years. If Matt was dead when he found him, then so be it. Right now he had to worry about his own life.

Deep in the woods lay an old man, coughing and spewing up blood. He'd made his bed on straw with an old ripped bedroll. He was comfortable with the smell of the woods, the dampness that comes from early dew, and leaves that have become rotten and piled on one another over time. The night sounds were surrounding him, making music that couldn't be written. The demons of loneliness tried to creep in but he pushed them away with a grunt. No one was getting in. Not for a while.

He closed his eyes and drifted into a deep sleep, not moving for hours. Way down in his mind Matt was floating around, but he pushed him back. The selfishness that overtook him long ago from years of being alone surfaced and bathed him in self pity and anger. It came from nowhere and would disappear at random. He'd learned to love the ebb and flow of it all.

He had no idea how much pain Hunter was feeling. He had no idea how lonely Matt was in the dark of the night. And if he'd allowed himself to think at all about the young man he'd grown to love, he'd have no idea how to bring the two men together.

Oddly, both the old man and the young man fell asleep with a hope that was dimming. And in the center of both their hearts was a man named Matt Collins. Only for the old man, time was moving at the speed of a runaway train and the years outside had wrapped their claws around his body, intending to pull him to the ground. Eating at him from the inside out. None of the elements that had aged his tired weakening body had a clue how tough this old man could be. And neither did he. Not this one night. For he felt like he was dying in the middle of nowhere and no one would know. But he was wrong.

CHAPTER 61

BRISTON MICHAELS PHARMACEUTICAL was the most powerful pharmaceutical company in the world and the leading manufacturer of antibiotics in the free world. Frank had been in New York pitching the company so I got Frank's car and drove to the airport to meet him. We were headed to the building we were about to lease to sign the deal together. The air was filled with high expectations as Frank and I loaded his luggage into the trunk and headed back to Destin. The trip back was just long enough for Frank to brief me as to where we stood with Briston. Frank was more jubilant than I had dared to hope.

"Matt, they are on board. If we can put together that nonprofit status that you talked about they will write us a check next Monday and it's gonna be followed by subsequent donations at regular intervals."

"I am so impressed, Frank. You did a great job! Have you told Seth yet?"

"No, I was hoping to surprise him. I never would have believed it would go so smoothly. They were looking for this kind of a charity to dump some money. They have more money earmarked for projects than we could ever spend."

The Florida countryside flew by us as we ironed out a few details about the funding. I glanced at the brilliant blue sky and palm trees that dotted the highway as we sped along. My stomach was full of butterflies. A year ago I couldn't keep a checking account open, and now I was going on the hook for a long-term lease and would be setting up an account to receive thousands of dollars in donations.

"Frank, we're gonna look back on this day and laugh. I can feel it; this is going to really be something to remember. I've asked Joe to meet us at the building with a camera. I want to chronicle this thing. By the way, did you have any crazy thoughts about getting high when you were in New York?"

"Matt, since Leslie got on board with us, I've been so high on this project that drugs would only ruin my buzz." We both laughed in agreement.

As we pulled off the highway, Frank did a quick zigzag into the parking lot of our new clinic off Bennington Drive. We parked behind the three story structure and I noticed that my stomach was still in knots. Jason Barnes met us on the sidewalk and had already unlocked the heavy, dark mahogany front doors. The place was clean and had the appearance of a well-kept office building in spite of the year it had sat empty. Jason spread the papers out on a table that was left behind by the previous tenants and we both looked over the lease. We had agreed upon a ten-year lease with another ten-year option. We added the option to purchase at the last moment. The owner had agreed with some hesitancy. Jason folded up the lease and gave us a copy, shaking our hands. He walked out strutting a little, probably patting himself on the back for renting to two suckers. But he couldn't have been more wrong. This was a dream come true for us.

I looked at the floors and noticed they were in pretty good shape. The foyer even had a regal look about it. I could hear Frank striding across the floor. Our footsteps echoed in the empty building. I tried to envision where the reception area would go and how all the rooms down the left hallway would work for exam rooms. As I glanced at Frank, I could see he was doing the same thing. As I walked down the corridors I could see a living, breathing clinic; the deal with Briston Michaels insured the place would be state-of-the-art.

My mind drifted as I thought of the poor and displaced people who would find help here and the knot in my stomach grew bigger. A nagging old fear that I couldn't either name or shake was back. My hands got clammy and as I walked back to the entrance Frank seemed to sense my stress level rising. I felt almost claustrophobic. I walked outside, knowing Frank wasn't far behind. He put his hand on my back as I stood there in the gravel. Finally he spoke.

"What's eating you, Matt?" I looked at him with a blank look.

"I don't know. I was picturing how our future patients would look and I saw the helpless look in their eyes. You know what I mean? They could be me."

"Yeah, like you were being pulled back into it."

"That's it buddy, I feel so fortunate to have been found."

Frank said nothing for a moment. He just looked at me as if he understood.

"Matt, we make choices every day. You've made a choice to jump back into life and now you have headed up a dream clinic where people can get real help. That's quite a jump, buddy. You should be proud."

I could see he was trying to find a way to get my mind off my fears and back to the task at hand.

"What are we going to call our clinic, anyway?" Frank couldn't hold back a smile.

I smiled and tried to shrug off the gloom I was feeling. "I had a couple of ideas."

Franks eyes fell on a couple of larger pieces of gravel that were lying in the sand. He bent down and grabbed two and tossed me a stone. We walked across the street and kept walking towards the water.

"How many times can you make that stone skip?" I asked, laughing.

With that he blurted out an answer. "Three!"

He bent and flung the stone and it hit the water, bounced up, and skipped again before it sunk. I grinned, feeling the challenge.

"I used to play this game with my brother Les up in Philadelphia." I reared back and said "four" and my stone bounced five times before sinking into the emerald waters of the harbor. Frank chuckled as he looked around for more stones. I was in a race to find the better stone first.

Suddenly we were two grown men picking up stones and skipping them across an unusually mild harbor. The plunk of skipping stones meeting the water was all we could hear. The sounds of the traffic faded. I was worried that Brother Joe was there by now, but we just couldn't let it go. We had a combined education of over twenty years of college between us and we were chucking stones like kids, laughing out loud at each other. I felt my fears slip away as the stones were swallowed up by the water. We never heard Joe approaching from behind; he had seen us and slipped across the highway. He came right up behind us with his dry humor intact.

"Oh, so this is how renowned surgeons behave just before opening a new clinic? I thought you guys all played golf or something?"

Frank and I snapped out of our stone-throwing trance and laughed with Brother Joe.

"Well, I can hit this target! Come on Joe, you want to throw a few?"

Joe just smiled and Frank and I stood to talk with him, the ripples in the water still spreading out and intersecting and crossing one another. Joe watched the water, seemingly lost in thought.

"Joe, I think we'll call this clinic 'Waterstone'."

"Now that's an odd name."

We stood there watching as the last of the ripples faded. Joe asked for the stone I still had in my hand. I grinned and handed it to him. Joe stepped back and threw a fast one that would've made Roger Clemens blush. The stone hit the water with a loud splash and the ripples spread into what seemed an eternity. Joe looked straight at me. "That's why I do it."

"Do what, Joe?"

"You asked me once why do I go out night after night with blankets and lunches, and this is why. Our lives are like the stones hitting the water. We don't know where the ripples will go, but they will cross and intersect and change the design of the water, constantly growing bigger and eventually reaching the shore. Matt, I had no way of knowing when I saw you on that bench that one day you would bring down a drug ring or start up a clinic. I just saw a cold man and gave him a jacket. We never really know where things are going to wind up. Look at you now! Not only have you grown and changed, but you are seeking to help others change their lives. The simple act of giving you a jacket has spread into something much larger than I could have imagined."

"I feel the same way, Joe. Frank and I have a good vision of reaching out and bringing in those who have no hope. I just hope we can have the effect on others' lives like you've had on mine."

"Open the doors of Waterstone Clinic and you will find the way. Frank, you've come a long way, yourself. I am thankful you've decided to come alongside Matt in this dream."

"I felt almost like I had no choice, Joe. Something pulled me in. I mean, Matt is a pretty impressive guy. It's hard not to like him. But when he shared his vision of this clinic, I really felt a pull. Waterstone is the perfect name."

"I agree. But in the case of men, it is our hearts that are the stones. So Waterstone will mean water washing over our hearts of stone." Frank and I looked at each other and nodded.

"I will say this to you two men; you never know who will walk through your door. God may have something in store for you that you least expect. Keep your eyes wide open. Turn no one away. One thing for sure, you never know who you will be talking to. Listen like you've never listened before. Past the words. Beyond the wound. And that is where the ripples will begin."

CHAPTER 62

———— ✦ ————

THE MAHOGANY DOORS felt heavy as I pulled them open to walk into the clinic. The air still smelled of fresh paint and newly waxed floors. I was still in a daze, having a difficult time believing this was real. It was a dream that floated around for a few months and suddenly began to take shape. I was still shocked that Seth had come on board, but I think he and Frank were reassured by the fact that they could keep their jobs at the hospital. I was the single one in the group so a substantial income wasn't as crucial. But those two men had families to support. Lifestyles. That was a private joke in my life. "Lifestyle." I had none. I owned very little even after nearly a year with Brother Joe. I was making just enough to buy food by working at RT's. Paul had been such a tolerant friend to me, allowing me to stand in during their gigs. It wouldn't have mattered to him if I'd faked playing the harp; he still would've allowed me to be there. And he would've paid me. No questions asked. Now that's a good friend.

I was at the clinic to set up the receptionist area and get it ready for the opening date, which we hadn't nailed down yet. Frank was successful in getting Briston Michaels Pharmaceuticals to fund our charity. I was astounded how quickly they got on board. Of course, Frank knew his stuff and could be pretty persuasive, but it was going to take a good bit of money to get us open. I had set up a bank account and the money was already transferred. I was about to phone Celeste to see if she was ready to come to work for me. I had purchased five large commercial filing cabinets to hold all of our patient files. She would need two standard file cabinets for insurance and correspondence. I was hoping she was skilled in accounting because our books had to be accurate. There would be no room for errors.

Her phone rang forever before she answered it. "Hello?"

"Celeste? It's Matt. Matt Collins. How are you?"

Silence. "Oh, hey, Matt. I haven't heard from you in a while; how've you been?"

"I've been as busy as a one-armed paper hanger! Just trying to get this clinic going. You know?"

"I've been thinking about you. How's that going?"

"Finally, we've had a breakthrough. A big pharmaceutical company has agreed to fund the charity so we are ready to get this clinic open. That's one reason I'm calling. I was wondering if you are ready to come to work for me."

I felt her smile. "You know I'm working at RT's, but I think I could find someone to replace me and slip right out and no one would notice."

"McKenzie would notice. But he's not around half the time, anyway. When could you be here?"

"Give me a week. I'll get things sorted out. What would I be doing, Matt? We talked some about it the last time I saw you, but not in detail. Now that you're ready to open, you may have a better idea of what you want me to do."

"I need a receptionist and bookkeeper. That's for starters. I really wish I could train you to work alongside me. But you'd have to go back to school to be a physician's assistant. Does that interest you at all?"

"I'm not sure. But let me get started and see how things feel. I've never thought about going into the medical field, but I'm not shutting out the idea."

"Just let me know when you're coming and I'll meet you over here and show you around. It's really taking shape and I'm excited about getting it open to the public. I've got two very talented surgeons who are on board with me. I'm about to hire some nurses and get the equipment in place. We've already purchased most of it, but it's a huge endeavor. The state of Florida has strict guidelines. You can imagine."

She blew out a long breath. "Yeah, I can. Good luck, Matt. I can't wait to help you in any way I can."

"Celeste, I'm so happy you're willing to work for me. You're going to fall in love with the people who walk through our door. I wish this kind of clinic had been available to me in my homeless years. And I saw many men out there dying over things they shouldn't die from. The hospitals can only do so much. With the cost of insurance, things aren't going to get any better."

"I agree. Matt, thanks for calling me. I'm really looking forward to this. I've about run out of things to do over here now that McKenzie's office is organized!"

"Talk to you soon. If you need to get in touch with me, you have my number."

I was so pleased that Celeste was going to work for me. I didn't allow myself the pleasure of thinking past that simple fact. I had a tremendous amount of work ahead of me and this wasn't the time for me to get romantic about a woman I hardly knew. But there was something there. Even when I didn't acknowledge it, there was a pull there. I was almost certain she didn't feel it, but that was fine because I wasn't ready for it, anyway. I had nothing to offer her but a job at this point. I needed to get my life in order and put some more time in front of that bench.

I wanted this clinic to represent our mission statement: *Every life matters. We will seek to treat the whole person and not just the wound.* Celeste might be the first person that the public speaks with, and I knew she would represent us well. She had the perfect voice and personality for the job. I leaned over the counter of the receptionist area and checked the refrigerator that was now humming nicely and making ice. I opened it and grinned at all the bottled water that was crammed in there. Each person would have that available to them. I also wanted to stock a snack area so food was available if needed.

I was working in the receptionist area, stocking the file cabinets with folders and the desk with supplies, when someone walked through the door. I looked up and it was Frank, smiling like he'd just won the lottery.

"Hey, buddy. What's going on in here?"

"Hey, man. How's it going? I'm setting up the receptionist area and doing some thinking about how we are going to represent our mission statement. We have to really think about the needs that we'll be faced with as the people start coming through our doors. It's exciting but reality is going to set in real fast."

"Oh, I know. I've been thinking about the same things. We really don't know what's going to come up until we've been open a while. So many different situations—there's no way to prepare for them all."

"I agree. But we do know that we want to treat the whole person if possible. That is our mission statement. We've already hired a full-time psychiatrist and a family counselor. And we are connected with a drug and rehab center in Fort Walton Beach. Those three things are major in dealing with the homeless or families who are struggling."

"I want to offer critical care to those who cannot pay; that's where my heart is."

"We're going to make a big difference in this community; I'm amazed how fast this all has come together. I'm ready, Frank. Are you?"

"Yeah. What about Seth? Has he been over to see the place lately?"

"He's going to come in in a day or two, as a matter of fact. He's really anxious to see the surgery rooms. They are filled with state-of-the-art equipment and the nursing staff is coming together. I've been able to pull some of the best nurses in the area, some of which had retired but were excited about getting back into the business."

"Sounds good. I can't wait to sink my teeth into a good surgery! I'm ready, Matt. It took some time for me to really get on board with you, but now I can't wait for it to open."

We heard sounds outside and walked to the front door. Gulf Coast Sign Company was getting ready to put up our sign. We went outside and watched as they raised the cherry-picker up to the second floor. There was a perfect space for the sign. It seemed surreal watching the name of our clinic going up on the side of a building that seemed to have been designed just for us. The whole thing seemed unreal. But it was happening and I knew then as the name Waterstone Clinic was placed on the building that it was finally going to happen.

We had a lot of work to do getting the place ready to open, and just standing on the sidewalk looking around, I could see three homeless people who needed help. I looked at Frank and he nodded. He had seen the men leaning against one of the tourist shops across the street. They were hidden but they were everywhere. Not to mention the families that kept their poverty a secret while they sent their young children to school with growling stomachs. I was even envisioning a dentist coming into the building. I had not said anything to Frank or Seth but I knew they would love the idea.

After the sign was up we took a photo and sent it to Joe on the computer. The Destin *Herald*, the local paper, was pushing to do an article about the clinic, so we needed to have our parameters set pretty soon. I decided to have a meeting with the three of us, adding Joe to the board for the stability he added. A fresh perspective.

"Frank, while you are here admiring the sign, let's go over a few things. The paper is really pushing to do an article on this clinic, so we need to nail down the opening date and also the parameters on what we will offer here. I just had a thought about trying to get a couple of dentists in the offices. We already are including counselors and a psychiatrist. A dentist would be the next step. What do you think?"

"I love the idea. Let's get Seth on the phone and have a short meeting tomorrow if he's available. Is Joe handy?"

"He'll make the time. The man is tireless. That way we stay one step ahead because these reporters are ringing my phone constantly and I haven't known quite what to tell them."

"I'm really pleased with the black sign. And I like the font. You did a great job picking that out. It is stately. Destin will be proud!"

"It fits this building so well."

"It fits our lives so well, Frank. I'm going in to call Seth. If you need to check anything else out, feel free. I have a lot more stocking to do and then I'm headed back to the house for a break."

After Frank left and I'd gotten an okay from Seth for the meeting tomorrow at 9:30, I finished loading the file drawers and put all the supplies in the cabinets. It was basically ready for Celeste to set up and I would be around if she needed help. I walked through the clinic one more time, checking all the windows and doors. There was nothing left to do except stock the bathrooms and the sinks in the exam rooms. The upper floors were empty but would be filled eventually as we offered other services to our patients. Things were going to move very quickly at this point and I felt like my head was swirling. A lot of critical decisions to make and while I was chomping at the bit to get open and treat patients, my mind was still a little sluggish from the years of abuse and laziness. After getting this far with a new venture that could change the inner structure of Destin and also impact other cities around us, encouraging them to open their eyes to the possibilities available, I was struck by how overwhelmed I felt at times with the daunting task ahead.

I longed for my family and wanted to share with them what we were about to do. I knew they would be proud of me now, and that feeling lifted my spirits as I locked the doors and headed back to see Joe. I had put in a full day and I was tired. But it was a good tired.

My cell rang in my pocket, but I'd turned down the ringer so I didn't hear it as I pedaled home. The streets were packed with tourists who were happy about being in paradise. But my eyes automatically scanned the landscape for the one who was hiding in the shadows. It was a habit I'd acquired that probably would stay with me for as long as I could breathe.

CHAPTER 63

Joe had taken care of a wedding and a funeral all in the same day. He was pretty tired as he fixed supper and was reading the paper when there was a knock on the door. Matt walked in smiling from ear to ear and hooked his cap on the chair across from Joe. They gave each other the high five and Matt plopped down and grabbed a roll. He suddenly was starving.

"Hope you don't mind me barging in like this! I have had a great day and wanted to share it with you. But first, how was your day?"

Joe grinned at Matt and shook his head. "Your living next door to me is like having a kid around all over again! I love it. And by the way, since you asked, I've worked hard today. A funeral and a wedding. The end and the beginning. Interesting day."

"Sorry, Joe. Didn't mean to sound flippant when I came in."

"No worries. So how was your day? What made it so wonderful?"

"I went to the clinic to stock the bathrooms and set up the reservationist's work area. There was much to be done and I was enjoying myself when Frank walked in. He really is ready to jump into this endeavor and I'm loving it."

"That sounds promising. You got a secretary yet?"

Matt laughed and poured himself some coffee. "Funny you should ask. Celeste is on board. Remember I told you about her. I interviewed her when she was really applying for a job at RT's. There's something special about her, but anyway, she's coming on board real soon."

"I love the name, Matt. I've been thinking about us standing at the water's edge, throwing those stones. Do you see how that all fell into place? It was perfect. I think you are in the right place in your life, Matt. This clinic was meant to be."

"Well, it's on the front of the building now, so it's permanent. It looks so good on that brick. What a building, Joe. The layout is excellent and workable for the clinic, and we're thinking we'll expand our services as we are directed towards the right people."

Joe set a plate of food down in front of Matt and sat back down to eat. The baked fish and slaw looked good.

"What were you thinking about adding, Matt? You already have psychiatrists and a counselor. What would you expand to?"

"I was thinking about a dentist. That is one area that is weak among the poor. Their teeth are horrible. They can hardly eat."

Joe was already nodding his head. He went to the kitchen to get dessert and heard Matt yell. He ran back into the room and Matt was pacing the living room floor talking on the phone.

"What do you mean he's in the hospital? What's wrong, Les?"

"Matt, Dad's had a heart attack. It's bad. Can you come home?"

"Me come home? Are you kidding? I have no money. There's no way I can go home now. Oh, man, Les. This is serious. How's Mom?"

"She's in a panic. I think you need to find a way to get home, Matt. This could be the end for Dad."

"Let me see what I can do. I haven't been home in so long I don't remember the last time I saw them. I'll do what I can, Les. Keep me posted. I've got my cell next to me but I'm gonna try to borrow some money."

"I'll talk to you soon, Matt. Get home any way you can."

When he put his cell in his pocket, Matt walked back to the table and sat down and put his head in his hands. He felt more frustrated than he'd ever felt in his life.

"What's going on, Matt?"

"Oh, man, this is bad. Joe, my father has had a heart attack. It's serious. That was my brother Les. He thinks I should come home. Do you know how long it's been since I was home?"

"A long time, I'm sure. Do you want to go, Matt?"

"I do, but in a way I'm scared. It's been so long. I have no car, no money. How in the world can I get there?"

"I can lend you the money, Matt. I know you are setting up your clinic, but you need to see your family. How about heading up there for a long weekend? You can tend to things and see about your mother. She would appreciate that, I'm sure."

"I know I will regret it the rest of my life if I didn't go. I'll pay you back, man. You know I will. I owe you my life. This sucks, Joe. It really sucks. I didn't expect it."

"Let's check flights and see what is available. I'll give you some money for the trip. You can pay me back when you open the clinic. How does that sound?"

Matt wiped his eyes and stood up. "I hate to keep taking from you, Joe. But this time I think you are right. I'll check flights and see what's available and call Les back."

Matt headed back to his apartment with a heavy heart. He immediately went online to see what flights were available to Philadelphia. It looked like he only had two choices so he chose departing early on a Thursday night and arriving in Philadelphia near ten p.m. He got on the phone to Les and shared the news.

"I'm coming home, Les. You really freaked me out with your phone call. Any news on Dad?"

"No news to report. I'm at the hospital with Mom and we are waiting on the doctor to come out and tell us what's going on."

"I'll be in Thursday night. But keep me posted. Should you put Mom on the phone or will that upset her more?"

"I think she would get upset just hearing your voice. Wait until you get here. She'll be so happy to see you that it just might compensate for any bad news we might hear tonight."

"Good idea. Can't wait to see you, Les. It's been a long time. I'll call when I land. It'll be late, though."

"It won't be the first time you called me late. Look forward to seeing you, Matt. Be careful."

Matt hung up and called Frank and Seth. If it had to happen, it was good that it happened now before they opened up the clinic. Matt knew he was going to be the main doctor there and taking off would be impossible for a while to get away. He was excited about seeing his mother and Les, but he was nervous about being in the whole area. It was where he had fallen the hardest. A lot of memories were going to come flooding back and he wasn't really prepared for that trip down memory lane.

He climbed into bed worn out and closed his eyes. Just as he was about to fall asleep, his cell rang again. He'd put it next to his pillow just in case Les called. It was Les.

"Matt. I got some bad news. Dad isn't going to make it. He may not make it through the night. Can you come sooner?"

Matt winced. "No way, Les. I only had two choices and I took Thursday night. It's Wednesday today. I just can't get there any sooner. Is Mom okay?"

"She's in shock, frankly. But I'll be here to help her through it. Just get here as fast as you can. I'm going to need some help. I'll keep you posted. Just wanted you to know what the doctor said. A bad heart attack. Really surprised he's lived this long. See ya soon, Matt."

Setting the phone down, he suddenly felt sick inside. *Dad is not going to make it.* He never dreamed he would lose a parent at this stage in life. But then, he hadn't been around his dad for years to see how he'd aged. How he was taking care of himself. The guilt poured in, or tried to. He might have been able to do something if he'd remained in Philly. But he tried not to own those thoughts. He did what he had to do, and then the years rolled into each other as he struggled to survive. He lay back on his pillow and closed his eyes. Exhaustion was setting in and he slept soundly for about four hours. When he woke up there was a message on his phone from Les. His father had passed away.

Matt hadn't cried in a long, long time. He hadn't allowed himself to cry when he was on the bench or when he had his heart attack. But now, alone in his apartment, he cried for his father. And the tears that came were filled with a lot of pain from the last six or seven years.

It was a healthy cry but it tore at his guts. If only he could have said goodbye.

Joe came early and opened his door, peeking in to see if he was awake. Matt was sitting at the kitchen table sipping a hot cup of strong coffee and staring into space. He was barefooted and his hair was a mess. Joe smiled and then his face went solemn.

"You okay, buddy? Did you hear anything last night?"

"Sure did. Dad didn't make it. He must have died around 3:00 a.m. I'm still in shock, I guess."

"I'm certain you are. What time is your flight?"

"Not 'til around 6:00. I've got all day to think about it."

"Settle down, Matt. You'll be fine. Your mother needs you now. And your brother. It will be good for you to see them and get away from here for the weekend. I'll watch over things. You know that. Don't worry about a thing. Just enjoy your visit with your family. It will be a healing time for you all."

"Not sure Mom won't be angry at me. If I'd been home, he might still be alive."

"Don't let your mind go there, Son. It's not true. Or at least you don't know that would be the case. He's gone now and you have to deal with what is. Your mother will need you for the next couple days."

"Yeah, I know. I just hope things go smoothly. It hasn't in the past. But I've changed and maybe she has, too. I will give it a chance."

"That's all you can do. I'll be here if you need to talk."

"I need a ride to the airport, Joe. And my return flight is Monday at 7:00 am. I'll get in here around noon. As long as I don't get laid over."

Joe shook his head. "I'll be here and I'll be glad to pick you up. Don't worry about anything but seeing your mother."

"Thanks, Joe. Guess I'll pack and check on the clinic. Frank and Seth were very supportive. I'll stop in when it's time for me to leave tonight."

"Sounds good, Matt. I'll say a prayer for you."

Matt sat at the kitchen table thinking about his father. He'd been a tough cookie most of his youth, hard on him and his brother. But there was a love there. His mother was the one who seemed to blame him for everything. He never understood why his father didn't stand up to her or defend him. But it was water under the bridge. His father had grown up alone on the streets. He was a self-made man who learned everything by reading a book. He was brilliant in his own way. But he was too passive. Matt was sick that he had no photographs to look at but he would be up there soon enough. He was nervous about seeing his mother and even being back in Philly. Where had the time gone? And what a life he'd wasted. All that work and now it was gone. Thank God for the new project he and Frank were working on. It really kept him from sinking.

The phone rang and it was Paul. He loved hearing that voice.

"Hey, dude. Hadn't heard from you in a few days. You still playing with us this weekend?"

Matt rubbed his face. He'd forgotten to call Paul. "Man, I forgot to call you. Things have been going nuts around here."

"What do ya mean, dude?"

"My brother phoned me last night and informed me that my father had just had a heart attack. He died at around 3:00 this morning. I'm heading up to Philly tomorrow."

"I'm so sorry. You need me to run up there with you? It'd be fun and you wouldn't have to face all that alone."

"What about your gig? McKenzie would have a fit."

"Yeah, he would. But it's sort of an emergency, isn't it? I'll see what I can do. Was the flight full?"

"No, but it was beginning to fill up. Better make up your mind pretty fast. Let me know, will you? I feel better already."

"Sure will. I'll get back to you shortly."

Matt hung up the phone and grinned. The gloom that had fallen on him was now lifting. If anyone could make a dreaded trip turn around it was Paul. And his mother would love Paul. He already knew it. He grabbed his suitcase and started packing. Realizing he needed to grab some things at the store, he slipped out and accidently left his phone on the table.

While he was gone, Paul phoned. "Hey, dude. You better hope I got a seat next to yours. You didn't think I'd allow you to fly north without me, did ya? Call me."

Matt came in an hour later and heard the message. Things didn't feel so impossible anymore.

CHAPTER 64

⚜

THE SPEED BUMPS at the entrance of the old Sundowner Motel were about as much of an obstacle as Jeff Bulinger's quarter-ton pickup could negotiate. The tiny old four cylinder engine sputtered to a stop in front of the rental office. Pauline, having heard the truck pull up, was at the glass doors secretly hoping it was Paco returning after coming to his senses. Her heart fell just a bit as the young scholarly looking fellow jumped out and headed for the office door. Pauline held it open for him as he entered. The dusty surroundings were just what Jeff had expected. The place seemed particularly grimy to the teacher as he looked at Pauline and stated his business.

"I'm looking for a man named Paco."

Pauline hoped that her face wouldn't betray her. *There's that name again.* To her it was like the small knife in her heart was being twisted.

"He's not here." She spoke in a stiff voice.

Jeff couldn't hide his disappointment. He'd been so eager to meet this guy Paco.

"When will he be back?"

"It don't look like he's coming back," Pauline stated. She turned her back to the stranger to hide the emotion in her face. "I'm afraid he's a bit of a drifter and might be hard for you to find."

Jeff pressed the point. "I'm sure he'll be back. He left this as a contact number, and I have news for him. It would be so disappointing if I don't get a chance talk to him soon."

Pauline turned and looked at the young teacher. "Disappointment follows guys like Paco, but if you leave your card, I'll see that he gets it if he ever comes back."

Jeff could see he would never get anywhere with the old lady so he pulled out his business card. "Well, if he comes back, please tell him I have information that's important to him regarding this Matt Collins fellow."

His voice trailed off as he looked at his watch. He had to be at work soon and couldn't open a second investigation. He'd have to end his pursuit; he'd run into a brick wall.

"Well, would you see that he gets my card? And if you hear where he is, please get in touch with me."

"I will," Pauline assured him. She knew in her gut that the odds were slim and none that she would ever see Paco again.

Jeff turned and left the lobby and climbed into his truck. He headed back over the speed bumps and was just about to ease out onto the road when he paused. He'd gone to sleep last night thinking there was an adventure about to unfold. But it was just another call. His life would move at the pace it had always moved. Nothing would change. As he exhaled, the thoughts and hopes he'd built up over the last twenty-four hours were released into the air and it was business as usual.

A few blocks down the road he saw a shabbily dressed man crossing the road ahead of him. Obviously a street person. He waited impatiently for the bum to cross the road before continuing his journey. As the vagrant looked in Jeff's direction, their eyes locked for a split second. Jeff had no way of knowing that the man crossing the road was the object of his now abandoned search.

Paco crossed the road and hurried back to the grassy out of the way spot in the woods he now called home. He glanced at the studious looking fellow in the truck as he walked by. His attention was quickly back on the stash he'd retrieved from the liquor store down the way. As he neared his spot his only thought was of getting out of sight and popping the top from his recovered treasure and quelling the pain in his head. There was a growing pain in his chest and gut. He sat on the ground and wrestled his backpack around and pulled out his bottle.

He was up as soon as the sunlight began to scatter its rays through the trees and overhead foliage that had provided him cover. The light brought with it a reminder of everything painful in his existence. His thoughts replayed the events of the last twenty-four hours. Having a room and a job had been great for a little while but it allowed people into his life. After weeks of that kind of life he had felt boxed in and crowded. He'd looked in Pauline's eyes up close and personal and had seen that his words had unfortunately had an effect on her. That information brought a fresh wave of responsibility. A burden he had been running from for years.

As the booze began to flow in his bloodstream he began to feel a slight sense of ease. He was becoming what he always strived to be, invisible. Like a child playing hide and seek with his parents, he felt as if no one could see him. Only Paco had played this game in the extreme. The more he stayed hidden, the blinder he became.

The haze of the liquor provided a barrier from the feelings that were welling up in his heart. Feelings like he should find Matt Collins, or that he should have gone to work. And a growing guilt was building that made him feel like he should have been friendlier to Pauline. These thoughts were among the clutter of noise and pain that was being drowned out by the heavy drink. He had enough money to stay this way for a while. The effects of such a binge on his health and well being were secondary to keeping the pain at bay.

He smiled because the realization that he was dying lost its urgency in the alcoholic haze that was his only shelter from the impact of those facts. As he settled back down he allowed sleep to overtake him. He smiled to himself knowing he had nowhere to go and all day to get there. Days would turn into weeks and nights would be long and dark. He pretended he didn't know how quickly life really was slipping away from him.

Paco suddenly woke from a long restless nap. He had no idea how much time had passed. He knew only that he needed a drink. He vaguely remembered a few trips to the store as he rummaged desperately through his belongings searching for his bottle. The growing pile of empties nearby told him he had been there a while. It felt like hours and he couldn't find any whiskey at all. He dug through his pockets and his worse fears were confirmed. He was out of whiskey and out of loot. He felt like he was being smothered in a prickly wool blanket and he needed to fix it. And he didn't have time; he could feel his heart racing already. He jumped up, brushing the leaves and grass from his clothing. His skin was clammy, his heart was racing, and the light hurt his eyes. He looked frantically around the campsite which resembled more of a nest and found some loose change scattered in little piles where it had eased itself out of his pockets during fitful sleep. A quick assessment told him he had enough silver for a pint. His eye for the cost of a pint had grown keen after years of experience.

His shirt stuck to him as he got up. His world violently whirled around as he stood in the fading sunlight. His body felt as if he were being tossed about in the bow of a tiny ship in a vast and violent ocean. He staggered as he took his first jittery step to the clearing. The traffic sounded like an airport; the noise and the light hurt. His stomach retched as he wobbled and took the steps he needed to find a break. A small sip of relief was all his body clamored for. His eyes were confused and unfocused.

He patted his chest for his secondary search something to smoke to calm his violent pain. He checked each pocket but it was futile. He was out of smokes as well. His face was pasty and white and sweat seeped through his clothing like blood though a bandage. His own voice was like a mantra: "Walk straight, Paco, stand up." His hands trembled as he found the stub of an old cigar. Bending down, he picked it up from the grass and in a single move he evaluated it for moisture. A smoke was no good if it didn't light. He stuffed the one inch butt in his mouth and shakily lit it. A cloud of smoke rose as he exhaled. It wasn't enough to calm him but it was better than going without. He trudged through the side streets of Biloxi, Mississippi like he was trudging through a snowy blizzard on the tundra. He kept repeating to himself that it was just a few more blocks.

As he walked he prayed earnestly that the store would be open. He judged by the sun disappearing in the sky and the amount of traffic that it probably was. This time he was correct. As the seasoned vagabond entered the store, the air-conditioned room felt like a balm on his face. He could breathe again.

The old man at the counter had made his living on the kind of pain that stood before him in the form of a hobo from Philly. Paco's dilapidated condition was not uncommon in his line of work. "Long night ahead of ya, buddy?" The gray-haired patron asked gently. Paco couldn't meet his gaze.

"Do ya have Old Grand-Dad in a plastic pint?" Paco quickly remembered the label from the pile of empties back at the nest.

"Yep, got 'em, $4.95 for the half pints." The old clerk softly broke the news.

Paco's head raged. He didn't have five dollars worth of silver in his pocket. A mild panic swept over him.

"How 'bout the O'Shaunessy?"

"Yep. $2.99." The old man assured him.

Paco smiled. "Man, you drive a hard bargain. I'll take one just so you can keep your lights on this month."

The old man chuckled as he retrieved the coveted beverage from a wall behind the counter. The liquor had been put there to protect it from the desperate people who would steal it. It would've been too tempting on the outside aisle.

"That will be $3.27 with tax." The old man spoke with a kindly smile.

Paco reached in his jeans pocket to retrieve the change like a jittery gun fighter before a duel. As he tried to place the change on the counter it scattered like rain on the floor. As if Paco's day couldn't get worse he smiled at the old man apologetically and bent down to retrieve the much needed loot. He was picking up quarters to pay his bill when his eyes lit on the most welcome sight he'd seen in a long time. A green tube of money sticking out of the sneakers Pauline had bought him that tumultuous night. His hand was quick to the task of grabbing the tiny roll and to his delight he found a twenty wrapped in a ten. Paco stood triumphantly.

"Let's leave that change for the sweepers. You sell Old Gold, as well?"

The clerk nodded in agreement and put the cigarettes next to the whiskey. Paco felt like he'd hit the lotto as he settled his tab and sauntered out the door with the first sense of jubilation he had felt all day.

The warm night's light was an eerie glow as the moon took over the sky. The old hobo had his drink and a new set of smokes, but he knew he wasn't going to make it back to the nest. His sweaty hands already screwing the top off his hooch, he staggered toward the back. His hobo radar told him there was a dumpster back there. He meandered to the back and spotted the bright green trash receptacle and knew he had found cover.

Paco had started to duck behind the metal dumpster hoping to get out of the sight of traffic when he was startled by the form of a ragged female opening a foil pouch that housed a day old discarded hamburger. It took a minute for the old man to recover from the shock of seeing another human being.

After greeting her and trying to sound as calm as he could be, he saw something familiar in her mannerisms. He had seen this young lady before but he didn't know where. He spun the top off his whiskey and took a swallow.

"Do ya mind if I catch my breath for a minute?"

Nodding, she cowered at his presence, embarrassed that he'd seen her resorting to the hunt for food. Paco's soft old ways worked to soothe the young woman and he drank his first gulp. A slow long exhale accompanied his having finally gotten his medicine in him.

As his nerves steeled themselves, her familiarity grew on him. He had seen her before. In a wave of recognition and affection he realized who he was seeing. It was Miranda, the young woman he had seen eating one day in a café. He was shocked at the sight of her and even more amazed at the odds of finding her again. The abusiveness of the day and the sickness he was fighting off suddenly dimmed at the prospect of having the company of a friend again. Maybe his luck was changing or God was smiling down on him, unearned either way.

The shock of her deterioration brought him back to reality fast. If there was such a thing as reality, this was pretty much it. Sitting behind a dumpster having a drink with a young woman who had no business being out alone behind a dumpster as night threw its blanket over the sun. His mind didn't want to grasp how long he'd been outside, but he knew one thing; he didn't want her to take that ride.

CHAPTER 65

IT WAS GOING to be a perfect night for flying. The weather report was favorable and Paul and I were already boarded on the plane. We were given seats in the midsection of the plane to sit and the plane began filling up fast. Shortly before takeoff, there were men checking the wings and walking around the plane. I started getting nervous. I hated flying.

"Hey, dude. Would you relax! They've got it, man. It's under control."

"I've never seen them checking the wings like that. Just seems weird to me."

"You scared or something?"

"Heck, no. I'm just anxious to get there, is all. I mean, Mom's going to be pretty upset. I want to get there in one piece, ya know."

Paul laughed and punched me hard in the arm. "Just relax, man. We'll be there in no time. Trust me."

I rolled my eyes and laughed but I didn't feel so sure about it. Something felt wrong. But it could have been that I hadn't seen my family in six years and I didn't leave in good standing with anyone. We finally taxied down the runway and slowly lifted off. Paul kept me talking so I wouldn't grip the seat, but no amount of conversation could curtail the growing fears of how this was all gonna go down when I saw my mother. And even Les.

"So how long has it been since you've seen the fam?"

I swallowed. My mouth was dryer than a cork. "Six years."

"That's a long time. Do ya talk to Les any?"

"I did call him not too long ago and we had a catch-up. At least the homeless part. I think it made him sick."

"It made us all sick, buddy. But you're done with that. I nearly went to that point myself. It's not all that hard to lose everything these days."

"I know. But I drank myself into it. I lost my whole life. Thank God I can still work as a doctor. I would die if I couldn't, man. Do you know how long I went to school?"

Paul chuckled. "Yeah, you told me enough times."

"Well, it nearly killed me. And paying for that loan will take me the rest of my frigging life."

"It'll be worth it now, dude. You're fixing to open up a free clinic and the whole world's gonna know about it. You're gonna be frigging famous."

I raised my eyebrows. "Is this altitude getting to you, dude? I'm not gonna be anywhere near famous. But I want to be successful in this venture. Frank is stepping out on a limb and so is Seth. Their good names are gonna be on the line. No one knows about me in Destin."

"Yeah, I know. But you are gonna be fine. It's a great concept and I can't wait to use the clinic! You said it was for poor people, too, right?"

I laughed and punched him back. "Yeah, dude. You can get your crippled self in there any time you need to and I'll work on you. But don't be dragging your raggedy friends in there!"

Paul bowed over laughing. He was getting loud. "You sit in my band and play for money and you're gonna sit there and call my friends raggedy? You got some nerve."

"Just joking, dude."

"You were just on a bench, for frigging sake."

"Yeah, don't remind me.."

" And it doesn't own you, dude."

"Tell me about it. But it sure felt like it not too long ago, when I was lying there looking at the stars. It was me and the bench. I talked to that bench for many a long night."

"Well, it didn't talk back, did it? Please tell me it didn't."

"I'm not that crazy! Anyway, I'll be glad when we get to Philly and deal with this family stuff and head back home. I'm sort of under pressure to get this clinic open."

We arrived in Philly in just under two hours and I was more than ready to get off the plane. We rented a car and drove down Interstate 476 to Montgomery Road. It felt strange to be driving these roads but very familiar. It all came back to me pretty fast. Paul was checking out the babes in the cars we passed, and I was just lost in the scenery and memories that came and went in my mind. Forty minutes later we were heading down Four Trees Lane where my parents' house was. My stomach was up in my throat. Les was going to be there so I would kill two birds with one stone. Paul jumped right out of the car like he was home.

"Hang on, Paul. Let's get our luggage out of the car."

"Oh, yeah. Well, I'm anxious to meet your mom. She's gonna love me."

"At least she'll love one of us. Now let's go inside. It's awkward enough for me to even be here. Guess I need to get it over with."

I knocked on the door and opened it. Mom was standing by the sofa talking to Les, and she turned around and yelled out my name. I saw her go down, but my feet wouldn't move. She was so shocked to see me it caused her to nearly faint. Les jumped up and grabbed her and we put her on the sofa. She was fine but I could tell right away she was excited and at the same time upset about dad's death.

"Mom, take it easy. I should have called but Les wanted me to surprise you. It's so good to see you!"

"You look wonderful, Matt. I was so worried about you. So worried. We didn't hear from you for so long. Why did you stay away?"

I was tearful but trying to stay strong. I glanced at Paul and he shrugged. He wasn't going to be much help. "I just couldn't talk to about it, Mom. It was too painful a time for me. It's so good to see you and Les."

I hugged Les and we looked at each other. Nothing had changed, really. He was shorter than me but similar in build. We both had dark hair and dark eyes. But I always got the girls, which put a rift between us when we were younger.

"Hey, man. Looking good. Great to see you!"

"You, too, Les. How's it going?"

"Pretty good. Mom is holding up great. It was just the shock of seeing you standing here in her living room. Too much for her, I guess."

"Yeah. Mom, I'm so sorry about Dad. Was this sudden? Or was he having heart issues?"

"He had several episodes that seemed like heart attacks but the cardiologist wasn't certain. So they were watching him. His cholesterol was a little high. But nothing serious. This was a killer heart attack. They said no one would've lived through it."

I shook my head. It felt weird not having Dad at home. "I hate this for you, Mom. I know you loved Dad. Are you going to stay in the house?"

"Oh, yes. I wouldn't think of leaving here. He wouldn't want me to. And Les is a phone call away if I need anything. Are you hungry, Matt? And you haven't even introduced me to your friend."

Paul stepped forward and shook her hand. He turned to Les and greeted him. "Sorry, guys. Matt is just excited about being here after all this time. Name is Paul. Paul Becker. We been friends for some time now. Just thought I'd make this trip with Matt; just wanted to be there for him."

"I think that's honorable of you, Paul. Thanks for coming. Now you guys come into the kitchen and sit down. We have a lot of dinner on the stove that I can reheat. I'll make up a couple of plates for you. We can talk all night, but only after you eat."

Mom had not changed at all. A little older but still so hospitable. She always felt better when she could see us eating her cooking. That made her the happiest. So on my first night back home, I ate like a teenager and watched her smile. It was worth it. I discovered that I really had missed her smile.

The funeral was on the darkest day I'd ever seen. Clouds were building and the forecast was for rain all day. Everyone had black umbrellas up at the gravesite and it looked like something I'd seen in a movie. I couldn't hear the pastor talking for all the thunder and rain that was coming down around us. More people than I'd expected came to the gravesite. Apparently Dad was a well loved man. He'd been pretty reclusive in his older years, working out in his shop and doing crossword puzzles. He loved to read and spent hours poring over math and science books. He wasn't really a people person. But because he was so intelligent everyone wanted to get to know him. He said little, but when he did, it was usually worth hearing. Unlike Les and I.

I looked to my left and I saw my mother sitting so still, so erect in her chair. Her face was solemn and her eyes stared into the air. I knew she was still in shock and she seemed almost frozen sitting there. I squinted and I saw one lone tear fall down her wrinkled face and hit her lap. One tear that meant a lifetime of love and memories was all she had. It killed me to see that tear. She was so stoic at times that it hurt my gut to see her so vulnerable. As the pastor finished his prayers and we all raised our heads up, they began to lower the casket into the grave. I think it was the hardest thing I ever did to watch my mother. After it was lowered, I walked to the edge of the grave and picked up a small shovel and dumped one shovelful of dirt down on the casket. It hit hard on the top and it had a horrible sound that echoed around us. The rain was coming down pretty hard and I was getting soaked. I turned and walked back to my seat and we all stood up.

The service was over. Les and I walked our mother to the car and I squeezed in beside her. She seemed so small and frail. I put my arm around her and for the first time in my life, she laid her head on my shoulder and cried. I held her for the whole trip home, and then Les and I took her into the house. Paul was waiting at the house for us. He thought it best that we had our family time. I couldn't have asked for a better friend than Paul. Food had been delivered to the house all week long so there was plenty to eat. Cousins were stopping in and family I hadn't seen in years.

A couple of hours later it was just Paul, me, Les, and Mom at the house. That was what I was waiting for. It was difficult to be around a mass of people when we were trying to accept the death of a man we dearly loved. It was harder to let go of my father than I had ever thought it would be. Perhaps because I'd been away so long. Or how we parted. We sat down and had a long conversation about our lives, our childhood, and all the good memories of Dad. We were pretty emotional at times but all of it needed to be said. As bedtime approached, Paul and Les decided to hit the sack early, I sat up with Mother and we talked until 1:00 in the morning.

"Matt, I hate that you thought I was against you when you were growing up. That makes me sad."

"I was the first son, Mother. I think you expected a lot out of me that I just couldn't deliver at the time."

"I guess I wanted perfect children. I don't know where that pressure came from. Your father certainly wasn't in that frame of mind. He was more lenient than I was. He would jump to your defense and I thought it was a conspiracy against me."

I laughed. "We didn't have a chance to win many wars with you, Mom. But I did need your support. I felt like I had to beg for it, and that made me just shrink away. I'm sorry if I let you down in my life. I admit I have had my share of struggles."

She looked at me and her eyes filled with tears. "I need you now more than ever. I know you've been through hell and back, but tonight I don't think I can hear about it. But tomorrow, your last day here, I do want to sit and listen to what you've come through and where you are headed."

"That's a deal, Mom. That's one of the reasons I came. I wanted to be here for you and be at the funeral. But I also wanted us to catch up with each other. It's been way too long."

"You have to make a promise to me that you'll never stay away this long again. Not ever."

"Fair enough, Mom. You got that promise. Now let's get you to bed and I'll be around tomorrow for whatever you need done."

We kissed and I headed to my room. I was worn out and full of emotions that I really didn't want to deal with. The dark in the room and the silence were conducive for a good night's sleep. However, I tossed and turned for most of the night, wrestling with the loss of my father, whom I deeply loved. When I finally went to sleep it felt like I had died.

I didn't move until late in the morning. When I opened my eyes I was aware of the sweetest fragrance in the world. My mother's cooking. Just as I peeked my head out of the door of my bedroom, I saw Paul coming down the stairs rubbing his eyes sleepily. It felt good to be home. Better than I'd dreamed. But I missed Dad. And he hadn't been gone but three days. How was I going to face the rest of my life without him?

CHAPTER 66

We awakened to the smell of bacon, eggs, fresh hot coffee, and straw-berries. Mom had made French toast and squeezed fresh orange juice. Les came down and ate a big breakfast with Paul and me and then headed out to run a few errands. Paul took off to check out the town, and that left Mom and I alone. Just what she had wanted.

"Matt, tell me about your life in Florida. I want to know the truth."

"I don't know where to start, Mom. So much has happened."

"You don't have to go into the gory details. But give me the long and short of it, will you? I don't like being the last person to know anything."

I smiled. Same mother I was used to. "Alcohol basically ruined my life, mother. You were around for that. I ended up in Florida and lived on a park bench. It wasn't pleasant but I was my worst enemy at that point. It seemed like I wasn't going to find my way back. I had a bad heart attack while I was living outside and really felt like my life was over. But I met a pastor named Brother Joe and he has given me my life back. I live in an apartment near the parsonage and eat breakfast with him most mornings. I get around on a bicycle right now but it won't be long before I purchase a car. I have actually been playing in Paul's band for quick money. But I am about to venture off into the medical field again, and Mother, I think you'll be proud of what I'm about to do. We are going to open a free clinic that will service most of the homeless people in the surrounding area. It is a huge endeavor, but after researching, we have gotten some huge financial commitments. It will be a 501-3C, and I am so proud of what we are accomplishing, Mom."

"That sounds like a tremendous amount of responsibility. And of course, I am very proud of you. But I just hope you are not taking on too much, Matt. It hurts me to think you've suffered like that, and even more that you wouldn't come home. I would've been there for you, Matt. Didn't you know that?"

"I was ashamed, Mother. I couldn't look you and Dad in the eyes. It hurt too badly. But now I've found my way back with the help of a few wonderful people. Paul included. Quite a journey. But setting up the free clinic is the greatest thing I will have ever done in my life. I'll send you photos of it after we get it going. I'm really pumped about it! I guess you can tell."

"Yes, I can tell, all right. How is your health? What are the doctors saying about your heart?"

"My cardiac surgeon will be on staff at the free clinic. He says I'm fine. I have had to change a few things about my life. No alcohol. No smoking. And a new diet, which I'm getting used to. I feel pretty good. Just tired."

"I know you are. You need to rest today because you're heading home tomorrow. I just want to stare at you, Matt. You look so good to me. It's music to my ears to hear that you've rebuilt your life and are going to be in the medical field again. I wish your dad had seen you before he died. He loved you so much."

A huge lump came up in my throat. "I know, Mom, and I hate that I didn't get here before he died. We did the best we could. I want you to know I'll be back soon. I'm not staying away anymore. And I want you to come down as soon as I get this clinic up and running. I have two great doctors on board with me, and we are talking about bringing in a dentist and maybe even an ophthalmologist."

"It sounds fabulous and I'm so proud of you, Son. We missed you and I was frantic at times, wondering where you were. We didn't know what had happened to you."

"I know, Mom. It bothered me that I couldn't call you and Dad. But somehow, I just couldn't face the damage. And it was getting worse by the minute. If it hadn't been for Brother Joe, I don't know where I'd be today. You have to meet this guy one day."

"I want to, Matt. He sounds like an interesting man. I owe him for saving your life."

"He watches over me like a mother hen."

"Nothing wrong with that."

"He doesn't miss anything, Mother. If I leave or come in late, he sees it. But he feeds me well and helps me make wiser decisions. So I don't mind his input in my life. He's my hero, if you want to know the truth. He has a heart for the homeless. And he looks for men who aren't out there so long that they won't come back. I almost didn't make it, but he snatched me back."

"Well, all I can say is that he must be something special to have talked you into changing. Because you can be one stubborn man."

We both laughed and I hugged her. Paul came in and we decided to ride around town so I could show him where I grew up. Where I had my practice. It felt good to get out for a minute and move around. We spent the whole afternoon checking out the town and ate at one of the better local restaurants. It didn't look like much, but Sally's Wheelhouse was the place to eat in town. All the locals ate there. Paul loved the rustic atmosphere and the yeast rolls. We settled into a wonderful and restoring conversation that smoothed out the emotions that had spread in every corner of my body and mind. I was never so glad in my life that I had Paul with me. He had turned out to be a gold mine of a friend. And those were hard to come by.

Les was waiting for me at the house when we got back.

"You been gone all day. You guys have fun?"

"Yeah. Ate at Sally's. It was packed. Just as good as I remember it."

"I remember it well. So how's it going with Mom?"

"Better than I expected. She's been a real doll. I'm worried about when we leave. How's she gonna handle Dad being gone?"

"I'll be a phone call away, Matt. Like always. I sort of resented you being away because it left me to deal with Mom and Dad. But now I guess it was a blessing in a roundabout way. She will need me for a while until she adjusts. I just wish you and I had been able to communicate a little better. Six years of silence is a bit much, man."

"I agree totally and I'm not proud of what I did. Or how I lived. It was lonely for me, Les, and I missed you more than you realize. I thought about calling you a million times. But I just couldn't dial the phone. Sometimes I had no money to call you, which presented its own set of problems. I didn't want you to see me like that. You can understand that, can't you?"

Les stood up and grabbed my arm and we hugged each other. First time in years. And it felt real good. He had been my best friend once and the memories we shared were priceless. And no one else could bring those back to my mind but Les.

"We are heading home tomorrow, Les. But you need to bring Mom and visit me. I'll let you know when things are more organized. I need to get this clinic up and running and make some money. It won't be long."

I looked at Paul and he was yawning. "Dude, you ready for bed? You've been a trooper all day. Let's go to bed early and get up and hit the road. How does that sound?"

"Hey, I've enjoyed this. Good to see where you came from. Your mom's the best. And Les, it was great to meet you. Matt has talked enough about you that I feel like I already know you."

"It's good to know Matt has an ally. But you've got the job of keeping him in line! You guys get some rest and we'll talk in the morning."

I lay in bed with my arms behind my head, thinking about the quick trip home. Mom looked pretty much the same. Maybe a little older. Les was like he was when I had I left him. Studious and responsible. I sure wished I could be more like him, and maybe, just maybe that was where I was headed.

Dad was gone. It echoed in my mind, the sound of the dirt falling on his casket. It hurt so much to hear that noise. My mind ran back to my childhood, recalling memories of fishing with Dad and watching him work on the cars. He was good with his hands, but so quiet you forgot he was in the house. It was one of Mom's pet peeves. She tried hard to engage him in an argument but he never crossed that line. Never took the bait. I wish I'd had more of his character in me. It would have saved me a lot of heartache.

The one thing I regretted was that we didn't talk as much as I would have liked. All the years I played ball and dated and learned to drive,

I had so many questions I wanted answered. He was busy working or building something. Playing golf. I didn't know how to approach him. I turned to the wrong things to deal with my frustration. He must have been blind not to have seen it. Mom had turned her head the other way. I drank in high school and on into college and medical school. So did all the guys. But mine was worse. I wish now I'd talked to Dad about it. I would have given anything to have heard his voice one more time. To hear that deep laugh and watch his eyes twinkle when he told a good joke. But that great voice that called out to us in the morning that it was time to get up for school was finally silenced. Never to be heard again.

I guessed if I had a quarter, even my last quarter, I would have called my dad if God would let me. Just to hear that voice one more time. In the dark of the bedroom, I closed my eyes with tears running down my face, and fell into a restless sleep. Tomorrow wasn't going to be any easier, telling Mom goodbye.

CHAPTER 67

⚜

THE ORGANIC COFFEE Bar was full of people. Every booth was crowded with college kids packed in like sardines. The noise was almost unbearable as Hunter waded through the crowd with Holly. The waitress had found them a seat in the far corner of the café, and Holly scooted across the red faux leather bench seat, catching her shorts on a torn edge. Someone had duct taped the rip but the seat had seen better days. There was a juke box at the front of the café that was playing '70s music at a level that could take your hearing out. They both knew a lot of the medical students sitting in the booths and standing by the coffee bar. It was a warm night and this was a perfect place to visit with friends. But Hunter had more serious matters on his mind.

"Hey, you. It's so loud I can hardly hear myself think!" Hunter smiled warmly.

"It's better not to think tonight. Rest your brain, dude."

"I want to plan our honeymoon."

"Well, you know I want to go to Destin just like you do!"

"We need to nail down a time so I can reserve us a place. A romantic beach cottage."

"You're killing me. I'd die to have that." She reached out and touched his hand.

"Let's check our schedules and see what time slot we have to zip down there for a long weekend. We wouldn't miss that much school."

They both pulled out their iPhones and looked at the hectic schedules that were the norm for medical students. It looked like August was going to be the window of time. The third weekend, to be exact.

"Hunter, check out the next to last weekend in August. That's good for me. What about you?"

"I was looking at the same time frame. I'll get online to see what's available. I found several rental companies that have fantastic houses on the beach. I'm sure they come at a price, though. My pockets aren't that deep, you know!"

"Oh, we'll manage. How bad could it be? We just want a few days. Just see what you can find out."

"I will. How'd you do on your chemistry test?"

"This professor is a piece of work. I think he's a little OCD. But I'm going to pass just to spite him. The questions on the test aren't even in the book."

"I'll be glad when we are in internship. I want some hands-on experience. Don't you?"

"Sure I do. I'm dying to get my hands dirty. Open heart surgery. Delivering a baby. I just wish I knew which way I wanted to go."

"You'll figure it out. I just want to be a surgeon. Not sure what to specialize in. But we have some time to figure it out. Can we take a break from that and enjoy our wedding? Is that possible?"

"Going to school and getting married is nuts. I want us to make it work. Do you hear me? We're not going to be one of those statistics."

Hunter was shaking his head. "No way, baby. I love you and that is forever. Now let's order and get out of here. I don't know how they'll squeeze one more body in this place."

He paused. "Wish I could talk to my father. You don't know how frustrating it is to be getting married and your mother is dead and you don't know where your father is. I feel like I'm floating. No one is attached to me but you."

"Have you heard anything from your friend Paco?"

"Nope. Not a word. I keep thinking any day now that I'll hear something."

"Well, don't give up, honey. He'll call you soon. I bet you anything he's getting closer to finding out something about your father. Just give him time."

"Do you know how old this guy is, Holly? He's ancient. He's been outside almost as long as we've been alive. How much longer will he survive out there? I mean, he didn't look too good that last time I saw him and that was a while ago. I'm worried he's not gonna make it."

"Hunter, relax. He's a pro at being homeless. That's in his favor, you know? Let's not think negatively about it. He's going to find your dad. I just know it. Now let's pin down a time for the wedding and call it a day. I've got tons of studying to do, and so do you!"

"Okay, I get you. We'll have just about enough time between that semester and the new one to tie the knot, enjoy a beach cottage for a weekend, and head back to school."

Holly smiled. Not her dream honeymoon, but it would have to do. "That sounds perfect. August 24 Let's tell the family and get things going. We don't have much time to pull this all together. And I don't have any extra time to plan a wedding. Mom is going to really have to help."

"Keep it simple. Don't let her make too big a deal out of this. We don't have tons of money and even less time. I just want you to be mine. I want to spend the rest of my life with you. That's all that matters."

"And a bite of wedding cake, you lughead. I know you are dying for that!"

"Yeah, a bite of cake. Or a bite of you. I'd actually prefer that."

"If that's a stab of being romantic, it's pretty pathetic. So let's head back to the dorm and I'll hit the books. I love you. I'm excited. Wish we had more time to plan, though."

"We'll make it happen, baby."

Hunter walked Holly back to her apartment and he headed back to the dorm. Lonnie would be waiting to hear what they'd decided as far as a date. His mind was all over the place. He really missed his mother and had so many questions about Matt. He felt frustrated that she hadn't shared anything with him about his real father. Why did she keep it all hidden?

As he poured over the books, his mind kept going back to what Holly had said about Paco. That he would find his dad sooner or later. It disturbed Hunter that he was relying on a stranger to locate his father. He was depending on a man who was undependable. Had he made a huge mistake in allowing that dream to develop? Was he walking down a dead end road?

Haunted by these thoughts, Hunter laid his head down on the desk and drifted into a fretful sleep. There was always a man in his dreams that was walking towards him but the sun was behind him and he never could see his face. He woke up feeling alone and frustrated. Foolish for trusting Paco. Foolish for wanting something that wasn't going to happen. He wasn't a child anymore. He didn't believe in Santa Claus. And hoping for his father to appear was just like believing in a man dressed in red. He sat up and rubbed his eyes and tackled the chapters he needed to learn in chemistry. He spent the next two hours studying for a test in anatomy and physics. Then he finally collapsed on his bed, noticing the light in Lonnie's room still on.

He whispered to himself as he fell into a deep sleep. "Paco, you better not let me down. I don't care how old you are, or how sick, you better find Matt Collins. I just want a chance to know who he is. You gotta give me that chance."

Hunter had a birthmark on his left ankle that was shaped like a half moon. He slept on his left side with one arm off the bed. And he liked his room totally black, not a stitch of light coming in. He craved math and science and hated cheese. He laughed at the Three Stooges and cried at romantic movies. But he was tough as nails inside. A heart of steel at times.

He didn't know there was someone across the miles who was a mirror image of himself. He had no idea that he walked in the footsteps of the man he was dying to meet. He had no idea.

CHAPTER 68

MIRANDA LOOKED LIKE she'd been hit by a truck, yet strangely, she was a welcome sight for Paco's sore eyes. The two of them together were an absolute train wreck.

"So you recognize me?" Paco asked without any expression on his face.

Conscious of how she must have looked, Miranda quickly nodded in affirmation. The two could see the suffering in the other but at this point they were nearly oblivious to their own. Paco took a medicinal pull on his whiskey.

"My name's Paco. Will you join me for lunch?"

"Yeah, I guess." Her mannerisms spoke more than her words.

Her clothes bore the familiar faded and dirty look that came with life on the street. Her hair was stringy and shapeless. Her face had a dull pallor to it and her cheekbones had become prominent from too many skipped meals. Paco couldn't look at her without it evoking a fatherly need to take care of her. The two walked to a nearby convenience store. She was too embarrassed to go in and too frail for Paco to insist. He quickly ran in and with the windfall he'd found tucked in his shoe he quickly returned with a bag of necessities. The two walked shakily back to his campsite in silence. In the bag was a four pack of cheap strong beer, a couple of Danishes and a can of Dinty Moore stew. After Paco had ingested enough beer and whiskey to quiet the screaming in his head, he pried the top off the can of stew and insisted that Miranda eat a few spoonfuls.

"You got to eat somethin'. Just a couple of spoonfuls at a time. No sense making your stomach hurt."

Paco fussed over her as if she were a newborn, which pretty much described her strength level. He moved carefully and quietly knowing that her nerves were as jangled as his own. After a while the two reclined in the grass and sipped their beer as if on vacation.

"I'm dyin' to know what happened to you. But you don't have to say anything."

"Not much to say. Boyfriend turned out to be a real creep."

"Yeah, that happens a lot. But you're okay now, right?" She looked pretty rough.

"Yeah, I'm pretty good, I guess." She spoke weakly, not seeming to know what "okay" really meant.

"How long you been out here on your own? Any idea?"

"Several months. I'm just learning the ropes."

"Takes a while. Watch out who you're hanging with, Miranda. Don't smoke nothing anyone hands you. And stay away from the pills that are being passed around. Beer is bad enough on you, but those pills are deadly."

The smell of the spring grass and the flow of booze had a hypnotic affect and the two felt lazy.

Eventually, Miranda's comfort level was high enough for her to speak. And she did so in soft tones that seemed to flow in a breeze to Paco's ears.

"Do you remember telling me to call my dad?"

Paco nodded lazily. "Yeah, you ever do it?"

"Yeah, and somehow you came up in our conversation." She sipped her beer slowly, playing with the rim of the can.

Paco's attention was arrested temporarily by a little yellow butterfly trying to land on a weed near his boot. His eyes grew narrow as if he were preparing for a nap.

"What did you tell him about me?"

"He said he knew you."

"Huh?" Paco's attention was reignited.

"My dad said he knew who you were."

Paco dismissed the information thinking the drink had gone to her head. Or whatever trauma she had been through had jarred a few brain cells loose. But he looked at her closely and as she spoke each word it captured more and more of his attention. *How would her dad know me?*

"See, my dad said he knows you from a bar in Philadelphia."

Paco was now invisibly squeezing her words like toothpaste, trying to piece them together before she got the next sentence out.

"Chic." The two spoke the name simultaneously.

Paco was now on his feet and his mind was whirling at the magnitude of the coincidence.

"He also said he needed you to call him collect. He seemed to think it was very important; something about a boy in med school. I have his number with me." Miranda's memory was as faint as her voice was weak.

Miranda fumbled through a ragged clutch looking for the paper with Chic's cell phone number written on it. Paco could no longer control his animation. He was pacing in a small circle. His head was pounding. Silently he asked himself, *Oh, man, how did I do this? What could he want?*

The barrage of his own questions was almost more than Paco could contain. After what seemed like forever, Miranda held out the tiny paper in her trembling hand. Paco retrieved it hastily and reviewed the number; it was definitely a Philadelphia number.

"We got to find a phone. Come on, let's find a phone! Oh, he's gonna flip out that I've found you again."

"I can't move. I need to sleep. I'll wait here 'til you come back; I feel safe with you. I'll lay here and watch your stuff."

Paco's eyes narrowed. He didn't like the idea of a girl who was obviously wrapped up in drugs watching over his belongings. But the enthusiasm for calling Chic overwhelmed his common sense. Paco could see she was not up to a trip to the phone or in any shape to run off with his stuff. So the two agreed he would go and call his old buddy while Miranda gathered her strength with a nap. She was looking very pale.

Paco raced madly down the street. By the time he got back to the liquor store he had Chic's number memorized, repeating it over and over. He burst in and went straight to the counter. There was a young guy standing behind the counter reading a book.

"Hey, dude. I need to borrow your phone for a moment. It'll be a collect call. I'll be brief, man. Just need to use the phone for a second."

"Well, we don't usually let anyone use the phone, but you seem to be in a panic." The young man reluctantly agreed and set his phone down at the end of the counter, away from where he was doing business. The automated voice introduced the call. Chic was on the other end of the line, freaking out that Paco was calling.

"Hey, Paco! I'd just about given up ever hearing from you! How in the world have you been, man?"

"I been everywhere. Worn out mostly. How 'bout you, Chic? Haven't heard your voice in quite a while."

"I'm good, man. But I'm sure glad you called. I got some really strange news for you."

Paco quietly listened, restraining his excitement.

"You know Matt Collins, the doctor you been looking for? Well, he's in Florida in a town called Destin. I tried to get word to you through the paper but guess you never saw the ad. Matt is in Destin and I'm sure of it."

"Wow!" Paco exclaimed loudly. "I was in Florida for a while; it was no picnic."

"Well, I'm sorry our buddy gave you a bad lead but he straightened it out the next time I saw him. I hate that you've wasted all this time."

"No problem. I made some money along the way. It's been quite a journey." Paco coughed and had to hold the phone away until he caught his breath.

"So you saw Miranda, eh? How is she?"

Paco felt a wave of discomfort wash over him as he now faced the very question he didn't wish to answer. "Hey, Chic, it's not my business, but you oughta come down and get her. She ain't good, man. Not sure what the whole story is but this girl needs her father."

"I'm not as surprised as I am concerned, Paco. The last time I spoke with her she was evasive. I knew she was with some guy. Guess that didn't work out."

Nancy Veldman

"Look, I got to get off this guy's phone but I'm gonna have Miranda call you. She isn't good."

"Drugs ?" Chic asked, sounding shocked to hear his daughter was doing so poorly.

"I hate to guess that, her being your daughter and all."

"Paco, just tell me, for God's sake! Is she okay?"

"Well, I think she's pretty sick. She's at my camp now so I'll have her call ya. Just know she may not tell you how bad she's doing. It's pretty common to lie about things like that. Especially to family. I'm just telling you that she's very weak and sick. I'm worried about how fast she's gone down since the last time I saw her, man."

"That really has me worried, Paco. I guess I need to get on a plane and get down there as quickly as I can."

"That would be my suggestion, Chic. I guess I'm heading over to Florida. Where is Destin?"

"Between Pensacola and Panama City. That's as much as I know about it."

"Okay, I got to get off this guy's phone. I'll have Miranda call you as soon as I get back."

Paco hung up and purchased another tiny bottle of liquor. It was nearly all the money he had but he needed it badly. He thanked the guy again for the use of the phone and hurried back to his camp. As he approached he could see Miranda lying under a tree on his other sleeping bag, fast asleep. He decided to be quiet so he wouldn't have to share his whiskey and rationalized that she needed the sleep more than she needed another drink.

He was worn out and wanted to just lie down and rest. His mind was reeling over the conversation he'd just had with Chic about Matt's location. He was blown away that he'd spent such a large amount of time in Biloxi for nothing. But then he would have never met Chic's daughter if he hadn't made a wrong turn in his search for Matt. Miranda needed help. She was such a lovely girl and his heart ached to see her in such a tough position. He really hoped Chic would make the effort to come down and see her. Take her back home.

He looked over at her sleeping and noticed that something about her looked different. As Paco looked closer, he noticed she was too still. Her chest wasn't moving and her skin had a waxy glow that told Paco he wasn't looking at his old friend's daughter, but at a corpse. Shock swept over him as he rushed to revive her. He pulled her up in his arms and tried to feel for a pulse. There was nothing. Her arms were limp and she was obviously not breathing. He worked on her, trying CPR, punching her chest, trying hard to get her heart to beat. But she was gone. He panicked, not wanting to leave her there. But at the same time, he needed to rush back to the store to use the phone again and let Chic know what had happened.

Once more he shook the girl. He blew air into her lungs over and over and pumped her chest. There was no pulse. She simply was gone. He laid her back down and closed her eyes. She was so beautiful, even though her hair had gotten dull and ragged. Her nails were dirty underneath. There was the typical homeless smell about her. But something else had gone wrong. She must have gotten some bad weed or drugs. There was no way of knowing until the medical examiner checked her out. He hated to even think about someone cutting on her body. He couldn't believe she was dead. He decided to tuck her into her sleeping bag and zip it up. Then he ran as best he could to the liquor store and slammed his fist down on the counter, panting and out of breath. The young man at the cash register raised an eyebrow and sauntered over.

"You need something?"

"Yeah. I need you to call an ambulance. There's a dead body in the woods by Smith Road. It's a young girl."

"How did you find her? Do you know who she is? Hey! Come back here!" The desk clerk ran around the counter but Paco was gone. He grabbed the phone and dialed 911.

Paco headed back to camp and picked up his sleeping bag and blanket. He cleaned up the area and made sure the zipper was up on the sleeping bag.

His stomach felt sick as he hurriedly left the camp, headed for the nearest pay phone. The uneasiness he felt about leaving Miranda was overridden with the urge to contact Chic. He had to let the man know that his daughter had died. But he also knew he couldn't stick around or he'd get tied up with the police about her death. He might even be seen as a suspect. It wasn't a good idea and he wanted nothing to do with the local police in Biloxi.

He headed towards the highway and found a pay phone at an old gas station on the side of the road. He fumbled around, found two quarters, and dropped them into the slot. This was not a call he wanted to make. Chic was a good friend, but it wasn't going to be easy telling him the bad news. Paco had hardened over the years and his emotions were hidden pretty deep. But seeing that young girl lying there dead had just about done him in. Maybe he was getting soft. Maybe the illness he was feeling in his own body had loosened him up a bit. Whatever it was, he had to get a grip when he talked to Chic. The man was going to lose his mind until he got down to Biloxi to get his daughter. And Paco didn't like being the one to drop the news on him.

The phone was ringing. Paco's hand was shaking. Chic picked up on the fifth ring.

"Hello? This is Chic."

Paco's raspy voice answered. "Chic. Paco here. Got some bad news. I headed back to camp after talking to you and I found Miranda dead. She's gone, Chic. You better get down here fast."

Silence on the other end. "Dead? Miranda's dead? How did that happen? I thought you said she was safe."

"She was safe. It didn't happen on my watch. She had already had some bad drugs or something. All we did was sip on some whiskey. But she looked rough when I saw her at the dumpster, Chic. She was pasty. I was worried then about her health. Look, I'm sorry, man. I hated to make this call. But get down here fast. The clerk at the liquor store called the cops. I had to get out, man. They'd nail me for this. They hate homeless people and this would be their chance to get me off the road."

Chic paused, thinking of what to do. He felt his whole body going down-hill. He wanted to die. His only daughter was dead, and this hobo was running away for fear of getting nailed for her death. He had sympathy for Paco, but his head was swimming. How did she die? Did Paco know and just didn't want to tell him?

"Do you know something, Paco? Are you holding back here? I need to know how she died."

"I don't know, man. All I know is that I came back to camp and she was dead. I worked on her. I tried to get her back. But she was gone. Just plain gone."

Tears streamed down Chic's face. *How did I let this happen?*

"Okay, Paco. Thanks for the call. I don't know what to say. You bet-ter get going. I don't want you arrested for her death. But I'm gonna want to talk to you when you get where you're going. I need to hear about your time with her. What she talked about. I want to get a clue as to how she has ended up dead. You know?"

"Yeah, I know. I'm sorry, Chic. It's tough out here. I'm one of the few who has lived so long."

"Take care, Paco. I'll catch up with you somehow. Call me. I need to talk to you."

Paco hung up the phone and hit the highway headed east to Destin. It would take him a long time to walk so far, but he knew he'd hook a ride here and there. He wasn't worried too much but he knew he'd better get out of town. His chest hurt and he was tired. But he put one foot in front of the other and walked through Biloxi to Ocean Springs. He made camp in a cluster of trees that had a lot of underbrush. He needed a drink so badly that he nearly cried. He felt sick and worn out. But he just needed to collect himself and think. This had ended up to be the worst leg of his journey. His health was deteriorating and he'd seen the death of a friend's daughter. He unrolled his sleeping bag and lay down to take a nap. Just before he fell asleep he checked his backpack and found a little whiskey left in the bottle he'd bought earlier. He took the last swig and fell into a deep sleep.

He knew, though, that needed more than a nap to revive his old body. He needed to find Matt Collins and make that magic call to Hunter. If he could live that long, it would be a great ending to his life. And that was a big if.

CHAPTER 69

⚜

WATERSTONE CLINIC WAS in full swing on its fourth day. There was electricity in the air and my heart felt like it skipped a beat each time Celeste handed me a new file. I was hugely aware that the clinic would not have been opened at all without the cash flow that the pharmaceutical companies donated. I was on my game and was overwhelmed with what had taken shape; the equipment and the confidence and compassion of the staff were beyond anything I had dreamed of in Philadelphia.

I watched as Celeste greeted every patient quietly and professionally. Many of them lacked proper identification; many had bizarre names or nicknames that had hung on for years and had become something of a persona for each of them. There was, of course, the initial avalanche of patients that only wanted to get their hands on some kind of narcotic that would provide a temporary lift from their painful existence. But they all came in hurting and Waterstone Clinic held its arms open like a shelter from a raging storm. Each person who entered received a warm greeting from Celeste or one of her trainees. And instead of being confronted by an onslaught of paperwork they were each addressed by volunteer staff. This staff member would walk them through the intake process, assuring everyone that their needs were important. The place had a buzz of excitement as people came in from every walk of life. Wealthy people came in to see how they could help. Many skeptical clergy members also came in to see where they could refer their poorer parishioners. Once inside, everyone seemed to want to get in on the excitement. The stack of volunteer applications quickly filled a file drawer of its own.

I threw myself into the venture with both feet. Each patient drew on all of my training and also on what knowledge I'd acquired from being homeless. I was dedicated to the task of allowing everyone access to the caliber of care that people deserved, no matter what their lot in life. The work flow was sometimes overwhelming but Celeste and I had an unspoken dance of efficient communication as each patient was seated. Celeste reviewed each file before handing it off to one of the nursing staff that Seth and Frank had recruited from each of their respective hospitals. The nurses would also familiarize themselves with the information in files before calling the patient by a number that was issued to protect each person's anonymity. As the patients were escorted to the exam rooms the nurse would get their concerns written on a Post-it note that was placed on each file. And that was the first thing I would look at as I retrieved the file from the acrylic holder outside of each door. As I entered I would always review the patient's concerns and take a minute to make sure I pronounced each name properly. I was a stickler for personal care and was vigilant about not letting anyone feel like they were being processed or pigeonholed. The team worked well together, and everyone took joy in their particular job.

I had decided to have a staff meeting after the clinic had closed for the day. I even insisted that the custodial staff was on hand for the meeting. I took a moment and reviewed the notes on my clipboard and made my way to the tiny wooden podium at the head of a large conference table. I smiled warmly and glanced around the room and saw Celeste, drawing strength from her. She had become something of a linchpin in the very short time we'd worked together. I took a deep breath and began my opening remarks.

"Take a look around this room. You're all surrounded by heroes. Each one of you is a staff member at the Waterstone Clinic and that makes each of you a hero. We named this place Waterstone because we are like a stone that drops into the water and the ripples touch any number of points in all directions. Together we can make a bigger effect than we can alone. And so these meetings are going to be aimed at building the cohesion of this team while addressing each individual need.

"Each of you is making history today. We are making history by addressing the needs of people who were about to fall through the cracks of society. Many have already disappeared from sight and will never rejoin society. Many are trying to get back on their feet and many never will. And some had no footing to begin with. None of that is our business. Our business is to meet each need as if the patient were the president of the United States. We aren't here to save anyone, we are here to provide a service. The more we stay focused on that service, the better that service will be performed. Now, in a minute I'm going to share my vision for the growth of this clinic. But we won't grow until we're doing a great job in the area that we are equipped to handle.

"Frank, Seth, and I are working now to include a social worker on staff to see that our patients can access all of the services the community already offers. We are searching for and offering a stable environment for continued healing in each patient. This week has proven that there are great needs are out there and we're alarmed about the number of STDs we've seen. An OBGYN will be recruited and staffed here. We are looking forward to the day when dental and optical care are offered here. The need is out there and we will find a way to meet it.

"The face of homelessness is changing rapidly, as well as poverty in general. This building has room to grow. Each of us has to grow in the performance of our duties. And we will pursue excellence together as a team or we'll suffer the consequence of mediocrity. And not just us but those we seek to serve, and they have seen enough mediocrity."

I looked at Celeste and could see I'd made my point. She gave me a mock salute privately that let me know I was being a little dramatic. We just had that way between us. I blushed quickly and finished my speech.

"Okay, okay, I'm not going to make any more speeches, but before we leave today I want to hear from the nursing as well as administrative staff so we can stay on top of our game. Each of you is important and your input is going to be noted. We want to increase our efficiency. Thank you all for coming!"

The head of each department weighed in while I sat in the back taking extensive notes. Celeste dismissed each person as she recorded the goals and needs of each member of the administrative staff.

I could see that if I wanted this venture to be as wonderful as Frank and I had imagined it to be, it was going to tax me. I had to keep an eye on expenses, on inventory, and also on morality. My blood surged as my list grew with each need that was stated.

By the end of the meeting only Frank, Celeste, and I remained behind, but there was an aura of excitement in the room. As I studied my notes again I realized what a huge endeavor this was going to be. But when I looked at Frank's and Celeste's smiling faces, I knew it would happen.

"So Frank, what do you think? How is this thing unfolding for you?"

Frank slapped me on the back. "Man, it's taking off like a bullet. Did you see the numbers of people coming in today? We haven't even advertised yet."

I grinned. I was starving. "What say we all grab something to eat. I'm hungry! How about you?"

Celeste nodded but declined to join us. "I've had a long day and I can't wait to get these shoes off and get comfortable. You men have a good dinner and I'll see you tomorrow."

My disappointment was obvious. "You sure, Celeste? You'll be missing a lot of good conversation and a few jokes that might not be worth hearing!"

"I'm sure, but thanks, anyway. I'll catch you guys another time."

She walked away rubbing her back. I didn't miss anything. I had really wanted to spend some time with her but she was worn out. Frank was watching but had the decency to act like he wasn't.

"Okay, buddy. Let's head out. I'll text Leslie and let her know I'm gonna be late. Maybe you need to let Joe know!" Frank laughed and headed towards his car.

I shook my head and grinned. *Sad but true. Joe would be the only one watching for me.* "Yeah, maybe I will. Hate to worry the old guy."

As I dialed Joe, Frank started the car and headed down the street. There were two choices: Hot Dog Heaven and Golden Moon Buffett. We flipped a coin and the buffet won. That was a good thing because both of us were starving. When we found a booth and sat our plates down, Frank noticed that we had put so much on our plates it was falling off the sides onto the table. We both laughed. I looked out the window at the street lights and got lost in my own thoughts. Frank waited for about three minutes and then tapped my arm.

"Hey, buddy. Don't go there. You're doing fantastic. You've reached a personal goal and our mutual goal. It's gonna be okay. I can see that far away look in your eyes. Where are you?"

I grinned and shook my head. " Man, this food smells good. Let's eat before you get a call from Leslie saying you better come home!"

As we dug into our food I acknowledged silently that things had probably moved too quickly for me to comprehend. As I looked down at my feet under the table, I recalled a time not so long ago when I had sat in this same restaurant, maybe even this same seat, with sand on my feet and nowhere to go. It was amazing what happened when someone had a little faith in you. Someone like Joe.

CHAPTER 70

———— ⚜ ————

THE LIGHT WAS on in the kitchen and a new pot of coffee was brewing. There were books piled everywhere and wadded up paper was on the floor next to the waste basket. Uneaten pizza slices were sitting in a box on the counter and two empty Coke bottles were sitting on the floor near the table.

Hunter was studying for the worst exam of his life. Organic chemistry. He was up to his elbows in formulas and was so tired he was having a problem focusing, much less keeping his eyes open. In the distance a dog was barking and he heard a police siren racing down Fisher Avenue. It didn't take much to distract him because he was so sleepy. He had just dug in to answer questions on a pretest and his cell rang. The sound jarred him and he grabbed it so the noise wouldn't wake up Lonnie, who had given way to the pull of sleep and climbed into bed an hour ago.

"Hello?"

"Hunter! It's Paco." His voice was so raspy, and the rasp turned into a fit of coughing which abruptly ended in a spit.

"Man, you sound horrible. Where are you, Paco?"

"It's good to hear your voice, Hunter. Don't worry about me. I've got some good news!"

"I never thought I'd hear from you again, dude. Where have you been?" Hunter frowned at the roughness of the old man's voice.

"I been looking for Matt Collins. Did you think I'd forgotten?"

"Yeah, kinda."

"Boy, it's all that's kept me going. I've some kind of crud in my lungs, but anyway, that's not why I called you."

"You said you had some good news, Paco. What is it?"

"I just got a call from a friend who said Matt is in Destin, Florida. Can you believe it?"

Hunter was shocked. That was where he was going for his honeymoon. The odds of him and Matt being in the same place were one in a zillion. What a coup! "I'm speechless!"

"Well, you better loosen up, dude. I'm gonna find this guy. I promised you I would. I just have to live long enough to find him. Thought you'd be more excited than that."

"Are you kidding? You blindsided me with this information! I was pouring over my chemistry book when you called. Studying for a tough exam. This was the last thing I thought I'd hear tonight! How did you find out?"

"Sheer luck. I been wasting my time in Biloxi because I was chasing a hot lead. But now I find out it was a rabbit hole. I'm in Ocean Springs now, headed to Destin. I got no money but I'm gonna find a way to get there."

"I got a little I could send you, Paco. How would I get some money to you?"

"You can't. I'm moving around too much. You could wire it to a Western Union, but don't worry about it. I'll find a way."

"Don't be stubborn, old man. You sound awful. Let me wire you some money."

"I'll figure out where there's one around here and call you back. May be tomorrow 'cause I'm pretty tired right now. I need to rest."

"You rest and give me a heads-up on where to wire the money. I don't have a lot but I can get you to Destin. You need to drink plenty of fluids, Paco. You got pneumonia or something?"

"Nah. Don't even think about diagnosing me over the phone. You study and I'll call you sometime tomorrow. If you don't answer I'll know you're in class. I'll call ya back somehow."

"Okay, Paco. It sure is good to hear from you. I had given up ever finding my father. Now I have hope again. Hey! I forgot to tell you something."

Paco broke into another fit of coughing but finally cleared his throat. "What you got to tell me, man?"

"I'm getting married in Destin at the end of August. So I'll be down there for a long weekend. It'd be cool if I could meet the guy when I'm down there. I'd like him to meet Holly, my fiancé."

"Happy for you, kid. Real happy. I gotta go. I'll talk to you tomorrow, man."

"Thanks, Paco. Take care of yourself. You really don't sound too good from here."

"It's the miles, Hunter. Don't give it a second thought. I'll be fine."

Hunter hung up the phone and sat at the table thinking. Paco sounded like he was very ill. Congestive heart failure or something close. He might not even make it to Destin. He pulled up a map of the coastline and checked to see how far Ocean Springs was from Destin. It looked like it was nearly two hundred miles. That was a long way when you were on foot. Or bumming a ride. His heart was beating faster thinking of the news about Matt. He really wanted to call Holly, but it was getting late and he knew she was studying like he was. The news could wait until tomorrow. But he doubted he'd sleep much. He tried to focus in on the chemistry questions and finish the pretest. When he'd worked about an hour, he called it a night and put on his tennis shoes for a quick walk. He had to get rid of the nervous energy he was feeling and the best way he knew to do it was go for a long walk.

Outside, he picked up his pace and headed toward Holly's. He'd decided that if he saw lights on he would stop and tell her the news. It was a star-filled night and the air was a little humid. There were still people out; students were always taking advantage of the night hours. When he turned down her street the house was dark and the blinds turned down. She'd already turned in for the night. He was a little disappointed and knew she would die if she found out he'd walked that far and not come to see her. But his common sense won over and he ran the rest of the way home, using the time to think about his father and what it would be like to meet him.

In spite of the rush of thoughts that Hunter had to tuck away so he could concentrate on the exam, he aced it within the two-hour window. It was one of the toughest exams he'd suffered. I guess some of the information I crammed into my pea-sized brain actually stuck, he acknowledged to himself. He watched as his classmates struggled through the exam and felt the sweat on his brow as he handed the test in to the professor.

He walked out of the classroom and headed straight to Holly's apartment. The fresh air felt good even if it was hot and humid. He just wanted to tell her the news about his father. He could hardly think of anything else. *It can't be a coincidence that our honeymoon is going to be in Destin, and that is where Matt is. What are the odds?* He walked up to her door and knocked. No answer. He opened the door and looked around, suddenly seeing her on the sofa sound asleep. She was beautiful asleep. Like Snow White. He tiptoed over to her and sat down on the edge of the sofa, watching her breathe for a second. Watching the drape of her arm hanging off the sofa. She was so relaxed. He knew only too well the late hours she'd kept studying for the same test he had. She was worn slap out. Without even asking her, he knew she aced it. She was way more intelligent that he was. He had to cram and she merely thumbed through the book. She picked up things by osmosis. He gently touched her arm and she stirred. He whispered her name and stroked her hair. One eye opened and she smiled. He turned to mush.

"You! What are you doing on my sofa? Watching me sleep?"

He laughed sheepishly. "Busted. You worn out?"

"Exhausted. How'd you do?"

"Aced the damn thing. You?"

"If you think for one minute that I'd let you beat me on that exam you're nuts."

"Oh, don't I know it. Girl, you're way smarter than I am. We've had this discussion before."

"Don't go there, Hunter. Your depth of knowledge is far greater than mine. I have a photographic memory. That gets me points. But in the long run, as a doctor you'll be the better one."

"Pooey. We'll see. Let's get through med school first!"

They both laughed and she bounded into the kitchen to get them two Cokes.

"I came by to share something with you. Guess who called?"

"Uh . . . I don't know. Who?"

"The one man who holds the answers to my past."

"Paco? Are you serious?" She sat down beside him and put her hand on his leg.

"Holly, this guy is ruthless. He sounds like he's on his last leg, but by damn, he's going to Destin."

"Destin? Why there?"

"'Cause that's where Matt Collins is supposed to be."

"Oh, my gosh! We're planning our honeymoon there! Maybe we should get married there, too. Wouldn't that be great if he could be in our wedding or at least see you get married?"

"Whoa, girl. He doesn't know I exist. I just want to shake his hand. I have no visions of having him as my best man. I dreamed of meeting him one day. It just may happen, Holly. You know what that would mean to me."

"I can only imagine what you feel. It does seem like you're going to get to meet him, Hunter. Wow. I know you're freaking out inside."

"I lost my mother. I need to know who my father is. I know we won't be close, but I'd sure like to meet him. It would help me move forward. I want you and me to have a good life and build a close family. If he ever wants more from me, I will certainly consider having a relationship with him. But that is dreaming right now. And I've done enough of that lately."

Holly wrapped her arms around him and kissed his mouth. "You're the best, Hunter. We are going to have a wonderful life together. That is, if we can get through some of the toughest courses on earth. One down, fifty to go!"

"You are the angel here. I feel so fortunate to have you in my life. I'll let you know if I hear anything else from Paco. He was going to call me today and let me know where I could wire him some money so he could make it from Ocean Springs to Destin. Walking isn't an option in his condition."

"I sure hope he makes it. Otherwise, you and I would have to track him down when we are there. I want to meet this hobo you are so attached to."

"I can't wait for you to meet him. He's going to look like death by the time he gets to Destin. I fear for his life. But knowing how tough he is inside, he'll make it just fine. Somehow he's learned how to survive. You and I would never make it."

Holly stood up and pulled him up beside her. "I gotta study more. I hate to end this time. It was so special of you to share this with me, baby. Now run, so I can hit the books. We both got a lot of studying to do if we're ever going to get away from here to get married. Our grades have to be top notch right now."

"We're shooting for excellence, babe. Excellence. I love you, girl. See you later."

Hunter studied into the night. He gave it his all. But in the back of his mind was the endless drive to know his father. To see him face to face. It was a drive that burned into his soul. It would not let go. It was a dream he'd had all his life, but now he could almost smell it coming true. He hit the pillow and was dead to the world for a few hours. And it was in those same hours that Paco was holding on for his life.

CHAPTER 71

---❖---

IT WAS A warm Friday morning and Joe was late waking up. His normal time to rise was around 6:00, but the night had been restless so he slept in. The sun was sending shards of light across his bed as he sat up and stretched. Since he'd aged, his sleep wasn't as restful as it used to be. He yawned and got out of bed and made his coffee. Matt was already at the clinic and that was where he was headed. He fixed a simple breakfast of oatmeal and toast and showered, dressed, and headed out the door. He was excited because he was going to see the clinic up and running. It felt like a new baby being born. There was a buzz in Destin that was spreading through the fishing village and excitement was growing. The building was impressive as a standalone structure. The mahogany doors were massive and opened into a marbled foyer and receptionist area. Joe couldn't wait to observe the clinic in operation.

It was heavy tourist season and the streets were full. A wreck happened at least twice a day in busy season on the main highway through town. Deputies were out in full force so Joe was careful not to speed. He tended to have a heavy foot, which always caused a snide remark from Matt. He accused Joe of having an "in" with God because he'd never had a speeding ticket.

The parking lot was half full as he pulled up next to Frank's car. Joe smiled when he saw Matt's bike locked up at a bike rack that had been placed on the side of the building. He was halfway thinking about buying Matt a used car, but had held off to see if the half-cocked dream of a health clinic would ever come to fruition. It not only began to develop but the lease of the building happened before Joe could really believe the dream was coming true. Matt was a very intelligent man and a visionary. He moved at a different pace than most, but had lost his way with the alcohol. Now he was moving forward at the speed of light and it was difficult for anyone around him to keep up. He worked tirelessly to get this clinic up and going. He was so enthusiastic that he sucked you in. Joe got out of his car and headed towards the door.

Just as he pulled the door open, Matt walked up to the Celeste and was speaking to her about a patient. "Hey, man! How's it going? I was dying to come and see this thing in action!"

"Hey, Joe! Good to see you." Matt smiled and walked over and slapped Joe on the back.

"I bet this feels good to you, Matt. You've worked hard for this."

"I have, Joe. But so have Frank and Seth. They are terrific with the boys on the street. Everyone feels so comfortable in here, and we've really treated a lot of people even though we've only been open a couple weeks."

"Still working the kinks out?"

"Haven't seen too many. A few changes need to be made to some of the exam rooms but that is small. I love the way this thing is running."

"Care if I walk around a little? I'm dying to see how it feels."

"Of course. And be sure to walk into the cafeteria and grab some food or coffee. It's really a nice place for the homeless to eat and the staff is enjoying it, too. The food is terrific. Hard to believe we could get such a talented chef that would be willing to work in a free clinic. He's on salary, of course. But you know he could make a lot more money if he worked in an upscale restaurant around here."

"Sometimes money isn't the motivation; of course you wouldn't know anything about that, I guess."

"Obviously." Matt smiled, and both knew he didn't miss the joke.

"I'll nose around and take a look. Don't worry about me. I really appreciate being able to walk through. I especially want to see the chapel. I'm going to enjoy stopping in to counsel people and pray with them. A lot of pain out there."

"I'll check on you in a few minutes. I need to see one more patient, Joe."

Joe walked away and began nosing around the rooms one at a time. The building seemed larger once he was inside. He found the cafeteria and grabbed a cup of hot coffee and headed for the chapel. It was dimly lit and quiet, with music playing in the background. A large cross stood up at the front and stained glass windows shed colors of red, yellow, blue, and green on the pews. He walked to the front and looked around and then something caught his eye. On the side, sitting very still, was a woman. She was crying softly and had her head down on the back of the pew in front of her. He walked over to her and sat down.

"Anything I can do?"

She didn't answer.

"I'm sorry you're upset. Can I help you at all?"

She turned to look at him and put her head back down. She was very thin.

"I'll get you some cold water to drink. Don't leave. I'll be right back."

Joe scooted out of the pew and hurried to find a water fountain and a cup. There was a side room away from the front of the chapel and when he opened the door there was a small desk and water fountain and cups stacked up on the large bottled water dispenser. He grabbed one and filled it with cold water and headed back to talk to the woman. She was still there but her crying had subsided.

"Here, take a sip. It'll make you feel better."

The woman swallowed some water and wiped her face. She was tired and dressed in ragged clothes. Her dress was too large and the hem was torn. Her hair was dirty and the hat she had on was worn and ragged. Joe put his arm on the back of the pew and sat there while she sipped the water. He wanted her to open up but there was no way to hurry it.

"Are you feeling better? Is there anything else I can do for you?"

"I'm so tired. The last food I ate was yesterday morning. I have no money. I don't know what to do."

"You've come to the right place, young lady. Let's go get you some food. This is a free clinic and they have a wonderful cafeteria around the corner. You up to that?"

The lady nodded and wiped her nose. "I'm very weak. Can you help me walk to the cafeteria?"

"Sure. But I want you to be checked out by one of the doctors here to make sure you are okay."

Joe helped her up and they walked slowly to the dining room. He led her to a seat and asked her what she wanted. He got a tray and picked out a hot meal for her and some iced tea. She was overwhelmed by his kindness and asked if he would sit with her while she ate.

"I'd love to sit here but I want to check with one of the doctors here. I'll be right back. You enjoy your meal and don't go away. I'll be right back."

She looked wary but started picking at her food, finally letting the forkful of food go into her mouth. She had few teeth but that didn't stop her from eating it. Joe hurried to find Matt and ran into him near one of the exam rooms.

"Matt, I've found someone I want you to see. She's a young woman that I found in the chapel just now. I took her to the cafeteria and got her some food. She's in there now, eating. Will you check on her? I'm worried that she might be ill."

Matt grinned. Joe was already doing his thing and he hadn't been at the clinic thirty minutes yet. "Sure! I'll check on her. Be right there."

Joe hurried back to the dining room and looked around. The woman had gone. He walked up to the table where she'd sat and he noticed that she had eaten a good bit of food. He scratched his head and frowned.

"Wonder where she went?" He spoke out loud.

Matt was standing right behind him looking at the empty chair. "Must have gotten scared. Some of them have not seen a doctor in years and they are afraid of what the doctor will find. They really aren't used to people poking on them. I can understand."

Joe looked at Matt and shook his head. "Yeah, I bet you can. But I sure was hoping she was going to be here when I got back. I'll look around the clinic to see if she wandered off."

"Let me know if you find her. I have one other patient to see and then I can grab lunch with you."

"Sounds great. Meet you back here shortly."

Joe took off hoping to find the woman, who had disappeared like vapor. He wandered back to the chapel and saw her sitting there. He walked up to her and sat down.

"Did you get scared? I brought Dr. Collins to see you but you'd left."

She looked up at Joe. "I'm dying, sir. There's no point in seeing a doctor."

Joe got quiet. He wasn't expecting that answer. "How do you know you're dying?"

"'Cause I can feel it inside. I was diagnosed with cancer years ago and couldn't afford the treatment. I fought it off but now it's taken over my body. I don't have a chance. Anyway, it don't matter 'cause there's no one who cares about whether I live or die, anyway."

"Let's have Dr. Collins check you out. Maybe you're not that sick. It would ease your mind to know that you are not dying, I'm sure. Won't you allow him to see you?"

"I could use a prayer. You are a pastor, right?"

"Yeah, I am."

"Good. That would make me feel better. A prayer."

Joe grabbed her hand and prayed for her. His words echoed in the empty room. The first prayers uttered in the new chapel were for a dying woman. Joe felt the gravity of the situation. He wished Matt had been there. He wanted the woman checked to see if she really was dying. But he knew he couldn't force her to accept that kind of help.

"Thank you so much for praying. I'm going now. And thank you for the food. It really did help."

"I hope you change your mind about seeing Dr. Collins. That is just what this clinic is for. People like you. I'll remember you in prayer tonight."

"Thank you again."

The woman left and walked out the front doors. Joe kicked himself for not asking her name. He went back into the chapel and noticed she'd left a bag on the floor. He grabbed it and ran to find her. But she had disappeared into the busy traffic on the sidewalks. He walked back into the clinic and headed for the dining room, hoping Matt was there. It was empty except for a couple of people eating in the far corner.

Joe sat down and looked into the bag. He was surprised to see a small bible, a photograph of a child, and a note that was folded up. He opened the note and read it slowly, a tear floating in the wrinkles around his eyes. She had written a goodbye note to her children. She really believed she was going to die. Matt walked up and saw Joe reading the note.

"What's that you're reading, Joe?"

Joe hesitated and then laid it down in front of Matt. "Here, sit down and read this. It'll make you sick."

Matt read the note and looked up at Joe. "Does this belong to that woman you wanted me to see?"

"Yep. She's gone now. Said she was dying. No need to see you."

"I see. You pretty upset about this, Joe?"

"Yeah. I may have seen her out there. At night. Didn't recognize her but I know she's been around here for a while. She knew where everything was when I talked to her. I hate that I didn't find her soon enough. That's the tough part about helping these people. Sometimes we are too late."

"I know how you feel. I have patients that wait too late to come in. And it's over for them. We make choices in our lives and we pay consequences. It isn't pleasant in any sense of the word. But it is life. You know that better than me."

Joe looked at Matt hard and put his hand on Matt's hand. He looked so serious that Matt was afraid of what the old guy was going to say.

"You know, Matt. It was a miracle I found you out there. A lot of men go unnoticed. I covered you with my jacket and could have walked away and never thought of you again. But for some reason you haunted me. You were on your way down."

Matt blew out a deep breath. "Man, Joe. You're getting heavy here. But I know what you mean. I'm more than just grateful for you finding me again. I am overwhelmed by your kindness. Why you cared about me is beyond the grasp of human understanding."

"I don't even know why I wanted to find you again. I was pulled toward you. You have turned your life around in such a short time."

"You have every reason to be proud, Joe. You have done more for me than anyone in my life, short of my parents. Don't feel bad about this woman. You did the best you could."

Joe shook his head. "No. No I didn't, Matt. I could have tried harder to help her. I know she has to want it. But when I see these pitiful things she left behind, it breaks my heart."

Matt stood there staring at Joe. What he was saying was slowly sinking in. "I will remember that in this clinic, Joe. It's the patient that may be the most difficult to deal with that really needs the help the most."

Matt shook Joe's hand and pointed towards the food. "Let's get some lunch because I have to go back to work."

The two men sat and ate quietly, laughing and enjoying their time together. Anyone watching would have thought it was father and son. Anyone watching wouldn't have guessed in a million years that Matt had ever had any children. And the funny thing was that in Matt's deepest of hearts he never thought for one moment he had a child wandering about in the world trying to find him. .

Joe left the clinic with a heavy heart. And Matt went back to his patients. The young woman who had left the clinic was lying in the bushes under a tree, getting sicker and sicker. Crying, but no one saw. She was right. She was dying.

CHAPTER 72

———— ⚜ ————

PACO NEVER MADE the phone call to Hunter. He hated borrowing money from the boy and made up his mind he'd find his own way to Destin. He was feeling terrible and the coughing was horrific. He needed something to drink and eat, and that was going to be his main target for the moment. He had to find quick work, but in the meantime he decided to hit the dumpsters to see if he could sort through the garbage for a morsel or two. He walked behind several fast food places and hid in the back, hoping to catch someone unloading food that wasn't used that day. Occasionally he had picked up half of a hamburger or French fries that weren't sold but tonight he wasn't so lucky.

He had learned patience and sat behind the dumpster until the restaurant closed. That was when they cleaned out the bins and the employees ate what they wanted and threw out the rest. At about midnight he saw two employees dressed in black come out of the back door with bags of food they were throwing out. His mouth was watering. He had to wait to stand up until they'd gone back inside, and then he jumped up on the dumpster and grabbed the bags. He was dying of thirst but the food would have to do for now.

After filling his stomach he began the hunt for water or a beer. He could panhandle and risk being taken to jail. Or he could just stand outside a diner and hope someone would offer him money or water. Either way was risky. He decided to sit on the sidewalk next to a busy intersection and watch the people going by. One young man walked by him and threw him a couple of dollars. That would buy one beer with change left over. So he got up and brushed the dead grass off his pants, nodded to the boy, and headed to the nearest convenience store for a cheap

437

beer. When he popped the top he couldn't drink it fast enough. But he also wanted to savor it. It might be his last one before he got up in the morning. He needed to find a place to camp and his body was worn out. He looked around and saw a clump of trees with a lot of ground covering and headed in that direction. He had to cross a main street but the traffic was light. A policeman whizzed by and Paco merely smiled. He'd been around so long that he wasn't nervous about the cops anymore. They didn't seem to see him; he'd learned to be invisible when he needed to. His clothes were pale natural colors and he blended in the surroundings no matter where he went.

As he headed into the woods someone jumped out and pushed him away. Paco was caught completely off guard.

"Hey, dude! Stay outta here! We been here a long time. This is our woods."

"Okay, man. Sorry. I'm new to this area and was just trying to find a tree to lie under."

"You not from around here?"

"No, just passing through."

"We kinda protect our camps around here. You gotta respect that. Someone else might be tempted to jump you and next time it might be pretty bad for you."

"Thanks. I'll remember that. I'm pretty tired. Need to go find a place to sleep. Got any suggestions?"

"Across the street between the two restaurants there's a stand of trees that will cover you pretty good. Just leave before daylight. You don't want anyone seeing you walking outta the woods. They'll report you to the cops and believe me, you don't wanna be arrested around here."

"I been down that road before. I'm too old to be jailed. All I want to do is sleep. Thanks a lot for your help."

Paco walked out of the woods and headed for the stand of trees across the street. His legs were weak but the food had given him new energy. He finally found a good tree to lie under and unrolled his ragged sleeping bag. That bag had been with him for at least ten years. It was in bad shape, but then, so was he. They sort of went together quite well. He wouldn't have given that sleeping bag up for anything. It was more like a friend to him. He gently laid the bag down on the ground, moving any sticks or small rocks so that his sleep would be uninterrupted. He didn't recall a time when he was so tired. His bones ached. He coughed up some blood and rolled up a shirt for a pillow. He was hot but felt chilled at the same time. He lay on top of his bag and turned on his side. Sleep came fast, but during the night but he woke up several times, disoriented for a moment about where he was. It had happened a lot on the journey to find Matt Collins. Sometimes Paco felt like he was chasing a ghost. Only now did he really feel he had a chance at finding the doctor.

The night sounds that would frighten most people wooed Paco to sleep. He'd stopped wondering about what was making the sounds over the years. Now they were like a symphony to him. Without the outside noises of nature he wouldn't have been able to fall asleep. Although he'd often slept in rundown motel rooms, he really preferred a good tree to lie under with the crickets and tree frogs singing him to sleep.

The night was long and the coughing kept him from going into a very deep sleep. He was thirsty again and even with that clawing at the back of his mind, he still managed to rest enough to get up the next morning with the desire to find work. It was critical now. He was broke. He had to have enough money to get to Destin. And if he had to die without a penny, he was not going to phone Hunter for the money.

As he climbed out of the woods, he brushed off his clothes and slung his backpack over his shoulders. It was time to wash some clothes and clean up his beard. Getting hired had moved its way up the ladder so everything he did was focused on that. He was a pro. He knew how to manipulate his environment to meet his needs. But he would need something for the cough. He stopped by a clinic on the edge of town near Gautier. It was crowded and the air-conditioning wasn't working. He waited for a while and paced back and forth, noticing the sweat dripping down his back. He felt sick. The intricate designs on the carpet were making him dizzy. The smell in the clinic was antiseptic and that helped to cover up the smell of sick, dirty people. Everyone in there was coughing, sniffing, and blowing their nose. Paco wanted to run out but the pull to get better caused him to remain. Finally his name was called and he went back to an exam room. The nurse took his vitals and wrote down answers to her questions, not smiling or looking at Paco one time.

A tall, thin doctor walked in. His name on his shirt was Dr. Juno. His words were blunt. "Paco. Is that your real name?" The doctor frowned, looking at his chart.

Paco frowned. Why did it matter? "Yeah. Paco."

"You homeless?"

"What do ya think?"

"I'm only asking because I need to know previous medical care."

"That's easy. None."

"Why are you here?"

"Need you to check my lungs. I know I'm sick. Can't take the time to go to the hospital right now. I need to work. So tell me what's going on so I'll know how long I have."

Doctor Peter Juno took a long look at Paco. He knew this man wasn't just singing Dixie. He sounded horrible.

"Sit up and let me listen to your lungs. Take a deep breath."

Paco nearly choked. "That's all you're gonna get, man. Can't breathe any deeper than that."

Dr. Juno moved away and looked at Paco. "Your lungs are getting full of fluid. You know that?"

"Yep. Been knowing it. But it's getting worse."

"Congestive heart failure. And you have no doctor?"

"Come on, man. How can I? I have no money. I move around a lot. Have to. Cops chase us out every time we make camp."

Dr. Juno shook his head. "You're not going to last much longer, the way your lungs sound. I'm not trying to be negative, but it's my job to let you know what you are facing."

Paco looked down and rubbed his beard. He knew what was wrong but hearing it said out loud hurt. "Well, can you give me anything for this cough? I just need to hold on a little longer. Come on, doc. Can't you give me something?"

"I can give you a steroid shot and an antibiotic. I know you can't be eating right, so there's no use in my talking about nutrition with you. But if you make any money, spend it on food."

"I hear ya. I'll take that shot, if ya don't mind."

"The nurse will give you a shot and I'll give you some samples of the antibiotic to take. Try to take it with food. That's all I ask."

Paco nodded and stood up for the shot. He winced when the nurse poked his hip, but he knew it was his lifeline. He took the samples from Dr. Juno and headed out the door. He felt better knowing what was wrong with him. It actually had a name. Congestive heart failure.

He pushed himself to think of where he was going. Gautier was a beautiful place with old Southern style homes and trees draped with hanging moss.. He wanted to find work and he needed a bath.

He spotted a truck stop and walked around until he spotted a trucker who looked friendly. He walked up to him and smiled. "Hey, dude. How's it going?"

The trucker looked at Paco and shook his head. "Man, you look like you're a dead man walking."

"Don't remind me. Say, you headed into the showers? I sure could use one. Hadn't had much luck finding a job lately."

"You didn't have to tell me that, dude. Follow me in there and I'll get you in. But keep your mouth shut, hear me? When they call my number I'm gonna take my shower with the door cracked. Then I'll let ya take yours and close the door. No one's really watching. But still, I don't want them on my case here. I come here a lot."

"Don't want to cause you any trouble. I'm just looking for a job and can't look like something the cat drug in."

"I hear ya. Come on. They're calling my number now."

Paco followed behind the trucker and stood next to the door while the man showered. As soon as he was through he stepped out in a towel and handed Paco a clean one.

"Hurry up. I can't stay back here too long."

Paco hurried into the shower and stood frozen as the hot water ran over his worn out body. He'd almost forgotten how good it felt to be clean. He felt revived and almost hated to put his dirty clothes back on. The trucker looked at him and grinned.

"You need some money to wash your clothes? I got a few quarters here. Go ahead, man. You may not get a better chance to take care of your clothes."

"Thanks, man. I really appreciate it. They're pretty dirty."

"Would stand in a corner if you took your pants off."

"Yeah. It's been a while. You know of a job around here I could do?"

The trucker shook his head. "Not really. I'll ask around, though. Going out front to get some coffee. I'll get you a cup and ask around. Be right back."

Paco wondered why the guy was being so nice, and it kind of made him uneasy. He hurried and washed a small load of clothes and dried them. It took nearly an hour. He walked out into the eating area and saw the trucker talking with some other men who'd just come off the road. He spotted Paco and waved him over.

"Dude, sit down here and have some coffee. I bought you some soup if'n you want it."

"Sure. I'll take it. Thanks, man. Haven't had food in a while, either."

"You been out there long?"

"Near twenty years."

"You ain't coming back, are you?"

"Nope. Too late for me. I'm probably not gonna live that long."

The trucker looked at the other men and shook his head. "Say, where you headed?"

"Headed to Destin. Where you goin'?"

"I'm driving to Tallahassee. You want a ride?"

"Are you serious, dude? 'Cause you know I ain't got no money."

"No problem. I got a few stops to make and you can help me unload. My back's been hurtin' a lot lately and it would help me out. Whaddya say?"

"Hell, yes. I was having a tough time picturing myself walking all the way to Destin. The soles of my shoes would be slap worn out."

The man laughed and shook Paco's hand. "Take care, dude. Hope you find what you're looking for in Destin. It's a tourist trap. They don't take kindly to hobos there."

"No place likes us tramps. But we gotta be somewhere. So I'm headed there to find someone. I been looking everywhere for him and I just heard he was in Destin."

"Must be pretty important for you to go to all this trouble, as sick as you are."

"It's all I got to live for these days."

The trucker stood up and waved Paco out the door. "We gotta get going, man. What's your name, anyway?"

"Paco. Just call me Paco."

"My name's Jenkins. Pete Jenkins. Let's go."

Paco followed Pete to the truck and climbed into the cab. His luck was improving and he was going to make sure he did nothing to set Pete off. He knew by what the doctor said that he didn't have much longer to live. He'd have never made it to Destin on foot.

It struck him hard to realize he was near the end of his life. But if he found Matt Collins, it would be worth all the effort. He laid his head back against the seat and dozed off, feeling the gentle rocking of the cab.

Pete was a quiet man and respected the old man's need for sleep. He had no idea what he was helping to bring about. For by what seemed like a cosmic event, two people were about to be brought together that would not have ordinarily met. And that one meeting would change the course of their lives forever. Just because an old tramp was determined to find a doctor who'd been under the radar for years and years. An unlikely meeting if he could make it happen. The "if" was getting stretched beyond the limits of fate. And that's just where miracles happened. Beyond the limits of fate.

CHAPTER 73

✦

IT WAS WAY past time for me to ask Celeste out for dinner. I'd been putting if off because I simply had no money. But now that I'd taken a paycheck, it was burning a hole in my pocket. I could at least afford dinner at a small café and a walk on the beach. She'd been terrific at the clinic even though I'd put more on her than she had bargained for. Actually, we all had had a heavy work load the first couple of weeks we were open. Now we were heading into the middle of August and summer was hot as ever. It had rained all day but now the clouds were parting and pieces of the sun were coming through.

I sat down at the kitchen table and looked at my phone. My nerves were screaming. I hadn't had a date in so long I couldn't remember when. And Celeste had been a little elusive since she came to work for me. I knew the protocol. Don't date employees. It usually fit, but this time I wanted to buck the rule. Chuckling, I recalled that this wasn't a new trait of mine. After a few moments of sighing, I dialed her number. All she could do was say no.

"Celeste? This is Matt. Did I catch you at a bad time?"

"No, not at all. Is something wrong at the clinic? Is there a patient in trouble?"

I laughed. "You sound like me. Relax. Nothing is wrong. I just wanted to see if you'd like to go to dinner with me. Something casual. Spur of the moment. And maybe a walk on the beach afterwards."

Quiet for what seemed like an hour. "Is that a good idea, Matt? I mean, I work for you now. Will that cause problems down the road? I need this job, you know."

I was caught in my own rebellion. "Well, I know the deal. And I've given it some thought. Couldn't we just have one dinner? What would that hurt? I promise you nothing will happen to your job."

"Mmm. I'm not sure if I want to take that risk. I really love the clinic and my work there. We're actually just getting started. I don't want to throw a wrench into something that could turn into a full blown career."

She was being way too sensible. "Celeste. Listen to me. I just want to eat something at the same table as you do! Can we do that? Let's call it a business dinner. Would that make you feel better?"

She laughed this time. But I didn't totally trust it. "Okay. You win. But don't be angry at me if down the road this ruins a good thing."

I blew out a breath. "How 'bout I pick you up at six o'clock? I'm going to ask Joe if I can borrow his car."

"Six o'clock? Okay. I'll be ready. Casual, you say?"

"Yes, very. Let's just have a good night and enjoy good conversation. We both have worked too hard."

"See you at six. Thanks for calling, Matt!"

That went a little easier than I thought it would. Although I did have to wiggle through the issue of her working for me. I knew I better be on my best behavior because I wanted to see her again. Of course I didn't tell her that. But it was definitely on my agenda.

I decided to head over to Joe's and ask for the car. I knew he would say yes, but I still had to ask. Never take anything for granted. That was my motto in my new life. I went out the door squinting as the glare of the sun shot through the darker clouds. It was almost blinding after a rain. The ground had been parched so the water was being soaked up like a sponge. My shoes were wet as I stood at his back door, knocking gently. He hated when I knocked. The door opened and he stood there with an eyebrow raised, looking at me like he was seeing the Prodigal Son.

"How many times have I told you not to knock? Come on in!"

"I know, Joe. I just do it to annoy you!" I stepped into the kitchen and grabbed a couple of warm chocolate chip cookies off the mound that was piled on a plate by the oven.

"Have a seat, Matt. What's on your mind?" I could see his writing on a paper near his coffee and knew he was preparing for his next sermon.

"Well, the time has finally come for me to ask to borrow your car! I've finally gotten up enough nerve to ask Celeste out and I need to have a car to pick her up! I don't think my bike would get us very far."

Joe paced around the room. He had a smirk on his face but he kept shaking his head. "I wasn't going to do this yet, young man. I had plans to wait until you were earning a living and really on your feet. But then, I guess you won't need it then. Come on. Let's get in my car. I have something to show you."

I was puzzled. What in the world had he done? "Joe, all I want to do is borrow the car. Is there something wrong? Are you okay?"

Joe laughed. "Sure, boy. I'm fine. Now quit asking me questions and get in the car!"

I followed him out and we got in the car. He drove slowly over to the church and went around to the back where there was a small garage. We got out and he walked over to the garage door and pointed to the handle.

"Go ahead. Lift this thing up. I got something to show you."

I lifted up the garage door and stepped back. A red Mustang was sitting in the garage. I looked at Joe and raised my eyebrow. "Okay. What in the world is this? You bought a new Mustang? What's it doing here in the garage?"

"Well, actually it's not mine, Son. It belongs to you."

I almost rocked backwards on my heels. "It's what? Mine? Are you serious? What have you done, Joe? You can't buy me a car!"

"Who says I can't? Now check it out. The keys are in the front seat. I been dying to give it to you but I was waiting for the right time. I guess a date with Celeste is as good a time as any."

I was shocked beyond words. This guy just didn't quit. "You've given me my life back. Don't you think that's enough? You didn't have to buy me a car, Joe! Really."

"What? You don't want it? I hardly think you'll turn down this red Mustang. Now go on, get in and drive it home. I want to watch you drive it."

I jumped in the front seat and looked around. Never thought I'd own a Mustang again. It was one of the first cars I ever bought. I couldn't remember if I ever mentioned that to Joe or not. The car started like a gem and the rumble was loud. I was going to be dangerous in this car.

"Man, how can I ever thank you! Thanks so much, Joe. I still can't believe you did this behind my back."

"It was fun and I couldn't wait for you to see it. Now go for a ride. Hey, wait!"

I rolled the window back down. "What's up?"

"Is your driver's license up to date?"

I smiled. He was always thinking. "Yes, relax. I have to renew it next year."

"Okay. Good! Go for it, buddy. Have fun! See you at home."

I pulled away from the church in a daze. My own car. Joe wasn't rich and this had to be an extravagant purchase for him. Why did he believe in me so much? How would I ever repay him? The car was fast and strong and I was going to love it.

I was starving to belong again. And I had a woman waiting for me tonight that I was anxious to get to know. Not a bad way to start a first date. A new car and a new friend. Maybe I could finally believe that my life was turning around. Maybe I could actually have a life.

CHAPTER 74

───────── ⚜ ─────────

MIKE AND DAN's Barbeque Grill was something to experience. First of all, it was colder than Alaska in there. Second, the people were friendly and always ready to meet a customer's slightest needs or wants. It was clean, it could be noisy, but this one night it wasn't very busy. I pointed to the corner booth and she complied with a smile. I scooted into the seat and watched Celeste as she adjusted her skirt and slid in. It had been a long time since we had sat across from each other at a restaurant. I had missed her eyes.

"You look lovely tonight. How are you?"

She blushed. "I'm good. Really. Surprised you called though. Love that red car! It's really nice."

"It was a gift. But I want to talk about you. How do you like your job? Everything okay at work?"

"What can I say? It's terrific. Busier than I thought it would be right off."

The waitress walked up and we ordered our food. I was so focused on Celeste that I really didn't look at the menu at all. I just wanted to make the most of the time we had together. I knew I couldn't count on it happening again because of her being employed at the clinic. We had to work through that fear.

"We have been busy. It's a reflection of the needs of Destin. I never thought the word would get out so quickly."

"I was shocked the first day when we opened the doors and there was a line going around the side of the building. I now realize that news travels fast in the homeless community."

"Not only the homeless but in those families who have children and no insurance for them."

"Yes. So tell me how you are. I still don't know much about you."

I gulped. If I was ever going to get close to this girl, I had to come clean about who I was. "What do you want to know?"

"Like where are you from? Where is your family? I think I heard your father passed away recently. Is that true?"

"Yeah. I was born in Philadelphia. I have one brother named Les. He's lives in Seattle. I went to medical school and was one of the highest paid surgeons in Philadelphia. I always drank in college but it increased as my career grew. I got to where I just couldn't handle life without drinking. I got a few DUIs and nearly lost my medical license. From there, it was history. I started my journey south and ended up in Destin. I lived on a park bench for several years, and had a heart attack. That was a wakeup call for me. I guess it would be for anyone."

She was still listening. "I hate that you had to struggle like that. It sounds terrible. How did you make it through that heart attack?"

"I had a good doctor. Guess who it was?"

She shook her head, smiling.

"It was Frank."

"No way!"

"Yep. Good old Frank. He saved my life. But I also was fortunate to meet Brother Joe at the Coffee House one morning when I was very hungry and stopped to get some quick breakfast. He sat down beside me and started talking while we ate our breakfast. He made me feel comfortable and offered me a place to live. I accepted and here I am. You cannot imagine what it is like living under his wing."

"He sounds like a wonderful man. I enjoyed meeting him the first time he came to the clinic. I haven't had a lot of time to talk with him since then. What a heart he must have."

"You don't know the half of it. He actually met me earlier when I lived on the bench. One night he was making his rounds among the homeless at night and found me sleeping on the bench. Apparently he thought I was freezing and took off his leather jacket and laid it across my back. I woke up with a jacket on me and never knew where it came from. He found me again at the Coffee House and gave me a place to

449

live. He said he really felt like I had potential. That I was different. I had to prove him right. It was a good while before I learned that the jacket was his. I was shocked."

Celeste had tears streaming down her face. I hadn't meant to make her cry. I actually had wanted quite the opposite on our first date. "Honey, don't cry. I'm so sorry. But you asked me about my life, so I told you. It's not a pretty story."

"No one looking at you would ever dream you'd been through that. You're an amazing doctor and you have such a strong character. It's an honor to be working for you. The vision you had for Waterstone Clinic is coming to life right in front of your eyes. I'm so proud to be a part of it."

I was loving her heart right across the table. It was hard not to reach out to her. But I didn't want to scare her away. She had a fragile way about her. I wanted to respect that. "Thanks, Celeste. I love what I do. Hope it comes across to the patient. That's where the gift is."

"I know you once said that dental was going to be a part of the clinic. Just talking with the patients that have visited us, I see that as a big concern for them."

"We can offer so much if we get the funding and also find qualified and willing dentists, psychiatrists, counselors, and ophthalmologists to fill those holes. It's exciting to see how this thing could grow."

She was eating slowly and glancing out the window from time to time. It gave me a chance to study her. I still didn't feel like I knew who she was. We were talking shop and not really opening up. Odd that I was thinking these thoughts as a man. I wondered if she was. The restaurant had begun to fill up and the noise level was rising. They were playing '70s music in the background. The place wasn't that big; maybe sat eighty people tops. But looking across at Celeste, I didn't notice anyone. Our waiter came and went and I was lost in her eyes, in her voice, and in the way her hair fell across her forehead. She was wearing a print dress in soft natural tones that had short sleeves. Her arms were showing signs of a slight tan. But her skin was fair. She would burn easy. When she was talking to me, I sometimes couldn't hear the words because I was lost in her beauty. I wished suddenly that we were finished eating so we could be alone. But inside I was afraid. It had been so long since I'd been close to anyone. My life wasn't as stable as I wanted it to be. I was afraid I would run her off. She was talking but my mind was racing ahead.

"So when do you think you'll move out of that apartment Joe has given to you?"

I was surprised at the question. "I haven't given it much thought. Sort of tied up with the clinic right now. But at some point I will want my own place."

"I know it feels good right now just to have a place to sleep. I still have a hard time seeing you as homeless. But it could happen to me real fast if I wasn't working right now."

"I wouldn't allow that to happen to you."

"You don't know me well enough to make that promise."

"I know I wouldn't let you sleep on the street."

"Well, it could happen to any of us at any time. You have shown me that. I really wasn't aware of homeless people around me, but now I find myself looking for them."

"You are too special to be homeless. I am glad you have a job now, and that I can share in your life in some way. I am so thankful we got this time tonight, Celeste. Was worried it wouldn't happen at all."

She raised her eyebrow. "And why is that?"

"Well, for one thing, I was afraid to ask you out. And secondly, you are in my employment. I don't want to ruin your ability to work for me in case you don't enjoy yourself on this date!"

"Of course I'm enjoying myself. How could I not? We're sharing a good meal together and having great conversation. I needed this."

"Oh, I have been waiting for this ever since I met you."

"You what? Come on, Matt. That's a line. Tell me it's a line."

I ducked my head down. "Not really, Celeste. I wanted to ask you out when I saw you in the parking lot at RT's. But that was pushing it, and I don't work that way. I wanted to wait until things were underway at the clinic before I asked you out. I wanted things to be perfect."

Celeste watched as I slowly looked up at her. "I don't know what to say, Matt. But you have touched my heart with your sincerity. I had no idea that you'd been thinking about me like that. I've never really had that kind of attention before. I'm speechless."

I collected myself and smiled at her. A cool, calm, collected kind of smile. "Sorry, didn't mean to sound so mushy there. What I was trying to say was that I was hoping we'd have such a good time tonight that we could do it again. Go out, I mean. I really want to know you."

She reached across the table and took my hand. "I guess some rules are meant to be broken. I have had a wonderful time with you and it would be great if we did this again. As long as you can promise me it won't interfere with my job! I really love working at the clinic and to be honest, I need the job."

I couldn't help but laugh, but I understood the reality of what she was saying. "You won't lose your job. Ever. Will you at least walk through this with me so that we can see where it's going? I mean, can we at least see if we like each other?"

I got a smile out of her. Almost a chuckle. "I'd love to. You are so much fun outside the clinic! Well, I didn't mean it like that!"

I raised my eyebrow at her and then laughed. "Let's finish our meal and leave. I want to walk on the beach with you before it gets too dark.

We held hands walking across the stretch of sand heading towards the water's edge. It was a little breezy so the waves were tumbling in to shore with a little more power than expected. Celeste had raised up her dress to keep it from getting wet and was holding her shoes as she walked at the edge of the water. We'd left her purse in the car and I was tempted to push her in the water but I didn't know if she'd find that kind of teasing funny and it might just kill my seeing her again. I was fighting the urge when she suddenly took off running. I flew after her, surprised at how fast she could run in the sand. Obviously she had done this before. And it was very apparent that I hadn't.

"Hey! Wait for me! You didn't tell me we were racing!"

She ignored my yelling and ran a ways down the sand. I felt a little pull in my chest and decided to slow down and not push it. One heart attack was enough. And the stents were holding nicely. Didn't want to conk out on our first date, either. I soon caught up with her and was glad to see she was breathing heavily.

"So you do this often, do you?"

"Yes. Actually I do! I try to run on the beach every afternoon when I get off work. Or at least walk a few miles. It's refreshing and I hate to be away from the water long."

"Well, it shows. I'm ashamed to say that I haven't taken advantage of the water since I moved here. I do love it and enjoy sailing and jet skiing. Snorkeling. Now with the clinic I won't have much time to do either."

"You'll have to find the time. You cannot work all the time, Matt. It will hurt your heart more than a good run would."

"You're right. But things need to get done in the beginning to make it easier for us all as time goes by."

I took her hand and we strolled back towards the car. I had brought a blanket along just in case.

"You care to sit here for a while and watch the sun go down?" I pointed to a spot on the sand and shook the blanket out and laid it down.

"That's a lovely idea. Looking at the sun now, we don't have much time before it sets."

I squinted at the horizon and nodded. It was going to be a quick visit at the beach, but the breeze felt so good on my face. I watched her as she laid her sandals down on the blanket and sat cross-legged beside me. I didn't want to let go of her hand, but I acquiesced so she could get comfortable. We watched the children playing near the water's edge and smiled as the boys dove into the water with their surfboards.

"Every night I'm here it's like the first time I have ever seen the ocean. It's different every time I come."

"I love that about this place. Celeste, you look lovely tonight. Did I tell you that yet?"

She blushed and looked the other way. "No. I don't recall you saying that, but thank you, Matt. You need to stop. You're embarrassing me!"

"Why? You're beautiful. I don't get to say that at work!"

She changed the subject. "I wonder what it would be like to live near the beach where you could wake up and see the ocean rolling in every morning. It would be breathtaking. What a way to start your day. I'd be watching people all day long. And then at night I'd want to walk the beach and maybe even sleep there."

I laughed at her last remark. "They don't look kindly on people sleeping on the beach. I can tell you that firsthand! And to tell you the truth, the sand looks comfy but it gets pretty hard lying on it. You're not even thinking about the night creatures that would be crawling all over you while you're sleeping!"

She shivered and I put my arm around her. Not a bad way to sneak that in. She pulled closer to me and we laughed, watching the families clear the beach as the sun dove into the horizon like a great dolphin, with the last bit of rays shining upward. There was an orange hue to the sky nearest the sun. In what seemed like seconds it was gone.

We pulled towards each other and snuggled for a moment. I was in heaven but I was afraid to breathe for fear she would pull away. She had no idea how long it'd been since I hugged a woman. I was shaking inside but hoped she couldn't feel it. I wanted so much to be a man and yet inside I felt so fragile. So afraid of messing this up. At least I was sober and now I had a wonderful career coming forward out of the mist. And tonight, this one night at least, I had the most beautiful woman in the world sitting beside me.

Gauging from my history, I wondered how long this would last. This new relationship with Celeste. How long before something stupid I did would drive her away? I shuddered for a moment and then shook off the thoughts of destruction. She seemed to feel something and turned and looked square at me. It was disconcerting but I couldn't pull away. And in one fleeting moment, when I was about to fall into her eyes—which had turned a mysterious lavender blue, she leaned forward ever so slightly. I thought I was mistaken it was so slow. But at last her soft lips pressed against mine and I lost myself in her fragrance. Those lips were like kissing a newborn baby. And it was such a surprise that it caught my breath. And then it was gone.

She sat up straight and looked out to sea. I was speechless, which was rare, and just sat there staring at her. How had she done that? How had she taken such a huge step across a crevice that waited to kill this moment, and kissed me as lightly as a feather, and then acted like it had never happened? It was huge for me. My mind was racing in a zillion directions at once. I felt like a teenager being kissed by the prettiest girl in class. Only the truth was I was in my fifties and had lived the last several years alone trying not to live. That kiss had awakened me somewhere down deep where I'd lost myself years ago. I got very quiet and still. Celeste turned and looked at me again, and a tear was rolling down her cheek. Her words were whispered, so faint that I could barely hear her against the noise of the waves coming in.

"I took that kiss because I was afraid you'd never make the move tonight. I hope you didn't mind. The ocean, the sunset, it all came down on me. And you were so close to me—I—"

"Shh. Don't explain it, sweetheart. I'm still in a daze from walking into your eyes. That was probably the sweetest kiss I've ever had. So pure. So simple. It caught me off guard, but it was perfect timing."

"You know how you wanted me to go out the first time you saw me? You know how you were afraid to talk to me because you feared you'd run me off?"

I looked at her wondering what was coming next. I whispered back to her. "Yeah, I clearly remember those feelings. I was petrified to call out your name. You were so pretty—so unreachable. I was practically homeless then. Coming off the street with nothing. No money. No home. No one. I—"

She put her fingers across my lips and shook her head. "I didn't see a homeless man. I saw a good man. Just like now."

I leaned into her and just sat there watching the darkness surround us. For a moment I lost track of time and then I remembered we had to go to work tomorrow. She must have remembered at the same time because we both stood up and I picked up the blanket and shook off the sand. I grabbed her hand and we headed back to the car, both of us lost in our own thoughts. I could hear the waves crashing into shore. I could hear the birds overhead. And before I got swallowed up in memories of sleeping outside near the water I reached the car and opened the door for her. When I took her home I was going to get out and walk her to the door. She shook her head.

"I'm fine walking to the door alone. You've been wonderful and I've loved this night. I want to remember it slowly. Thank you for a lovely time, Matt. I'll see you tomorrow bright and early."

She leaned over and we kissed for a second. And then she was gone. I sat there for maybe ten minutes not wanting to ruin the spell she'd cast on me. But my watch told me I'd be turning back into a doctor in nine hours so I pulled away from her house and drove home. When I let my head rest on my pillow, with all the lights out in the house, and the covers pulled up to my neck, I let myself relive the softest kiss I'd ever had in my entire life. And I thought I would die in the remembering of it.

CHAPTER 75

PETE JENKINS ROLLED his big rig carefully down the highway as Paco dozed off and on. He felt his hope rising as they neared his destination even as his strength was ebbing away. Paco awoke slowly as his body felt the momentum of the big rig cranking out the miles, his sleepy eyes watching as the odometer clicked off mile after mile. He instinctively reached for his back pack, trying to quench a deep thirst inside his gut. Pete saw him stir and spoke quietly.

"Dude, if you need a drink that bad, you're gonna have to walk. You know insurance companies frown on alcohol in the cab. I love my job too much to let a few drops of whiskey put me at risk of losing it."

Paco shrugged and looked out the window, feeling the sweat gather on his forehead.

"We gonna stop and drop a few crates in Mobile and then we'll get some coffee and doughnuts. Then it's on to Tallahassee. I can drop you at the Destin exit on I10; they should have a bus that will take you into Destin. They call that town Crestview. If you feel strong enough to help me unload in Mobile, I'll give you a couple of bucks for helping me so you won't show up in town flat broke."

Hope flooded Paco's heart as his pulse grew rapid from lack of booze. The mid July sun warmed the windows and strained the air conditioning in the clean smelling truck. Paco found himself craving the stale stench of a smoke but he swallowed it along with his desire for a drink. He busied his mind on the scenery that was passing them at seventy miles per hour. As they passed a work truck from the Alabama Corrections Agency, they saw a crew of prisoners cleaning up the highway, cutting the grass and bagging up debris. Paco nodded his head but kept his gaze steady at the men alongside the road. Pete looked at Paco as if he knew Paco's history.

Paco grunted. "Been there done that."

Pete just grinned. "We all have our own prison."

Paco seemed amused at the statement and looked as if he wanted to break into a lecture, but Pete simply repeated himself: "We all have our own prison, man."

Paco chuckled and then chimed in. "Yeah, but thanks to you, I'm wearin' a clean jumpsuit."

The two laughed as the road broke into six lanes. Pete eased the big rig into the northernmost lane and the engine roared as he lowered his speed to fifty five and downshifted. Suddenly the daylight vanished as they entered a tunnel, taking the pair out of downtown Mobile. The sun was blinding when the darkness of the tunnel ended and the sky came into view.

Soon they would be near the edge of town, dropping two crates of auto parts at a collision shop before navigating the busy city streets back onto the highway. Mobile looked like every other city, yet it had an unusual feel that was all its own. In the summer, it had a Gulf Coast sort of flavor that set it apart; the big ships in port that were visible for miles let the two men know this wasn't your average city. Pete jumped out of the semi, leaving it running. Paco clutched his backpack, remembering his ordeal in Tampa. Yet something about Pete was different from that other driver. There was a warmth and compassion that allowed Paco to trust him.

Paco spotted a store and a dumpster and after they were unloaded he stole his way over to the store. Pooling his change, he purchased a tall can of beer and raced over to the dumpster after making sure Pete was still inside tending to business. The cold fluid washed down his throat, instantly quelling the butterflies that were beginning to feel more like a bee's nest to the old bum. Safely out of sight he recovered the unused portion of a cigarette that an unknown patron had discarded. He inhaled the stale acrid smoke and as he tipped up the last of the beer Pete's face popped into view. Paco swallowed the beer quickly with no intention of giving up his contraband. He might give up his soft ride to Destin but he wasn't giving up the momentary relief of that last cold swig. He was surprised that Pete had found him so quickly but before he could ask how, the old trucker spoke quietly.

"Predictable."

When Paco opened his mouth to protest the old trucker just smiled. "Been there done that. If you're done with the beer, get in the truck. Let's get you to Crestview."

The two began to walk across the parking lot, Paco was shaking his head in disbelief that such a good plan could have been uncovered so easily. Again, before he could speak, Pete spewed out more wisdom.

"We only deceive ourselves. We think no one can see. But the only ones we fool are ourselves."

As they closed in on the truck something new stirred deep in Paco's gut; a wrenching that he had never felt before. Before he could think he doubled over on the pavement in a fit of coughing, blood coming up and fluid from his lungs. He knew then that he'd better hurry to Destin, because his time was short. Pete saw him coughing up blood and shook his head.

"Paco, get in the cab. We need to keep goin' or we're never gonna reach Destin. I told you earlier that you needed to rest. You're sick, man. Real sick. I don't know how you keep on going."

Paco looked at Pete and shook his head. "Haven't you ever been driven to do something?"

"Yeah, I'm driven to gettin' you to Destin."

"I'm talkin' about something really important. This thing that I am doing is for a young man who has never met his real father. It is the one drivin' force that keeps me going. I know how much it's gonna mean to this kid when he sees his father for the first time. That's a life-changin' event there. Ya know?"

Pete nodded and pushed the pedal down hard. The rig took off and the gears kicked in one at a time until they were up to speed on the highway. "I get what you're doing, Paco. But if you are about to die, it doesn't make much sense to push like that. Give yourself time to heal a little.

That kid wouldn't want you dying on the witch hunt. You don't really know if this guy's alive, do you?"

"I got good information that he's in Destin. I have to look. I cannot waste any more time than I already have tryin' to get to him. It's now or never."

"That's a true statement. 'Cause you're not gonna make it much longer. I hate to be so crude but I've seen you cough up blood. Man, that's usually a sign the end is near."

"Don't ya think I know that? I live inside this used up body, man. I'm ready for it to be over. I've lived my life pretty much how I wanted to. I chose to live the hard way. Some people would shake their head, knowing what education I've had. But I got burned and it did something to me. I've never been the same since. I just want to do this one thing before I go. I promised that kid I'd find his father, and by damn, that's what I'm gonna do."

Pete smiled and shook his head. "I believe you're gonna do it, Paco. You're so determined that I believe you just might pull it off. Now buckle up and sit back and rest. I'll get you to Destin. Trust me."

Paco leaned his head back on the seat and blew out a deep sigh. He was tired. But as the miles clicked by, he got sleepy and dozed off again.

Pete was also getting tired. He hadn't slept well last night and as he pulled in to Crestview he found a rest stop around Milton and pulled in. He smiled when he saw a huge Blue Angels Hornet in front of the Welcome Center. He started to nudge Paco but decided against it. The plane wasn't that important. The old man needed to sleep more than anything.

Pete got out of the cab and headed to the restroom. It felt good to stretch his legs again, and he was thirsty. He got a Coke and walked back to the cab. He hadn't been gone ten minutes. When he opened the door to the cab, he noticed Paco was gone. He looked around the truck and stood away from his rig to see if Paco had headed to the restrooms. He was puzzled at how Paco could have disappeared so quickly. Where had he gone?

Twenty minutes later it hit Pete that the old hobo had taken off on his own. He couldn't understand why, because Paco was so ill. He waited around for a few more minutes and climbed into the back of the truck and dozed off for about two hours. When he woke up, he was disoriented for a moment but soon remembered that Paco had disappeared. He couldn't believe that he hadn't shown up, but he knew in his gut that the guy was gone. He started the rig and pulled out of the truck stop. It felt eerie to be traveling alone but maybe Paco had another plan. He kept his eyes open as he headed towards Tallahassee. It was late afternoon and he knew he'd make it by dark. He was ready to get out of the rig for a day or two. But he couldn't get Paco out of his mind. Why was the man so determined to do things the hard way; why did he want to hoof it to Destin instead of taking the ride? Nothing made sense. Absolutely nothing.

Paco was already walking his way to Destin. He'd had enough of the truck and Pete, even though he liked the man. He owed him for the help and appreciated his comments about his health. But he needed to be outside and breathe the fresh air. He needed to keep on moving or he knew he would die. So he thumbed a ride part of the way and just kept walking. He would get there before morning if he could keep on going. It gave him plenty of time to think.

Ugly as it was, he could only stand so much talking. And Pete was a talker. But Pete had gone out of his way to be nice and Paco wasn't ungrateful. He was a loner. Plain and simple. His legs were tired and his chest was hurting, but the drive to see Matt was keeping him going. He was out of money and needed a quick job. So his mind was on work and the elusive doctor. He would settle both of those dilemmas when he got to Destin.

Hours went by and darkness fell; it was so dark he could hardly see where he was going. He thought about stopping to rest but knew if he did, he might never get back up. A red pickup stopped and he caught a ride for about twenty miles sitting in the back of the truck. The wind in his face was refreshing and it felt good to rest his legs. When the truck stopped, he hopped off and took for the road as fast as his legs would carry him. Soon he was on Highway 98 and he knew it wouldn't be too long before he would see the lights of Destin. He yearned to lie down, and he was dying of thirst. So his first thought as he saw the signs of the small fishing village full of tourists was to panhandle enough money to buy a beer and a bite to eat. The first gas station was his target. He dodged a cop car and ducked into the shadows of an awning near the side of the gas station. When he saw a man stop to get gas he walked over to him and just asked him point blank for enough money for a bite to eat. The guy pulled out a five dollar bill and smiled at Paco.

"Here, man. Go get yourself something. You look like you've seen better days."

"You're right. I'm about on my last leg. Thank you for your help."

Paco walked away and purchased a beer and a bear claw pastry. He swallowed the food whole and gulped down the beer. He almost bought another one but decided against it. He headed for some woods to bed down for the night. He was worn out and as soon as he'd made camp he fell into a deep sleep.

His body ached and he coughed blood up all night. But he had made his destination. He was closer to finding Matt and that was all that kept the old hobo going. That and the love he had for Hunter. He couldn't wait to make the phone call that was going to change Hunter's life. He had to hang on just a little longer. He was almost afraid to fall into a deep sleep for fear he wouldn't wake up. But in spite of his fears, morning came and the sun that had risen early came bursting through the trees to warm his face. It was going to be a hot humid day and he got up and brushed the pine needles from his clothing. He couldn't remember feeling so tired and worn out. But a glimmer of hope stirred in his belly as he rolled up his sleeping bag and tied it to his back pack. He needed some hot coffee badly. As he walked out of the wooded area, cars were already on the road. He could smell the salt air and took in a deep breath, which caused a coughing spell. But nothing, not even the red blood he saw on the ground, would deter his journey now.

As Paco walked around a section of Destin, he was feeling worse by the minute. He headed into another gas station and asked the lady at the check out if he could have a cup of coffee. She took one look at him and raised her eyebrow.

"Man, you look like you didn't go to bed last night. You okay?"

"Not too good today. You got a coffee for me or not? I'm pretty sick."

"I'm not allowed to give out coffee for free. We have cameras here. "

"I got some change." He was aware of the cameras as he walked to the coffee machine and fixed a large cup. He put sugar and creamer in it and walked back to the register to pay.

"Take care of yourself. It's going to be a hot day out there."

Paco nodded. "May be the best day of my life."

Paco shuffled out of the gas station and headed towards the water. There was a stand of trees and scrub oaks that would make a good shade from the heat that was pushing away the coolness of the morning. He was feeling worse by the minute and decided against a long trek on hot pavement searching for Matt. It would have to wait until he felt stronger. The last stretch of his journey had been hard on his body. He was worried now that he might not even make it.

He leaned against the tree and shut his eyes. He could hear other men in the woods talking. He knew better than to say anything to them. He was the new guy on the scene and usually that wasn't a good thing. He closed his eyes and allowed his body to rest again. But his brain was moving at the speed of light. He didn't want to give up. He couldn't.

CHAPTER 76

———— ⚜ ————

BROTHER JOE WAS out late for a Friday night. The air was sticky and there wasn't a blade of grass stirring except near the water, which was barely moving in and out as he made his way among the giants on the street. He'd worn shorts, which was unusual for him even on the warmest of nights, but he was grateful for the decision as he felt the sweat trickling down the back of his neck. The mosquitoes and the pesky yellow flies were out and he spent most of his time swatting them away and wishing for a can of Bug Off. He walked up on a group of men who were sitting down against a fence smoking cigarettes. He nodded to them and approached slowly, knowing they'd be uneasy about a stranger walking up. He saw a few of them grab their pack of cigarettes and hide them. Always afraid of someone taking what they had.

"Hey, guys. Everybody doing okay tonight?" His voice was low and gentle. He smiled as he moved closer.

"Doing okay, thanks. You Brother Joe? I heard about you from some men on Beach Drive. They said you roam around at night bringing food or water or sleeping bags. Is that true?"

Joe nodded and squatted down so he could chat with the men. His knees were weak but it was the only way he could get real with them. He would nurse his wounds later at home and curse the effort he made that didn't produce the results he wanted. But at the moment he was happy to look into their eyes and gather as much information about their needs as he could. They all said they were fine and that they didn't need anything. But he knew they were thirsty and probably had eaten only one meal that day. On weekends it was worse. No shower and no food were offered. He grabbed the water he had in his back pack and handed them out to the men. "Yeah, I try to help out when I can. You guys got any news? Anything happening out here on the street?"

They mumbled something between themselves and shrugged. Finally one of the men on the right side whose beard and hair were so mingled you could hardly see his face spoke up. "I heard there was a new man on the street today. Came all the way from Philly. That's what they're sayin'."

Joe's ears perked up. "Really? You haven't seen him around?"

"Not yet. But we're aimin' to find out who he is. 'Cause we can't allow him to take over our territory or anything. We worked hard for this spot and we ain't gonna give it up to some newcomer."

"I can see why." Joe smiled and looked around at the men. "What did he look like? This new man you talk about."

"Kind of scruffy. Not too tall. I heard he was an old man."

Someone else chimed in. "Heard he was near dyin'."

Joe nodded again and stood up. His knees weren't going to hold up long if he kept squatting down. "Okay, I'll get going now. If you guys need anything just get word to me. I have a few clothes, food, and a couple of bicycles that have been rebuilt. I'll come around Saturday night and then again on Monday. Sundays I try to rest."

The men quietly nodded and watched as the old preacher walked away. Joe wasn't too surprised at the news of a new homeless man on the scene. They came and went like gypsies. Some of them were gypsies. But Destin police were continually forcing people to move around so they wouldn't bother the tourists and some of the homeless left and went to other locations less desirable. Less populated. Often it was to their demise because less was offered them and they were left on their own to survive. He walked through the parking lots and crossed over towards the beach. Some of the park benches next to the park were full of beer drinking hobos. They were harmless but often got arrested if they were too loud or anyone complained. They waved at Joe because he was well known among them. He tried to offer them food but they shook their heads. Beer was the item of the night and even a protein bar just wasn't going to cut it.

As he headed towards a small stand of trees he noticed an older gentleman sitting under one of the larger trees. He had a backpack and tent and his shoes were showing signs of wear. He had a lot of hair sticking out from under a ball cap and had his eyes closed. It was hard to see his face but the street light down the hill was casting a small glow around the bottom of the tree where he was sitting.

"Evening, sir. Don't mean to bother you. Do you need some water?"

Paco stirred and looked up at the older man standing in front of him. "Nah. I'm good." He closed his eyes.

Joe could tell by the way he was breathing that he wasn't well. "You sure? It's awful hot out here tonight."

"You an angel or something? What are you doing out here? Passing out water?"

"Pretty much. I come around here a lot at night to check on the men who sleep outside. You been here long?"

"No. Just arrived. Not feelin' all that well, so not up to much talk."

"Gotcha. I won't bother you then. But if you need anything, I'll be around tomorrow night about the same time. Make sure you drink enough liquid. It's easy to get too dehydrated. You look like you know the ropes out here."

"'Bout twenty years is all. I'd say that was long enough to figure it all out."

"Well, you're still alive. That's proof enough. Take it easy, old timer. See you later."

Joe walked away as Paco stared at his back. Each man was wondering about the other.

Matt was late coming in from his date with Celeste and noticed Joe's lights on. He walked across the lawn swatting mosquitoes and cursing. Using the usual way to get in, he opened the side door that went into the kitchen and shut it quietly. Some leftover rolls were sitting out and he poked his head in the refrigerator and found some cold roast.

Suddenly he was starving. He cut some of the roast beef and stuffed it into a roll and took a huge bite. Just as he was chewing his first bite Joe came through the door.

"Hey, you. Making yourself at home?"

"Pretty much. Where ya been, old man?"

"A little respect would be nice. I been out looking for hobos. Found a new one tonight. He's not doing too well."

Matt raised an eyebrow. "Someone I need to look at?"

"Not sure he'll allow it. But maybe at some point. I left him water but he acted like he didn't want to be bothered."

"Well if you see him again, just let me know. I'll check him out for you."

"Mighty kind of you, with your mouth full and all. Not a bad roast, huh?"

"Delicious! Not like I didn't eat already or anything."

"You have a good time with Celeste?"

"It was perfect. I tell you Joe, she's one of a kind. And so is that red car!"

Joe laughed and grabbed a few slices of roast and stuffed it into a roll. "I'm tired tonight. It's been a long hot day and the night hasn't been much cooler." He looked at Matt and shook his head.

"What?"

"Nothing. Really. Just can't get that old hobo out of my mind. I'm sure it's nothing. So tell me about your date."

Matt grinned. "We had a good dinner at Mike and Dan's Barbeque and walked on the beach. I had tucked a blanket under my arm so we sat down and watched the sunset. It was amazing, as usual. But you wouldn't believe how easy it was to talk to her. She was adorable. And she really loves her job at the clinic."

"I can tell you really like her. Sounds impressive. So what's ahead for you two? You gonna ask her out again?"

Matt slung his legs over the arm of the leather chair in the living room and watched Joe clean up the kitchen. "Yeah. I'm just trying to figure out how to wait a few days before I call. Don't want to seem too eager and all, but I'm really dying to see her again."

Joe chuckled and sat down on the sofa near Matt. "Son, you act like you've never been on a date before. You're fifty something years old. Of course I know it's been a while since you were in a relationship. That right there could cause some excitement!"

"Okay. You keep on ribbing me and I'm not going to tell you anything."

"Just joking, boy. Relax."

"I know you're as tired as I am. Let's both get a good night's sleep because tomorrow's coming pretty fast."

"Agreed. Breakfast at seven. You coming?"

"Have I ever missed one yet?"

"Good point. See you in the morning."

Matt walked to the door and looked back. "Thanks for the snack. It hit the spot."

Joe just looked at him with a slight grin. *The boy has some potential.* He finished cleaning up the kitchen and turned the lights out. As his head hit the pillow he acknowledged for the millionth time that he was lonely. Not because he didn't see enough people in his day, but because he'd never found anyone to share his life with. Maybe because he'd been so busy helping people. It didn't bother him often, but this night it caused him to have a restless sleep remembering a couple of women he'd left with a broken heart because he was too stubborn to allow that kind of love in.

CHAPTER 77

———————— ⚜ ————————

WITHIN A FEW days of arriving in Destin, Paco had figured out the pecking order on the street. There were several groups of homeless, most of which stayed pretty clear of him. But one man, who was also a loner, shared with Paco the ins and outs of the underground world. Tourists were oblivious of the homeless and most of the population of Destin had no clue homeless people were around. It was critical not to look homeless, so most of the men were difficult to spot in the daytime. At night the scenery changed. Paco learned quickly that was when the men drank and grouped together. After a few drinks, they no longer cared who saw them. They hung out in public places and sat on benches lined up on the side streets. The police were constantly cruising by them and knew most of them by name. Paco was the new one and word got back to the police each time a newcomer arrived. He was ID'd twice when he'd been drinking too much and sat too close to a thriving business.

Mostly, he hid in the many stretches of woods that were scattered on Highway 98. He sat his tent up and cleaned out a location that was close to a church that served lunch. There was a shower on the side of the church that was available for three days a week. He was getting sicker by the day and knew his time was getting short. But the drive to find Matt was pushing him beyond what his body could stand. He felt weaker and unsteady on his feet at times. His mind was getting foggy and he was losing his appetite. But thinking of how much Hunter wanted to meet his father kept him going even when he felt like dying. The odd thing about it was that no one would really know if he died.

His life didn't mean much, and his death even less. So that didn't scare Paco. He'd dealt with it years ago when he made the decision to

469

remain on the street. When people asked him why he chose to remain outside, he had a difficult time answering them. There didn't seem to be a clear cut-and-dried reason. He just didn't want to go back to society. He worked when he needed money and bought only what he could carry. Early on he enjoyed eating good food at nicer restaurants, but as the years passed he was satisfied with less and less. His teeth were bad, what little he had left, and his face looked older than his years. His clothes were clean but ragged. His shoes had walked so many miles that the soles were thinning in spots. He had moved the plastic bag holding the letter addressed to Matt Collins from his old shoes to the ones he wore now. But they were wearing out to the point where he was thinking about splurging for a new pair. He had let himself go so far down that he didn't have the energy to pull himself back up.

The week had been long and hot and Paco was worn out. He had picked up a little money helping a boat captain clean barnacles off his boat. He held on to it like it was gold. It was Saturday night and all the men were drunk. He had been sitting under a huge live oak tree enjoying a light breeze when a man they called Wolf walked up.

"Dude. You got a light?"

Paco looked up and raised his eyebrow. "Sure. Hang on." He reached inside his backpack and pulled out a lighter, handed it to Wolf and watched as he lit up the piece of cigarette he held gingerly in his fingers.

"You're new around here. I've been hearing stuff about you."

"Yeah, came in a few days ago. Trying to stay away from the herd, if you know what I mean."

Wolf nodded and squatted beside Paco. "That's cool, man. They're a bunch of drunks and are constantly getting arrested for public drunkenness. It would pay you to stay away. 'Less you want to end up like them, in the tank all the time."

"No plans for that. I got a reason for being in Destin. And I aim to get it done pretty soon here."

"I figured you won't be around long. Just stopped by to get a light. Loners aren't too welcome around here. This group is pretty tight. You prob'ly picked that right up."

"Frankly, I don't care whether they like me or not. I'm not here to fit in. I'm here to find a doctor named Matt Collins. Until I find him, I'll be hiding in the woods out of everyone's way. That's my plan."

"You hungry?"

"Always hungry."

"I got some fish I'm cookin'. Let's go eat some of it before the cops smell the fire."

Paco pushed off the tree and stood up, wobbly. He had had too much to drink and needed something in his stomach. It was getting late but the fish sounded good. He followed Wolf into a part of the woods behind a huge empty building. It was a perfect spot to hide. But the smoke was curling up above the trees and was going to ruin a good campsite if Wolf didn't put out the fire pretty soon. The aroma of fish on an open fire was stirring hunger pangs in Paco's belly. He squatted down and stabbed a piece of fish and waited for it to cool.

Wolf pulled his hat down but was watching to see if Paco liked the fish. He took a big bite and nearly swallowed it whole. There was plenty for both men to fill their stomachs but the meat was dry and Paco was getting thirsty. Wolf reached around the tree and pulled out a cold beer. He smiled at Paco and offered him one. Paco was amazed and laughed.

"You got a regular diner here, man. Nice of you to share it with me. Why did you do that, anyway?"

"'Cause you're a loner like me. And besides, I couldn't eat all this here fish."

"True. Thanks, man. It hit the spot. I was hungrier than I thought."

Wolf nodded and put out the fire. He grabbed the last little bit of fish and popped it into his mouth. He licked his fingers and put dirt on the fire. Paco stood up and turned to walk away. Wolf stopped him dead in his tracks.

"You say you're lookin' for that Matt Collins guy?"

"Yeah. Been lookin' for him for a long time."

"I know where he is."

He had Paco's attention. "You say you know where Matt Collins is?"

Wolfe smirked and nodded. "Yep. Exactly what I'm sayin'."

"Well what do I have to pay for that information?"

"How much does it mean to ya?"

"It means a hell of a lot."

"What would ya give me if'n I was to tell you where he is?"

"I reckon I could find him on my own. If you know where he is, so do a lot of others, I'm guessin'."

"That's a risk you'll have to take, I guess."

"Thanks for the fish. I'll find the guy on my own. Everything's got a price."

"Shore does. You take care now, Paco. Nice talkin' with ya."

Paco lay down against a small tree under the eave of an old broken down shed. The mosquitoes were gnawing on every speck of exposed skin. The alcohol level in his body was working against him, and he passed out quickly and slept through the night. His tent gave him respite from the night creatures and he would have slept until noon but the morning sun shot through the trees, heating up the inside of the tent like an oven. He woke up sweating profusely and unzipped the tent to allow some air to come in. There were thunderheads on the horizon and a slight smell of rain, so the promise of a cooler day was whispering in the breeze that blew the tent flap and stirred the leaves on his tree.

As he climbed out of his tent his stomach was growling. He headed towards the Coffee House to grab a cheap breakfast, putting out his cigarette as he entered the door. There were people coming in behind him and he noticed two doctors eating in the corner. Soon the place was crowded and Paco kept his head down, enjoying the smell of bacon and eggs that wafted up from his steaming plate. He sipped strong coffee and ate his last bite of raisin toast. The coffee warmed his sick stomach but wouldn't sit well later in the day.

He decided spur of the moment to call Hunter. It was only fair to let the kid know he was in Destin, alive. Well, barely alive. His stiff fingers dialed the number and waited for that voice that haunted him constantly. On the fourth ring he answered.

"Hello? This is Hunter." The voice was clear as a bell.

"Hey, dude. You sleeping all day?" Paco laughed but ended up coughing blood up. Not a good sign.

"Geez, Paco! Where you been? I been sick with worry about you. You were supposed to call and—" Paco butted in. "Hang on, kid. I'm here, ain't I?"

Hunter laughed. "Yeah, guess so. But, geez. You need to call and let me know where you are. I'm just a kid, ya know?"

"How could I forget? Now listen. I wanted you to know I'm in Destin. Just ate some breakfast and was going to scout around. Not feeling too well, though. When you coming down here anyway?"

"You sound terrible. Have you gotten anyone to check out your chest? What's going on with your health?"

"Don't worry about me. I'm not gonna be 'round much longer, Hunter. The main thing is I made it here. So tell me, when is your wedding? When you coming my way?"

"Next weekend. Can you hold out until then? It sounds like you're on your last leg."

Paco laughed but cut it short. "Nah. I'm good, man. I'll take it easy until you get here. But I'm gonna find your dad. He's here somewhere. You can count on it."

Hunter felt his stomach knot up and he had a lump in his throat. "I'm not counting on anything, Paco. So don't worry about that. If you find him, that'd be great. If not, I'll live."

"Yeah, yeah. I hear ya. I also hear how badly you want me to find him. I saw that in your eyes, remember? My memory isn't that bad, dude."

"Well, it sure is good to hear your voice. Although I wish I could check out your lungs. I thought you stopped in a clinic not too long ago? Did you mention that to me?"

"Not sure, but I did see a doc not too long ago. He said I was good. Main thing is to eat and get enough rest. I'm coughin' up some blood but not too worried 'bout it. I'm gettin' around just fine. How's school? Enough about me."

"I'm working my ass off, Paco. It's hard. But Holly and I are pushing through it together. We can't wait to get to Destin, even for a couple of days. I can't wait to see you, Paco. It's been a long time."

"I feel the same way, boy. I'll keep you posted on what's going on down here. And I want you to count on one thing, Hunter. You're gonna get the chance to meet your father if it's the last thing I do. You got that, man?"

"Paco, I know you've tried your best. You don't have to push so hard. I'd love to see the guy but it's not worth your life, man. You gotta think about yourself right now."

"It's too late for me. But you're just beginning your life. And I can make that promise because I know he's around here somewhere. I just have to find him. My one fear is that I'll die before I get to him! That'd be my luck, Son."

"Don't say that, Paco. I want Holly to meet you. Just take it easy and stay out of this heat as much as you can. Your body isn't going to hold up much longer if you keep punishing it like you are. Can't you stay in a motel to get out of the heat for a while?"

Paco sighed. There was no explaining it over the phone. "I'm used to livin' outside, Hunter. Don't cater much to being boxed in, ya know? Don't worry. I'm gonna make it just fine. I'll talk to you soon. Good to hear your voice. See you soon, boy. Looking forward to it."

Hunter hung up the phone and stood looking out a window near the hall phone. He brushed a tear off his cheek. Why did he think he wasn't going to ever see Paco again? A chill came over him as he walked back to his room. Lonnie was sitting at his desk cramming for a biochemistry test. He was pushing hard for an A on this one. Hunter was greeted with a quick nod and a belch. Hunter noticed he was drinking a large Coke and another pizza box was sitting on the counter. The guy just never changed. Here he was studying to be a doctor and eating junk food.

"Man, you gonna die before you ever become a doctor. You ever heard of vegetables?"

Lonnie glared at him. "Listen, dude! I'm cramming for the worst test of my career and you're gonna jump my butt for eating pizza? Come on, man."

Hunter retreated to his room and sat on his bed. Lonnie was right. He had overreacted because he was upset over Paco. He was worried the guy was gonna die before he could get down there to thank him. And in the back of his mind, if he was real honest, he was afraid Matt Collins would not be found.

Paco hung up the phone with a renewed determination to find Matt Collins. He spent the rest of the day wandering the streets of Destin, not realizing he was missing the one area of town that would have caused his journey to come to an end. He crashed early, feeling more tired than usual, and went to bed hungry. His cough was worse and he had a fever. But he was tough. He knew how to survive. And he also knew he was playing around with fate, which wasn't a good bedfellow to have around. For the fear was that the arm of fate would reach its hand into his life at a moment when he least expected it and take him out. Like the flame of a candle being snuffed out. However, the drive to find Matt Collins was so strong that it kept the old man going beyond any doctor's predictions or worst prognosis. He was a dead man walking and he didn't care. Because he loved a young boy he'd seen in the worst of circumstances, and that love was what kept him alive.

CHAPTER 78

———— ⚜ ————

HUNTER HAD THE car packed and was leaning against the side waiting for Holly to find the one pair of shoes she just had to take with her. He was getting used to having to wait. It seemed like an enigma to him. No matter how much time a woman had, she still at the last moment had to do one more thing that would make a person late. He smiled at the thought of her rushing around in a frenzy. The trip to Destin was going to take them about seventeen hours, give or take a few, depending on how many stops they made. He knew she would want to stop in Nashville overnight and that was fine with him. But the constant stopping for shopping malls and ice cream and restrooms could stretch the trip into three days.

He was nervous about the wedding, but not the commitment. They were facing some of the toughest years of their life in med school and they'd both been warned about the need to wait until they were out before they got married. It was mostly him pushing it. He wanted a family. He wanted to belong. His mind was running full speed when she came flying out of the door with a frown on her face, the wind blowing her hair all over the place. It couldn't be good news.

"I'm sick and tired of looking for those stupid shoes! I know they're in the house somewhere but who knows where. Someone could have borrowed them and not given them back. I'm so frustrated."

Hunter held back a laugh. "Come on, Holly! Take it easy. What's one pair of shoes going to hurt? I mean, really. I'll buy you a new pair, how's that?"

Not the thing to say. "Are you serious? Do you know how much I loved those shoes? They were perfect for this trip to the beach. I never get to wear them here and I was so looking forward to it. And besides, we'd never find them now. I bought them last year."

Hunter was stuck. He would lose now no matter what he said. "Let's get going. I'm sure we can stop at many of the malls we'll pass on the road. You'll find something even better, I promise."

Frowns and grunts were all she could manage. She plopped into her seat and buckled the seat belt and glared at him. He didn't understand why she was so negative toward him. "What? It's not my fault you can't find those shoes."

"No. But you don't understand how important those shoes are. You keep trying to pacify me."

"Well, at least I'm trying. Okay. I'll shut up. I want us to have a great time on this trip, and no pair of shoes is going to ruin it for us. You hear?"

Big sigh. "Okay. I will keep it down. It's just so darn frustrating. So are we aiming at Nashville? I'd love to stay overnight there."

Hunter grinned. At least he was right about one thing. "Yeah, that's where we're headed. I sure wish Paco would call me. I have no idea where he is now or what he's doing. He sounded so sick the last conversation we had that I fear he might have died."

"Well, we won't know unless he calls. Too bad he doesn't have a cell phone. Say, have you heard from Aunt Jenny? Is she going to make this trip?"

"She hasn't called in the last couple of days. The last I heard she was planning on being there. I can't imagine her not coming. She's my only real relative."

"She'll be there. She was so excited about us getting married that she was about to freak out. Remember?"

Hunter laughed and reached over and touched her hand. "Yeah, I do remember. Are you nervous at all about the wedding? About our life together?"

Holly blew out a big sigh and looked at him, wrinkling her nose. "I'm nervous, excited, and full of so many emotions. But I really want it over with so we can get back to a normal schedule. School consumes both of us. It's hard to relax for a few days and enjoy the wedding stuff."

"I feel the same way. We need time to get relaxed and then before you know it, we'll be heading home. I hope we can enjoy being on the beach. Waking up to the view of a massive Gulf. The water is supposed to be emerald green. Ever seen water like that?"

"Nope. But I'm really looking forward to walking in the sand and feeling the coolness of the water. It's been so hot this summer . . ."

"Holly, we are making the right move here, aren't we? I mean, you don't feel pushed to do this, do you?"

"Hunter, we've been over this a million times. It's the best solution for us. I know others don't agree. But you and I are settled enough with each other that I don't think we'll feel the crunch like another couple might. We've talked it through as best we can. Now we're going to just enjoy the weekend and deal with things when they come up as maturely as we can."

"That's why I love you. You are so even tempered. So calm. I need that in my life. I hope I am as good for you as you are for me."

Hunter pulled onto the expressway and the road opened up into four lanes. He pressed down on the pedal and the car took off as they both settled into a casual rhythm of conversation. Hunter turned on the music and they sipped on their coffee, trying to let the tiredness that had accumulated drift away.

Paco was up and walking down near Benning Drive early Monday morning. The sun was warm and he was sweating. He was weak and light-headed and his coughing had increased to the point where he could barely talk. His throat was sore and his chest hurt every breath he took. He was so tired that he considered taking off his backpack. But then everything he had would be gone. He wasn't quite ready to let go of the little he had. As ragged as the backpack was, it held all he owned.

He saw a huge building on the corner of Benning and Highway 98. As he turned the corner he looked up and saw a sign on the front of the building. It said "Free Clinic." He was amazed at the size of the building;

it was unlike any clinic he'd ever seen. Especially a free one. He decided to stick his head inside, and as he pulled on the great mahogany doors his chest felt like it had caved in. He fell through the door and landed on the floor in the foyer.

Celeste came running up to him and called out to a nurse who had just walked by. "Go get a doctor. This man's very ill."

The nurse nodded and scurried down the hall. Frank Harrison appeared out of nowhere and knelt down to check on Paco. A stretcher was brought by two male nurses and they took Paco to one of the examination rooms. Frank leaned over Paco and tried to find a pulse. Paco stirred and opened his eyes.

"Man, what happened? I—"

"Don't talk right now, sir. Let me see what's going on." Frank listened to his chest and hooked him up to an EKG machine. A nurse was standing by and assisted him hurriedly.

"Mary, we need to see if this man's having a heart attack. Let's read the EKG quickly and see if it'll tell us what's going on."

He turned to Paco and spoke quietly. "Sir, can you tell me your name?"

"Name's Paco." Paco's voice was raspy and weak.

"You have any health problems? Ever had a heart attack?"

"Got congestive heart failure. Never had a heart attack. No, sir. But coughin' up blood lately."

Frank nodded as he watched the EKG. It didn't look good. The old man's heart was going fast.

"We need to run some tests on you, Paco. You okay with that?"

"Yeah. But it's a waste of time, doc. I'm dyin'. I already know that."

"Well, let us be the judge of that. I'm going to take you into the operating room and do an angiogram on you. I want to see what's going on in those arteries of yours. We'll do an MRI also."

Paco closed his eyes. He knew he was in good hands. But right before he remembered to ask about Matt Collins, he blacked out and didn't wake up until he was in the recovery room with all kinds of tubes hooked up to him. He was groggy and a nurse told him to stay quiet and calm. He closed his eyes and drifted off in a deep sleep. Matt came in and checked on him several times. He called Joe when the night was coming to a close.

"Joe, just wanted you to know I won't be coming home tonight. We got a new man in here and I want to stay with him tonight. He's pretty fragile."

Joe was quiet for a moment. He was wondering if it was the new homeless man he'd met. The guy had been so fragile. It would be a shot in the dark but he had to ask.

"What's the guy's name? Just a stab in the dark here, but I was wondering if it was the same guy I met."

"Paco. His name is Paco. Is that the guy?"

Joe was astounded. "Yeah, that's him. How is he?"

"Not good. I'm worried that he may not make it. That's why I want to stay."

"Mind if I come down for a bit? I'd like to pray for him."

"Not at all. If you're up to it, come on. I'd love to have the company."

Joe hung up and shook his head. He really felt bad for the old hobo. But he was in a good place. He was in good hands. If there was a chance to be had, he would find it with Matt as his doctor.

Paco drifted in and out of a groggy sleep. He was struggling inside, wanting to ask a question. But he couldn't get his eyes open long enough to ask it. Something was bothering him but he couldn't remember what. And time was running out.

CHAPTER 79

———— ✦ ————

THE CLINIC WAS quiet in the middle of the night. Matt was moving from the recovery room to his office, checking on Paco constantly. His condition had remained critical. He was in the last phase of congestive heart failure. His heart was just giving out. His lungs were filling up with fluid. He was quiet and seemed peaceful enough when Joe showed up.

"Hey, buddy. Glad you came. Paco seems very calm right now. I'm just glad he made it to the clinic before he had his heart attack. Can you imagine this happening on the street?"

"Yes, I can. You had one, remember?"

Matt laughed and shook his head. "How quick we forget! He seemed so fragile and I guess I never felt that way about my own life."

"This man's been out there a lot longer than you were, Matt. He's been outside for many years. He has no one. I wish I could speak with him. Is there any way you could rouse him so that I could ask him a few questions?"

Matt and Joe walked into the room where Paco was and Matt went over to the bedside. Paco had his eyes closed but he was moving his hands a little. He seemed frustrated. Against Matt's better judgment he reached over and touched Paco's hand. At first there was nothing. But Matt squeezed it again and Paco opened one eye. Then the other. He looked around the room and then at Matt and Joe. He had no idea who they were.

Joe spoke up first. "Paco, I met you the other day when you were sitting under a tree near the ocean. Do you remember me?" His voice was deep and soothing.

Paco squinted at Joe and waited a few seconds. Then Joe's face began to look familiar to him. He nodded slowly. "I do . . ." His voice was weak.

"It's okay, my man. Don't try to talk. I just wanted to pray with you, if that's okay."

Paco nodded. As he turned his head to see who the doctor was, his eyes were a little blurry. He blinked a few times and then Matt's face came into view. He looked at Matt's face and then his eyes moved down to the name on his white coat. He squinted carefully and saw "Matt Collins, M.D." on the badge.

He froze. The look on his face was one of shock. Pure surprise. Matt moved in closer to him and checked his eyes with a small light. He listened to his heart. His pulse had increased.

Paco tried to talk. "Matt Collins? Is that you?" He whispered hoarsely.

Matt barely could hear what he was saying. He leaned in and asked Paco to repeat it.

"Are you Matt Collins? Is that you?"

Matt was taken aback by the question. "Yes, I'm Dr. Matt Collins."

Paco was getting anxious and trying to sit up. Matt held him down and tried to calm him.

"Paco, you can't get up right now. You're very sick. I need you to try to lie still."

Paco wouldn't listen. His eyes were lit up with energy. "Matt, I've been looking for you—for a long time. I can't believe . . ." He could barely get the words out.

Matt patted him to settle him down. He was so agitated. "It's okay, Paco. Stay as calm as you can. Now what is it you wanted to talk to me about?"

"Where are my shoes, Matt? I need my shoes."

Matt shook his head. "You don't need your shoes now, Paco. You're not leaving here. Do you realize how sick you are?"

Paco nodded. "Get me my shoes, dammit! I need to show you something."

Joe couldn't help but laugh. "Guess he showed you who's boss."

Matt grinned. "Okay. I'll get your shoes."

He went out in the hall and found a locker with all of Paco's things in it. He pulled out his boots and walked back into the recovery room. He set the boots on the bed and looked at Paco.

"I need you to look inside the left boot. There's a plastic bag there."

Matt looked inside the left boot and pulled out a plastic bag. He looked at Paco and raised his eyebrow. "Now what do you want me to do with this filthy bag?"

Joe couldn't help but grin.

"I want you to open it and pull out the letter that is addressed to you."

Matt was surprised. "What do you mean, 'a letter addressed to me'? How in the world did you get a letter that was meant for me?"

"It's a long story. . . .I don't know if I have enough energy to tell it. Read the letter first, will ya?"

Matt pulled the letter out. It was dirty and tattered on the edges. He read it slowly, his eyes trying to absorb the meaning of each line. The ink was dim and part of the side of the letter had been torn. His life was ripped apart as he read the handwritten note from a woman he'd nearly forgotten until now.

Dearest Matt;

I realize this will come as a great shock to you, but I chose to wait until now to share something with you. We parted suddenly and I know you probably remain angry with me even now. I was never able to explain to you why I wanted to back out of your life, but I am writing this letter to let you know why.

Matt, we had a son together whom you have never met. His name is Hunter. He is a wonderful young man who is now in medical school. He is much like you, which made it very difficult for me as I raised him. I saw you in his eyes every single day. I am very ill and dying so I thought perhaps I better let you in on this secret now, even though I honestly thought it was best you never found out. You had made it very clear to me that you never

483

wanted children. So how could I have remained in your life with a child in my belly that you didn't want?

Please do not be angry with me. I hope you find each other somehow. Some way. It would be the greatest gift you could give me as I lie here dying if you would find your son and get to know him. I'm sure he will be a light in your life as he has been in mine. I hope this finds you well and happy. Most of all I pray you will share a part of your life with Hunter. For he has longed for you his entire life.

Love, Lara

Matt was stunned. He glanced down at Paco and tears were wetting the pillow under the old man's face. Matt's hands were shaking and he set the letter down on the edge of the bed. In his mind he knew Paco was very frail. He knew professionally this wasn't the time to unload on him when he lay there dying. But the look in Paco's eyes pulled him in past the medical knowledge of what he was doing into the realm of human survival.

Paco whispered in a low voice, but it was steady. "I know this comes as a shock to you. I'm sorry you had to find out this way. I was afraid I wasn't gonna live long enough to tell you. I never read the letter but my guess is that Lara pretty much explained about your son. I want you to know I've met your son. He's a wonderful boy. I wish he was mine."

"How in the world did you meet him? Where is he now?"

"We met on a bus. He was going to see his Aunt Jenny. And I had nowhere to go. I was obnoxious and reeked of liquor and unclean flesh. Your son was gracious and befriended me for the short time we were on the bus. We shared about our lives and his yearning for you touched my life. Touched me to the bone. I've been driven to finding you, Matt. I can't believe I walked in here and now you are leaning over me while I am dying."

Matt sat there shaking his head. "So you talked to Hunter? Where is he? I want to find him."

"Believe it or not, he's either heading to Destin or already here. I called him to let him know I was here, and he could tell I was very ill. I have no cell phone, so he'll be looking for me. He'll hit the hospitals in the area because he knew by my cough how sick I was. He warned me I didn't have much time."

"This is like a dream. I can't believe I am sitting here with you talking about my son! I didn't even know I had a son! And I'm smiling like an idiot. I never wanted children. And I find out that Lara had a child and never told me! She had every reason to hide it. I told her in no uncertain terms that I didn't want children. But now, after all I've been through, I need family. I need to meet my son."

Tears were streaming down Matt's face. He was weeping openly and Joe was wiping tears from his eyes. Paco closed his eyes and tried to breathe. It was getting harder and harder. Matt checked him and patted his arm. He knew Paco didn't have long on this earth. His time had come.

"Matt, promise me you'll find Hunter. He is here with his fiancé. They are getting married here. It was his dream to find you and I have worked hard for months to make that dream come true. He's a good boy, Matt. He'll suck you right in. I warn you of that."

"I promise you that I'll find him. I'm not sure where to look; was he booking a hotel room or a beach cottage? Did he say?"

"I don't know. He didn't talk about that with me. I just know he'll be looking for me. As a med student he'll hit the hospitals first. He isn't aware of this clinic but there's a chance he'll find it." His voice trailed off.

"Paco, I am going to make you're as comfortable as possible. I don't want you to suffer. You've done a great thing bringing me this letter. By listening to you talk I know you've had some education. I don't know your story but I want to know."

"Ask Hunter—Matt. He'll tell you all about me. Ask Hunter—"

"I will. Now you settle down and hang in there. Try to rest and breathe as deeply as you can. You're on full oxygen and I hope that helps you breathe. I'm sorry you are suffering, Paco. I know Hunter is going to want to see you."

Celeste arrived early and opened up the office. She noticed that Matt's office light was already on and went in to see what was going on. Matt shared with her immediately about what had transpired during the night.

"Celeste, I wish you could have been here. Paco is a homeless man and has traveled long distances to find me. He ended up here in Destin and had this heart attack not realizing I worked here. Can you imagine how this all came together in a matter of hours? He's been looking for me for months!"

"That's amazing. Why was he looking for you? I am confused."

Matt laughed and shook his head. "Join the club. This whole thing has been confusing. He handed her the letter from Lara and watched as she read it. It was obvious she was surprised when she read he had a son.

"You have a son? You didn't know she was pregnant?"

"No, we separated so quickly that I had no idea. She seemed to be eager to end it all, so I let her go. I never was clear on why she wanted out of the relationship."

"Now what are you going to do? How will you find him?"

"I have no idea. I'm going to start with the hotels and then the beach rentals. It'll be a shot in the dark but I have to try. Would you start calling for me, Celeste? His name is Hunter Bentley. Let's see what you can find out; check all the motels and hotels. Then hit the beach rental companies in Destin. Let me know if you find out anything at all."

"I'll get on it right now. The lobby is filling up already. Looks like it's gonna be a busy day. Keep me posted on Paco."

Matt walked out the door and into the recovery room where Paco was sleeping. His pulse was weak and his vitals were virtually disappearing. The old man wouldn't last much longer. Matt was shaking from the news that Lara had shared with him. He had a son. His mind and heart were racing. He wished more than anything that he could have more time with Paco to talk. But time was slipping away.

CHAPTER 80

※

HUNTER WAS DRIVING around Destin searching for a hospital. It was a hot humid afternoon and Holly was ready to hit the beach. But she knew how important Paco was to Hunter, so she bit her lip and chose to help him find this incredible hobo who'd given up so much of his time to finding Hunter's father. Her job was to watch the right side of the road for any clinic or hospital. They'd already hit a few to no avail.

"Damn, you wouldn't think it'd be that difficult to find him. I mean, how many places could he be? He was pretty sick. I'm sure they wouldn't try to treat him at a walk-in clinic."

"Take it easy. I mean we've just begun to look. Why don't we just go straight to the main hospital in the area. Wasn't that Sacred Heart?"

"You're right. We're wasting our time this way. I'll head that way now."

Hunter weaved in and out of traffic trying to save time, and breathed a sigh of relief when they pulled into the hospital parking lot. He jumped out of the car, making sure Holly was behind him, and walked quickly through the front doors. He was impressed with the hospital immediately.

"Good afternoon. I hope you can help me. I am looking for a home-less man who might be here. His name is Paco."

"Paco? Does he have a last name?"

"That's the only name I have. Would you please check to see if he's here?"

The sweet elderly lady sitting behind the desk could tell Hunter was agitated and she tried her best to help him. But after making a few phone calls she shook her head. "There is no person in this hospital with the name' Paco.'"

Hunter was openly disappointed. "Well, thank you so much for your help."

He and Holly turned and walked back out the double doors into the sweltering heat. He stood there feeling hopeless and then headed towards the car. Holly could tell he was getting discouraged.

"Come on, Hunter. Let's head into Destin. There may be a clinic we haven't seen that took him in. It's worth a try."

"Okay. Sorry to be so glum. I just feel like I'm looking for a needle in a haystack. He didn't give me his real name. Or if he did, I don't remember it. I've always called him Paco. People look at me like I'm crazy but that's his name. He was so ill. I'm worried he's already gone."

He pulled out of the parking lot and slipped into bumper-to-bumper traffic. There was no point in being in a hurry because they weren't going to go any faster by getting angry. They passed a few clinics that were small and then came to a red light. On one side was a gas station and on the other there was a three story building that was beautiful with heavy wooden double doors. From the light Hunter couldn't see the name on the front of the building. When they went through the intersection he finally read the words "Waterstone Clinic" on the front. He glanced at Holly and she shrugged.

"Wouldn't hurt to check this out. It's big enough to handle more serious cases. Let's go in and see by chance if Paco is there."

Hunter was impressed by how imposing the building looked. It looked stunning on the outside. He opened up the heavy mahogany doors and the familiar smell of antiseptic hit him as he headed for the receptionist. Celeste was typing and getting insurance forms filled out for the patients who had coverage. She looked up and saw a handsome young man come in with a young woman. She smiled and greeted them.

"Hello! I'm Celeste. Can I help you?"

Hunter smiled nervously. "This sounds like an odd request, but do you happen to have a man here by the name of Paco?"

Celeste's face froze for a second. She gathered her composure and responded with a weak smile. "Why yes, we do! Do you know Paco?"

Hunter's broke into a big grin and nudged Holly. "He's a good friend of mine. Is there any way I could see him? I've been worried sick about him."

She got up and held up her hand. "Hold on a second. I'll talk to a doctor and see if he can have a visitor. He's pretty ill."

The worry showed on Hunter's face as he looked at Holly. "Did you hear that? He's very ill. I knew it! I'm so glad he's here getting the care he needs."

"We're fortunate to have found him in time. I know you're relieved."

"I won't be relieved until I see his face. That man has searched a long time for my dad and I want to thank him. He hardly knows me, Holly. He's amazing. What a heart!"

"I know you care about him, Hunter. I hope you get your chance to see him before he dies."

Celeste came around the corner with a doctor who introduced himself as Dr. Frank Harrison.

"Are you here to see Paco?"

"Yessir, I am. We've come a long way and I was hoping I would be able to see him before he died. I know he's very sick. Can I just see him for a moment? I promise not to disturb him."

"I'm going to take you back there now. I warn you he is very ill. Very fragile. We've been watching him 'round the clock, trying to keep him as comfortable as possible."

The three of them walked down the hallway to the recovery room where Paco was sleeping. Matt was standing by the bed listening to his chest when Hunter walked in. He stepped back as Frank came forward and led Hunter to the bedside. Hunter leaned over Paco and shook his head. His friend didn't look good. He was pale and his breathing very shallow. Hunter leaned lower and whispered into his ear.

"Paco! It's Hunter. I'm here, man. I came as fast as I could. Did you hear me? It's Hunter."

Paco lay very still, barely breathing. Hunter tried one more time.

"Paco! It's Hunter. Can you hear me?" Hunter took his hand and placed it in Paco's hand. He squeezed lightly and waited for a response.

He had just about given up when Paco squeezed back. Hunter broke into a smile. He knew Paco had heard him.

"Can you open your eyes for me, Paco? I want to say goodbye to you."

Paco lay dead still but suddenly his eyes popped open and he looked at Hunter square in the eyes.

"Paco. I love you, man. I'm so glad to see you. You've been so good to me and I just had to thank you."

Paco whispered something but Hunter couldn't hear him. He leaned in closer and asked Paco to repeat what he said.

"Hunter. I found your father."

Hunter looked puzzled. "What? What are you talking about, Paco?"

Paco raised his finger and pointed to Matt, who was staring at him with a shocked look on his face. He was frozen.

"This is your father, Hunter. Matt, meet your son. He's the young man I've been telling you about."

Hunter stood up and looked at Matt. His eyes were filling with tears. "You mean you're my father? You are Matt Collins?"

Matt grabbed Hunter and hugged him. Hunter pulled away and looked at him. "You're my father? I don't believe it! I've wanted to meet you all my life, and here you are taking care of Paco! How in the world did this happen?"

Holly put her hand on his shoulder. She could see he was getting upset. "It's okay, Hunter. Matt's as surprised as you are."

Matt grabbed Hunter and hugged him again. "Hunter! I just found out yesterday that I had a son! Paco handed me the letter your mother wrote to me years ago. She told me she had a son named Hunter and had withheld that information all these years until she was dying. I've been in shock all night and had Celeste calling all around Destin to find you! I can't believe you just walked into my clinic to find Paco!"

Hunter wiped his forehead and shook Matt's hand. "It's so glad to finally meet you! You have no idea how happy this makes me."

Suddenly Paco made a loud gasp and all four people turned around. He was gone. But on his face was a slight smile. He knew that his journey was over. He'd done what he meant to do.

Hunter knelt down and leaned over the bed and cried for Paco. His body shook and he felt so sad. Matt put his hand on Hunter's shoulder and comforted him. This was a traumatic reunion for Hunter and no one really understood the ties he had with the homeless man.

Matt pulled Hunter up and they walked out of the room with Matt's arm around his shoulder. "Hunter, I know this is tough for you. That dear man brought us together after all these years. He's a true hero. He used his last breath to bring you to me. I will owe him the rest of my life. You don't know how happy I am to see you."

"You have no idea, Matt. This man sacrificed so much to find you. I was so afraid I wouldn't get here in time to talk to him before he died. I've been worried sick about him."

Hunter hugged him again and pulled Holly over to him. "I want you to meet my fiancé Holly Carrington. We're getting married down here. I'd love for you to come to my wedding!"

Matt shook Holly's hand. "You two look so happy. It's so nice to meet you, Holly. I'd be honored to come to your wedding, Hunter. Is your Aunt Jenny going to be there?"

"Yes, as a matter of fact she is. Say Matt, what will you do with Paco's body? I mean what kind of funeral will he have?"

"Usually homeless people are cremated here if there is no family to contact. Did he have family?"

"I think he did, but I wouldn't know how to go about contacting them. I don't even know his real name."

"We'll take care of that. We can check with the police department in Philadelphia and they'll run his prints to see if he has a record. I bet they'll track down his family."

"It seems weird but he's sort of been family to me. We've talked a lot on the phone and I've trusted him like a good friend. I'm so sad that he died just when I finally got to see him again. He's had quite a journey, Matt, to find you. I mean, what are the odds of his coming into your clinic?"

"It's even more amazing than that, Hunter. He fell through the doorway and had a heart attack on the floor in the reception area. He would've died had that happened on the street. We tried to save his life but he was already in the last stages of congestive heart failure. There was really nothing we could do after the heart attack but make him comfortable. He finally told me about the letter and the rest is history. I'm standing here looking at you and we both are in shock. We have a lot of catching up to do, Hunter."

Matt took down some contact information and they talked for a while, sharing stories and laughing. It was awkward at first but the past seemed to merge with the present and the two men bonded quickly. Hunter went into the recovery room one more time to tell Paco goodbye and then he and Matt hugged each other after Hunter stepped out of the room.

"Matt, I sure am glad I found you. When I heard you were here I was overwhelmed with the urge to see you. I still can't believe I'm looking at you face to face."

"Son, we have so much to talk about. I want you and Holly to get settled and let me know what time the wedding is. I'll be there. I'm so happy to meet you—and to know you even exist. That's going to take some time to sink in."

They both laughed and Hunter and Holly left the clinic and headed to the car. They didn't stop talking all the way back to the beach house where they were staying. It was afternoon and they both were starving. So they drove to one of the restaurants on Old 98 and Hunter talked all the way through lunch. Holly had never seen him so animated. They were sitting at a picnic table outside on a deck overlooking the Gulf. The water was emerald green and people were everywhere. It was a beautiful place to have a wedding and honeymoon. They were both tired from all the exams and pressure of school and it felt good to just relax. But finding Matt had turned their world upside down.

"I been sitting here thinking, Holly. Do you think Matt would be my best man? I mean, I know it's fast, but it would mean so much to me for him to do it."

"You'll just have to ask him, Hunter. But going by how he reacted this morning, I bet he'll say yes. I can tell he really wants to get to know you."

"Yeah. I guess he does." Hunter was blushing and Holly smiled.

"You're a lucky man, Hunter Bentley. You're getting married and you found your father all in the same week!"

"I'm the luckiest man alive, Holly Carrington. Don't ever think I don't realize that. You're the most beautiful woman I've ever met and now you're going to be my wife!"

Matt picked up the phone in his office and dialed Joe's number. He leaned back in his chair grinning ear to ear. He couldn't wait for Joe to pick up the phone.

"Hello?"

"Hey, man. How's it going?"

"Going pretty good. How's your day been? Anything wrong? You hardly ever phone me in the middle of the day. You're usually too busy."

"Two things. Paco died. Not too long ago."

"Oh, man. I'm sorry, Matt. He seemed like such a nice guy. Too bad he was so ill. I'm glad we got to take care of him and you made him feel as safe and comfortable as possible."

"Second thing. I met my son."

Dead silence on the other end. "You what? Did you say you met your son?"

Matt laughed. "I knew that one would get you. Yeah, I met my son, Hunter. Can you believe that? He walked right in here to see Paco. It blew me away, Joe. He's wonderful. Such a cute kid. He's even asked me to come in his wedding."

"I didn't know you had a son! Where did this come from? How did he find you? That meeting was ordained. You happy about it? Did things go well?"

"He had no idea he would find me when he came in to see if Paco was here. We both are pretty much in shock. I couldn't believe how we both just jumped in and talked our heads off. I couldn't talk fast enough and neither could he. This is going to be one of the most important times in my life, having the opportunity to have a relationship with my own son. Meeting you was huge. It changed my life, I'm here to tell ya. But this comes right up against you pulling me off the bench. I actually have a son who wants to get to know me. It just thrills me to no end."

"I'm happy for you, Matt. You have wanted family around you and now it's coming to fruition. Be careful what you ask for! So when do I get to meet him?"

"I want you to come to the wedding with me. He's got to meet you. I mentioned you to him earlier. He doesn't know the whole story but he will."

"I'd love to come. Just let me know when and where."

"Great! I'll call you shortly."

Matt hung up the phone and sat in his office thinking about Hunter. In the other room Paco's body was covered with a sheet. The coroner had been called and a search would be done to locate his family. He closed up some files on his desk and turned out the light but he just sat back down in his seat. Joe was waiting on him, but his mind just couldn't wrap around the concept of having a son in his life. He was blown away with the letter from Lara. He had no idea she'd been sick. He'd lost touch with her on his way down and never tried to find her again. Of course, she wouldn't have talked to him, anyway. *Hunter looks so good; she did a great job with him. A medical student! She had said he reminded her of me. How kind.* He'd been a real jerk to her. So selfish. But then, that was what had caused the crash in his life. Selfishness. Now he had a chance to make it up to her by loving their son.

He stood up when the coroner opened the door. He moved Paco out quickly and headed to the mortuary to get his fingerprints so they could establish next of kin. Matt locked up the clinic and walked to his car.

Man, life can take a turn in a nanosecond. This is going to change my life forever. Until I die. He waited a long time to find me. I sure hope I won't be a disappointment to him. I know one thing; I'm gonna love him like I've never loved anybody. I don't know how he'll take my being a homeless man for a few years, but I'll try to make him proud of me now.

Wouldn't it be a neat thing if he stayed here and worked with me in the clinic?

Matt laughed at himself and pulled out of the parking lot and headed home. *If I'm gonna dream, I might as well dream big. And the way things have been happening around here lately, anything could happen.*

CHAPTER 81

— ⚜ —

THERE WAS A generous wind blowing and the Gulf was choppy. It was partly cloudy with the sun shining through big billowy clouds. The wedding was on the beach in a missionary style Gulf front home. There were only a handful of people coming to the wedding, which included Holly's parents, Fred and Brenda Carrington. Joe had been asked by Hunter to perform the ceremony because he'd had no luck in finding a pastor on such short notice. This blew me away because I so wanted Hunter and Joe to meet and get to know each other.

It was early when I walked up to the beach house and Hunter greeted me at the door. "Hey, Matt. So good to see you again! Come on in. You look terrific in your black suit."

"You look pretty handsome yourself. Are you nervous?"

Hunter smiled. "No! Not at all. But I got a favor to ask of you, and I'd sure hate for you to turn me down on my wedding day!"

I smiled and looked at my son. "What do you need, Son? I'll do anything I can to make this day memorable for you."

"Well, uh, I'd like you to be my best man."

I was totally blown away. "Be your best man? Are you serious?"

"I know it's too soon in our relationship, but, man, I've waited so long to find you. It would mean the world to me if you'd stand up beside me at my wedding."

"Hunter, I'm speechless. That's such an honorable position and I don't feel I've earned that place in your life. But if you would like me to be there with you, I'm there. You can count on it."

Hunter grabbed my hand and shook it. "You have no idea what this means to me. As you know, my mother is gone. I have no one here but Aunt Jenny."

"Say, you got a minute? I'd like to share something with you."

"Sure. Let's go sit down in the living room where we can talk in private."

I followed Hunter into the house and we plopped down on the sofa, sitting next to each other. I jumped right in because I knew we didn't have much time.

"Hunter, I don't know how much you know about my past. There are some things I'm not too proud of and I want to get them off my chest before I stand up with you at your wedding. You know I am a doctor. A surgeon. I lost everything because I was an alcoholic. When I left Philadelphia, I headed south and lived as a homeless man for several years. I simply stepped off the world for a while and lost myself in an underground way of life. Joe found me sleeping on a park bench one night and covered me up with a leather jacket he had on. Later he found me again eating at the Coffee House and offered me a place to sleep. He basically gave me a new start on life. I couldn't have made it without him.

"I want you to know I'm back on my feet and have started this free clinic to help those who are poor or homeless. I've gotten my stride back and am so excited about this new venture. I hope you can be proud of your father at some point. I'm not proud of how far down I fell."

Hunter looked at me and shook his head. "Matt, I've wanted to know my father all my life. I shared that with you the other day. I knew you struggled. I didn't know how much. But I'm proud of what you are doing in that clinic. I cannot imagine how much work it took just putting that thing together. You have two great doctors working with you and I love the whole setup. It would be a dream come true working in a situation like that. So don't ever worry about what I think of you. I guess if I'm honest, I have loved you for years. I just hadn't met you yet."

I wiped the tears from my eyes and put my arm around my son. "I can't wait to stand with you at your wedding. This is one of the most exciting days of your life and I get to share it with you. What more could a father ask?"

Hunter stood up and faced me, and I saw for the first time a little of Lara in his face. It caught my breath for a moment, as I remembered the love we had shared long ago. "There is one more thing that I'd like to ask of you, Matt. And I don't know how to say it other than to just blurt it out. Since I've waited so long to meet you I really don't want to call you Matt. I know we just met and all, but for some reason I feel closer to you than that. I don't know quite how to say it, but I—"

"What is it, son? What do you need to ask me?"

"Well, I was wondering if I could call you 'Dad'? I hope I'm not stepping over any boundaries here. But we've lost so much time, and I need you in my life."

I was speechless again. The boy had not been in my life seventy-two hours yet and he was already taking over my heart. I never thought I'd be called "Dad." I had never wanted it. But now it felt like a gift. "I would love for you to call me 'Dad.' Hunter, your acceptance of me is overwhelming. And I feel so fortunate to have you in my life. Let's get ready for this wedding, son. I want this to last forever for you and Holly."

Joe walked up and looked at us both. "You two together are trouble, I can already tell. How's it going, Hunter? You ready for your big day?"

Hunter smiled. He looked at Matt and then at Joe. "Brother Joe, I have some good news. My dad has agreed to be my best man. What do you think of that?"

Joe smiled and turned his head to wipe his eyes. "Your dad, huh? Well that's the best news I've heard today. Come on, boys, let's not keep the lady waiting."

I watched Hunter walk away with Brother Joe, and my heart was about to burst. How lucky was I to have such a wonderful man like Joe in my life! When I was at my absolute worst he lifted me up. He gave me hope. And he showed me the way out. At my lowest point I had no dreams. I had no desire to live. *Now I want to live a long, long time because*

I have the most wonderful son in the world. I did nothing to deserve his love, but I will do everything I can to keep it.

And he called me "Dad." I smiled and looked up, because I thought I could feel Paco smiling down on me. *It's because of you, Paco, that I ever met my son. I'll keep my promise to you. I'll love him the rest of my life. And I'll never forget you, Paco. Did you hear him call me "Dad"?*

Epilogue

A YEAR FROM the day Hunter met Paco on the bus, on a cool spring day when the azaleas were in full bloom and the seagulls were feeding readily at water's edge, Celeste and Matt said marriage vows and were married near the ocean, leaving their own footprints in the sand.

There was a salty wind blowing on this wedding day. Matt smiled as he looked into Celeste's eyes, which were the color of the water that was washing up on shore. He would live out a new life with her, letting those eyes calm him when he was stressed. He was ever thankful for finding his son and couldn't wait to spend the rest of his life loving Hunter, making up for the years he'd missed.

In all the time he'd spent in Destin, the one person who had made the most impact on his life was Joe. A somewhat private soul who took each day as his call to serve others. Tirelessly, he was a picture of a servant. And for one second, as his eyes rested on Joe waiting to bless their marriage, to the group of people who had gathered at the wedding. He let his thoughts go back to the time when a leather jacket came to rest on his cold, worn out body. Joe's jacket. And in that one act of giving, there were remnants of hope and a belief in a homeless man who had nowhere to be. No one to love. And nothing to hold on to.

In the end, it was the unselfishness of Joe that gave Matt his life back. He owed him his life. And he would spend the rest of his days giving back to others, so Joe would see that he had learned that one thing from him. But what he really gleaned from the older man whose shoulders had begun to sag, and whose hair had turned totally white, was a love for the One who whispered the call that caused Joe to give up his life to serve others. For in that one whisper that Joe had heard, he saved the life of a man who had no life. And Matt, scarred and broken, had somehow retained enough intelligence to decipher where that call had come from. Not because he had heard a sermon but because he had seen it lived out.

After the wedding had passed and Matt and Celeste had moved into a new home on Seagull Lane, Matt went to visit Joe. He was growing weary and not feeling all that well. But when he saw Matt his face lit up and he smiled. And the voice he spoke with, a little deeper and raspy, made the hairs stand on Matt's arm. For in a moment of time an unexpected window into Joe's soul opened up and Matt stepped through that window and came into a deeper understanding of this giant of a man who had saved his life.

It wasn't long before Joe passed away quietly in his home late one Saturday night. Matt felt like a part of him had been taken away, and for a time he couldn't breathe. He had a fear that welled up in him that somehow he couldn't make it without Joe. But when those doubts would creep in, and they did, Matt went to the closet and pulled out the brown leather jacket and breathed in the smell, and remembered the man that saved his life.

Matt and Celeste would wander to the beach often and sit on the bench that held many memories. After many years he turned the clinic over to Hunter and came to work less and less. His interest was elsewhere in his old age. He found himself wandering around at night among the homeless, carrying blankets and food, and giving out water. Listening to the cries of the weary men. And often, when the light was low and the moon was covered by wispy clouds, Matt would remember the man he loved so dearly who walked among the sleeping giants, meeting needs. Caring for the men that no one would touch.

And one cold night when the wind had a chill, he was walking through the camps looking for anyone who needed a blanket. And he came up on a man who was sleeping on the ground under a huge tree. He was shivering and talking in his sleep. His hair was cut short and his beard trimmed, but he lay in the dirt with his face against the roots of the tree that gave him shelter. And Matt pulled off his jacket, the leather one that Joe had given to him, and without hesitation he reached over to the man and silently laid the jacket across the young man's weak shoulders and quietly walked away.

About the Author

Nancy Veldman

NANCY VELDMAN LIVES in Destin, Florida with her husband. She has two daughters, he has two sons, and they have ten grandchildren. She has owned Magnolia House for twenty three years and is an author, pianist and watercolor artist. And she is listening even now. You can visit her Website at magnoliahouse.com or write her at nancy@magnoliahouse .com.

Is this all there is?
No.
But you will have to give
until you have no more,
cry until there
are no more tears,
listen,
laugh,
and learn to love
even when you get nothing
in return.
Until our last breath, there is more.